# PRAISE FOR ALYS CLARE'S HAWKENLYE SERIES

'A worthy heir to Ellis Peters'          *Poison in the Pen*

'This is no murder-by-numbers writer. What seems a fascinating subplot, about a forest people who adhere to the old pagan ways, gradually becomes central to the investigation. Clare draws utterly believable characters who have warmth and humanity. And she introduces another knight whose character keeps us guessing until the final chapter. Don't let the fact that this is the sixth in a series put you off. But I bet, like me, you'll be ordering books one to five when you've finished.' *Derby Evening Telegraph* on *A Dark Night Hidden*

'Cunningly shifting sympathies among virtually all the players, Clare spotlights first Helewise, then Josse, in a detecting competition that lifts the partners above their predictable gender roles . . . immersing them in a suddenly engrossing tale.'          *Kirkus Reviews* on *Whiter than the Lily*

'It's gripping stuff, and it's sure to keep you hooked throughout'          *Daily Post* on *Ashes of the Elements*

'They are actually rather good'          *Publishers Weekly*

## THE HAWKENLYE MYSTERIES

Fortune Like the Moon

Ashes of the Elements

The Tavern in the Morning

The Chatter of the Maidens

The Faithful Dead

A Dark Night Hidden

Whiter than the Lily

Girl in a Red Tunic

Heart of Ice

The Enchanter's Forest

## ABOUT THE AUTHOR

Alys Clare is a history enthusiast and full time author. She lives in Kent, where the Hawkenlye mysteries are set. The most recent include *Whiter than the Lily*, *Girl in a Red Tunic* and *Heart of Ice*. To find out more, you can reach her on her website: www.alysclare.com

ALYS CLARE

# The Enchanter's Forest

HODDER

First published in Great Britain in 2007 by Hodder & Stoughton
First published in paperback in Great Britain in 2008 by Hodder & Stoughton
A division of Hodder Headline

A Hodder Paperback

1

A CIP catalogue record for this title
is available from the British Library

ISBN 978 0 340 92386 3

Typeset in Plantin Light by Hewer Text UK Ltd, Edinburgh
Printed and bound by Mackays of Chatham Ltd, Chatham, Kent

Hodder Headline's policy is to use papers that are natural, renewable
and recyclable products and made from wood grown in sustainable
forests. The logging and manufacturing processes are expected to
conform to the environmental regulations of the country of origin.

Hodder & Stoughton Ltd
A division of Hodder Headline
338 Euston Road
London NW1 3BH

For Alex Bonham,
with my grateful thanks for her infectious enthusiasm
and all her hard work

*Cytharizat cantico*
*dulcis philomena,*
*flore rident vario*
*prata iam serena,*
*salit cetus avium*
*silve per amena,*
*chorus promit virginum*
*iam gaudia millena.*

The sweet nightingale
sings like a lyre;
the flower-filled meadows
are laughing for joy;
a flight of birds soars up
from the enchanted forest;
the maidens' chorus
promises a thousand delights.

*Carmina Burana;*
*cantiones profanae*

Author's translation

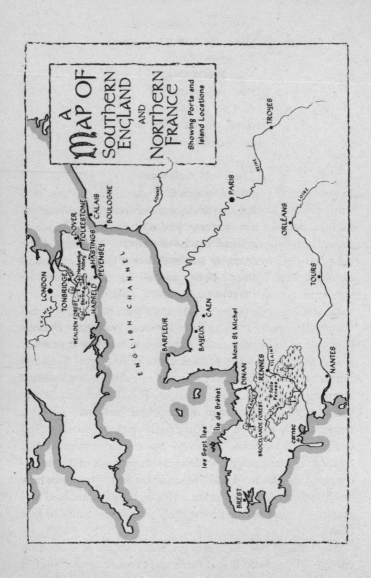

A
MAP OF
SOUTHERN
ENGLAND
AND
NORTHERN
FRANCE

Showing Ports and
Island Locations

# PROLOGUE

*Spring Equinox 1195*

In the forest the new season was flourishing. The air was loud with birdsong as male chaffinch, blackbird, thrush and warbler each proclaimed their territory and advertised for a mate. A recent heavy shower had increased both the intensity of the light and the sweet spring smells of tender young grass and unfolding leaf. Nature's power was all but tangible and the very trees seemed to rejoice.

In stark contrast, the young man who was slowly and dejectedly making his way from the deep heart of the forest back out to its fringes could not have been more miserable. Today was his fifth trip to the interior of the Great Wealden Forest and he had been on the same hopeless mission that had taken him there the previous times. He'd heard that, a few years back now, some men out poaching had come across a treasure trove of coins and, despite the fact that he knew full well what had become of them – those who related the tale dwelled with fascinated ghoulishness on *that* part of the story – his greed and his need had overcome his fear. Five times now he had managed to master his terror as he had scrabbled and dug in what had seemed to be likely places; five times he had failed.

The trouble was that he never really stayed in there long enough. He guessed that if there *was* treasure to be found, it would be in the secret, dark areas that lay hidden miles away from the outside world, where they said mysterious beings lived who shunned mankind, preferring to keep to their own sort, their own ways, even their own religion. They also said that these strange people did not take kindly to outsiders poking their noses in where they were not wanted. Most certainly they would not approve of someone scratching about beneath the roots of those vast and majestic oaks of incredible antiquity searching for loot. Look at what had happened to those wretched poachers . . .

Each time he had found a likely spot and taken up his mattock to break the soil and start digging, initially the hope of finding what he was so frantically looking for would carry him for a while, fuelling him with nervous energy and desperate optimism. This time, he would think to himself, this time I'm going to strike lucky, and he would try so hard to make himself believe it that he could almost see his eager hands gathering up piles of glittering gold coins, feeling their wonderful weight in his palms and watching with fascinated eyes as they fell through his fingers.

Each time, sooner or later, the moment would come when he could no longer ignore the dread feeling that someone – perhaps some*thing*, for there was no sense at all of a human presence – was watching him. It would begin with a chill down his spine; a chill that, given that he was working hard enough to bring him out in a sweat, really should not have been there. Then he would think he heard some small noise, only when he stopped his digging to listen, there was no sound other than those that were natural to the forest. When he resumed his work, slowly, steadily the conviction would grow that something was creeping up on him, stealthily, silently, poised to pounce on him as he bent to his digging. He would try to ignore his fear, command himself not to let his imagination run away with him, but always, sooner or later, he would fling aside his mattock, draw his dagger and spin round to face his attacker.

There would never be anything there.

And the only sound would be one that nobody but he could hear, for it was the silent scream of terror that echoed inside his head.

But he had to go on trying, for if he did not find himself a source of ready wealth, he would be left with no option but to kill himself.

It was all because of his wife.

As he stumped along, against his volition his thoughts turned to her. She was young and clever, with an arrogant tilt to the chin that she had inherited from her French mother, along with the withering glance from those dark and captivating eyes that seemed to say, *You?* What on earth have *you* got to offer someone like me? She was also utterly lovely, with a neat little figure and round, high-set breasts that felt surprisingly heavy in his eager hands. Her power over him was absolute for if he did not do as she wished she withheld herself. Now, because she was so angry with him about the money he had given to the ransom fund, she had refused him admittance to her bed and her body for more than six months, and that last time he had caught her unawares and all but raped her. It was going to be a long time before she let him forget about that, even though at the time he would have sworn she enjoyed it as much as he did.

What she could not – or probably would not – understand was that, over the matter of the ransom, he had had no choice. Great merciful heavens, did she think he had *wanted* to give away a quarter of his income purely to recover a king fool enough to go haring off to Outremer and allow himself to be captured on the long road home? She had accused him of hurrying to give his contribution when a wiser man might have held back hoping to be overlooked, but he had told her roughly that there was no point putting any hope in *that* naïve idea since everyone knew him and his very conspicuous wealth and his was one of the first doors on which they would come knocking. It had been better by far to appear a loyal subject who just could not wait to offer his contribution to the fund while he prayed earnestly day and night for his sovereign's safe return.

The real trouble was that, in his desperation to prove to her that he was a very rich man and thus the best choice as husband out of all of those who offered for her hand, he had exaggerated his wealth. Once having convinced her and her mother that his means were far more than their true value, he had been forced to go on living the lie. For the two years of their marriage he had consistently spent more than his income and, devastatingly, the ransom contribution demanded from him appeared to have been based on what he boasted of possessing rather than what he really owned.

The simple outcome was that he was now flat broke and heavily in debt. Ruin and utter humiliation were staring him in the face, not to mention the loss of his glorious wife, who would no doubt take pleasure in kicking him good and hard when he was down. If, out of the last vestiges of love for him, she managed to hold back, then for certain her mother would show no such restraint. Her mother's sneering, disdainful expression haunted him; there was no need for her to say *My daughter is far too good for you* because it was written all over her face. Sometimes he would hardly dare to go home in case the old tyrant had spirited her daughter back to France . . .

Oh, dear God, if only he had some *money*! What wouldn't he do!

His wife could have the solar she'd been demanding for the last God knew how long, and some good jewellery and a few lengths of the most costly silk for her summer gowns. He could put in an offer for that pretty bay palfrey she had her eye on.

He could buy her all those things and more, then she would slide naked into their wide marriage bed, open her arms and her legs to him and, with that seductress's smile on her beautiful face making the bewitching dimple dance in her cheek, invite him to join her.

*Aaah!*

He was swamped by lascivious thoughts of what he would do to his wife – and what she would do to him, for she had tricks that he had never come across before and that drove him wild with lust – once he had earned her favour once more.

Then abruptly he came out of his fantasy world and returned with a painful jolt to reality. None of it was going to happen because he was broke.

Today he had really believed he was on to something, for he was all but sure he had stumbled across the very place where the poachers had found their coins; there were undoubtedly signs that someone had dug there in the fairly recent past. But if they had, then whatever hoard they had stolen from had now been removed; he had found nothing but earth, roots and stones.

Sick, overcome with a sudden urgent need for daylight that was not filtered through a million young green leaves, he had turned and fled from the place. Now, almost weeping with despair and disappointment, he was trudging along, head down, too miserable to care very much where he was going.

He was jerked to attention by the abrupt shock of coming up against a barrier. His heart began to race and he stared around him, skin tingling. But he couldn't see anything: no fence, no hedge, nothing. Angry suddenly – it was strange how his emotions seemed so volatile – he pushed against whatever was holding him back and after a moment it yielded. With the sense that he had thrust himself through some sort of mystical portal, he plunged on and found himself in a clearing that he was quite sure he had never been in before.

He stopped, let the head of the mattock rest on the springy grass and looked around him. It was a strange sort of a clearing; unnaturally quiet, very regular in shape and encircled by oak trees that were placed at such equal intervals that they might almost have been planted. But that was silly – he smiled grimly at his own folly – for this was a forest and the oak trees just grew wherever the acorns happened to fall. And, he reassured himself – for the sense of unease was quickly growing – wasn't it often the case that an old oak left to its own devices became circled by its own offspring so that, when the ancient father oak eventually died, a natural circle would have formed around the place where it had once stood?

Yes. Even though the smooth grass in the clearing was uninterrupted by any vast old tree stump, that must be what had happened here.

Mustn't it?

He was afraid. Shouldering the mattock, he decided to set out across the clearing and head for the faint boar track that led off through the trees. He would follow it and, sooner or later, he would find himself on a familiar path and then he would make his escape.

Or so he fervently hoped.

He knew he must get going but for an appalling moment his body seemed petrified and his legs would not obey his will. There was dead silence in the clearing and then suddenly it was broken by a profoundly deep, indescribably strange sound like a single huge heartbeat.

There was enchantment in the air.

He took a deep breath, tensed his muscles and threw himself forward. The spell was broken.

He began to run, needing more than anything in the world to get away, out from that still, silent, spellbound spot and back into the open air beyond the last of the trees where he would be able to breathe freely again and where there was not this dreadful, constant sense of being watched. He had an idea that the forest fringes were not far away now; he just had to control himself, try to bite down on the panic and just keep running till he was free, then he could—

It was at that moment that he fell.

He was right in the centre of the circle at a place where the ground dipped into a long, shallow depression about an arm's length across. He had noticed it when looking around the clearing but, since it was plain and quite featureless, had paid it little heed. Now he cursed it, for it had interrupted his flight to safety; perhaps even his flight for his life. I might want to die, he thought grimly, but if I make the decision to end my life it'll be at a time of my method and choosing and for sure I don't want to be terrified to death by some malignant forest ghoul.

He sat up, rubbing at his shoulder; he had fallen headlong and hard.

Still slightly dazed, he patted the ground around him. He was sitting in the depression and it seemed to him that some insistent thought was knocking at his mind, something that he should have noticed but hadn't.

A depression. Right in the middle of the clearing. Where once a great oak tree might well have stood.

And where had those poachers found their treasure?

*In the hole left by an uprooted oak.*

Hope flared up in him, searing through him and raising his spirits like the rising sun on a morning after a night's rain.

Filled with sudden energy, he leapt up, raised his mattock and began to dig.

# I

The devastating news reached Hawkenlye via a tinker.

His name was Thomas and he and his solidly built handcart had been a familiar sight in the wide vale between the North and the South Downs since time out of mind. He could turn his deft hands to a wide diversity of tasks and was possessed of the useful ability to mend virtually anything. The well-used tools of his trade he carried in a wooden chest nailed to his cart; surrounding it were habitually to be found boxes and sacking parcels of various sizes containing anything from magic charms to nit combs. What he did not carry with him he could acquire; it was common for a housewife casually to mention some obscure item that she lacked and forget all about it, only to have Thomas the Tinker turn up again a month, a season or a year later triumphantly flourishing the desired object (and, with his twinkling, friendly and disarming smile, asking a price commensurate with the trouble he had been put to in his search).

There was another role in which Thomas served his community: he supplied them with news. People did not travel far from their doorsteps and consequently knew little about the wider world unless someone came and told them and, ever since he had been a lad, Thomas had revelled in doing just that. He kept his eyes and his ears open and he had a prodigious memory for facts, faces and, particularly, for gossip. He was, in short, a Godsend and there was not a home in the land where he was not welcomed with something to eat and a drink, hot or cold depending on the weather, to wash it down.

He turned up at Hawkenlye Abbey one sunny midday towards the middle of June. First he called at the gate house, for on his cart was a packet of precious beeswax for the Abbess and a consignment of needles and threads for the endless mending that the infirmary nuns carried out in their spare time. Then, having passed the time of day with Sister Ursel, he set off down the sloping track to the valley where the monks tended the shrine and looked after the pilgrims who came to take the holy waters in the hope of curing whatever afflicted them. Thomas had a set of roughly made pottery cups for Brother Saul (it was amazing how many they got through down in the Vale; people were just so careless) and, being well aware of the hour, he was hoping with quiet confidence that Saul would invite him to stay and eat with the brethren.

Saul haggled amicably with the tinker over the cost of the cups and, with business concluded to the satisfaction of both men, told Thomas he was welcome to join the monks for their midday meal. With alacrity Thomas sat down at the long bench and, for the duration of the simple repast, listened to the monks' news and ventured some of his own.

He saved the ripest plum for last.

'I'm on my way south now,' he announced as he got up from the bench. 'Far side of the Great Forest.'

'Indeed?' Brother Erse said, eyes alert with curiosity. 'Anywhere in particular?'

'Oh, yes.' Thomas took his time, looking round the circle of monks and lay brothers to make sure he had their attention. 'Oh, for sure.'

'Where?' several monks said together.

Dropping his voice to a dramatic whisper, Thomas said, 'I've got nails and needles, soft satins and a silver cup on my old cart and I must make haste to reach my destination while the light is good and bright. I've been entrusted with a special order – an *important* order – and the man who awaits me is impatient for his goods.' He eyed the group, gratified to see that they were hanging on his words. 'It's going to change things around here,' he went on, 'you see if I'm not right, for news is spreading like the tide through a breached dike and there's an air of excitement everywhere I go. Oh, yes, it's going to change things all right!'

'What is?' breathed young Brother Augustus.

Thomas turned to him. 'They've found something,' he whispered. 'Unearthed it from the ground, put up a shelter to keep it from the elements, spread word that there's been a miracle discovery and organised a place for folks to refresh themselves and stop overnight.' Eyes widening in feigned amazement he went on, 'Why, it's much like this here settlement in the Vale, now I come to think of it!'

Alarmed now, the monks were muttering to one another. A ripple of unease spread through the company.

'You mean – you're telling us that somebody has found another source of holy water?' It was Old Brother Firmin who courageously voiced the unthinkable.

'No, not exactly that,' Thomas said, turning to the elderly monk with a kindly smile. 'It's bones, see. That's what's been found: great, heavy bones, like as if a giant's buried there.'

'And . . .' Brother Saul paused, swallowed and tried again. 'And the bones work miracles?'

'Oh, aye, I reckon they do that all right,' Thomas assured him. 'Leastways, that's the claim. Whether they do or not' – he shrugged lightly – 'well, we'll just have to wait and see, won't we?'

'Whose bones are they?' Brother Micah whispered, glancing nervously over his shoulder in case some higher authority stood there about to punish him for indulging in dangerous gossip.

'Didn't I say?' Thomas asked innocently. 'Dear me, no, I don't believe I did!' He shook his head at his careless omission. 'Well, you'll know the name right swift enough when I tell you and you'll readily understand, clever and learned men that you are, why this here discovery has led to the construction of the shrine I'm heading for with my goods and why it's going to bring about all the fuss that'll follow, sure as my name's Thomas.' The remark, long-winded even by Thomas's standards, left him slightly breathless.

'Who is it?' cried Saul. 'Whose skeleton's been dug up?'

Thomas looked from monk to monk, meeting each anxious pair of eyes for a moment. Then he told them.

Josse d'Acquin, King's man and long-time friend to Hawken-lye Abbey, learned of the news sitting in a cool, shady corner of his neighbour's garden contentedly supping a mug of ale and watching the antics of the children of the family.

Brice of Rotherbridge had wed Isabella de Burghay in the summer of 1193 and she had born him a daughter, Fritha, the following April. The baby girl, now a couple of months past her first birthday, was laughing infectiously as her elder half-brother and sister played with her beneath the sweet chestnut tree. As Josse watched the trio – all three were attractive children and Roger and Marthe were well-mannered into the bargain – he and Brice were joined by Isabella.

She walked gracefully across the grass towards them, a jug in her hand. Her heavy, dark blond hair was neatly braided and covered by a small veil held in place by a narrow silver circlet and she wore a gown of dark green whose sleeves, lined with paler green and flaring widely at the cuff, trailed almost to the ground. Her full breasts and the beginnings of a bulge under her waistband suggested that she was pregnant again; in fact Josse knew this to be true for Brice had just told him. He got up from the rough bench on which he and Brice were seated and with a smile indicated to Isabella that she should take his place: 'You should rest, my lady, in this heat,' he said solicitously.

Isabella returned his smile. 'Brice has told you, then,' she said.

'Aye, and right glad I am,' Josse replied earnestly. Both Brice and Isabella had suffered tragedy in their lives; to see them married and so happy together, the new baby girl and the older children whom Isabella had born her first husband close-knit into a real family, made his heart glad.

It also made him realise how lonely he was and how purposeless his life had become.

But now was not the time to dwell on that.

'Do you wish for a boy or a girl?' he asked. A little too heartily, if the concern in Isabella's eyes as she shot him a look was anything to go by; he had forgotten how very perceptive she was. She moved closer to him and briefly took hold of his hand as if trying to give him her understanding and her support.

'For my part, I do not mind one jot as long as the child is healthy,' Brice said.

Isabella laughed. 'Don't you believe him,' she said lovingly, 'for, already having a daughter, he would dearly love a son.'

'I'm quite sure—' Josse began.

Isabella put a hand on his arm. 'Do not worry, Josse,' she whispered, 'for the baby that I carry is indeed a boy and we shall name him Olivar, after Brice's late brother.'

'How can you know it's a boy?' Josse hissed back.

But Isabella's only answer was a serene smile. Then she reached for his and Brice's empty ale mugs and refilled them.

They sat together on the bench beneath the chestnut tree for some time, the heat making them too lazy for anything but the most trivial conversation. There was a soft but constant humming in the air, as if a thousand invisible insects were close by. The sweet scent of gillyflowers lay on the summer air. The ale combined with the excellent meal that Josse had just consumed, making his eyelids heavy so that he found himself nodding; the sounds of the children and the baby seemed to drift further and further away . . .

. . . and then he heard the word *Hawkenlye* and was suddenly wide awake.

'Hm? What was that?' he demanded, making himself sit up straight and blinking his eyes open.

Brice chuckled and Isabella said kindly, 'We were speaking of the new shrine on the southern fringe of the forest, Josse. Brice was saying that Hawkenlye Abbey will have to take care that it does not lose all of its pilgrims.'

'What new shrine?'

'Have you not heard?' Brice sounded surprised. 'They've found some bones – large ones, or so I'm told. Some young lordling has cleared the ground around the site and he's put the word around that there have been some miracles – cripples throwing away their crutches, deaf old women suddenly regaining their hearing, barren women becoming pregnant, that sort of thing. He's built a shelter and he's offering food and drink. For a price,' he added.

'They're saint's bones?' Josse asked. He was both amazed at something so extraordinary happening so close to home and, at the same time, very apprehensive because of what this new discovery might mean for the Abbey. In particular – she was very dear to him – for its Abbess. She fought a constant battle with what to him seemed a perfectly natural pride in the Abbey and its place at the centre of life in the vicinity and any threat to it would be like a direct threat to her . . .

Brice and Isabella exchanged a glance. 'Not exactly a saint,' Brice said.

'Whose are they, then?' Josse asked, with some impatience.

Isabella looked down at her hands and then said quietly, 'Josse, are you familiar with the Matter of Britain?'

'Er . . .' The phrase was familiar but it took Josse a few moments to gather his thoughts and recall what he knew about it. 'It's to do with King Arthur, isn't it?' Isabella nodded. 'Aye, and he's meant to be sleeping in a hollow hill somewhere with all his knights, ready to come to England's aid at our hour of gravest danger.'

Brice smiled. 'In brief, you have it,' he said. 'There is, however, rather more to the story.' He looked at his wife. 'Isabella is the expert,' he continued. 'I am sure that she will explain further, if you would care to hear?'

Josse was unable to see what this Matter of Britain had to do with a sudden threat to the Abbey but if enlightenment was on offer, then he was going to take it. 'My lady?' he said.

Isabella sat quietly for a moment or two, as if collecting her thoughts. Then she said, 'I have always loved tales pertaining to our land and its turbulent past. You, Josse, knowing as you do the unusual circumstances of my childhood and youth, will readily understand that it was probably these very circumstances that predisposed me to that love.' Josse nodded. 'Aware of my interest, my dear Brice here obtained for me a most welcome gift on the occasion of our marriage; he commissioned the monks at Canterbury to make my very own copy of Geoffrey of Monmouth's great work, the History of the Kings of Britain.'

'A most generous and enviable gift, my lady.' Josse, who was no reader, did his best to put enthusiasm into his voice but Isabella's quiet laughter suggested he had failed.

'For me, nothing could have been more welcome,' she said, still smiling. Her voice filling with eagerness, she went on, 'Geoffrey's story begins with the arrival of Brutus, who was the great-grandson of Aeneas the Trojan, and tells of how he established a dynasty of kings at New Troy, and the story proceeds to cover a thousand years of our land's history and . . .' She stopped herself. Her eyes had been on Josse and he realised that his smile of polite interest was probably looking a little fixed. 'But I must not risk boring you. The point is that Geoffrey's thrilling account concludes with the tale of King Arthur and his magnificent court, of his valour and of how he kept the invader at bay, of his death at the hands of his treacherous nephew and of how his body was taken to the Isle of Avalon to be cured so that he may answer Britain's call when we have need of him.'

Josse, watching her as she spoke, noticed how her sea-green eyes had lit up with excitement. He realised that she believed in her story; for her, quite clearly, the prowess of the legendary Arthur was as much a legitimate part of England's history as the arrival of William the Bastard and the stormy reign of Henry II.

Which was going to be a ticklish problem of diplomacy, since Josse didn't credit a word of it. Memory had returned and information concerning King Arthur, his castle, his knights, his wife and his hunt for the Holy Grail was now flooding Josse's mind. There had been other works by this Geoffrey of Monmouth; Josse had met folk who had eagerly consumed every word the man and his imitators had written. Copies of the manuscripts were readily available, although their cost made them the preserve of the wealthy. It was said that Queen Eleanor and the late King Henry had been fascinated by the tales and had made a royal visit to Glastonbury, a site closely associated with Arthur.

Glastonbury. Bones. Pilgrimage. Something was knocking loudly and insistently on the door of Josse's attention, demanding admission.

'Excuse me, my lady,' he said, interrupting Isabella, busy outlining the wonders of Arthur's court. He bowed briefly in apology. 'If all this is leading up to an announcement that King

Arthur's bones have been unearthed in the Great Wealden Forest, then that can't be so because they were dug up by the monks of Glastonbury Abbey five years ago.'

'That is quite true,' Brice said gently. 'The Glastonbury monks found the bones of both the King and of Guinevere his Queen, buried in a huge, hollow tree trunk beneath which was a stone and an inscribed lead cross. The Queen's long, fair plait of hair was found, although it fell to dust when it was touched.'

'Hm.' Josse fought to keep his cynicism under control; any belief that he might have originally had in the monks' miraculous find had been tempered by the realisation that Glastonbury Abbey had suffered a devastating fire shortly before the bones had been found and was consequently in desperate need of the money that pilgrims would bring pouring in. But out of deference to his hosts – who were also his good friends – it did not seem polite to mention that fact.

'The inscription on Glastonbury's lead cross is clearly legible,' Isabella was saying. 'It's in Latin: *Hic jacet sepultus inclitus Rex Arturus, in insula Avalonia.*'

'Here lies entombed the famous King Arthur in the Isle of Avalon,' Josse translated softly. To himself he added, how very convenient for Glastonbury, that the bones were so clearly labelled.

'The Isle of Avalon is the old name for Glastonbury and the place to which Joseph of Arimathea brought the Grail,' Isabella said eagerly. 'They say that the area was once under water and that the hill of Glastonbury stood out like an island. There is magic in such sites, Josse, for there the water meets the land, although the boundary between the two elements is ever shifting, ever shrouded in mist. And now we've got such a site of our very own, and it too is located on a magical boundary, for it is where the trees thin out and fade into open heathland and it is exactly the sort of place where such a person would have been buried.'

She was, Josse thought, thrilled and entranced by the discovery. He could understand her reaction, for life in the country tended to stroll along at a fairly even and unhurried pace and anything new was always greeted with enthusiasm. This tale of ancient and highly distinguished bones that could work miracles was news of the most exciting kind; people would be falling over one another to go and have a look, even if they were in no more need of healing miracles than he was and went along out of plain curiosity.

Isabella was still speaking of mysteries and magic. Her voice, he noted, had taken on the hypnotic tone of the story teller who ensnares her listener in the web of her spell . . . Josse blinked, shook his head sharply a couple of times, and the illusion disappeared. She was Isabella, his friend, the wife of his neighbour, and there was no danger present whatsoever.

'So,' he said decisively, 'someone's unearthed King Arthur again, this time in the Wealden Forest.' Brice tried to interrupt but Josse was well into his stride now and did not allow it. 'The man behind the whole business must be – who is he, by the way?'

'His name is Florian of Southfrith,' Brice supplied. 'He's a rich young man, well set-up, handsome, and he lives with his beautiful wife in a modest but very fine manor house near Hadfeld. You know it?'

'The name is familiar but I cannot recall any details.'

'It is the area where the dense trees give way to heath. The forest lies to the north and to the south are the green valleys that eventually rise up to meet the South Downs.'

'And from whom does this Florian of Southfrith hold his lands?' Josse asked. 'His overlord, presumably, will be claiming a goodly portion of the takings?'

'I imagine he holds tenure from the Clares of Tonbridge,' Brice replied mildly. 'Richard de Clare has interests in that direction, although, come to think of it, I cannot say for sure that Florian is his tenant; the lands may belong to Canterbury for all I know.'

'Hmm.' What was I saying? Josse asked himself. I was about to make some point when I was diverted. Ah, yes. 'This Florian is bragging of his miraculous bones in the hope of attracting the sick, injured and needy to his shrine and the people, I would guess, are as one diverting their attention to the new wonder and away from Hawkenlye Abbey.'

'You have it,' Brice agreed. 'It is said that scarcely anyone visits the Hawkenlye shrine any more, so eager are they to see the new discovery for themselves and share in its power.'

'But that's terrible!' Josse said furiously. 'These poor fools must be protected from their own folly, for the dubious claims made for a pile of bones out in the forest can hardly be compared to the skill and care freely on offer at Hawkenlye! As well as the holy water down in the shrine that they give so freely, there are kindly monks and lay brothers to feed and care for those in need, as well as an infirmary full of nursing nuns whose reputation for herbal remedies and healing is well known throughout the land!' It was an exaggeration, but he did not care. 'The very purpose of that magnificent Abbey and its hard-working, selfless people to be cast into the shade by an upstart with a false claim? It is not to be borne!'

He heard the echoes of his furious words die away. He felt ashamed for having shouted; all of this was no fault of Brice's or Isabella's, who had merely relayed the news. He could not in fairness be angry with either of them, for if they chose to believe in something which he himself viewed with the greatest suspicion, then that was their choice. And, from what they had told him, it would seem that their view was the popular one; to have such a discovery made virtually on the doorstep would, for the local populace, be the sort of awesome and exotic event that they could only dream about. Word would spread like fire in a hay barn and soon the whole country would be beating a path to see the new wonder.

He, it appeared, would be in a minority of one.

No.

His would not be the sole voice that spoke out against the new attraction, for he could think of another who would be shoulder to shoulder with him. And *she* most certainly did not stand alone.

Abruptly he stood up, experiencing a brief wave of dizziness; he had been sitting in the heat for too long. For all that the bench was in the shade, the summer afternoon was hot. And two large, empty jugs testified to the amount of ale that he and Brice had downed.

'I must be on my way,' he announced. 'Thank you, Isabella, for your hospitality; thank you both for your entertaining conversation.' He bowed, first to Isabella, then to Brice.

Both of whom, he noticed, were hiding smiles.

'You will be on the road again early tomorrow, I'll warrant,' Brice said.

'Eh? Well – er – I—'

'Don't tease, Brice,' Isabella admonished. 'Dear Josse, your affection for the Hawkenlye community is well known and we merely surmise that you would wish to support them in their time of trouble.'

Josse turned worried eyes to her. 'That is so, my lady. Any help that I can offer is hers – is theirs to command.'

'The new shrine may be but a passing attraction,' Isabella said.

'Especially if the supply of miracles starts to run out,' Brice added cynically.

Isabella frowned at him. 'If the discovery is true, such will not be the case.'

Her remark recalled to Josse something that had been worrying him and he spoke it aloud. 'Tell me one thing: just how can these bones be those of Arthur when we are told that Arthur and Guinevere are buried at Glastonbury?'

Again, the exchange of glances between Brice and Isabella. Then, at a faint nod from his wife, Brice took Josse's arm. 'Florian is not claiming to have found Arthur's bones,' he murmured.

Despite the heat, a shiver seemed to run through Josse. Fearing that he already knew the answer, he whispered, 'Whose, then?'

Brice's eyes were oddly sympathetic. Softly he replied, 'It is said that they belong to Merlin.'

# 2

Josse rode in through the gates of Hawkenlye Abbey in the middle of the morning of the next day, having covered the familiar road from New Winnowlands in what was probably record time. He had been awake early, anxious to speak to the Abbess. He had dreamt of her; she had been floating on a moonlit expanse of lake and she had held up a hand to him, pleading for his help. Reaching down, he had found her surprisingly strong and had been helpless to save himself as she pulled him down into the bright water. He had woken shaken and sweating and offered a brief, panicky prayer that the dream was not an omen.

Now the hot June sunshine had dispelled night fears and as he handed Horace's reins to Sister Ursel, the Abbey porteress, he was more than ready to exchange the usual mildly flirtatious remarks with the stout old nun. She, however, was not; he could tell from her very demeanour that something was wrong.

'What's the matter, Sister?' As if he did not know. He put a hand out to touch hers.

But she shook her head. 'Better talk to the Abbess, Sir Josse. She'll tell you.' And before he could ask again, she had clicked her tongue to Horace and was leading the big horse off in the direction of Sister Martha's stables.

Leaving Josse to wonder where the Abbess was and how quickly he could find her.

He spotted her quite soon. She was coming out of the Abbey

church and what looked like the entire contingent of Vale monks followed behind her. As he watched, she turned to exchange a few words with them, giving them all what from long experience he recognised as her best, bracing, chins-up smile. The monks bowed to their superior and headed off for the rear gate and the path that led down to the Vale.

The Abbess turned, saw Josse and, her face now beaming in a genuinely happy smile, hurried to greet him.

'What luck that you should arrive, just when I have been praying for your company!' she said, reaching out to take both his hands in hers. 'Sir Josse, rarely have you been more welcome!'

Flattered that she should have been praying he would turn up, nevertheless he thought it only right to explain that, as far as he knew, it was not divine intervention that had brought him. Hastily he said, 'My lady Abbess, right pleased I am to see you, too, but I know what it is that troubles you and that makes you glad of my presence.'

Her face fell. 'You do?'

'Aye. I was with Brice and Isabella – she's expecting another child, by the way – and they told me.'

'I am so happy for Isabella, and for Brice.' Even in her anxiety, the Abbess appeared genuinely delighted at that part of his news. Josse, recalling that she too was aware of the couple's history, felt sure she would include Isabella in her prayers until a healthy baby was safely delivered. 'But, oh, what are we to do about Merlin's Tomb?'

They had begun to walk away from the gate and off in the direction of the Abbess's private room at the far end of the cloister. But, before they reached it, she took hold of his sleeve and indicated a bench, half in sunlight and half in shade, that ran along the wall. 'Let us settle here,' she suggested. 'The morning is too lovely to waste it sitting inside.'

They sat down side by side on the bench. Then he said, 'You notice an effect already, then?'

'Oh, yes!' She turned to face him, distress evident in her expression. 'From towards the end of last month, we began to see a diminution in our visitors. Brother Firmin mentioned it to me – he prepares the Holy Water, as you know, and he was wondering why he did not seem to be as busy as usual. Then Brothers Saul and Augustus began to check on the daily tally of pilgrims and they brought me the results. Usually our numbers are anything from half a dozen to as many as twenty a day – it's the season, Sir Josse; people save their travelling up for fine summer weather and long hours of daylight whenever they can. But now, well, the average was at first closer to three per day. Then two, then, last week, only four people for the entire week. This week' – she gave a pathetic little shrug – 'so far, nobody.'

'*Nobody?* No pilgrims at all?' He was amazed that the rival attraction should have had such a devastating effect so soon.

'Not a one. Here we all sit, ready and eager to fulfil our purpose in life by giving aid to all who come seeking it, yet nobody comes. And oh, Sir Josse, I am so afraid that when word gets round that the people now go elsewhere for succour, as no doubt it already has, then all those who support us so generously will think again.' Lowering her voice to a whisper, as if she could not bear the thought of anyone else hearing the humiliating words, she said, 'We need the funds, you see. We cannot charge for the care that we give; that would be unthinkable, for we do the Lord's work. Yet we must have money to survive and one of our main sources of income is the gifts that the wealthy bestow in exchange for Hawkenlye's prayers and its beneficial, healing presence within the wider community. If our benefactors choose to support a rival foundation, then with a huge and unfillable hole in our income and, far more crucially, without the needy, the lost, the sick and the desperate to care for, we shall no longer have a reason to exist and we are lost.' She looked down at her hands, folded in her lap, and her coif cut off his view of her face. Leaning forward, he saw that she had her eyes tightly shut, as if trying to blot out the dismal prospect before her.

'What shall we do?' he said. 'What *can* we do?'

She turned to him, a smile spreading over her face. 'Dear Josse. Thank you for the *we*.'

He waved away her gratitude, embarrassed, as he always was, when she accredited him with altruistic motives when what he was really doing was to ensure that, for the foreseeable future anyway, he would be near— No. He made himself arrest that thought. 'I know the name of the man behind this tawdry scheme,' he said gruffly.

'*Do* you?' She seemed amazed. 'Sir Josse, you *are* well-informed – I have asked whomsoever I can for details of this dreadful business but they appear to be scant. Who is he?'

'He's a young man named Florian of Southfrith.'

'Southfrith. He is a local man, then, for the Southfrith lands are close by. Yet he made his discovery on the far side of the forest, where the woodland peters out and the heathland begins.'

'So I'm told. Giant bones, apparently, and this Florian seems to have sufficient evidence to prove that they belong to Merlin. My lady,' he turned to her with a frown, 'what puzzles me is how it is that all the people who now divert like brainless sheep after the bellwether to this new shrine know the name of Merlin!'

She looked surprised. 'But Sir Josse, everyone has heard of Merlin. I would warrant a small wager that if we assembled my nuns and monks and asked for a show of hands, all but those with their heads permanently in the clouds – and I own that we do have a few of those – would raise their arms and say, Merlin? Oh, yes, I know of Merlin. He was King Arthur's magician.'

Greatly taken aback – was he in truth the only person in

England not to be fascinated by this Arthur and his companions? – Josse shook his head wonderingly. 'I see.' His voice
sounded dejected, even to himself. Then: 'My lady, I do not
believe for one moment that these vast bones belong to Merlin.
Do you?'

She hesitated. 'I would like to be as sure as you, Sir Josse,
but I do not think that I can. For one thing, it seems that
miracles have already been reported and attributed directly to
Merlin's intervention.'

'But—' He had been on the point of saying that miracles
always happened at shrines; in his own view, he had a vague
and barely formed notion that when people genuinely believed they were going to become well again, quite often they
did. The healing water, or the saint's finger bone, or the
splinter of the True Cross, or the phial of the Blessed
Virgin's milk, might be the impetus that brought about that
belief, but the cure itself was merely the body doing what it
was best at.

However, recognising that his own ideas were quite irrational and probably blasphemous as well, Josse firmly closed
his mouth on his objection.

'But?' the Abbess prompted.

He shook his head. 'Nothing, my lady.'

After a while, she spoke again. 'Brother Firmin said something comforting,' she said slowly.

'Aye? And what was that?'

'He is remarkably sanguine about the whole thing. I was
relieved – I had thought that he would be deeply distressed at
this apparent shunning of the precious Holy Water that has
become almost his life's blood. And he is still weak, you know,
after the sickness last year.'

'Aye.' Privately Josse was amazed that the old monk was still
alive.

'I asked him why he seemed so unconcerned,' the Abbess

went on, 'and he replied that as soon as the pilgrims realise that the new shrine doesn't work, they'll be back.

'But it does work,' Josse protested. 'You have just been telling me of the recent miracles.'

'Brother Firmin maintains that they are false. He was very apologetic about what he saw as wishing disappointment on those who think they've been cured, but he says that what appear to be miracles are just the excitement of the new attraction.'

'Does he, now?' Good for Firmin, Josse thought, quite surprised that the old boy should demonstrate such clear-eyed objectivity. 'Well, my lady, that is an encouraging thought. But since we can have no idea of how long it will be before people discover their mistake, and since the Abbey which you and I both love is suffering in the meantime—'

'*And* people are being seduced away from the true source of help,' she put in. 'If it is true that these are the bones of Merlin, then I am a little surprised that they should have brought about healing, for Merlin was a sage and a magician but not specifically a man who was renowned for the working of miracle cures. Whereas our Holy Water spring was discovered via the direct intercession of the Blessed Virgin herself who, as you will recall, Sir Josse, appeared to a party of French merchants dying of fever and told them that the water would cure them, as indeed it did.'

'Aye, I remember, and indeed there's that too . . . Where was I? Oh, yes. We can't just sit back and wait. We must *do* something.'

'*Yes,*' she cried, as fervent as he. Then: 'What?'

He thought for a moment. Then he said slowly, 'My lady, you keep in your mind room for doubt, I think; you will not say definitely that these bones are not what they are claimed to be.'

'No-o,' she agreed tentatively.

'I am less charitable and I am all but certain that this is

nothing but a scheme cooked up by a clever man to rob the credulous of their money.'

'But you can't be sure!' she protested. 'What if the bones are genuine and are really capable of doing good and helping those in need?'

Thinking that he'd eat his cap if they were, Josse said, 'I will try to keep an open mind, my lady. What I propose to do is to present myself at Merlin's Tomb as a pilgrim. That way I shall experience exactly what the ordinary man or woman experiences. I shall listen when I am spoken to, kneel before whatever sort of display has been set up, express my awe at being in the presence of such a wonder and proclaim myself cured of whatever I have stated ails me.'

'What good will that do?' she demanded. From her faintly aggrieved tone, he guessed she was reluctant to dismiss Merlin's bones as a total sham. He made a mental note to bear this attitude of hers in mind; he did not want to risk hurting her feelings by speaking too bluntly.

Yet.

'Well, for one thing I'm not in fact suffering from any ailment, God be thanked' – the exclamation was in response to the swift glance she shot him, as if warning him against taking his sound health for granted and not giving credit where it was due – 'and so I will not have the sense of desperation that may blind other visitors to what is really going on.'

'Many will be there purely because they are curious,' she said. 'They may not be desperate either.'

'Aye, you're right, but I'll warrant I'm probably the only man there who is out to prove the whole thing is false.'

She studied him intently. 'You have no faith at all in these being the bones of Merlin, have you?' she murmured.

He tried to decide between tact and honesty. Honesty won. 'No.'

He thought she was about to reprimand him for his

cynicism. But then she began to laugh. 'Dear Josse. What would I do without you?'

Full of confusion, he felt the hot blood flush his face. 'My lady, I—'

She waved a hand. 'Sir Josse, no need for explanations. We must agree to differ, but I must admit in fairness that I am more than grateful for your disbelief. You are the very person to do what you propose and pay a visit to the tomb.'

'Thank you. I—'

But she was not in the mood for small talk and polite remarks. Interrupting him, she demanded, 'How soon can you set off?'

They decided that Josse's pretence of being a simple pilgrim with a bad back would be made to look more credible if he rode the Abbey's old cob instead of the magnificent Horace and exchanged his fine tunic for something less distinguished. The monks in the Vale and the nuns in the infirmary were conscientious in their vow of poverty and did not waste anything: whenever someone died in their care they would, in the absence of any other claimant, remove the clothing and inspect it carefully. If the garments were capable of salvage – often people died in rags – the nuns would launder, darn and mend until the clothes were once more fit for wear. Then they would be folded away in a large chest in which small linen bags of lavender were scattered as a deterrent to moths. Accordingly, Josse's present need was easily met by a visit to Sister Emanuel, who ran the retirement home for aged nuns and monks and who, among her other duties, was in charge of the clothing chest.

Josse, in common with just about everybody else in the Hawkenlye community – including its Abbess – was a little in awe of Sister Emanuel. She was highly intelligent, educated and reserved; the pale skin of her face had a strangely smooth and unlined quality, as if the woman had seldom been affected by the sort of emotions that make normal people frown in anger, screw up their eyes in distress or crease every part of their faces in hearty laughter. As he entered the retirement home, Josse noticed that she was instantly alert to his presence; she got up from where she had been seated at the bedside of a very old and incredibly tiny woman and, her step steady and unhurried, glided over to the door to greet him.

'Good morning, Sir Josse.' Her voice was low-pitched but clearly audible; she would, Josse thought, be used to dealing with the deafness of the very old. 'How may I help you?'

'Good morning, Sister Emanuel,' he returned. He explained his request and she gave a brief nod, turning on her heel and, beckoning to him, stepping over to the left of the door where, in a recess, stood a large wooden chest.

Opening it, she knelt and carefully checked through the folded garments. A sweet scent of lavender rose to Josse's nostrils and he breathed in deeply, reflecting in passing that such an impulse was not one you would normally wish to indulge in an old people's home. But Sister Emanuel, he knew, would not permit the stench of urine and unwashed flesh in her domain; what luck, he reflected, to be cared for by one such as her at the end of a long life.

She stood up, a bundle of soft, moss-green woollen cloth in her arms. Shaking it out, she held the garment against Josse: it was a tunic, generously cut if a little short. 'I think this will do,' she said, bending down to see just where the hem fell. 'It was once a fine garment, but has been worn for rather too long.' She pointed to several neat darns.

'It is just what I want,' Josse assured her. 'A decent fellow fallen on hard times, that's me.'

She risked a very small smile. Delving back into the chest, she extracted a leather cap. 'And what about this to cover your head?'

He tried it on. It fitted perfectly. 'Thank you, Sister. I am grateful.'

She bowed. Then, as if eager to return to her charges, she courteously showed him to the door.

Josse and the Abbey cob were old friends. Being in no great hurry, for his destination was probably only eight or ten miles distant, Josse did not press the aged animal but was content to jog along at a pace that was mostly an ambling trot. His path curved round to the east and then turned southwards, then south-westwards, following the outer perimeter of the Great Forest. It would have been more direct to ride straight through the thick woodland but Josse, like everyone else in the area, avoided going into the forest unless he really had to.

Sister Basilia in the refectory kitchens had packed up some food for him and after an hour or so he stopped in the deep shade of an oak tree and, leaning against its trunk while the cob grazed nearby, ate his bread and cheese and drank the flagon of small beer.

He had been given only vague directions to the new shrine but he was reasonably confident of finding it. He rode along slowly now, the path following a slight rise in the heathland to the south, watching the densely growing trees and undergrowth to his right and looking out for a break that would give access to the interior. As it turned out, he could not have missed the spot even without such careful attention: a steady stream of people was tramping along the track, making for the shrine, and all he had to do was follow the herd.

The trees on the edge of the forest had been thinned to allow clear access. About a dozen large trees had been hacked down, their raw, wide trunks testimony to the size and age of the amputated trees. Across the space that they had left was a path, clearly marked by stones set at regular intervals along each side.

Into Josse's head flew the thought: the forest people will not like this.

He pictured Joanna, who lived away on the other side of the forest but who nevertheless, he knew without a doubt, would be well aware of this violation. Then he thought of the strange, otherworldly woman known only as the Domina, and a shudder of fear went through him. The Domina had power and the Great Forest was her land. What would she do in response to this abomination?

For abomination was what it was. Dismounting and leading the cob – there were many people on the path, young and old, and Josse did not want to push through on horseback and make them leap out of the way – he saw with horrified eyes just what Florian of Southfrith had done.

He had desecrated a venerable and beautiful area of ancient forest for what Josse firmly believed was entirely his own gain. If it was true that he had come across something of genuinely grave importance, if they really were Merlin's bones lying there in the tomb, then surely there was a better way of sharing the discovery. Florian ought to have first reported his find to Hawkenlye, Josse thought angrily, possibly also involving the secular authorities, and someone should have brought the forest people in on the discussions. That way, arrangements could have been made for the people to visit the tomb in a controlled manner and there would have been no need for this violence against the forest. As it was, one selfish man thinking only of his own pocket had forged ahead with such ruthless speed that it had left the rest of them breathless.

Horrified, furious, he walked on.

The felled trees at the forest edge were only the start of it. At the place where the path terminated, some twenty or thirty paces within the woodland, many more trees had been roughly cut down and a great swath of undergrowth had been swept away, the leaf mould of hundreds – thousands – of years untidy with heaps of sawdust, bits of broken branch, leaves and twigs. Despite the fact that a considerable sum of money must have been spent on the place, everywhere there was a depressingly rough, uncaring look, markedly in contrast with the mature and dignified nature of the native forest.

A raw-looking fence had been erected, split chestnut rails nailed to uneven uprights. It had all the hallmarks of something done in haste and not very well. Where the path met the fence there was a stout gate, now standing open. The heavy chain hanging from it suggested that it could be firmly locked when necessary; nobody, it seemed, was going to visit Merlin's Tomb unless Florian of Southfrith said they could.

A thick-set man in a leather jerkin stood by the gate. As each visitor approached, he was demanding something . . .

Just as I expected, Josse thought.

Florian had gone one step further than merely to make money from the refreshments and accommodation he was offering. He actually had the nerve to demand an admission fee.

Josse reached into his pouch and prepared some coins. When he was face to face with the mean-looking man on the gate, he offered a couple of clipped silver half-pennies, hoping that one of them would suffice. Both were quietly taken from his open palm. The man gave him a quick grin that was no more than a stretching of his lips and curtly nodded him through.

Within the enclosure another man came to take the cob; he, too, was heavily built and he bore the facial scars and flattened nose that suggested a life of fighting. Reckoning that it was no doubt the large amounts of money being made that necessitated so many guards – for that was surely what they were; there were three more of them loitering just inside the fence – Josse handed over the horse's reins.

He edged along the path behind an old woman supporting

an even older man. Turning, she gave him the time of day. Her expression was tense, her sunken blue eyes bright with excitement.

'What's up with you, then?' she asked.

'My back.' Josse adopted a crouch and put a hand to the small of his back.

'Ah-ha!' She grimaced understandingly, as if she knew all about bad backs. 'My old man here' – she gave the man beside her a nudge in his skinny ribs – 'he's all but blind.' The old man turned to peer at Josse through cloudy eyes and gave him a nod. 'But that'll soon change!' the woman added happily.

Josse felt a stab of pity for her hopeless optimism. 'You expect a miracle?'

'Oh, yes,' she said confidently. 'It's Merlin, isn't it? He's magic, he is, and he's one of us.' Lowering her voice, she added in a whisper, 'He and his magic were here long before the other lot came. They may have their fine abbeys and their holy springs but they can't stamp out the old ways, now, can they? And now here's our Merlin returned to us and back in his rightful place!' She smiled her satisfaction. '*Now* we'll see some wonders!'

Not entirely sure what she meant by *the other lot* – it sounded disturbingly as if she was referring to the Christian church and perhaps Hawkenlye in particular – Josse murmured a meaningless acknowledgement. Just then the line moved on several paces and he said, 'I wish you luck!'

'You too!' the old woman called.

He shuffled slowly on, one hand on his back, face screwed up in pretend pain, letting a gap develop between himself and the elderly couple. He wanted to take his time in studying the whole area. The path led on to a second, higher, fence, also gated; this second fence was solidly built with hazel hurdles and underbrush and Josse could see neither over nor through it. By the open gate stood a man.

He was younger and far less heavily built than the toughs on the outer fence. He was also much better dressed, in a tunic of bright scarlet velvet trimmed with heavy gold braid. His boots were of soft leather, fitted him like a second skin and looked brand-new. His hair – bright chestnut and gleaming with cleanliness – was neatly cut and his light grey eyes shone with health. He was clean-shaven and extremely handsome. He was, undoubtedly, Florian of Southfrith.

Josse approached him and gave him a low bow, as befitted an impoverished man with backache greeting a young and wealthy lord.

A long, pale hand was extended, resting on Josse's shoulder in a brief touch. 'Rise up,' intoned an educated voice, in the tone of a priest bestowing a blessing, 'for your suffering will soon be at an end.' Josse straightened, looking the young man in the face. Florian appeared taken aback at such a bold stare; hastily Josse lowered his eyes.

'Thank'ee, Master,' he muttered.

'When I tell you to do so, you may walk on to the sacred spot,' the soft voice went on. 'Make your appeal, leave whatever offering you have brought, and then make your way past. You will be shown where to go.'

'Thank'ee,' Josse said again. He very much wanted to have another look at young Florian, but he had learned by his earlier mistake. The poor, the humble and the afflicted did not habitually meet the eyes of their lord.

There was a short wait, and then Florian tapped Josse on the arm and said, 'You may go on now.'

Josse walked forward along the path.

It turned abruptly left, and then right; whatever lay at its far end was designed to be out of sight until a visitor reached it.

Stepping out into the open, Josse was faced with a stunning sight.

The ground had been cleared and stamped down and the

forest floor here was now bare earth. The trees and the undergrowth had been cut back for some four or five paces in each direction, so that the sun shone down into the glade. There was a trio of thorn trees standing on the perimeter; pieces of coloured rag and ribbon had been tied to the lower branches. The ground sloped gently, higher to the far side of the clearing, falling away to the near, southern side. Right in the middle of the open space was a long, deep scar.

Josse went closer.

Now he could see over the lip of the steep-sided hollow into its dark interior. The pit had been walled with stones and its base appeared to be one vast slab. Stretched out on the slab, arms by its sides and fingers gently curved over the wide palms, was the huge and intact skeleton of a man who must in life have been a veritable giant.

Whatever else might be a lie or a false claim, these bones looked real enough and, despite himself, Josse was awestruck. His eyes ran over the huge bones – large dome of the skull, with the brow ridges elegantly curved; long, heavy arms, deep ribs; wide pelvis, femurs and lower leg bones stretching endlessly. He glanced down at his own legs then back at the skeleton, calculating that the giant's legs must have been at least an arm's length longer than his own. Which would have meant that had Josse and the giant stood side by side, the giant would have towered over him by perhaps almost as much as a quarter of Josse's own height.

He did not know what to make of it. Expecting a very obvious fraud – a pile of bones scavenged from some old, forgotten burial ground, perhaps, or even the cast-offs from a slaughter house – here he was faced with a real human skeleton, moreover an unusually large one. It was . . . disturbing.

Josse realised as he stood there in silent, entranced contemplation that something was happening: there was a definite sense of power emanating from the skeleton and he could feel the hairs on his arms tickle his skin as they rose in response to his atavistic dread. *It's not Merlin!* he shouted silently, fighting his sudden alarm. It can't be; Merlin is nothing but a legend. Am I to be like some ignorant peasant, deluded by a clever man's trickery? For trickery it is, he told himself, struggling to keep a clear head and a rational outlook. Whatever power these huge bones may possess, Florian of Southfrith is claiming it to be something it isn't and in my view, Josse thought grimly, that amounts to deception.

But argue with himself as he might, still Josse's body defied his brain as the fear and the awe flooded him.

He tore his enchanted eyes from the bones and caught sight of the faint gleam of some dull, dark metal on the far side of the tomb. Moving around the head end of the pit so as to have a closer look, he saw that it was a plaque, probably made of lead. It was roughly in the shape of an equal-armed cross, pitted and broken at the edges as if it had, in truth, spent six hundred years in the ground. The inscription was in Latin and read *Here lies Merlin, magician to King Arthur. Look upon his power and fear him.*

Trying desperately to shake himself free of the spell, Josse took a pace – two, three paces – away from the tomb. And abruptly the dread left him.

He stumbled on, following the path as it curved away, concealing the tomb once more. His breath came more easily now and he felt the sweat of fear drying on his back. By the time he reached the huddle of tables, benches and low, rudely fashioned huts where the pilgrims took their refreshments, he was breathing normally again.

Almost.

# 3

As he rode thoughtfully back to Hawkenlye Abbey, Josse tried to distract his thoughts from his reaction to the strange power of the bones by attempting to calculate just how much money Florian of Southfrith must be making out of his convincing and seductive new venture. There was the admission fee; he recalled the not inconsiderable sum of two silver half-pennies that had been extracted from him, although it was possible that those pleading extreme poverty might get in for less. How many visitors could there be in a day? Twenty? No, more, surely, for they had been arriving steadily throughout the time span of Josse's approach, arrival and departure. Forty, then, and that estimate was surely on the low side. Even if every one gave just half a penny, that was twenty pennies. It would take a working man three weeks to make that much.

Then there was the food and drink that was on offer after the pilgrims had visited the tomb. Hot and thirsty after the journey, surely it would have taken either a strong will or an empty purse to resist the mugs of beer and the plates of bread, dried meat and cheese invitingly spread out. Josse had succumbed to temptation; he had been surprised to find the small beer pretty good, although the bread was hard and the meat had what looked like a maggot hole in it. His meal – served up by another of the strong-looking guards – had cost him another half-penny.

Assuming the same forty visitors, of whom perhaps thirty took refreshments, then that was another fifteen pennies.

Some people clearly made use of the overnight accommodation; Josse had observed that one of the huts contained a pile of straw palliasses and a heap of blankets. Goodness only knew what the charge was for spending the night in Florian's hut. And then there would probably be another half a penny for food and drink in the morning; people were reluctant to start a long walk with nothing in their bellies. Perhaps a penny for accommodation and breakfast? If only one family spent the night, that was at least another shilling a week.

Was there anything else? Josse thought it over. Oh, yes – the offerings. There had been a depression in the ground between the tomb and the refreshment tables, at the bottom of which a little spring welled up out of the earth. The stony bed of the spring had, by the time Josse passed by, been already covered with coins and with what had looked like pieces of jewellery and other small metal items such as pins and pocket knives. Doubtless people felt that Merlin would be more likely to answer their prayers if they gave him something and Florian was obviously encouraging them in this belief; Josse himself had been invited to leave his offering, although in fact he had not done so.

There was no way that he could accurately judge just what Florian was making each day. What was absolutely certain, however, was that it was a very great deal.

Keeping that fact at the forefront of his mind and pushing firmly aside the memory of how Merlin's Tomb had affected him, Josse kicked the cob into a surprisingly sprightly canter and headed for the Abbey and the Abbess.

Helewise looked up from her work to see Josse standing in the open doorway. With a smile of welcome, she indicated the stool that she kept for visitors and invited him to sit down and tell her all about it.

She heard him out in silence, nodding occasionally. When

he had finished, she said slowly, 'Sir Josse, it is far, far worse than I feared, for the crowds whom you describe who queue up so patiently and so optimistically to view the tomb are clearly not to be deterred by reasoned argument. Even if we made a direct appeal – and, believe me, I have been contemplating such a move – I do not think that anyone is at present in a mood to leave the thrilling excitement and promise of the new for the unchanging reliability of Hawkenlyc.'

He seemed to be on the point of speaking but appeared to change his mind; probably, she thought grimly, because, although he would like to protest, *he knows I speak the truth.* She thought for a while, did some mental calculations and then said, 'If I reckon aright, this Florian of Southfrith must be making roughly twenty shillings a day.' As the enormity of that sum struck her – why, a chaplain only earned twice that in a *year*! – she realised she must have made a mistake. 'But that cannot be right,' she added.

But Josse was nodding glumly. 'No mistake, my lady. That's what I worked out too. And, believe me, I was cautious in my estimates and so the likelihood is that he's coining in a great deal more.'

'He is surely unlikely to go on making so much,' she said doubtfully. 'As the proverb has it, a wonder lasts nine days, and then the puppy's eyes are open.'

'Hm.'

She had expected a more emphatic endorsement of her remark; had he not sat outside this very room only this morning and claimed firmly that the whole Merlin's Tomb business was nothing but a hoax? 'Sir Josse?' she said enquiringly. 'Do you not agree that people will soon tire of this new attraction and see it for the money-making scheme that it is?'

He met her eyes. 'I am not so sure, my lady,' he admitted.

'Oh? How so?'

He cast his eyes around the room as if seeking inspiration. Then: 'I expected to feel nothing or, if anything, disgust and contempt for a clever piece of dupery. Yet when I stood by the tomb looking down at those enormous bones—' He broke off, shrugged and then said, 'They give off a force. I felt as if I were in the presence of a great power that I did not understand.'

'*Josse!* Oh, then there *is* something in all this and it is not just a fraud!' She put her hand to her mouth, horrified by his admission. If he of all people had been so affected, then what of the more credulous? Oh, dear Lord, they would go from Merlin's Tomb straight home to their towns, villages, hamlets and hovels, tell their family, friends and neighbours how wonderful it had been and in no time all those whom they told would be setting out too. The present steady stream of people would become a river, a torrent, a full-moon *tide*, and nobody would ever come near Hawkenlye again . . .

With some effort, she made herself stop.

But Josse, dear Josse, must have seen the terrible vision that she saw. 'My lady, do not despair,' he said softly.

She managed a small smile. 'I see very little reason not to.'

He had stood up and was pacing to and fro across her small room. His restless presence, as always, made it seem even smaller. 'Florian of Southfrith must be made to stop,' he announced.

'But why?' she demanded. 'If there is a power in these bones, and if it is benign' – she suddenly appreciated that this was quite a big *if* – 'then what right have we to come between the people and a source of succour? Times continue to be hard, Sir Josse. It is but two years since everyone in the land had to give far more than they could afford in order to buy back our King. Yet what have they in exchange for their enforced generosity? King Richard stayed in England less than two months and then set off campaigning again and we have seen neither hide nor hair of him since. Purchasing the King's freedom has cost the people dear and it will, I fear, take them a very long time to regain any sort of security. Some will never achieve it and will live in wretched poverty and miserable uncertainty until they die.' She heard her voice rise with passion and took a moment to regain her composure. Then she said quietly, 'If they find comfort and help in this Merlin's Tomb, then should we try to stop it?'

'If it is based on a fallacy then yes, indeed we should.' Again, Josse did not sound as certain as she would have liked.

'The crucial question being whether or not it is a fallacy,' she murmured.

'Aye.' He gave a gusty sigh.

She thought for a while and then said, 'Sir Josse, if these bones are not Merlin's, then they have to be someone else's.' He smiled briefly at the simplicity of her argument but did not interrupt. 'Then perhaps we should turn our efforts to discovering whose the bones are,' she went on.

'They're very large,' Josse put in. 'The man in that grave would easily have stood head and chest above me, if not more.'

'That much taller than you!' She was shocked, for Josse was no midget.

'Well, maybe not quite,' he admitted.

'Who on earth *was* he?' she murmured wonderingly. She had always dismissed tales of giants as nothing more than fairy stories. To have the skeleton of one found not ten miles away was disturbing, to say the least . . . 'If it is true that Florian did not make this miraculous find on the forest fringe with its lead cross helpfully providing identity—'

'I'll stake my reputation that he didn't,' Josse said.

'—then he must have found the skeleton somewhere else, manufactured the lead cross, dug a hole in the forest floor, lined it with stone and placed a slab in its base, then transported the bones. He would have had to wait a while for the grave to lose its air of raw newness—'

'Not so long at this time of year,' Josse put in. 'In May and June everything grows so fast and signs of recent labour would soon have been covered up.'

'Very well. Let us say he waited a few weeks. Then he chops down the trees to make his clearing, puts up fences and huts and then makes the announcement. You and I both know full well how news travels, especially when it concerns a miracle. All Florian would have to do was sit back and wait.'

Josse was frowning and she wondered if there was some point with which he wished to take issue. 'Sir Josse?'

'My lady, I was thinking of something prompted by the first part of your proposed account.' He glared at her, although she knew his anger was not directed at her. 'The trees,' he said bluntly.

'The trees?' She tried to follow. Then light dawned. 'Oh, I see. You are thinking of the forest people.'

'Aye. We have seen in the past how they react to unnecessary felling of trees. I am thinking, my lady, that I would not wish to be in the shoes of the man who roused the wrath of the Domina.'

'Neither would I,' she agreed fervently.

There was a short silence in the little room. He, she imagined, was thinking the same as she. Who would be the first to put the thought into words?

It was Josse. 'I should seek them out,' he said slowly. 'The forest people, I mean. I'll go into the forest and try to locate one of them, and ask to be taken to her. The Domina,' he added, as if he could have meant anyone else.

But he could, she suddenly realised: he could have meant Joanna.

Joanna lived in the Great Forest. She was one of the forest people and Helewise had good reason to know that her powers had been steadily growing until she too was a force to be feared. She also had reason to know that to speak of Joanna was difficult for Josse.

But speak of her she must.

'Joanna too will be greatly disturbed by this intrusion,' she said softly. 'Should you, do you think, seek her out too?'

He turned pained eyes to her. 'She is not always there to *be* sought out,' he said. 'Since I found out about Meggie, I have sometimes tried to. She said I might,' he added, as if he needed to excuse his actions. Not to me, Helewise thought quickly. Why should a man not wish to see his natural child, *and* the woman who bore her?

'You have tried to go and visit, but found her away from home?' Helewise prompted.

'Aye. Three times now, since that business with the Eye of Jerusalem.'

'She saved my life, and that of others,' Helewise observed. 'I have never thanked her. Perhaps I ought to.'

Josse was watching her. 'She'd probably be at home to *you*,' he said roughly.

'Oh, Josse, don't—' She could feel his pain and instantly wanted to comfort him. But she did not know how to. She bowed her head.

After some time she said, '*I* will go into the forest, with Sister Tiphaine as my guide.' Sister Tiphaine was the herbalist; rumoured still to be part-pagan despite all the years she had spent as a nun, she was known to have contacts and friends among the Forest Folk. 'We shall try to find the Domina and also perhaps Joanna, if she is there to be found, and speak to them concerning their views on Merlin's Tomb. It may be that Hawkenlye and the Forest will unite in their opposition, and both be the stronger for having a powerful ally.'

He nodded slowly. 'Aye. And it can surely do no harm to discover what they think.' Tearing himself away with an obvious effort from thoughts of the forest and those who dwelt within it, he said, 'As for me, I shall don my true identity

and visit Florian's home, then return to the wider area around
the tomb. If it is as we conjecture and Florian has transported
bones from elsewhere, then perhaps I shall be able to find out
where he found them. If that fails, I shall consider approaching
Florian himself to demand some explanations.'

She looked at him. 'Be careful,' she warned. 'He is making a
great deal of money and he will not be willing to discuss the
whys and wherefores with anyone, even a well-armed knight
such as yourself.'

'I am a King's man,' he said with a hint of pride.

'So you are but, on your own admission, Florian surrounds
himself with bodyguards.'

'Hm.' He looked as if he would have preferred it if he had
kept that fact to himself. 'Very well, my lady. I shall be careful.'

'I will pray for you,' she said gently. 'Once again, you take
on a force that threatens the Abbey and, once again, we are in
your debt.'

He grinned. 'Don't feel too much indebtedness until you
know it's warranted,' he said. 'I may achieve precisely nothing
in my endeavours.'

'That I doubt,' she returned. 'When will you set out?'

'First light tomorrow.' He stretched. 'For now, I will reclaim
my own clothes and return these garments to Sister Emanuel.
Then I shall visit the monks in the Vale and ask them to
provide me with some food and a bed for the night.'

He made a sketchy bow, headed for the door and was gone.

The next morning Helewise sought out Sister Tiphaine immediately after Tierce. She made her way around to the herb
garden, where the neat rows of plants were growing abun-
dantly under the June sunshine. Sweet, potent smells floated
up to her and she breathed in deeply, enjoying the sensation as
some of the plants' power surged into her lungs.

The herbalist was standing inside her little hut. The door

was propped open and the soft sound of Sister Tiphaine's humming could be heard. It sounded more like a chant, as if the herbalist were making some incantation to empower whatever remedy she was working on . . . Wisely, Helewise decided not to enquire.

'Sister Tiphaine!' she called out as she approached.

Abruptly the humming broke off. 'My lady Abbess,' Sister Tiphaine greeted her, wiping her hands on a spotless piece of white linen and coming to stand in the doorway.

'Sister, I have to go into the forest,' Helewise said without preamble – she was feeling quite apprehensive and the best way to deal with qualms was, in her experience, to ride straight at them – 'and I need you to be my guide.'

'Of course, my lady.'

'It's this wretched business of the new shrine.'

'Merlin's Tomb, they're calling it.' There was scorn in the herbalist's tone.

'Yes, indeed they are. Well, whether it is or not' – she could have been mistaken but she thought she heard Sister Tiphaine mutter, 'It's not' – 'it is giving us a very great problem because it is diverting the pilgrims who would otherwise come here. Since a large part of the reason for our very existence is to care for those who come to take our healing waters, this is not a situation that I wish to see continue for any longer than can be helped.' She realised that she was sounding pompous. Looking straight into Sister Tiphaine's deep eyes, she said simply, 'For their own reasons, the forest people must be equally distressed at this intrusion. It is my hope that I might meet the Domina and discuss our position. Can you – will you – help?'

Sister Tiphaine did not answer for a few moments. Then she said, 'My lady, you say *our* situation, yet I believe that the interests of Hawkenlye and of the Forest in this matter are not similar.'

'That's as may be,' said Helewise with some impatience,

'but I would guess that both parties would like to see an end to this Merlin's Tomb.'

'Indeed,' Sister Tiphaine muttered. Then: 'I will guide you through the forest, my lady. I cannot say whether we shall meet the Domina, although I feel sure that she is close.' She frowned. 'As you surmise, the violation that has been perpetrated by Florian of Southfrith deeply disturbs and distresses those who guard the sanctity of the trees.'

'Quite.' Helewise was surprised that Sister Tiphaine, who kept herself to herself and did not indulge in Abbey gossip, should know the name of the man behind the Merlin's Tomb trickery. If, indeed, trickery was what it was . . . Oh, what she would give to be absolutely sure! 'Well, let us be on our way, then,' she concluded briskly, 'and you must do your best.'

Sister Tiphaine bowed. 'Very well, my lady.'

Tiphaine led the way along the forest path, turning her head now and then to ensure that the Abbess was still close behind her. Although she had said she was not sure of being able to locate the Domina, in truth she was pretty certain that she could, for that Great One of the people was bound to be in the area. As Tiphaine had hinted to her superior, the Forest Folk had reacted furiously to what Florian had done. There was the question of the felled trees and the great swathe of raw ground where he had ordered his workmen to hack away the undergrowth; there were also those two crude fences and the tacky, badly built huts that would blow apart in the first strong wind and that probably already let in the rain.

Worse, far worse, was the skeleton now lying exposed in an open grave for no better reason than that an unscrupulous man wanted to make money. A great deal of money. The forest people – and Tiphaine herself was sufficiently tied to them to feel the same strong emotion – were carrying the fact of those huge disinterred bones like a permanent hurt, a growing pain that nagged and bit and refused to let go.

The Forest and the Abbey both would like to see an end to it, the Abbess had said. Oh, thought Tiphaine now, she does not know how truly she spoke!

They came to a wide clearing a mile or so within the forest. Tiphaine stopped, looking around and sniffing the air.

'Where are we?' the Abbess asked, coming to stand beside her. 'I do not know this place.'

Tiphaine glanced at her. The Abbess, she knew, was no stranger to the forest; living so close beneath its shadow, she had had occasion more than once to enter deep within its mysterious interior when the interests of Abbey and Great Forest coincided.

As indeed they did now.

'It is a place of meeting, my lady,' she said, keeping her voice low. 'Usually a watch is kept on this glade so that word may be passed on when someone comes here.'

'You mean we're being observed?' The Abbess glanced around and Tiphaine felt her apprehension.

'Aye, but not with any malicious intent. They know you, my lady, and respect you.'

'Oh!'

Tiphaine hid a smile; one of the things that she most admired about her superior was her absence of grandeur. It was true that she could be prideful in small matters, but her evident surprise at being told she was held in esteem by the Forest Folk was typical of her. Abbess of a great foundation such as Hawkenlye she might be, but she did not expect everyone to fall on their knees and grovel at her feet because of it.

'Shall we wait, my lady, and see what may happen?' Tiphaine suggested.

'Yes.'

They moved across to where a fallen log made a convenient bench seat – which in fact was exactly why it had been placed there – and made themselves comfortable. Tiphaine, happy to be out in the forest and breathing in its good air, closed her eyes in bliss. Then, remembering just who it was that sat beside her, she opened them again and looked at the Abbess. With amusement she observed that her superior had also closed her eyes and was sitting with her face turned up to the sun, apparently taking the same keen pleasure in her surroundings as Tiphaine. Relaxing, Tiphaine shut her eyes again and let the forest take her over.

Presently there was a small sound.

Tiphaine's eyes shot open to see the grey-clad figure of the Domina standing before her. Instinctively she rose to her feet and, forgetting for a moment that other superior who sat beside her, made a reverence to the woman who was one of the Great Ones of the forest people.

To her surprised pleasure, the Abbess did the same.

The Domina extended her hands, briefly touching those of Tiphaine and the Abbess. Then, looking at the Abbess, she said, 'I knew that you would come and I know why.'

'I thought you would,' the Abbess replied. 'This business affects us at Hawkenlye badly, diverting as it does those seeking help and comfort and taking them instead to a place whose prime purpose is to separate them from their money. But you of the forest are affected far more grievously, for I am told that this Florian of Southfrith has felled trees and cleared ground in pursuit of his dishonest scheme.'

The Domina's eyes were fixed on the Abbess. 'The man Josse has visited the place,' she stated.

'Indeed. He went there yesterday,' answered the Abbess.

The Domina nodded. 'It is known.'

And was, Tiphaine thought, probably the reason why the Domina had expected a visit from the Abbess.

'I assume I am right in believing that you and your people wish to see an end to this Merlin's Tomb?' the Abbess said.

'Yes.' The single word was uttered with quiet force. Then: 'It is sacrilege.'

There was a pause. Tiphaine wondered if the Abbess had been about to ask the Domina to elucidate but, if so, then clearly she thought better of it. Instead she said, 'What can we do?'

The Domina sighed. 'There are many things that *could* be done and that may indeed be done,' she said after a moment, 'although whether they *should* be is another matter.'

'You mean—' But the Abbess broke off. With a faint smile, she said, 'Better, I think, that we do not speak of such things.'

The Domina nodded. 'Perhaps the most sure path would be to prove to the people who now flock to gape and wonder that these bones are not what Florian of Southfrith claims them to be.'

'Yes,' the Abbess said eagerly. 'If there is a way of proving that Florian has brought in the bones from elsewhere and it's not Merlin at all in the tomb, then they'll all realise they've been duped.' A smile spread over her face. 'Perhaps they'll demand their money back.'

'Such an action would be only fair,' the Domina agreed, 'although success would, I fear, be unlikely.'

'Quite.' The Abbess frowned. 'It might, however, be a matter for the Tonbridge sheriff if it could be proved that Florian was taking money fraudulently.'

The Domina gazed at her. Whatever profound thought was running through her head, Tiphaine, watching the two powerful women with close attention, could not guess. 'The bones are not those of Merlin,' the Domina said. 'Be quite sure of that, Abbess Helewise.'

'You . . .' The Abbess hesitated, as if reluctant to ask for further assurance. Then, squaring her shoulders – she was slightly taller than the Domina, Tiphaine noticed – she said, 'I am sorry if I appear to doubt you, but I must ask how you can be so certain. If we are to press ahead with our plans to discredit Florian's scheme, I have to be absolutely sure that we are acting fairly and honestly. Otherwise – if, that is, there is a possibility that the skeleton is that of Merlin and that the bones are therefore capable of working miracles – then it would be wrong to close down a source of comfort and relief when our people so badly need all the help they can get.'

For some time the Domina did not reply. Tiphaine, who knew rather more about what lay behind the affair than she had revealed to her Abbess, waited.

Eventually the Domina said, 'They are not the bones of Merlin. If miracles have happened, then this may be because of people's expectations.' Tiphaine could detect the care with which she was choosing her words. The Domina continued, 'For one such as Florian of Southfrith to make money out of the exposure of bones that he falsely claims are those of Merlin is not only cruelly dishonest; it is also dangerous, for there is a force in that place that has been desecrated with which it is folly to meddle. For both reasons he must be stopped.'

'*Dangerous?*' the Abbess echoed, and Tiphaine saw her eyes widen in alarm.

'Be assured, Abbess Helewise,' the Domina continued implacably, 'that the entity known commonly as Merlin has nothing whatsoever to do with either the bones or the miracles.'

And with that, it appeared from the Domina's demeanour, the Abbess was going to have to be content.

After some time the Abbess spoke. 'How do we prove it?'

'I believe,' said the Domina, 'that, as far as the people are concerned, it is a matter of proving that Merlin is in truth entombed elsewhere.'

'*Is* he?' demanded the Abbess.

'They say so,' replied the Domina enigmatically.

'And his tomb is there for all to see?' the Abbess pressed.

'Oh, yes. I have seen the spot where they say Merlin lies entombed with my own eyes. There is a spring that bubbles out of the ground whose water is ever cool and sweet. Above it is a great slab of granite, shadowed by a thorn tree. It is told, is it not' – she had fixed the Abbess with a penetrating stare – 'that Nimuë penned the enchanter up beneath a hawthorn tree?' Before the Abbess could speak, the Domina pressed on, her voice now low, hypnotic. 'There is a long white banner tied to the thorn bush and it floats and dances in the breeze. They come to worship and they scare themselves, daring one another to stamp on the great granite slab and then running wild in horror when the power is unleashed.' There was a pause as the echoes of her dramatic voice faded and died. 'But,' she concluded in her normal tone, 'they come to no lasting harm.'

'And this – this place of which you speak, it is in truth the burial place of Merlin, magician to King Arthur?' The Abbess pressed the point.

'So they say, lady.'

'Is it nearby?'

'No.'

'But it is possible to visit there?'

'Yes.'

'Then – then I should go and see for myself,' the Abbess said decisively.

The Domina eyed her and Tiphaine thought she saw a certain admiration in the look. 'It is far away and to go there necessitates a voyage over the sea,' she warned. 'You would be absent from your Abbey for considerably more than a matter of a few days, Helewise.'

'Oh. I see.' The Abbess's face fell. 'Then I shall ask another.'

Her eyes lit up. 'One who I know will agree to accept the mission.'

'You speak of Josse,' the Domina commented.

'Yes.'

The Domina nodded. 'I believe that he is a wise choice,' she agreed, 'and I in my turn will propose a guide who will ensure that he reaches his destination safely.' She was watching the Abbess closely; Tiphaine, who had a shrewd idea what was coming, thought she could guess why.

'Who is this guide?' the Abbess asked. 'Josse will not be in any danger, will he?'

The Domina shrugged. 'There is always a certain peril in travel but he will be at no greater risk than anyone else. As to his guide, the person whom I have in mind has visited the place where they say Merlin lies buried and will not have any difficulty in recalling the way. Moreover, the presence of this guide will ensure Josse's safety in realms where it could be perilous for outsiders to tread. He will be taken to the spot, shown the granite slab and the spring that they call Merlin's Fountain. He may then bring the account of his visit back here to you and you may do with the information as you see fit.'

The Abbess was nodding her enthusiasm. 'Yes, yes, of course,' she said eagerly. 'The word of Sir Josse that Merlin lies buried elsewhere, and that he therefore cannot possibly be the skeleton on the far side of the forest, will suffice to raise doubts as to Florian's claims. People are less credulous than men such as Florian believe; Sir Josse's word added to the fact that Florian has been making so much money from the supposed tomb will surely convince all but the most unintelligent that the whole arrangement is nothing more than a fake.'

'So it is to be hoped,' the Domina said.

'You said that this place lies over the seas.' The Abbess returned to the practicalities. 'Where is it? In Ireland, perhaps?'

'Not Ireland,' the Domina replied. 'It is in Armorica.'

'Armorica?' The Abbess frowned.

'You may know the land as Brittany,' Tiphaine supplied.

'Brittany!' exclaimed the Abbess. 'Merlin lies buried in Brittany?'

But the Domina did not answer.

The Abbess was looking doubtful now, as if she were entertaining second thoughts about the wisdom of sending Josse off on such a trip to a place so far away.

Perhaps reading the thought, the Domina said softly, 'Remember, he will have a sound guide with him.'

'Yes, of course, so you assured me.' The Abbess sounded relieved. 'Who is this man? One of your own people?'

'One of our people, yes. But not a man.' The Domina's face was expressionless. 'I speak of a woman. She has been to Armorica and has stood beside the great granite slab. She of all people will ensure that your Josse achieves the journey there and back again as safely as it is in her power to make it. And she is powerful: be in no doubt of that.'

'It's Joanna,' the Abbess breathed. 'Isn't it? You mean to send Joanna to be his guide.'

And the Domina said, 'Of course.'

# 4

Unaware of what was being planned for him by the two powerful women out in the forest, Josse had dressed himself in his habitual tunic and hat and set off on Horace for the heathlands to the south and east of the Great Wealden Forest where he understood that Florian of Southfrith had his home. *He lives with his beautiful wife in a modest but very fine manor house near Hadfeld,* Brice had said. Well, the man's name and the place where he had his abode ought to be enough for Josse to locate him.

He had followed the same path that he had taken the previous day for the first part of his ride then, when he emerged on to the open, heathery country on the far side of the forest, branched off to the south-east. The going was easy and he let Horace amble along at a steady, unhurried pace. While he remained close to the dense woodland behind him, withies, hazel and rowan grew alongside the track, giving him some shade, but as he progressed further into the open countryside, the trees finally gave out and he felt the full strength of the morning sun beating down on him. Now it was the gorse that held sway: the gentle slopes over which he rode were glowing with the dense yellow of the flowers, so that the air was redolent with the sweet, heavy, intoxicating scent. Horace's big hooves brushed the wild thyme, which contributed its own clean smell. Josse could hear the delicate twittering of linnets and he spotted a pair of wheatears – white arses, as they were commonly known – flying low over the heather.

It was, he decided, a perfect day for riding and he wished that he had no fixed purpose but could saunter on until fatigue and hunger finally drove him home. But he did have a purpose, and an urgent one at that. Clucking to Horace, he increased his pace to a smart canter and set himself to the task of finding Hadfeld.

Presently he noticed that the landscape was changing. Encroachments had been made into the heathland and there were increasing numbers of assarts, where the untamed countryside had been claimed and converted into farm land. Sheep grazed the wiry heathland plants and there were large areas of bracken, fenced off like a crop, and Josse guessed the plant was being grown for fuel. Nothing ate bracken; he recalled Sister Tiphaine once telling him that it caused sickness in most animals but that, in small doses, it was useful as a contraceptive. He smiled to himself; whatever could they have been talking about to have prompted her to tell him *that* interesting little fact?

He came to a hamlet of four or five low, huddled little dwellings, outside one of which a couple of women sat over a huge basket of nettles. Observing as he approached, Josse noticed they were tearing the tops from each stem and throwing them into a cooking pot, setting the remaining stems and leaves aside in another basket. One of the women looked up and gave him a grin; she was a round-faced woman in perhaps her mid-twenties, pleasant looking except that she was missing all but three of her teeth.

'You have a good harvest there,' he remarked, returning her smile.

'Aye, and the blisters to prove it,' she said with a bubbling laugh. 'But nettles is free, sir knight, and ours for the picking, and the tender young shoots make a tasty meal. The rest of our haul will go for nettle beer.' She winked at him as if anticipating the pleasures of an evening of mild intoxication.

'I wish you joy of it,' he said. 'Am I on the right road for Hadfeld?'

'Aye, more or less. Keep on till you reach the stone cross and then turn left, then right. That'll take you to Hadfeld.'

'Who are you after?' the other woman asked. She was older but had the same features; an elder sister? 'I'll wager it's young Florian.'

'Aye, it is,' Josse agreed.

'Thought as much.' The woman nodded sagely.

'Do many folk come seeking him just now?'

'Aye, but most of them in truth are seeking Merlin's Tomb, which is nowhere near Hadfeld but lies just within the forest, some—'

'Thank you; I know where the tomb is,' Josse interrupted.

'Been there already?' the first woman asked.

'I . . .' Josse hesitated, reluctant to discuss his business with two inquisitive strangers.

'He'll be after our young Florian to demand his money back,' the woman said to her companion in a whisper deliberately pitched loud enough for Josse to overhear. Glancing up at him, she added, 'The cure lasted but a day and then back came the troubles, double fold.'

Despite himself, Josse laughed. 'I am not sick, thank the good Lord, and it was not to seek for help that I visited Merlin's Tomb.'

'Then you're the lucky one,' the older woman said, all levity suddenly absent from her voice and her face, 'for there's more 'n one family hereabouts lighter in the pocket and still tormented by worry over whatever it was drove them to the forest tomb in the first place. People ain't best pleased with young Florian,' she added darkly. 'If you're a friend of his, sir knight' – the look she cast at Josse suggested she would think the less of him if he were – 'then maybe you should warn him to watch his step and his back.'

He met her gaze levelly. 'I am no friend of his,' he said quietly. 'Now' – he deliberately changed the subject – 'Florian's dwelling is indeed at Hadfeld, as you imply?'

'Aye, it is,' the first woman confirmed. 'You'll likely find him away from home, since he spends each and every day down at his tomb. But his wife will be there. You could wager that fine horse of yours on that, *and* your hat.' Both women chuckled.

'Thank you, both of you,' Josse said. With a courteous nod of the head, he kicked Horace and went on his way.

The reason why the women had been so sure that Florian's wife would be at home became evident as soon as Josse rode up to the house. Building work was under way and a woman stood on a mounting block very near to where the workmen were toiling, closely watching every move they made.

Josse dismounted and tethered Horace to a ring set into the wall beside the open gates. The house was not large but it was well-built and compact, with a pleasing symmetry to its dimensions. Flower beds had been placed either side of the door, beneath small windows set high above them in the smooth stone. There were lilies and gillyflowers in bloom, sweet-smelling and sending out a strong perfume. Outbuildings on the far side of the house appeared to have been carefully repaired. Money had been spent – recently, by the look of it – and must, judging by the buzz of activity and the gang of workmen, still be pouring out.

Walking across the courtyard, Josse approached the woman on the mounting block. He swept off his hat and said, 'Madam? Have I the honour of addressing the wife of Florian of Southfrith?'

Without so much as glancing round, the woman said, 'He is not here and is unlikely to return until the light fails. You'll find him at Merlin's Tomb.' The bored resignation in her tone suggested that this was not the first time she had made the remark that morning. In addition, the woman spoke of her husband so scathingly that Josse thought he detected dislike.

'Aye, so I have been informed,' Josse said, maintaining a polite tone; he did not find it easy when the woman had not the manners to turn and address him face to face. Recalling the reason he had thought up for visiting Florian's home, he went on, 'They told me your husband is having a solar built' – it had been a good guess, as had just been proved – 'and I wanted to ask him if he's satisfied with the builders he has engaged and, if so, what the name of the master builder is.'

'He's over there' – she pointed, with a long, fine hand bearing a large garnet set in a gold ring, towards a thin, dark, nervous-looking man standing on top of a partly built wall with a plumb line in his hand – 'and he's called Josiah.' She spoke with an accent and Josse guessed that her native tongue was French. 'As to satisfaction, it is not possible to say until the work is complete.' At last she turned to look down at Josse and he saw a pale face, the smooth skin very slightly olive in complexion, the black eyes almond-shaped under fine, dark brows. She was unsmiling and she stared at him as if he were something smelly on the sole of her narrow calfskin slipper. Lifting her delicately pointed chin in a gesture of pure arrogance, she said, 'And just who are *you*?'

In no hurry to answer, largely because he could tell she found it irritating, Josse studied her. She was not tall – petite would be the word, he decided – and the slim-fitting silk gown showed a narrow waist and hips but surprisingly generous breasts; the bodice looked as if it had been designed for a woman even better-endowed. The gown was of a pale pearly grey and the colour must have been chosen with care, for it complemented the woman's skin tone perfectly. Her eyes, he now saw, were not black but very dark blue. What he could see of her hair, which was drawn back off her face and covered by a circle of fine silvery net held in place with a silver circlet, was glossy, smooth and black as midnight.

She would have been one of the loveliest women he had ever set eyes on. But beauty, in Josse's opinion, needed a smile: the scowl that the woman wore drew her brows together, etched downward-sloping lines in the beautiful face and soured the wide mouth; in short, she had the look of a malevolent child thwarted of its latest unreasonable demand.

'I am Josse d'Acquin,' he said eventually.

'I see.' The frown eased a little. 'And you say that *you* are wanting to build a solar?' She sounded as if she found the suggestion faintly risible.

'Er – it has been suggested.' That was the truth; Josse's servant Will had been dropping hints these five years past at least and more than once a local mason had just happened to pass by – undoubtedly summoned by Will – to propose to Josse the same idea.

'New buildings don't come cheap,' the woman said rudely. She eyed his garments minutely, from the feather in his favourite and well-worn broad-brimmed hat to his comfy old riding boots.

Refusing to be drawn, Josse merely said, 'So I imagine.'

She took hold of a fold of her skirt, swishing the gorgeous silk to and fro so that it made a soft, rustling sound. He caught a glimpse of an underskirt in a deeper shade of silver grey and saw a flash of exquisite, pure white lace, stiff and costly. She tapped her slim foot in its soft leather slipper. 'Of course,' she said languidly when she had evidently reassured herself that Josse had noticed every item of the display, 'my husband is a *very* wealthy man.'

'Indeed,' Josse said mildly.

'Oh, yes.'

'That must be quite delightful for you, my lady.' He wondered if she would detect the irony.

'Naturally, it is.' Apparently not. 'My husband claims that it is his privilege to give me pleasure by buying me whatever I desire.' She gave an artificial little sigh, as if she could not quite believe her generosity in allowing her husband the huge favour of allowing him to spend his money on her.

'Perhaps he is fresh to marriage?' Josse asked. 'It is well known that a new bridegroom often indulges his bride.'

'We are two years wed,' she said sharply. Then, forcing a smile that went no further than her lips: 'Florian likes to ensure my favour, sir knight. I had many suitors and he does well not to forget that he had to face much competition for my hand.'

Watching her, Josse thought but did not point out that her former popularity was hardly relevant now that she had made her choice and was married to Florian. It seemed highly likely that she used the reminder of it as a stick with which to beat the unfortunate Florian whenever his attention slipped from his decorative, spoiled wife and his purse-strings began to draw closed.

Josse was beginning to feel very sorry for Florian of South-frith.

It was hot in the courtyard. The sun was beating off the flagstones and the walls of the house and the air was dry and full of dust. The woman on her mounting block, predictably, had taken the only patch of shade. A better-mannered person would, Josse thought, by now have invited him inside the house and offered him something cool to drink. Florian's wife contented herself with staring at him impatiently and making it perfectly apparent that she wished he would go away.

'I am grateful for your kindness and your time, lady,' he said, increasing the irony. Bowing, he added, 'I will leave you to your overseer's duties.' And that, he decided as he straightened up, was verging on plain rude; to suggest to a rich man's wife that she was forced to labour like a workman was an insult.

Colour flew swiftly into her face. She seemed about to make some vitriolic reply but, with an effort, she controlled herself. Then she turned her back.

Josse walked back across the courtyard and out through the gate, freeing Horace's reins from the hitching ring and swinging up into the saddle. Looking back, he saw the door to the house suddenly open from within. A woman dressed in black emerged on to the steps; she wore a long veil whose edge came down low over her eyes so that Josse could not see her face clearly. However, her figure, her posture and the harsh voice which called out in French suggested strongly that she was the young woman's mother.

'*Primevère, que fais-tu là au plein soleil?*' demanded the older woman. Primevère, Josse thought. Primrose. A singularly unfitting name for Florian's haughty wife, whose looks and nature were far removed from the simple prettiness of a primrose. '*Tu seras bronzée comme une rustre!*' The older woman spat out the pejorative word like an oath.

'I am not in the sun, *Maman*,' the younger woman called back. 'There is no danger whatsoever that I shall start to look like some rustic lout, so there is no need to make such a fuss.'

The older woman had just noticed Josse.

'*C'est qui, lui?*' she demanded of her daughter, jerking her chin in Josse's direction.

Primevère turned to stare at Josse. 'His identity is not important,' she said dismissively. 'He is just leaving.' Then she climbed down gracefully from her mounting block, took her mother's outstretched hand and went with her back into the house, slamming the door behind her with a loud and eloquent bang.

The second part of Josse's mission was less straightforward: there did not seem to be any obvious way of discovering where Florian had found the bones that he had transported to the clearing in the forest. Where, Josse wondered as he rode along in the sun, trying to distract himself from his growing thirst, would a man go to find bones? A burial ground? Some grave sunk beneath the aisle of a church? A wealthy family's private vault? He had no idea which suggestion, if any, might be the right one.

He caught sight of a small church ahead, set beneath trees to one side of the track. He saw as he drew nearer that someone was sitting on the step of the open door; the priest was taking his ease in the cool shade with a mug of beer and a thick hunk of dark and dryish-looking bread.

'Greetings!' the priest called out as Josse rode up. He waved the mug. 'Will you take a drop? It's as cold as my subterranean cellar can make it! There's water in the trough for your handsome horse, too.'

Deciding that this was probably not the happy priest's first mugful, Josse willingly dismounted, tethered Horace in the shade beside the trough and went to seat himself on the doorstep.

'A-a-ah!' he said with deep pleasure as his buttocks encountered the cool stone.

'Good, eh?' the priest said with a smile. 'Here.' He handed over a second mug and Josse drank gratefully.

'That's worth a long, hot ride,' Josse said when he had taken the edge off his thirst.

'You've come far?' asked the priest.

'From Hawkenlye Abbey.'

'I see.' The priest eyed him shrewdly. 'Come to have a look at the rival attraction?'

'Aye.' There seemed no point in denying it.

'Do you believe what is being claimed for those particularly large bones?'

Josse paused. 'I do not *want* to believe,' he said, 'but I am forced to admit that there is a power to the place – to the bones, perhaps – that I cannot explain.'

The priest sighed deeply; all happiness had abruptly left his cheerful face. 'That's what they all say,' he muttered glumly.

'Father,' Josse began tentatively, 'let's say for argument's sake that those are not the bones of Merlin but that Florian of Southfrith found them elsewhere and took them into the forest, then claimed to have unearthed them there and to have discovered that they are miraculous.'

'That would amount to fraud, which is a very serious allegation,' the priest said warningly.

'Oh, I make no allegation' – Josse spoke swiftly – 'I merely outline a hypothesis.'

'Go on.' The priest sounded guarded.

'Well, if it happened that way, I'm asking myself where on earth such bones might have been found? Are there any such within your church and its immediate surroundings, for example?'

Now the priest was studying him closely. 'There are, but no grave has been disturbed.' The smile breaking out again, he said, 'I checked.'

Josse laughed briefly. 'You have entertained the same thought, then, Father?'

And the priest said very quietly, 'Yes.'

After a thoughtful pause, the priest spoke again. 'You ask where a man might find a skeleton. Sir knight, such a task is difficult but not impossible. The chalk downs to the south of us were long inhabited by our forebears and, like all men, in their due time they died. Now it is an interesting thing, but it is my observation that sometimes our ancestors burned the bodies of the dead, for I have seen for myself how some graves contain burned bones bundled up in small spaces, accompanied by offerings to the pagan gods that the people worshipped.'

'The bones in the tomb are not burned,' Josse put in.

'No, no, I am told not, but I was about to say that there are also to be found upon the Downs burial sites and barrows that contain whole skeletons, carefully laid out as if with reverence. In much the same way, indeed, as we bury our own dead, save that it was the custom of our forefathers to lay bodies north-south and not, as we do, with their feet to the east so that they can rise up and face the Holy City on the Day of Judgement.'

'You have seen such skeletons on the Downs?' Josse demanded eagerly; if this priest had come across such a thing, then why should not Florian have done so too?

'Yes,' the priest admitted. 'Yes, I have.'

A thought struck Josse. 'The burial place that you speak of – is the skeleton still within?'

'Yes.' Again, the disarming smile. 'I checked that too.'

'But that's only one such grave,' Josse said, determined not to have this exciting new possibility dismissed out of hand. 'Florian could very well have found another similar grave and—'

'—and robbed it of its occupant.' The priest nodded slowly. 'Yes, sir knight; that is exactly what I find myself thinking.'

Josse shook his head, troubled and confused. A thought struck him, one that he had not considered before. 'Has it actually been stated that the bones at Merlin's Tomb are capable of working miracles?' he asked. 'And if so, was the word spread by Florian of Southfrith or by popular rumour?'

The priest eyed him steadily. 'That I cannot say,' he murmured. 'What I will tell you, sir knight, is this: it was those ruffians now doing guard duty at the tomb who first emerged to tell of the wonderful discovery in the forest. I saw them and I heard what they had to say, and their words made me angry for they were sacrilegious. They spoke of Lazarus being brought back from the dead and of the raising of Jairus' daughter; of the healing of the blind and the dumb, of the man who took up his bed and walked, of the release of those possessed by devils.' He leaned forward and, in case Josse had missed the point, said vehemently, 'Those are the miracles of Jesus Christ, sir knight, and of him alone! The ruffians had been well trained and none actually said that the new tomb could perform such feats, but then they did not need to, for the implication was there and more than enough to convince the simple and the desperate.'

'I see,' Josse said. If what the priest said was true – and there was no reason why it should not be – then this new information amounted to yet more damning evidence against Florian. To imply a miracle-working ability to his fraudulent tomb rather than to state its healing power outright – as the Hawkenlye community did about their holy water – was both cynical and clever and also typical of what Josse was coming to recognise as Florian's nature.

*You should warn him to watch his step and his back,* the woman at the roadside had said.

How right, Josse thought, she was.

Helewise half longed for and half feared Josse's return. She was keen to hear what he had to report of Florian of South-frith's home and household but she dreaded having to pass on to him what had been decided for him.

It had not occurred to her that he would refuse the task. She thought about it now as she waited for him. After quite a short time she found she simply could not imagine him saying no.

He arrived late in the afternoon and came into her room looking hot, tired and dusty from the road. His tunic and undershirt were unfastened almost down to the waist and she could see his strong neck and chest. As if he noticed her eyes upon him, hastily he straightened the garments and secured the leather lace.

'I am sorry to appear before you covered in sweat and muck,' he said, 'but it has taken me some time to rub down and settle Horace and I did not want to make you wait while I saw to myself as well.' He grinned. 'I thought you might be impatient to hear how I got on.'

She answered his smile but experienced a sudden surge of guilt; poor Josse, here he was, diligently trying not to keep her waiting longer than he must, yet in so doing, lessening the time between his present frame of mind, whatever that might be, and how he was probably going to feel once she had told him what had been decided. 'Oh, I don't mind a little honest sweat,' she made herself say.

His grin widened. 'Quite a lot, actually.'

'Hm?' She wasn't really listening.

'Quite a lot of – oh, never mind.' Approaching her and leaning with his hands on her table, he said excitedly, 'I went to Florian's house. He has a very decorative crosspatch of a wife upon whom he's lavishing everything he's making out at Merlin's Tomb. She has a brand-new gown and slippers, her mother has moved in and they're building themselves a solar!'

Helewise said, 'Oh, really?', sounding pathetically uninterested even to herself.

He noticed too. 'Well, *I* thought it was relevant,' he muttered. Then, before she could answer: 'That's not all. I met up with a priest down near Hadfeld and he reckons it'd be reasonably easy to locate a skeleton out on the Downs and transport it into the forest.' Eagerness spilling out of him in spite of her lack of reaction, he said, 'This is how I see it, my lady. Florian needs money – I've seen his wife and, believe me, a man with the misfortune to be wedded to such a creature will always need money – and, like everyone else, he's been knocked back hard by what he had to pay towards the King's ransom. His wife threatens to withhold herself unless he starts bringing home the little and the not-so-little presents that she's used to and young Florian is racking his brains for a means of making some cash. He's out riding on the Downs one day and notices a piece of bone sticking out of the ground – aye, all right, my lady' – she had made an involuntary sound of disbelief – 'I'm not saying it's what *did* happen, I'm only saying it *could* have done – and, jumping down from his horse, he digs around for a while and discovers that he's unearthed an intact skeleton, moreover that of a particularly large man. Now, this is where it becomes *really* interesting!'

She could not help but catch the edge of his fervour. 'Yes?'

'My lady, you are familiar with what has happened at Glastonbury?'

'The monks have found the bones of King Arthur and his Queen and now the Abbey is a place of pilgrimage.' She spoke as briefly as she could, not in the least wishing to engage in a long discussion of the rights and wrongs of the issue.

'Aye, that's it! Well, you know of it, I know of it, so the likelihood is that Florian does too. You agree?'

'Ye-es,' she said. She had an idea she knew exactly where this was going.

'An enterprising and unscrupulous young man desperate for money finds some unusually large bones. He thinks, why not claim that these belong to someone very famous? Why, you said yourself that everyone knows about Merlin, so maybe the old enchanter's name was the first one to pop into Florian's head. He digs up the bones, smuggles them by night into a suitably awe-inspiring and tucked away place in the forest, creates a realistic-looking tomb and makes a lead cross inscribed with suitably confirmatory lettering. He covers up the bones, allows a couple of weeks or so for the undergrowth to grow back – and at this time of year that wouldn't take long – then back he goes to make his discovery. He hires a few strong men to fell some trees so as to make access easier and to build a couple of flimsy huts, presumably promising to pay them out of the proceeds. Then he spreads the word that Merlin's secret and long-lost burial site has been found, and the rest we know.'

'The rest,' she said slowly, 'is that Florian is making twenty shillings a day or more out of pilgrims visiting a shrine that is nothing but pretence. If, that is,' she added, 'these bones are not those of Merlin.'

'Aye,' he said heavily. 'Aye, that's the crux of the matter.' He gave a deep sigh. 'My lady, every instinct tells me that they are not and yet . . .' He shrugged. Then he said, 'But I cannot deny there is a force to the place or the bones, or perhaps both, although whether it's what Florian claims it to be or something else entirely, well, I just don't know.'

'Ah.' What had the Domina said? *There is a force in that place that has been desecrated with which it is folly to meddle.* Oh, dear God, and now here was Josse talking about some frightful force whose origin he did not even try to guess!

But he was waiting and she must collect herself and speak.

'Sir Josse,' she began tentatively, 'I have spoken to the Domina.'

'My lady, forgive me!' he cried. 'I have been so busy expounding on my own actions this day that I have omitted to ask you about yours! Please, tell me what happened in the forest!'

She looked up into his trusting, anxious face and her guilt waxed hot. But there was nothing for it but to report what had been decided. 'After some discussion,' she said baldly, 'we reasoned that the surest way to disprove Florian's claim is to provide proof that Merlin lies buried elsewhere. The Domina's people have some idea that he has a shrine or a tomb or some such thing beside a fountain deep in a forest far away, and we—'

'I'll go there,' he said instantly. 'Tell me where it is and I'll find it and bring back word of it.'

'That was what we had in mind,' she acknowledged. 'We thought that proof of the location of the true Merlin's Tomb, plus the revelation of just how much money Florian is making out of the false one, would convince the people that they are being tricked.'

'Aye, you're right!' Josse exclaimed. 'I'll set out as soon as I can, my lady. I'll make a start with preparing my gear – I can get everything ready very quickly once I've decided what I'm going to need – and I'll make sure Horace has a generous feed. The pair of us will get a good night's sleep, and then—'

'Sir Josse, there is something else,' she said gently. She could not bear to hear him make his plans so enthusiastically when he did not know the whole picture. 'The place of which I speak is far away,' she hurried on, 'in fact, in Brittany, which the forest people know as Armorica.'

His face had gone stony. 'Armorica,' he repeated dully. She knew then that he had guessed what was coming.

'You will need a guide who is familiar with the terrain and who will be able to intercede between you and the guardians of the tomb.'

'The guardians are of the Domina's people,' he murmured.

'Yes, indeed.' She took a deep breath. 'The Domina has proposed such a person and it's Joanna.'

And Josse, his expression a touching mixture of distress and joy, said, 'I guessed as much.'

# 5

The knowledge that Joanna was to escort him to Brittany initially caused Josse pleasure and pain in almost equal measure. The prospect of having her company – and that of his daughter as well? Oh, but surely she would bring Meggie with her, wouldn't she? – for however long the journey might take was nothing other than wonderful. But then, what would happen when they got back to Hawkenlye? How would he, having become accustomed to living with her, be able to live without her again?

He went to his bed that night with the dread of that destiny filling his head. But in the morning his pragmatic nature had reasserted itself: he *had* to make the trip, and with Joanna; he had no choice, for the mission was fundamental to the future of Hawkenlye Abbey and he could not let the Abbess down. Therefore he would go with a happy heart, extract what joy he could from being with Joanna and Meggie and let the future take care of itself.

He washed and dressed – some kindly soul had addressed him or herself to the problem of his sweaty chemise and dusty tunic, for both had been laundered and were now fresh and smelling faintly of lavender, and his boots had been polished to a high shine – and presented himself before the Abbess. Without preamble he told her that departure would have to be delayed until later that day at the earliest, more likely early the following morning, since he first wished to visit the sheriff of Tonbridge.

'I think I can guess why you wish to see Gervase de Gifford,' the Abbess said.

'Aye, no doubt you can,' he replied. 'I believe we should alert him to our suspicions regarding Florian and the tomb in the forest. If we are wrong – which I admit I doubt – then Gervase can dismiss the warning as if it had never been uttered. But if we're right, then the sooner he knows about all this, the better.'

The Abbess was nodding. 'Yes, Sir Josse, I agree that it is a wise precaution to speak to Gervase. I – er, I had not in truth envisioned that you would be leaving today; I am not sure that the Domina will as yet have—'

'She won't yet have given Joanna her orders?' He felt his face twist in a grimace that seemed to turn all by itself into a grin. 'Oh, my lady, I expect she'll be doing that right now. And Joanna travels light: if I can be ready in not much more than an hour, then so can she.'

Not entirely pleased with the Abbess just then – although he had not dared to get to the bottom of exactly why that was – he gave her a polite bow, turned and left the room.

He found the house of Gervase de Gifford in a state of confusion. Two horses stood in the shade out in the courtyard and a young groom was walking one of them slowly to and fro; returning Josse's greeting, he said, 'She showed up lame yesterday and s'morning she's just had a new shoe. I've to ensure she's all right now 'cos some day soon she may have a long journey in front of her.'

Josse was on the point of asking where Gervase was going – and who, indeed, was going with him – but stopped. It was none of the groom's business and Josse would do much better asking Gervase. 'Your master is within?'

'Aye,' the lad confirmed. 'Go on in, sir.'

Josse tethered Horace and ran up the steps to the door. He heard voices: an old man, a young woman and Gervase.

Pausing, he identified the first two: Sabin de Retz and her elderly grandfather.

They were Bretons from the town of Nantes and they had fled to England in February of the previous year when their lives were in danger. Gervase had taken them under his protection and he and Sabin had promptly fallen in love. For the past fourteen months or so, Sabin had been trying to make up her mind whether to return to Nantes or remain in Tonbridge. She was an apothecary, taught by her grandfather; he had brought her up after the deaths of her parents. He was now all but blind and his unwillingness to face the long journey back to Nantes was one of the factors affecting Sabin's decision. She had steadily built up a clientele in and around the town and her fame was spreading; there was a living for her and old Benoît in Tonbridge and it was hers for the taking.

But the pair of them had also had a fine and rewarding life back in Nantes, where they had been the confidential servants of an important figure. Josse, aware of the bare bones of Sabin's dilemma, had sympathised with the young woman: hers was not an easy choice.

He went on into Gervase's hall. The argument stopped and Gervase and Sabin hailed him; Benoît's quavery tones demanded, 'Who's that?'

'It's Josse.' Josse went up to him, bending down so that the old man, seated on a bench by the fireplace, could peer into his face.

'Josse,' Benoît said on a sigh. 'Josse, they're going off and leaving me all on my own! They'll be away so long – why, I might very well be dead by the time they return! *If* they return,' he added dismally.

'Grandfather, *of course* we shall return!' Exasperation was apparent in Sabin's voice as she swept across to kneel at the old man's feet and take hold of his hands. 'And as for leaving you on your own, you know that isn't true. Gervase's servants have been given detailed orders on how you are to be looked after.'

'It won't be the same. Won't be like having my own kin at my side,' the old man moaned.

'I'll be back as soon as I can,' Sabin said. 'But I have to go – you know that as well as I do, Grandfather. We sent word to the Duchess explaining our absence, and I'm sure she has realised by now that we're not going back. But, for the trust that she placed in us in the past and for the affection that grew between us, I cannot rest until I have seen her and explained myself to her face to face.' Abruptly she dropped Benoît's hands, throwing herself away from him. 'Oh, *try* to understand!'

Gervase, eyeing Josse, gave a faint apologetic shrug. Then, turning to Benoît, he said firmly, 'You understand very well, I think, Benoît.' The old man had the grace to look ashamed. 'It is only natural that you do not like the prospect of Sabin's absence but, knowing what this trip means to her, you will surely give her your blessing.' It sounded more like a command than a question and Josse hid an admiring smile; Gervase appeared to have the measure of the old man.

'I don't know about blessing,' Benoît muttered, narrowing his red-rimmed eyes and peering up in Gervase's general direction.

Gervase moved closer, adopting Sabin's former position at the old man's feet. 'She has made up her mind at last in the matter of a decision that has been extremely hard,' he said gently. 'Your welfare has been a major factor in her consideration and she was willing to give up what she herself wanted if you did not wish it.'

'I don't want to go back to Nantes!' Benoît wailed. 'I'm too old for such a journey and it would be the finish of me!'

'Which,' Gervase said – and Josse could almost hear the gritting of teeth – 'is precisely why you're going to stay here.

Sabin will be back with you again very soon, but first you *must* let her do what she has to do. She will not rest easy until she has spoken to the Duchess.'

Benoît gazed into Gervase's eyes. 'You'll take good care of her?' he whispered.

Gervase smiled. 'You know that I will. I give you my word to protect her with my life.'

'Hm.' The old man turned his head to where he thought Sabin stood. 'Sabin?'

'Here, Grandfather.' She hurried to his side.

Benoît gave a dramatic sigh and, placing a hand on each of the two heads before him, one brown, one fair, he said, 'Go, then, and may the good Lord above keep you in his care. Do what you must, Granddaughter, and then return to me.'

There was a short silence, and then Sabin murmured, 'Thank you, Grandfather.'

The old man dropped his hands back into his lap and Gervase and Sabin stood up. Then Benoît got to his feet with a groan – Josse noticed how both the two young people instantly went to help him – and said, 'Now, all this has tired me. I shall retire to my bed and take a nap.' He shrugged off the helping hands and shuffled off towards the doorway at the rear of the hall. Reaching it, he turned.

'Oh, Sabin?'

'Yes, Grandfather?'

'You say you intend to fetch back from Nantes as many of the tools of our trade as you can carry. Well, while you're at it, bring the smaller of my two herbals, will you? I would dearly like to look at it again before my sight fails entirely.'

And with that remark, punctuated by a couple more sighs, he went through the doorway and out of sight.

Josse heard a quiet sob; Gervase heard it too and went to Sabin, taking her in his arms and whispering words of comfort. After a few moments she wiped her eyes and, giving Josse a smile, said, 'I apologise for my tears. Grandfather has the ability to make me feel so very sorry for him and, although I know full well he knows exactly what he's doing, still it affects me.'

'I understand,' Josse said. 'It's hard to ignore the appeal of blood kin and to do so would take a sterner heart than yours, Sabin.' He returned her smile with genuine affection; he had developed a high regard for her. Then: 'So you've made up your mind?'

Now her smile was radiant. 'Yes. I shall return to Nantes to see the Duchess and collect what Grandfather and I require of our possessions there. I have work enough and more here in Tonbridge to keep myself occupied and, there being still a great deal that Grandfather may teach me of our craft, he too will have a useful and fulfilling life.' She shot a glance at Gervase and her face flushed pink. 'There is one more thing to tell you. Gervase and I are to be married.'

Josse held out both hands and Gervase took one, Sabin the other. 'I am not in the least surprised but I confess myself quite delighted,' he said warmly. 'You will be an asset, dear Sabin, to both town and husband.'

She laughed, leaning forward to kiss him on both cheeks. He noticed, as he had done when first he met her, the faint and attractive smell that he guessed to be a melange of the herbs that she worked with. It was, he thought absently, the trade-mark of the apothecary . . .

'. . . just finished briefing my men and Sabin and I are off to Brittany as soon as we can,' Gervase was saying.

'*What?*' Despite having listened to the discussion of this trip that had just been batted to and fro, Josse had not made the connection. 'But – I am bound for Brittany too! I am aiming to leave at first light tomorrow.'

Gervase and Sabin looked at each other, and then back at Josse. 'Why?' Gervase demanded. Quickly Josse told him about the problem of Merlin's Tomb, adding that the reason for his present visit to Gervase had been to inform him that, in Josse's opinion, the whole operation was almost certainly fraudulent. He explained that the decision had been made for him to be shown the real tomb of Merlin, over in Brittany, and that this was why he was being sent there. 'So you go on a mission for Hawkenlye Abbey,' Gervase mused, 'where the monks and the nuns and the good Abbess must for sure be missing their usual pilgrims?'

'In part, aye, but it is also to prevent a great many people paying out hard-earned money to a trickster,' Josse returned promptly.

Gervase bowed his acknowledgement. 'Of course.' Then: 'Do you agree to our riding together, Josse? I have given my word to Benoît that I will take good care of Sabin' – he gave her a loving look – 'but how much safer she will be with you also at her side.'

'I agree right readily,' Josse said, 'I plan to leave tomorrow: can you be prepared to depart by then?'

Gervase looked at Sabin. Shooting a swift glance at the doorway through which her grandfather had gone and biting her lip, she said, 'Yes. Of course.' Then, taking a breath so deep that it raised her tense shoulders, 'The sooner we leave, the sooner we shall return.'

'I must inform you,' Josse said, 'that I will not be alone.'

'Who is to accompany you, Josse?' Sabin asked. 'Somebody from the Abbey?'

'No. If I'm to find the location of the true burial place of Merlin I'll need help, for I am told it lies deep in a forest. A guide has been arranged for me.' He met Gervase's eyes and read in them understanding and pity. 'Joanna is going to show me the way.'

Gervase nodded. 'The obvious choice, of course. And how do you feel about that?'

Josse frowned, then suddenly smiled. He said, aware that it was something of an understatement, 'Fine.'

Joanna stood just outside the gates of Hawkenlye Abbey, Meggie sitting on the ground beside her yawning hugely, and tried to calm her rapid heartbeat. I will be better, she kept telling herself, as soon as I have seen him and we have acknowledged one another.

Oh, hurry up, Josse, she pleaded silently. Where are you? What are you doing, that keeps me waiting in this painful suspense? To take her mind off her anxiety, she thought back to the extraordinary happenings of the past twenty-four hours.

It had begun with a visit from the Domina to Joanna's little hut deep in the forest late in the evening two days ago. Not that there had been anything in that to alert Joanna to what was to come, for the next day was Midsummer's Eve and Joanna had an important role in the ceremony that would take place that night as the Sun moved from the constellation of Gemini into that of Cancer. It was a special night for her people, even more special than usual, for this year there was a clutch of powerful planets in the summer signs of Gemini, Cancer and Leo. In addition, the ascendant was in the fire sign of Aries and was not Aries the very symbol of the Sun himself?

But the Domina had not come to issue any last-minute instructions concerning Joanna's role in the forthcoming ceremony. Instead, the moment that Joanna straightened up from her low and respectful bow, the Domina said, 'A fraudulent Tomb of Merlin has been set up on the Forest's southern fringes. We wish to stop this sacrilege and therefore you will go to Armorica, to where the Fountain of Merlin issues out of the ground close to our healing place of Folle-Pensée. With you will go the knight Josse and there, with one of our Great Ones, you will lead him to this place so that he will be convinced it is the true burial site of the magician Merlin. On

Josse's return, his word will be sufficient for the false tomb to be exposed.'

Shock coursed through Joanna and she felt the fast, alarmed thumping of her heart. 'But I—' *I cannot*, she wanted to cry. *I must not be with Josse, for the sweet pain is more than we can bear and hence I have arranged matters so that we remain apart.*

One did not, however, say *I cannot* to the Domina. Joanna bowed her head.

'Very good,' the Domina murmured. 'Tomorrow night we celebrate the Solstice. Before that you must prepare yourself and your child for departure early the following morning. You will make your way to Hawkenlye, where you will find the man Josse awaiting you.'

'I may take Meggie?' Joanna raised her eyes and stared at the Domina, hardly able to believe what she had just heard.

The Domina smiled faintly. 'Yes, Joanna. You go on a mission whose success is vital to your people' – to us? Joanna wondered; she could appreciate how a spurious Merlin's Tomb could badly affect the Abbey, which explained Josse's involvement, but why did it matter so very much to the Forest Folk? – 'but it is not likely that there will be danger and so there is no reason for your child to be robbed of her mother's company and care.'

'Thank you,' Joanna said meekly. Her question must remain unanswered; one did not say *why?* to the Domina any more than *I cannot*.

'Besides,' the Domina added, with a wry look, 'it would be a brave woman or man who undertook to keep your little girl happy when you were not there.'

Uncertain whether this remark implied praise or criticism – she rather thought the latter – Joanna bowed again and with courteous ceremony escorted the Domina across the clearing to where the path led away into the forest.

Knowledge of what was to come – and a considerable

amount of trepidation – meant that Joanna threw herself all the more fervently into the festival of Midsummer Eve. She needed help and giving all of herself to this night of honouring her gods was the best way that she knew to ask for it. It was not the practicalities that bothered her; the help that she would be begging for was in working out how on earth she was going to cope with being with Josse.

She was fairly certain that she could find her way to Folle-Pensée, for she had been there before and in the course of her long training she had been taught to learn a route thoroughly the first time she took it so that she would not forget if she had to go back. Once there, the Domina's scant orders had implied that someone else – one of the Great Ones, no less – would be instrumental in providing whatever it took to persuade Josse that Merlin lay buried there. This Joanna found a great relief for, as far as she could recall, her people were ambiguous about whether or not this was true, despite the local Armorican people's firm belief in both Merlin and his miraculous powers.

It was a relief because Joanna realised that she would not be able to tell Josse a lie, even if the Domina herself stood over her and gave her a direct order.

And that, she thought uncomfortably, might be more than a little awkward

She packed up her leather satchel, folding up a change of clothing for herself and Meggie, her small portable pack of herbal remedies, certain charms without which she never strayed far and a suede bag containing items for her own and Meggie's personal care. She also squeezed in some strips of dark, dried meat – she only ate the flesh of animals if she was desperate, but a long journey might well throw up such a situation, even in high summer – and a handful of the small, sweet apples that Meggie loved. Then she put the satchel aside and turned her thoughts to the ceremony.

\*

It had been spectacular. The enormous fire had been lit at sunset, its great light blazing forth as if to implore the Sun's presence and draw down His light. Joanna had wondered whether any reference would be made to her forthcoming mission to Armorica – perhaps a prayer asking for its success and her safe return – but she ought to have known better, for the forest people were secretive even amongst themselves.

A highly respected bard had told one of the ancient myths, accompanied by a group of people dressed in black, their faces masked with green leaves, who enacted the dramatic events of which the bard sang. Their dark silhouettes against the fire-light had inspired fear and awe. There had followed dancing and feasting, then, at a signal from the Domina, all of the people had followed her to a small hillock deep in the forest, where a winding path circled its way up to the summit. At the peak they stood and waited and there, eventually, the first light of the new-born Sun appeared.

Joanna had been awarded the honour of taking the first flame from the Domina's torch and bearing it back to the clearing where the festivities had been held. She had worked very hard and was word perfect in the long chant that she sang all the way; the moment when she led the people back to the light of the dying fire, and suddenly they all joined in and sang with her, would stay with her for ever.

She had finally crawled on to the sleeping platform in her little hut more than two hours after sunrise, only to be woken by Lora – who had cared for Meggie while Joanna was doing her torch-bearing duty – far too short a time later.

Now, standing as straight and as still as she could outside the Abbey gates, Joanna felt the excitement and exertion of the night catch up with her. Meggie was leaning against her mother's legs, slumped and almost asleep; it would not have taken much for Joanna to have lain down on the grass and joined her.

But suddenly she heard voices and the sound of horses' hooves on stone; squaring her shoulders, she moved slightly until she could get a clear view of who was approaching.

Josse was walking along at the side of a fair-haired young woman who was laughing in response to a remark of Josse's. She looked very happy, as if something very nice had just happened. Josse was leading his big horse – Horace, wasn't it? – and the woman held the reins of a dainty grey mare whose wide eyes and delicately arched neck suggested good blood.

Pain scorching her, Joanna thought, ah, I see! Josse and his fine lady are to ride and I am to trudge along behind like the hired help! Oh, how *could* he!

Giving Meggie a nudge to rouse her, Joanna raised her chin and stepped forward to greet him.

Josse saw her standing in the gateway and felt as if some unseen hand had grasped hold of his heart.

She stood tall and proud, her dark hair neatly braided and the two plaits hanging down to her waist. She wore a robe of fine wool, dyed to a shade of green that seemed to mingle the colours of the forest and blend them into a shade that somehow carried something of them all. The gown was fastened at the shoulders with gold clasps. On her feet she wore beautifully sewn leather sandals, substantial enough for a long journey, and a satchel hung from her arm. Protruding from its flap was a short wooden rod into one end of which had been fixed a translucent brown crystal. At her feet was what appeared to be a soft woollen blanket, rolled up neatly and tied with a cord.

Meggie, looking heavy-eyed, stood beside her, her thumb in her mouth. She was tracing shapes in the dust with one foot and did not look up.

Joanna did. Her dark eyes were glaring up at Josse with such ferocity that he stopped dead.

'Joanna,' he said huskily; he cleared his throat and tried again. 'Joanna, it is good to see you. This is Sabin de Retz' – he touched Sabin's arm, noticing as he did so that she was rigid with tension and guessing that she too had noticed Joanna's expression – 'and she is to ride with us since she too has business in Brittany.'

Joanna said nothing.

'We – er – we should start as soon as we can,' he went on. He handed Horace's reins to Sabin and advanced towards Joanna, feeling the burning power of her eyes fixed on him.

'Ride on, Josse,' Joanna hissed caustically. 'I'll follow along in your dust.'

He realised all of a sudden the impression that he must have made and simultaneously he understood the false conclusion to which she had leapt. He put a hand on each of her shoulders – touching her sent a shock of terror through him, as if her very flesh could somehow harm him – and said very quietly, for her alone, 'Joanna, don't. It is not as you seem to think. Sabin is to marry Gervase de Gifford, who is sheriff here and a good man. He will be with us very soon; he is in the stables fetching his own horse and also your mare Honey, who has been in the nuns' care.' He gave her a little shake and, his inexplicable fear of her vanishing as quickly as it had come, leaned closer and whispered, 'D'you think I'd let you walk when I rode? Silly girl!'

Then, at last, she smiled.

Sabin saw the smile and let out the breath she had been holding. There had been something in the air, something that she did not recognise and that scared her, and it seemed to emanate from the fierce eyes of the dark woman in the beautiful green tunic.

Who was she? If she was the woman Josse had spoken of, and surely she must be, then Josse had referred to her as

Joanna. Yesterday Gervase had appeared to recognise the name; Sabin had asked him later later but all he had said was that she was a woman of the forest people who was a friend to Josse and to Hawkenlye Abbey. She was a healer, he'd said, and Sabin had detected admiration in his voice. Wondering if this Joanna might also be good-looking, she had awaited the meeting with excitement.

Joanna *was* good-looking; she was, Sabin now thought, almost beautiful. She had not expected Joanna to have a child with her, a girl child of about two and a half years, if Sabin were any judge.

Now, still feeling the sweet relief that had flooded her the moment when Joanna smiled, she thought again about what Gervase had said. A woman of the forest; a healer. Add to that, Sabin thought wryly, someone with the power to alter an atmosphere by her very presence and it adds up to a woman of whom to be very, very wary.

She was about to risk a friendly greeting, perhaps address a remark to the sleepy little brown-haired girl, but then she heard the sound of horse and human footsteps and, turning, saw with unexpectedly vast relief that Gervase was approaching, leading his own familiar bay and a smaller, gold-coloured mare who was dancing on her toes with excitement. He met Sabin's eyes, gave her a smile and a wink that heartened her still further, and then walked on towards the woman in green. Sabin watched him.

He put Honey's reins into Joanna's hand. 'Your mare, my lady,' he said with a bow.

Joanna took the mare's reins, gave Gervase a word of thanks and, lifting the child, set her astride in front of the saddle. Both Josse and Gervase stepped forward to help Joanna mount but she swung herself up behind the child without their aid. Sabin suppressed a smile as the two men stood there, their hands still outstretched and their mouths open.

She felt Joanna's eyes on her.

Nerving herself, she met the frank stare. With a swift glance at the two men, she looked back at Joanna and raised an eyebrow as if to say, sweet, aren't they? And, unless she was very much mistaken, on Joanna's stern face as she glared down there appeared a very faint grin.

Sabin had the distinct feeling that Joanna's senses worked rather more efficiently than other people's and that the woman of the forest had observed all that there was to observe in the little scene that had just been enacted. Whether or not that was true, for some reason Sabin felt that the woman's initial animosity had subsided.

Which, considering the long journey in each others' company on which they were about to embark, was probably just as well.

Helewise heard a soft tap at her door.

'Come in.'

'They are ready to leave, my lady Abbess,' Sister Ursel said. 'I am sorry to disturb you, but you did say that you wished to see them off and bless their journey.'

'Indeed I did, Sister Ursel. Thank you.' Rising, Helewise indicated to the nun that she should go on ahead back to the gate. After taking a couple of steadying breaths, Helewise followed her.

With an appearance of calm serenity that she was far from feeling, she walked up to the quartet at the gates. Josse had yet to mount; she went up to him and said softly, 'Thank you, Sir Josse, for what you are about to do. Good luck in your endeavours and let us all hope and pray that you meet with success.' Then, suddenly afraid for him: 'May God bless you for your willingness always to be a friend of the Abbey, and may he keep you in his care and bring you safely home.'

Josse closed his eyes for a moment and muttered, 'Amen.'

'God's speed, Gervase,' she said, moving on to the sheriff,

who removed his hat and gave her a bow. 'And to you, Sabin' – she turned to the fair young woman on the grey – 'and I congratulate the pair of you on the happy announcement that you are to be wed.'

'Thank you, my lady,' Sabin said meekly.

Lastly Helewise turned to Joanna, sitting silent and still on the golden mare. The child sat before her, watching Helewise with heavy-lidded eyes. 'This little one will be asleep before you've gone half a mile,' Helewise said softly, smiling up at Joanna.

Joanna smiled back, deep, dark eyes seeming to reach right into Helewise's mind as if seeking briefly to touch on memories that both she and Helewise knew were hidden within. 'Yes, my lady,' she replied. 'Meggie was awake for much of the night.'

'She'll soon catch up on her lost sleep,' Helewise said, grateful to Joanna for speaking of normal things. 'They are so very adaptable at that age, aren't they?' she added.

'Yes. They tell me the trouble really starts when they're a little older and start to question everything with *why*?'

Helewise laughed. 'How true,' she said. 'I recall it only too well!'

She reached out and touched the child's springy brown curls. 'Go safely, little Meggie,' she said softly. Then, eyes on Joanna's, she whispered, 'May I give you a blessing too?'

There was a split-second's hesitation, then Joanna's face relaxed and she said, 'Yes, my lady. I should welcome it.'

Helewise leaned close to Joanna and Meggie and quietly uttered a brief but urgent prayer for their safety. She thought she heard Joanna murmur 'Amen', but she could have been mistaken.

Then she stepped back, waved a hand to Josse, now mounted, and watched as the four adults and one child rode out of the gates and off on the road that led to the coast.

# 6

The early start, combined with a warm, dry day that was ideal for a journey, meant that the travellers reached the coast in the mid-afternoon. They made for the port of Pevensey, busy now in high summer with the arrival of many small ships from across the narrow seas and beyond. Josse left the others in an inn yard, where they would take care of the horses and then see about ordering a meal, and he set out along the quayside in search of a captain who would take the party over to France; preferably to some port as far to the west as possible.

After several refusals, uttered with varying degrees of civility, Josse found a man from Harwich who was about to set sail. The captain's itinerary included several ports on the north coast of France, after which he would round the Breton peninsula and, on its southern side, sail up the wide Loire estuary to Nantes, then on southwards, hugging the coast, as far as Bordeaux. He was carrying English wool and Flanders cloth; at the mouth of the Seine he would stop to take on board a cargo of luxuries – tooled leather goods, spices and silks – that had been brought upriver from the market at Troyes, then he would sail on to Barfleur and then—

At this point in the captain's apparently endless narrative Josse interrupted and enquired very courteously whether or not the man took passengers.

'Passengers?' He sniffed, eyeing Josse dubiously. 'I take those who can pay.' He jerked his head in the direction of a group of half a dozen men in the simply cut, dark and hooded robes typical of monks, who were sitting in the shade by the wall that ran along at the rear of the quay. One man sat a little apart from the others and he seemed to be watching the comings and goings with avid curiosity; perhaps, Josse thought vaguely, this was his first excursion outside whichever walls usually penned him up. Near to the monks an elderly man sat gazing vacantly into space, his lips moving as if in prayer. Or he might have been talking to himself.

'Have you space for more?' Josse asked. 'Four adults, a child and four horses?'

'I have room,' the captain said. He pointed along the quayside to where his ship lay berthed, her deck and the two gangplanks busy with the comings and goings of the crew. 'My ship is generously sized and adapted for the accommodation of horses. Where do you wish to go?'

'Two adults of the party are bound for Nantes; the others and the child for' – Where *were* he and Joanna bound? He realised that he had only the vaguest idea – 'er, for Brittany.'

The captain smiled. 'Nantes is in Brittany.'

'We wish to go north of Nantes.' He was pretty sure that was right, anyway.

'Well, then perhaps I will drop you off at Dinan.'

'Dinan? Aye, very well, if that is what you advise,' Josse agreed.

The captain shrugged. 'There is no need to decide now. I will take your party, sir knight, although it will not be cheap.'

He named a price. Josse gave a dramatic cry of horror, throwing his hands in the air as if he'd just been informed he had missed the Second Coming, and offered half. After some haggling, they agreed at a figure that was roughly three-quarters of the captain's original sum. They shook on the deal and Josse agreed to hand over the coins (the Abbess had insisted on funding his and Joanna's travelling expenses from the Abbey's coffers; Gervase and Sabin also carried money sufficient for their journey) as soon as all of the party were aboard.

Then, satisfied with the arrangements, Josse returned to tell the others that they would be sailing that evening as soon as the tide turned.

The ship was called the *Goddess of the Dawn* and she was a clinker-built cob whose design showed clear signs of its long-boat origins, although she was shorter and rounder in shape. She was some thirty paces long; her planks, set parallel on the widely curving ribs, ran from the high prow to the equally high stern in precise, even lines that drew the eye and spoke aloud the ship's beauty. A tall mast stood amidships, the square sail at present neatly furled. From the front of the prow extended the bowsprit, to which could be fastened the bowlines attached to the edges of the sail that enabled a canny captain to sail close to the wind. Along the gunwales was a row of holes, for the use of oars when the wind failed and for manoeuvring in estuaries and rivers. The rear quarter of the deck was covered by a wooden construction, on its roof a railed-in aft deck. A door gave access to a dim interior, beneath which a companionway led to the storage area where the horses were also accommodated.

On the ship's high prow there was a figurehead, skilfully carved in pale oak, depicting a woman with flowing hair and a fierce expression. As befitted a goddess, she was accorded deep respect by her captain and crew.

Watching from the quay some time after sunset as the horses were led aboard, Josse observed his companions as they stared at the ship to which they were about to entrust their safety and their lives. Sabin, noticing the figurehead, gave a small gasp and, furtively making the sign of the cross on her breast, muttered something inaudible. Gervase, as befitted a man deeply in love, turned his attention from staring up at the tiny platform right at the top of the mast and gave Sabin a reassuring hug. Joanna's expression was unreadable; Meggie, held tight in her mother's arms, was clamouring to get down and rush off to explore.

'Come on, then,' Josse said bracingly. 'We'll go aboard and settle ourselves in, then we'll eat the supper we've just purchased as the ship sails.'

Without giving anyone time to protest, he strode up the gangplank; the sound of footsteps behind him indicated that the others were following. But then why would they not? he asked himself; all of the party, with the possible exception of Gervase, had crossed the narrow seas before and the two women had both done so quite recently. They'll lose any fear that they have once we're on our way, he told himself.

The captain, who introduced himself as Harald, offered to show the women to their cabin; the men would have to make themselves comfortable on deck, he told them, since the second cabin was his and anyway far too small for more than one person. But the weather seemed to be set fair and Josse thought privately that he would much prefer to bed down out in the fresh air beneath the stars than in some fusty cabin. He and Gervase found a place immediately behind the main mast, where the fresh water barrel stood protected by a small roof, and, setting down their bags and bedrolls, laid claim to it.

'Should we not have a better view up in the prow?' Gervase said.

'Aye, maybe, although there will not be much to see once night falls out in the middle of the Channel,' Josse replied. 'But my reason for selecting this spot is because if it's rough out there, the middle of the ship will have less motion than the ends.' He made a seesaw movement with his hand, the centre of his palm remaining relatively still; he was aware that he had not used the correct seaman's words but Gervase understood.

'Of course,' he murmured. 'Josse, I am glad that you and your experience are with us.'

The women rejoined them quite soon. Joanna did not speak but Josse heard Sabin mutter to Gervase that the cabin smelt of stale sweat and she was sure she had seen a rat run away as they entered. With a private smile – he was quite glad not to be the recipient of her complaints – he announced he was going below to make sure the horses were being adequately cared for.

As he came back up on deck, having satisfied himself that the horses were all right, he felt the planks beneath his feet give a sort of a lurch; looking down on to the quay, he saw that they had untied and were under way.

Taking a bracing breath – despite the experience to which Gervase had referred, Josse still hated the sea – he went to rejoin the others.

The wind was from the west and the captain utilised it and ran before it almost due east to Boulogne. Although its force lessened as the night went on, still it was sufficient to fill the sails and drive the *Goddess of the Dawn* on at a fair speed. Opening his eyes at first light – despite the padded bedroll, a wooden deck was not a place conducive to prolonged, deep sleep – Josse saw straight ahead the line of the French coast. He got up quietly so as not to disturb Gervase and walked soft-footed back along the deck on the starboard side, where the captain stood talking quietly to the steersman.

'Good morning,' Josse murmured.

The steersman nodded a greeting. The captain said, 'Sleep well, did you?'

Josse shrugged. 'Not bad.'

Harald laughed softly. 'Not like our holy brethren up there.' He nodded in the direction of the half-deck above the cabins. 'One of them – maybe more than one – is snoring fit to wake the dead.'

Josse listened; aye, the captain was right. The sound of steady, rhythmic and loud snoring could be heard above the rushing of the sea and the various creaks and groans of a wooden ship under canvas moving at speed. 'Sounds like a chorus to me,' he observed.

Harald grinned. 'Maybe it's a version of plainsong and they throw the sound back and forth between them.'

'Where are they bound?' Josse asked.

'Mont Saint Michel. D'you know it?'

'I've heard of the place. Set in a bay where the sea rushes in like a galloping horse, they say.'

'Aye, it's a wild and bleak place all right. Cut off by the sea except at low tide, shrouded in mist more often than not and home to nobody but the monks.' The captain shook his head. 'Wouldn't do for me.'

Josse agreed. Then: 'How soon do you expect to dock in Boulogne?'

'Hour or more yet. We'll have to take in sail as we near the coast – there's some shallows there where the sand banks up and we'll take it carefully.'

Thanking him, Josse made his way forward and stood up in the high prow, his elbows resting on the rail beside the Goddess's large wooden head. He would wake the others presently but, for now, he took pleasure in some time alone to stare out at the reassuring sight of the coastline ahead. It was irrational, he knew, for a man could drown as readily three paces from the shore as three miles, but somehow he always felt much safer once he was in sight of land. He glanced at the stern profile of the Goddess beside him then, after a quick check to see if anyone was watching, stretched out his hand and patted her firm, rounded shoulder. 'Look after us, Lady,' he muttered.

The Goddess, naturally, did not reply.

*

The party spent another five days and nights aboard the *Goddess of the Dawn*, during which time the ship came to feel almost like home. The winds remained predominantly from the west or the south-west and, since this was the overall direction in which the ship was sailing, progress was often frustratingly slow. But Harald was a skilful sailor and, although often sailing almost straight into the wind, he usually managed to find a tack that ensured forward movement.

Joanna abandoned the cabin after the first night; Sabin followed her after the second. For the remainder of the voyage the two women spread blankets on the deck beneath the mast beside Josse and Gervase where, at night, Meggie would be securely placed between them. The weather stayed fine and the ship kept quite close to the shore. The sea was for the most part calm and when rough waters were encountered, such as at the wide mouth of the Seine, the ship's motion proved to be no worse than a steady rocking and the spray was no more than a refreshing mist on the face.

On the morning of the fifth day, Joanna sat with Meggie on the aft deck, watching the dancing waves and telling her a story about a city that drowned when the seas rushed in. To Joanna's quiet delight, the little girl showed no fear – which might have been understandable even in an older child, bearing in mind that they were at sea and therefore not in the ideal place for a tale with drowning as its theme – but instead sat with wind-flushed cheeks and a fascinated half-smile staring out over the deep green water.

Aware of eyes upon her – Joanna's sensitivity had grown fast during the years of her instruction – she turned and saw that one of the monks was staring at her. She met his gaze for a split second – his face was shaded by his hood and she could not read his expression – and then he bowed his head.

Returning her attention to Meggie and picking up the story,

Joanna wondered why the small encounter had upset her. She had felt malice coming from those shadowed eyes; of that there was no doubt. One arm around Meggie's waist as the child sat on her lap, Joanna reached inside her gown with her other hand and found the bear's claw set in silver that she wore on a silver chain. Holding it firmly, she asked for protection from whatever it was that threatened her; after a few moments, she felt reassured.

She finished her tale and Meggie relaxed against her, half asleep and no doubt wandering happily in daydreams of magical drowned cities. Joanna wondered again about the monk; she risked a quick glance and saw that he was still there, although now the others had returned to their habitual place and were sitting muttering together. Perhaps they were praying.

She closed her eyes and went back to that moment when she had felt the monk's malevolent thought directed against her. Was it simply that he heard her story and, judging her to be a pagan, instantly hated her? It was quite likely; one of her anxieties over coming on this journey had been over the inevitable proximity with Outworlders – her people's name for those who lived beyond the forest – that it would bring. She had been given training in how to go unnoticed when with Outworlders and she could make herself so unobtrusive as to be to all purposes invisible; yet he – that monk – had glared at her as if he knew exactly who and what she was and both loathed and condemned her for it.

She risked another quick look at the group of monks. The one who had stared at her sat a little apart and she realised that she had already noticed something about him: he did not join in conversations or eat the sparse and not very appetising meals with the others. Was he being punished? Joanna was not very familiar with the ways of monks but she had an idea that temporary ostracism might well be the penalty for some piece of behaviour unacceptable to the community. With a faint smile she amused herself by wondering what the shunned one had done. It served to distract her from her moment of fear and soon she had forgotten all about it.

The ship had put in at Barfleur – Josse had told his companions that the port was favoured by their King and his mother, a fact verified by the excellent state of repair of everything from hawsers and bollards to the quay itself – and, since Harald said that it would take some time to complete the unloading and loading procedures, Gervase suggested that the party go ashore. Their horses were brought up from their accommodation below and for a happy hour the party enjoyed a ride on the fresh green grass above the town. Sabin spotted a street market on the way back to the quay and, handing her mare's reins to Gervase, stopped to purchase some provisions.

As the *Goddess of the Dawn* sailed out of Barfleur and prepared to round the Cherbourg peninsula, the four adults and Meggie enjoyed a simple meal of bread, cheese, apples and a flagon of cider that nevertheless tasted like a feast.

At noon on the sixth day out of Pevensey, the ship reached Mont Saint Michel. Since the little island could only be approached at high tide, the *Goddess* stood off for an hour or so then, with the small waves now lapping at the rocky feet of the Mount, she put in briefly and tied up at a rickety wooden jetty. Josse and the others watched with amusement as the party of monks was ushered swiftly and unceremoniously off the ship by the clearly anxious Harald; 'I'm surprised he didn't chuck them in the sea half a mile off and make them swim for it,' Josse observed. With haste, the crew prepared to put to sea again, every man of them, the captain as well, working with fierce concentration in that perilous place that tested the most experienced seamanship.

Josse and the others watched them intently, admiring their efficiency; Josse for one was relieved when at last they were done and the ship began to pull away from the jetty. So total was the absorption of both passengers and crew upon the task in hand that hardly anybody noticed the strange behaviour of one of the monks, the last one to slither down the gangplank and in the rear of the rest of the party by some fifteen or twenty paces. A couple of sailors, anxious to draw back the gangplank, went to hurry him up; abruptly he turned and ran back along the narrow plank, now stretched over the gap of water that was already appearing between the ship's sides and the wooden supports of the quay. With a brief nod to the sailors, who were watching him indifferently as if passengers changing their minds at the last moment were all in a day's work, he sprang up on to the gunwale and ducked down out of sight into the companionway leading down to the cargo deck. His brother monks, already some twenty paces away, did not notice any more than most of those on board the ship had done. Even if they had, it would not have concerned them overly.

The man was the monk whom Joanna had thought was being ostracised.

He was not in fact a monk at all.

Late in the afternoon the *Goddess* entered the estuary of the river Rance. She sailed for a mile or two up the wide waters of the river's mouth but the captain knew that he could not approach the port of Dinan, perhaps another six or seven miles upstream, until the tide was once again coming in and the sea building up towards high water.

Joanna, seeing Sabin standing up in the prow, went to join her.

'How are you feeling?' she asked her quietly; Sabin had been very sick during the first night in the stuffy cabin. She had asked Joanna not to tell Gervase and Josse, explaining with a wry smile that she was meant to be the healer, not the patient. She had dosed herself with a remedy of her own making – Joanna had been interested in the ingredients, the main one of which was root of ginger – and she had not felt as bad again, although she had been frequently upset by the ship's motion and had consequently felt queasy for most of the voyage.

Sabin smiled. 'Better now that the end is all but in sight,' she said.

'You and Gervase intend to disembark at Dinan too?'

'Yes,' Sabin confirmed. 'Gervase was for sailing on round to Nantes, but I have heard that the sea gets rough around the Breton peninsular and I was very reluctant to encounter anything worse than we have already experienced.'

Joanna was about to point out that the sea had been flat as a pond almost all the way, but it would have been unkind and so she didn't. She had noticed that, while some people quickly grew accustomed to the way a ship pitched and tossed and were soon no longer nauseated by the motion, others could sail all their lives and still lose their most recent meal at the first wave. 'So you will continue your journey by road?'

'Yes. The captain sent for one of his sailors, a man who knows the area, and he told us that the road from Dinan to Rennes is good. The one from Rennes to Nantes, as I know from my own experience, is even better. At this time of year, we shall make good progress and perhaps even beat the *Goddess* into Nantes.'

'Even if you don't,' Joanna observed, 'you'll arrive feeling better than if you've just rounded Armorica on a sailing vessel.'

'Armorica?' Sabin queried. 'A Breton myself, I know the word, of course – it is the ancient name for Brittany – but I was not aware that anyone still called the land by that name.'

Joanna could think of no reply; a short, trite answer would have served, only she did not want to fob Sabin off with the trivial; the full explanation would have taken far too long. 'I – er, I must have heard someone use the term somewhere,' she said vaguely. Sabin eyed her curiously for a moment then, with a faint shrug, turned away.

The *Goddess of the Dawn* tied up at the quayside in the port of Dinan just as darkness fell. The journey upriver had been slow and tedious, especially for the crew, who had manned the oars for the last stretch. Their labours had been aided by the incoming tide, which sent the water flooding in up the river, but the men nevertheless had been hard put to it to keep the ship steady in mid-stream. Watching the swift expertise with which the hands secured the vessel to the quay, Josse thought that to a man they were undoubtedly looking forward to going ashore for a hot meal and a well-earned drink or two.

The captain sent four of his crew to bring the horses up from below and as Gervase and the two women set about stowing their bags and bedrolls behind the horses' saddles, Josse went to say farewell to Harald.

'When d'ye expect to return to England?' Harald asked. 'That is, if you're intending to return?'

'Aye, we'll be going back,' Josse confirmed. 'As to when . . .' He shrugged. 'I cannot say. It depends on how long it takes us to see to our various missions.'

Harald nodded sagely. 'Men of affairs, then.'

'Er – aye.' It seemed easier to agree than to enter into extensive explanations which were, in any case, nobody else's business.

'We'll not be calling in here on our return,' Harald said, 'but we'll be bringing a consignment of wine up from Bordeaux to the monks on the Mont, so you might catch us there if you've a mind to. Won't be for more than a fortnight at the very least, however, and longer than that if these westerlies keep up.'

Josse was hoping to be safely back in Hawkenlye before that. 'Thank you, captain. We'll see how we go.'

And, with a bow, he took his leave of both captain and ship and went down the gangplank to join the others.

They climbed the winding, cobbled street that led up from the port, leading the horses because of the steepness of the incline; in addition, the stones were slimy with the refuse of a day's traffic and, despite the cobbles, more than once one or other of the horses slipped. The incline flattened out slightly as the road approached the town walls and, in single file now, the party went under the great arched gateway, its iron grille at present raised. Joanna, who had been here before, glanced up at the darkening sky: twilight was fast falling and within the hour it would be fully dark and the gates would be secured for the night.

She had not anticipated coming back to Dinan when she had agreed to accompany Josse to Armorica. In a place close by the town she had endured the worst time of her life: pregnant by one of the most famous men in the western world, she had been married off to an elderly lord and sent to live with him in his ancient family manor. For six years he had made her life hell and then he had taken a fall out hunting and his death had released her. She had fled, taking her young son, a few personal possessions, the boy's pony and her own mare and taking ship to England, to seek refuge with the only person in the world whom she trusted.

And look, Joanna thought as she panted up the last steep incline of the Rue du Jerzual, what that flight has led to . . .

She became aware that Josse was speaking and hastily began to listen.

'. . . find a place where they'll provide a good meal and beds for the night?' he suggested.

He seemed to be asking her; presumably he too remembered that she used to live in the area.

'I do not know Dinan well,' she said, 'only having visited on rare occasions. I am sure there is decent accommodation to be found, although I cannot say where.'

Josse, she noticed, had flashed her a look of sympathy and understanding; she tried to recall exactly what she had told him of her life with Thorald de Lehon and, embarrassed, thought that she might have included a few details that she would have done better to have left out.

'There's an inn down the street to our left,' Gervase said. 'Shall we try there? Plenty of people seem to be going in, which is always a good sign!' He spoke lightly, as if he too felt Joanna's unease.

She looked in the direction of the inn. It was indeed busy, and the sound of voices and laughter floated out into the street. She nodded. 'Very well.'

Gervase went in beneath the arched entrance to the inner yard and engaged a harassed-looking man in conversation, pointing back at the others standing in the street. After a few moments the man gave a shrug and nodded. Gervase beckoned, and Josse led the way into the yard. The man had whistled up a couple of lads, who took charge of the horses, and Gervase explained that he had secured a room for the women and Meggie and space in the communal dormitory for himself and Josse.

'It's not perfect, but it will serve, I think?' He looked anxiously at Sabin.

'It's fine,' she said. 'Can we eat here too?'

Gervase smiled. 'Oh, yes. That was the first thing I asked – I'm starving.'

Joanna looked around the small room that had been allocated to herself and Sabin. There was one bed, not very wide, and although the bedding looked reasonably fresh it had clearly been used. I'm going to hate this, she thought miserably; accustomed to nights in the fresh cleanliness of her little hut in the forest, where the invigorating air blew gently through the unshuttered window, to be forced to sleep in a confined space with the smell of other people in her nostrils was anathema to her. And she would have to share her bed not only with Meggie – which she was used to and which she loved – but also with Sabin. And as yet she had not decided whether she even *liked* Sabin . . .

Sabin had removed her gown and under-shift and was washing vigorously, bending over the basin and splashing water over face, neck, breasts and armpits. Drying herself on a small piece of linen from her bag, she grinned at Joanna. 'That's better. There's plenty more water in the ewer if you want to wash too.'

'Thank you. I'll see to Meggie, then use up what's left.'

'Don't be long,' Sabin said. 'The men are keen to eat.'

'Very well.'

Quite soon Joanna was finished and she and Sabin set off along the passage towards the eating area, where Josse and Gervase could be seen downing large mugs of something no doubt cool and refreshing and probably also alcoholic. Sabin began to make some comment but just at that moment she caught her toe on an uneven flagstone and tripped, lurching against the wall and throwing out a hand to save herself. There was a ripping sound; looking down at her upper body, Joanna saw a large tear in the bodice of Sabin's gown. An area of creamy white flesh was visible, together with one rosy nipple.

Despite herself, Joanna giggled. 'I don't think you can go in to dinner like that.'

Sabin muttered something in her own tongue, then smiled ruefully as she tried to pull the torn edges together. 'No, I can't,' she agreed. 'I can mend this, but it'll take quite a while to do a good job.'

'Have you another tunic?'

'Yes. You go on – I'll go back to our room and change.'

Joanna walked on into the dining area. She swiftly explained what had happened and said that Sabin would join them as soon as she could; Gervase, nodding, indicated a long table at the far end of the room and suggested they sat down and ordered some food.

Gervase sat with his back to the room, and Josse and Joanna sat against the wall, Meggie between them. The child was tired and hungry and consequently on the edge of being fractious; Josse took her on his lap and entertained her with the peek-a-boo game, contorting his face into the alternate happy and sad expressions with each passage of his hand. Meggie found this quite fascinating, wrinkling up her own little face as she tried to copy him. Joanna was in the midst of laughing at the picture that the two of them made together when suddenly she felt as if she was being stabbed; the sharp pain between her eyes was exactly as if someone were attacking her with the point of a dagger.

Recognising the sensation, she bent forward briefly, pretending to straighten Meggie's tunic, and unobtrusively drew forward the small veil that she had put on when they came ashore, careful to make sure that it concealed her face. Then slowly she raised her head and let her eyes wander around the crowded room.

She saw him almost immediately. The force of his expression horrified her; no wonder it had caused her pain, for malice poured out of him, honed to a fine point that was aimed straight at her.

She thought quite calmly, I have to get away.

She leaned close to Josse and murmured, 'I'll go and see if I can help Sabin,' then, getting up with unhurried grace, she left the room. Once out of sight of anyone within it, she ran as fast as she could along the passage to the bed chamber.

Bursting into the room, she found a flustered Sabin struggling with the laces at one side of a pretty grey-blue gown; the braid had got itself into a knot that she could not untie. Sabin looked up as Joanna flung the door closed and, panting, leaned against it.

'What's the matter?' Sabin's eyes were round with amazement. 'You look terrible – what has happened?' Her face paled suddenly and she seemed to sway. 'Oh, God, it's not Gervase? He's not hurt?'

Registering with a part of her mind how deep was Sabin's love for Gervase, if even the thought of his having come to harm affected her so badly, Joanna hastened to say, 'No, Gervase is perfectly all right – they all are.'

'What is it, then?' Sabin looked only partially reassured.

Joanna took a breath, trying to steady herself. Then she said, 'I used to live near here. I was married to a man – Thorald – whom I hated and when he died I took my son and we ran away. His younger brother thought I had killed him and was after my blood, only he never found me.'

'Oh, how terrible! He was cruel to you, this Thorald?'

'Yes.' She was not going to elaborate. 'And Césaire – he's the brother, the one who thought I'd killed Thorald – is right at this moment eating his supper in the tavern.'

Sabin rushed to her side. 'Has he seen you?'

Joanna's terror broke out of her control and flooded through her; dropping her face into her hands, she whispered, 'Yes.' She removed her hands and stared at Sabin. 'He won't let me go again. He'll have me arrested and they'll probably hang me.'

Sabin put her arms around Joanna. 'No they won't,' she said bracingly. She gave her a little shake. Then, after a moment's swift thought, she said, 'Listen. I've got an idea.'

# 7

Josse watched Joanna return to the dining room. She edged her way through the jostling crowds of people, the folds of her veil falling gracefully and concealing her face. She reached the table and took her place beside Josse. Leaning towards her, peering around her veil to look into her face, he was about to tell her what there was to eat when suddenly he stopped, his mouth opening in surprise as an involuntary exclamation rose to his lips. She shook her head, a minute gesture that only he could see; puzzled, eyeing her warily, he subsided. Gervase, busy trying to get a singularly dim-looking lad to understand what he was trying to order for the party to eat and drink, had greeted Joanna's arrival with no more than a vague nod.

Josse clutched Meggie closer and tried to keep her attention on the little stick man that he had made from a piece of the straw that was strewn on the floor. Obliging child that she was, she studied the little figure to the exclusion of everything else; praying that whatever crisis was currently being enacted would not last too long, Josse risked a quick glance around the room.

A man was pushing his way towards their table. Of medium height and running to fat, he had long, lank dark hair surrounding a bald crown and his thin face was set in an expression that was an unpleasant mixture of disgust, hatred and triumph.

Gervase had seen him too. It was apparent that whatever had aroused the man's fury had to do with their own party, for now he was standing beside their table and his hand was on the handle of a long knife in a scabbard hanging from his belt.

Gervase half rose. 'What do you want?' he asked.

The man did not look at him. 'Her,' he said tersely. 'Come along quietly, Joanna; best in the long run if you don't make a fuss.' He fingered the knife. 'We don't want people getting hurt, do we?'

Josse grasped her arm as if to keep her from the stranger by force; she shook him off. She sat with her head lowered, the concealing veil falling forward.

'Joanna!' the man hissed. 'I don't know why you've come back but, by God, I'm glad you have! It's too many years that my poor brother has gone unavenged but at last the day of reckoning has come. Stand up, woman, and come with me, or must I call someone who will force you?'

At last she raised her head. Staring the man full in the face, she said haughtily, 'I do not know who you think I am but let me tell you that you are mistaken. I am not this Joanna, whoever she is, and you will kindly go away and leave us alone.'

And Sabin de Retz, anger in her bright blue eyes, fixed the stranger with such a fierce glare that his own eyes fell. But, apparently unable to accept defeat, he raised his head again and gave Sabin another long, hard stare. 'You *were* her,' he murmured, a bewildered frown creasing his sallow face. 'How did you . . . ?' Fear twisting his expression, he hissed, 'It's witchcraft. It must be, for how else was I deceived into seeing a woman who now turns before my very eyes into another?'

Josse, deeply alarmed by the mention of the word *witchcraft*, was about to do what he could to prevent the situation getting even worse but Gervase got in first. Standing up and straightening his shoulders, he said quietly to the man, 'This lady is Sabin de Retz and she is a native of Nantes. She is a renowned apothecary in her home town, where she has in the past numbered the great and the good among her patients. She is under the protection of myself and of this knight' – he indicated Josse, who had also risen to his feet – 'and she is to be my wife.' In case the stranger had missed the point, Gervase added, 'Do not further insult her by your unwelcome attention, for it is displeasing to all of us.'

The man closed his mouth with a snap. Pointing a shaking finger at Sabin, who was staring at him as if he were a rat, he muttered, 'You've done magic. It's enchantment. I—'

'You,' Josse said loudly, squeezing past Sabin and grabbing the man by the arm, 'have taken too much ale and it has addled your wits. It is high time you went home.'

'But—' the man protested.

Josse ignored him. To the amusement of several bystanders, he grasped the man by his upper arms and, lifting him off his feet, carried him to the door and, once out in the street, promptly dropped him and shoved him on his way. The man took a couple of steps, stumbled and collapsed on to the ground, where he sat looking bemused and shaking his head in disbelief.

'Go home and sleep it off,' Josse advised. 'We won't make any complaint against you if you do. But if you return to bother the lady again . . .' Josse left the remark unfinished; somehow it sounded more threatening that way.

The man stared up at Josse's tall, broad body filling the doorway. Then he got slowly to his feet and staggered away.

Josse returned to the table at the far side of the dining area to find Gervase sitting next to Sabin, Meggie beside them chewing on a piece of bread and eyeing with evident glee the steaming dish that had been set before them: the food had arrived. Gervase was holding Sabin very closely and from the frown on his face, it appeared he had just been remonstrating with her. Sabin glanced up at Josse with a faint smile.

'Joanna saw someone she did not wish to meet,' she said quietly. 'She seemed in fear of him and so I suggested we exchanged clothes. I came back in here, hoping that the man would make his approach, as indeed he did. Seeing that I was not Joanna, with luck he will believe he was mistaken and leave us – her – alone.'

Josse squeezed her shoulder. 'You think quickly, Sabin,' he remarked. He was about to express his profound thanks for the resourcefulness that had saved Joanna but remembered in time that she did not know – or at least he didn't think she knew – about what lay between him and Joanna. Collecting himself, he said decisively, 'We'll take our supper along to your room, Sabin, with your permission. That way, Joanna will get her meal without having to risk showing her face out here again.'

'That's sensible,' Gervase commented, helping Sabin to gather up the trenchers, bread basket and serving dish. 'Come on, Meggie – you'll have your supper soon, I promise.'

Later that night, when Josse and Gervase had gone off to find what comfort they could in the communal sleeping accommodation and Meggie was fast asleep, Sabin propped herself up on one elbow and, looking down at Joanna lying beside her, said, 'Now it's time to tell. Since I saved your skin earlier this evening, I think, don't you, that I have a right to know what all the fuss was about?'

Joanna, who had been prepared for such a demand, smiled to herself in the faint light of the nightlight candle that they had left burning beside the bed. She turned on to her back, made herself comfortable and, supporting her head on her crossed arms, said, 'What do you want to know?'

'For a start,' Sabin said, 'what happened to your son?'

Joanna sighed. She had not been in Ninian's happy company for three years now, although not a day went by that she did not think of him and send her love and her blessing to him. He would be nine years old this year. He was turning into a fine-looking boy; tall and with the promise of breadth and strength in his chest and shoulders, with his father's brilliant blue eyes and penetrating, discomfiting stare. His hair, glossy and grown almost to his shoulders, had the colour and sheen of a ripe chestnut.

Joanna knew what her son looked like for she used her scrying bowl regularly, enduring the terrible, nauseous headache that always followed because it was worth the pain to watch her son growing up.

'I gave my son into the care of strangers,' she said baldly. 'A place was found for him in the household of a good man, a knight to whom Ninian is page until the time comes for him to begin training as a squire.'

'Why did you give him up?' Sabin asked. 'I know it's quite customary for well-born boys to be raised in other men's households, and I only ask because it's quite clear how much you love your daughter. Loving your son equally, how could you bear to part with him?'

'I had no choice!' In her fervour Joanna spoke too loudly and Meggie stirred in her sleep. Reaching out to stroke the child's forehead with a gentle hand, Joanna went on more quietly, 'When I fled from Brittany I went to England, to seek out my – to find a woman who had looked after me when I was little, a servant in the house of my kin in England. She took me in and cared for me and taught me to live as she did.'

'She was a wise woman?' Sabin breathed.

'Yes. That was the name given to her by those who live in the outside world. She was one of the forest people; as I have since learned, one of their Great Ones.'

Sabin was nodding her understanding. 'And you became one of these Forest Folk too; that is why you look and seem so strange. Oh! I am sorry! That was very rude.'

Joanna was chuckling. 'Rude but true,' she acknowledged. 'I had discovered what my destiny was; I think I had always known, although I did not set my foot on the path that was meant for me until I had lived for more than twenty years in another life, a very different one. But the life of a forest dweller was not right for my son, in whose veins flows royal blood.'

'Whose?' whispered Sabin.

Putting her lips right up against Sabin's ear, Joanna told her and watched with amusement as her eyes widened. *'Oh!'* she exclaimed. Then: 'Does Ninian know?'

'No, and nor will he, for almost all of the people who know the secret are dead.' She shot Sabin a quick look. 'You and I know, of course . . .'

'I won't tell!' Sabin shook her head vigorously.

'I know,' Joanna replied serenely. 'That's why I told you.'

'In time, then, your son will grow up and become a knight,' Sabin went on, apparently unaware of how great a compliment Joanna had just paid her, 'and – will you know how he turns out and what he does when he's a man? Have you – can you see him?'

So Joanna explained about scrying. Again, Sabin's astonishment was wonderful to watch. 'I have heard tell of such things,' she said wonderingly, 'but never thought to meet and share my bed with one who can actually *do* them.'

Joanna knew what Sabin would say next before the words were uttered.

'Can you do some magic now?' she asked in an excited whisper.

'What shall I do?' Joanna whispered back. 'Conjure a spirit? Turn you into a badger? Make a flying potion so that you and I can fly high over Dinan and watch the good people settle down in their beds for the night?'

'You can do these things?'

Joanna laughed, and the tension broke. 'No. Well, I could

make you believe that I was doing them, but that is not quite the same thing. They're just tricks, Sabin. The true power is saved for when it is really needed and it comes at a heavy price.'

'You saved the Abbess!' Sabin exclaimed. 'It *was* you, wasn't it? There was a lot of talk about this mystery woman who came in the night and brought Abbess Helewise back from the dead.'

'She wasn't actually dead,' Joanna murmured.

Sabin was looking at her with deep admiration. 'I'm honoured to be with you,' she said simply.

Joanna, embarrassed as she always was when the subject of her strange powers was discussed, paused for a steadying breath and then said, 'Sabin, the honour is mine. Your quick thinking and your courage saved my life this evening. If ever you are in need, remember that you have a friend out in the forest. You'll be living quite close once you are settled in Tonbridge and all you will have to do is go to the Abbey and ask for me; there are those in the community who know how to get in touch with me.'

'I shall not forget.' Sabin's voice was husky with emotion. After a pause – it was as if both of them needed a moment – she said, 'Meggie must have been born after you began your life in the forest.'

'Yes. She was born in the little hut deep within the shelter of the trees where I live.'

'You bore her alone?' Sabin sounded horrified. 'Weren't you very scared?'

Joanna smiled. 'I was scared, yes, as I believe all women are in childbed. But I had good friends with me and they reassured me and braced me when the pain seemed too much to bear and my courage was low.'

'Women of the forest?'

'One was an elder of our people; the other was a nun.'

'From Hawkenlye?'

Joanna chuckled. 'Of course.'

They had been hedging round the question that Joanna knew Sabin burned to ask. But when it came, it was not in the form that Joanna had expected. Perhaps it was the intimacy of lying in the half-darkness together; perhaps – and this, Joanna thought, was the more likely – it was just that Sabin was a woman who spoke her mind.

She said, 'Meggie is Josse's child, isn't she?'

Joanna hesitated only for an instant. Then she said quietly, 'Yes.'

'Yet you do not make your lives together and, when in each other's company in public, you behave civilly but distantly towards each other as if you were mere acquaintances.'

'It is because . . .' Joanna paused to think. Then: 'Josse and I lead such different lives. We could not make one another happy, for to live together one of us would have to give up the life they have chosen.'

'Is there no compromise?' Sabin asked.

'There's— No.' Joanna spoke with finality.

'Does he know that she's his child?' Sabin's voice had dropped as if she feared the sleeping Meggie might overhear.

'Yes. He found out last year, when the sickness came.' Turning to look at Sabin, she said, 'How did *you* find out?'

Now it was Sabin who laughed. 'It's obvious, for they are so alike. Not that I realised immediately – for a long time I was in awe of you and did not like to stare at either you or your child, enchanting though she is. I suspected one day on the *Goddess of the Dawn* when I heard Meggie laugh, because she sounded like a treble version of Josse. Then tonight, when she sat on his lap and he made that little stick man for her, they had their heads close together and they were both intent on the plaything. I saw that their eyes are the same shape and colour – that particular sort of brown with golden lights in it, like sunshine on peaty water. Then I knew for sure.'

Joanna thought about that for some time. Then she said, 'Does Gervase know?'

'I have no idea. I have not asked him and I certainly haven't told him of my observations.'

'Thank you.'

'For what? For not gossiping and spreading unsubstantiated rumours like a fat goodwife in the market?'

Joanna grinned. 'For precisely that.'

There was silence between them for some time, broken by the sound of Meggie's deep, steady breathing. Then Sabin said, 'I'm going to marry Gervase.'

'I know. He's a fine man. He has a true heart.'

'You know him?' Sabin sounded surprised.

'No, Sabin. I met him for the first time when we embarked upon this journey.'

'Then how can you say with such certainty what sort of a man he is?'

'I'm doing one of my magic tricks,' Joanna said ironically.

'*Are* you?'

'No. Sorry, Sabin – I really shouldn't make jokes about it. No, magic has nothing to do with it. I've been trained to study people and to look beneath the façade that they present to the outside world. They – the people who taught me – explained to me that—'

'How do you do that?' Sabin demanded eagerly. 'Can you teach me? I'd love to be able to see right into people!'

'I could teach you, yes, but it would take months.' Ruefully Joanna thought back over the hours and hours of instruction that she had received. But then, thinking that her reply had sounded a little dismissive, she added, 'You can make a start by watching how people look when they speak. For example, a man who either stares fixedly and intently into your eyes or keeps evading your glance is probably lying. You could also study what they say; someone who talks incessantly about themselves and never asks about you is likely to be self-centred and selfish. Watch how others are in their company. Someone with whom little children and animals are instantly at ease is usually trustworthy, for creatures and the young of our own species use all their senses and see with clear eyes.'

Sabin was slowly shaking her head. 'It's logical, isn't it, once it's explained?'

'Yes,' Joanna agreed. Then, for she found herself liking the outspoken young woman beside her more and more, 'We'll meet again, Sabin. Be sure of that. Then, if you wish, I'll teach you some more.'

Sabin gave a satisfied sigh. 'I'd *like* that.' Then she yawned, turned on her side and said, 'Goodnight, Joanna. I can't keep my eyes open any longer.'

'Goodnight,' Joanna returned. 'Sleep well.'

But presently Sabin whispered, 'Did you really kill him?'

'Thorald?' Joanna felt herself stiffen at the very name. 'He was a bully who beat my son and repeatedly raped me. But I did not exactly kill him.'

'What does *that* mean?'

Why not tell her? Joanna thought.

So she did.

'I put a stone in his horse's shoe in the hope that the horse would stumble and throw him. Then I sat in a darkened room and, with my eyes closed, visualised over and over again the same scene, in which the horse pulled up very suddenly and Thorald flew straight over its head, landed hard and broke his neck.'

'And was that what happened?'

'It was exactly what happened.'

There was a silence. Then Sabin said warmly, 'Good for you.'

Silence descended again. Sabin's breathing deepened and she began to snore faintly. With a smile, Joanna reached across and gently turned her on her side.

Joanna lay awake for a while longer, thinking about Sabin, about Gervase, about the bright sunshine that was going to bless their wedding day and the garland of ivy and wild flowers that Sabin would wear in her pale hair. Her thoughts turning to tomorrow, and to the prospect of setting out on the road to the forest with Josse beside her, eventually she too slept.

In the morning the party met up in the dining area. The inn served a hearty breakfast and, thinking of the long roads that lay ahead, all of them ate plenty. Then they went outside to where the horses were standing ready for them, and soon were setting off out of the shady inn yard and into the bright morning sunshine, heading through the busy streets towards the town gate that opened on to the south.

The party stayed together for some miles, following the road that wound its way south-eastwards to Rennes. For the first part the road followed the river Rance, taking the same line along the river valley, and the going was level, steady and easy.

Looking ahead, Josse could see the dark outline of a dense forest; it seemed to take up the entire horizon. Calling to Sabin, he said, 'Does your road lead through the forest?'

'I think that Gervase and I must veer off to the east,' she replied. 'I do not know the road, for this is the first time I have been so far north in Brittany, but I asked at the inn and they told me to turn left, on the road that bends away from the river.' Standing up in the stirrups, she gazed ahead. 'I believe that I can see the place where the road forks, and indeed it appears that our road leads through an area where the trees are thinner.'

The party came to the junction and drew up. 'Josse and I must follow the river a little further and then turn to the south,' Joanna said.

'Then this is where our paths part,' Gervase said. Reaching out, he took Josse's outstretched hand, then leaned close to Joanna and gave her a kiss. 'Look after this little girl,' he added, patting Meggie's cheek, 'and each other!'

'We will,' Josse replied, kissing Sabin in his turn. Joanna and Sabin embraced. Then Josse and Joanna watched as Gervase and Sabin rode away. The pair turned once or twice to wave, then rounded a bend in the road and were out of sight.

Josse took a deep breath. Then he said, 'Well, Joanna, now it's just you, me and Meggie.'

She turned and gave him a smile. He was both surprised and delighted by its intensity; whatever happens over the next few days, he thought as they urged their horses on down the riverside path, I am going to make absolutely sure that I enjoy it.

# 8

The Brocéliande felt subtly different from the Great Wealden Forest. Riding in the patchy sunshine, watching Joanna in front of him carefully picking her way, Josse tried to work out what the difference was.

There was much more water here, for a start. Back in England, the Great Forest spread itself high up on the ridges, on uplands where the land was well drained and where it was rare to come upon even so much as a thin trickling stream, never mind any standing water such as a lake or a pond. Here in Brittany the forest was lower-lying and it was filled with small meandering rivulets; the air was alive with the hypnotic sound of running water. There were many places where springs came bubbling up out of the rocks and at some of these sites anonymous visitors had left small offerings, presumably as gifts to whatever spirit they believed resided in the spring. Riding gently along, his eyes half-closed and his mind and body filled with joy, Josse could well believe there were spirits all around, moreover ones whose present mission was purely to make him happy through every one of his senses.

In addition to being noisy with the sound of water and alive with numinous spirits, there was something else that made this place so different from the sombre woodlands of the Weald. The Breton forest seemed . . . Josse screwed up his face as he tried to put a name to the impression he was receiving. It feels *younger*, he thought, smiling at himself for his whimsy. You can wander in the Great Wealden Forest and think yourself back in some age before time began and where man had yet to plant his footsteps. The Old Forest is unchanging and ever watchful and it does not like intruders. Whereas this place feels green and young and so full of life that it makes a man want to sing aloud from sheer happiness.

His eyes on Joanna's bottom as she rode ahead of him, he wondered if his sudden desire to sing might have more to do with her than any benevolence he might or might not be receiving from the trees around him.

He was still trying to get used to the headiness of being alone with her. Well, alone except for Meggie, but her presence was an enchantment in itself. This morning she was riding with her mother on the golden mare – he could have spent all morning simply watching his child's lithe and graceful little body and the way the sun caught glints of gold in her dark hair – but, during much of the long journey from Hawkenlye, Josse had been in the close company of his daughter for hours at a stretch and their fascination for each other had not faded; quite the opposite, in fact. Well, it was not to be wondered at since they were making up for the first sixteen months of Meggie's life during which neither had been aware of the other's existence.

Josse listened to Meggie's fluting voice as she asked her mother yet another question; the 'Why?' game was a current favourite and could, as Josse well knew, go on for hours if the child was not distracted. Aye, he thought, his daughter was a delight and he already loved her profoundly. Regarding Joanna, he was aware that neither the situation nor his own emotions were quite so straightforward. Travelling from England in the company of Gervase and Sabin, the other couple's presence had been a barrier to any intimacy between him and Joanna and it had seemed quite natural to treat one another politely but with the reserve of near-strangers. Joanna, indeed, had spent quite a lot of time sitting in the prow of the ship staring out at the sea, and Josse, after initially feeling slightly hurt that she should so detach herself from the rest of the company – oh, all right, from him – had finally understood that, given what he knew of her usual habits of solitude, she was probably finding the constant presence of other people quite difficult to cope with.

Then there had been last night in Dinan and that business in the inn. Josse had not liked the look of the man who had come blustering up to their table and he had felt the threatening presence of danger lurking somewhere just beneath the surface; in him, as it always did, this instinct had set his fighting response in readiness and in the aftermath, once the confrontation had been avoided, he was for quite some time left feeling jittery and jumpy. But Joanna had dismissed his anxiety, saying only that she had known the man when she lived in the area and that he had reason to hold a grudge against her. Josse was not reassured; the man had said something about his brother having gone unavenged and what was more there could be no question of mistaken identity because he had called Joanna – or the woman he had believed to be Joanna – by name.

Besides, Josse knew very well what had happened to Joanna when she had lived in the Dinan area. When they had first met, she had told him how, wed to a bully of a man many years older than herself, she had fervently wished to be rid of him and even gone so far as to insert a stone in his horse's shoe in the hope of bringing about a fall. Josse had no idea what sort of power the brother of Joanna's dead husband might wield locally but, even given that it was extensive, then surely he would be on very shaky ground if he went ahead with trying to brand Joanna a murderer on such slim evidence and for a crime committed so long ago?

Josse thought about that. Then the aspect that worried him more slid into his mind and he remembered how the furious man had said there was witchcraft involved.

Witchcraft.

Now it might not be feasible to prove that Joanna killed her late husband. But if anyone came at her with accusations of witchcraft, that was a different matter. She wouldn't deny it for one thing or, if she did, she'd do so in terms that to an outsider would be equally damning.

Witchcraft.

Oh, dear God, and they were on the wrong side of the narrow seas for accusations of witchcraft. Here, if you did not obey the dictates of the church you were excommunicated and if you persisted in your heresy you were executed in one of the worst ways imaginable.

They burned witches in France.

It would only take one interested observer of that nasty little scene in the inn to pass on what he had overheard to the religious authorities and the might of the church would be on their trail.

And then . . .

Biting at his lip in his anxiety, Josse felt a sudden slight flow of blood as the skin broke and he winced at the small pain.

I must stop this worrying, he thought. Look at Joanna; is she concerned? No. We're out of the city now, we'll have shaken off anyone who might have tried to follow us and in any case, in all likelihood the man realised he was mistaken and has given up the pursuit. Joanna and I are out in the forest, going deeper into its sanctuary with every step. Nobody can touch us here; we're quite safe and I might as well relax and begin to enjoy myself.

When, a little later, Joanna turned in the saddle and said, 'Meggie and I are ravenous. Let's stop by that inviting lake up ahead and eat,' he agreed with alacrity. And, as the three of them made a secluded and comfortable temporary camp in the shade of the sheltering trees, he gave himself up to the various profound pleasures of the moment.

*

It was not through any relaxation of Josse's watchfulness that the unseen presence in the trees went unnoticed. Although he was a big man, the secret watcher was very, very careful to keep himself hidden; nobody saw him if he did not want them to and, even had Josse scoured every inch of the surrounding woodland, it would have made no difference. The man was dressed in garments of soft, muddy shades and he was accustomed to adapting his movements and his breathing to the rhythm of the natural world. In his hiding place he sat perfectly still and watched. Presently, as Josse and Joanna packed up the remains of their meal and prepared to depart – the watching man noted with approval that they were careful not to leave any sign of their presence – he leaned infinitesimally over to his right in order to see which way they set out.

Satisfied that he knew enough to be sure he would be able to follow, he sat still once more and waited until it was time to set out after them.

Josse and Joanna rode on through the long afternoon. It was less than a fortnight past the summer solstice and there would have been light enough, even in the forest, to have gone on for some time yet. But Meggie was clearly tired and, as Joanna pointed out, they were in no desperate hurry and there was therefore no need to ride beyond the endurance of any of them. So, when her searching eyes found what she was looking for – a sort of apron of land set within the loop of the meandering stream that they had been following for some miles – she suggested to Josse that they stop and make camp for the night.

He reined in his big horse and sat looking at her. She met his eyes briefly and then looked hastily down at the ground; straight away he knew the same thoughts ran in her mind as in his. He paused, took a steadying breath and then said, in what sounded remarkably close to his normal voice, 'This looks a good place. Shelter from that stand of trees and water in the stream.'

'Yes, and the stream loops round on three sides of us, with the thicket across the neck of the loop forming the fourth side,' she added quickly, as if as eager as he to speak of ordinary things. 'Anyone approaching will alert us either by splashing across the water or breaking through the brambles.' Glancing in that direction, she said with a grin, 'And I wouldn't suggest *that* as the best way.'

He echoed her smile. Dismounting, he said, 'What shall I do? Cut some branches or something to make a shelter?'

'*No!*' She sounded horrified. Quickly she explained. 'Sorry, Josse, but we never abuse the forest by taking living wood. I'll see to the shelter and I'll make a fire. Could you – er . . .' Watching her frown, he realised with amusement that, since she would doubtless be used to seeing to every aspect of a night under the stars all by herself, he was quite redundant and any task she came up with for him to do would be to save his face rather than to help her out. 'What about the horses?' she suggested, her expression lightening. 'They look as if they could do with a rub down.'

'Then they shall have one.' Pausing, he said, 'Do you want Meggie's help? Or may she come with me?'

'I can manage without her. Meggie, would you like to help me or Josse?'

With not an instant's hesitation Meggie said, 'Josse.'

Josse and Meggie finished their appointed task and, sitting down on the springy grass, Josse took his daughter on his lap and they watched Joanna putting the final touches to their night's lodgings. He was full of admiration for the speed and efficiency with which she had worked; in no time she had put together a simple framework of dead wood – mainly old leafless branches – over which she had placed bunches of bracken tied on to the frame with lengths of twine. The finished shelter was in the shape of a shallow arc, its base secured to the feet of two young birch trees and its top curving out and covering a space large enough for three people to lie down. She had taken note of the direction of what wind there was and the shelter had been placed so as to protect them from it. She had found several granite chunks, each about the size of a fist, which she had set down in a circle in front of the shelter; within the circle a fire had been lit. On the fire a small cooking pot sat, propped up on three more stones. Water could be heard bubbling in it and there was an appetising smell carried on the steam that issued from it.

She met his eyes. 'That's our supper,' she said.

'Mm. What is it?'

'A sort of broth. It's mostly barley grains with onions and herbs, and when it's nearly done I'll add some dried pork strips.'

'I didn't imagine you would eat meat,' he remarked.

She smiled. 'I don't unless I have to, but we're on a long journey and it's demanding a lot of energy. I won't be much use if I'm faint from hunger and, away from my home, I have to make the most of what's available.'

'I see. It's like being on campaign – soldiers say that you're never choosy again once you've really known hunger.'

'Quite.'

'How are our supplies?' he asked. They had brought provisions before leaving Dinan, adding these to what remained of the purchases they had made at various ports along their sea route.

'We've got plenty for now.'

'How long—' He stopped. He was enjoying himself far too much to want to know how long before they reached their destination.

'Yes?'

He looked up at her – she was approaching with a flask in her hand – and said softly, 'Nothing. It doesn't matter.'

As if she knew full well what he was thinking – she probably did – she gave him a very sweet smile. Then she went back to her broth.

They ate their simple supper, finishing off with slices of a spicy apple tart brought from a Dinan baker. Meggie played in the shallows of the stream for a while, Josse holding tight to her hand, until it was time to settle her for the night. Warmly wrapped in her soft blanket, her stick doll cuddled in the crook of her elbow, she was heavy-eyed and almost asleep even before her parents had finished saying goodnight to her.

Josse and Joanna went to sit on the top of the bank above the stream. Josse, at a loss as to what to do next – he knew full well what he wanted to do, but whether or not he should was another matter – drew up his legs and clasped his hands around his raised knees. His eyes fixed on some vague point in the middle distance, he felt rather than saw Joanna lean closer towards him.

Then, her head suddenly on his shoulder, she put her arms around his neck, turned his face towards hers and kissed him.

The surprise quickly ebbed and soon he was kissing her back, the frustration of days in her company when he couldn't touch her combining with his deep love for her – the love that had been a part of him since first he met her – to give an edge of hunger to the embrace which he sensed she felt too. When, after a considerable time, they broke away, she looked into his eyes, grinned and remarked, 'Oh, but I've been longing to do that!'

There was so much that he wanted – needed – to ask her. What her life was really like out in the forest. What her people did, how they lived, what they believed. Whether she spent much time with them or was in the main alone. Whether she

had made friends, female or male. Whether there was anyone—

But she was unfastening her tunic. Slipping it over her head,
laying it carefully on the ground. Removing the white under-
gown. Standing naked before him – he noticed, among half a
dozen far more imperative impressions, that she wore a charm
of some sort, a claw, perhaps, on a chain around her neck –
and pulling him to his feet.

'Josse, I'm hot and sweaty and I need a good wash. Shall we
bathe together in the steam? There's some deep water down
there, on the outside of the bend, and a gently sloping pebbly
beach where we can get in and out easily.'

He could not take his eyes off her. Her body was not exactly
as he remembered – well, she has borne another child since last
I saw her naked, he reasoned; my child – and her breasts were
heavier. But the life she led had put its mark on her, for she was
lithe and strong and he could see the line of long, powerful
muscles lying beneath her smooth skin. She watched him
looking at her and did not move until at last he raised his
eyes to meet hers. Then, opening her arms, she said, 'Dear
Josse, you are a little overdressed for bathing. May I not help
you remove your garments?'

Then he was laughing for the joy of it, accepting her help
with the laces of his tunic, feeling the sudden surprise of the
cool evening air on his bare skin as she stripped away his hose
and lifted his undershirt over his head. Very soon he too was
naked. Together they slid down the low bank, stepped into the
stony shallows and immersed themselves in the peaty, green
smelling water of the forest stream.

He did as she did, working up a lathery, milky liquid with
the leaves of a pretty pink-flowered plant that grew on the
stream banks – she said it was called soapwort – and using it to
wash his hair and his body. It was a novel sensation and he felt
his skin tingle.

The sky was darkening. Lying on his back, floating in the cool water, Josse looked up and saw the first of the stars appear. Then she was beside him, the warmth of her against him making him realise that he was becoming chilled. As if she knew, she took hold of his hand and led him out of the water, where she fetched lengths of linen with which to dry themselves.

He did not know what to do next. She had kissed him, aye, and then taken off her clothes and stood before him without a stitch on before helping him out of his garments too, but then that had been as a prelude to bathing and maybe it did not mean anything among the people who were now hers. Maybe they all undressed as a matter of course and it was not taken to mean that – er, to mean anything. If she would just give me a clue, he thought desperately, because if I make a move and it isn't what she wants, then spending further time together will be—

But what it would be went out of his head because she stepped forward into his arms, folded her own around him and, pressing against him so that he could feel every inch of her from her breasts to her firm, rounded belly and her strong thighs, she stretched up so that she could whisper softly in his ear and said, 'Josse, we could make love if you wished.'

Then there was no more speech between them, just the sounds, soft at first but quickly becoming urgent, of two people who care deeply for each other setting about demonstrating their love. She had spread blankets on the grass and gently he laid her down upon them, cradling her head on one arm while with his free hand he traced the outline of her features, only then letting his fingers follow the line of her neck downwards until he was touching her breasts. Her response was swift and, delight flooding through him, he felt her sure touch on his chest, his belly and down into his groin. It was as if she remembered exactly what gave him the most pleasure;

fiercely aroused, hungry for her, he sensed that she was as ready for him as he for her and it was soon over.

They lay wound in each other's arms. Her head was on his chest – her hair was still damp – and he could feel the warmth of her breath on his skin. He had envisaged getting up, dressing in their undergarments and creeping in beneath the shelter to settle for the night beside Meggie, but, when he made a move to rise, she shifted her weight so that she lay right on top of him and he could not move.

He could just make out the laughter in her dark eyes. She said softly, 'Spent and ready for your bed so soon, sir knight?'

To which, as he felt his body stir again, there was really only one answer.

Later, lying snug in the shelter with Meggie's soft breathing and the gently rhythmic tearing of grass as the horses grazed nearby the only sounds, he had to say what was uppermost on his mind. 'Joanna,' he whispered, his mouth right up against her ear so as not to disturb the child, 'should we have – I mean, I hope that I did not take another's place out there just now.' Full of confusion, he did not know what he was trying to say. Or, he thought honestly, the trouble was that he *did* know, all too well, but was afraid that he had not the right to ask.

There was a pause before she replied. Then – and he thought he heard the love in her voice – she said, 'Josse, I understand what it is you want to know, or I believe that I do. You are asking whether or not there is another man in my life. It is not easy to answer you, for reasons that I hope to be able to make clear to you in time. I have lain with another since I lay with you' – despite his best efforts he could not prevent his instinctive reaction, although he managed to restrict it to what sounded like a faintly disapproving grunt – 'on two occasions. But' – she hesitated, and he sensed that this was not easy for her – 'it is not quite what you must be thinking. He – it was someone who is of great importance among my people and it's as if I was being awarded a great favour by being the recipient of his attentions.'

'He didn't make you do something you were reluctant to do?' He of all people, who knew the particular horrors of her past, needed to ask that.

'No, dear Josse, I was as eager as he.' She reached out for his hand and gave it a squeeze, as if aware that her words would hurt. 'He gave me this' – Josse felt his hand being raised up to her neck, where she clasped his fingers around the pendant that she wore – 'and I have his protection.'

'It's a bear claw, isn't it?' Josse said.

'Yes. He is a bear man.'

There was silence as he tried to make sense of those last five words. Then: 'What do you mean?'

'He's a power figure. Someone who has trained so extensively in the ways of our people that he has acquired strange abilities quite outside the realm of what humans usually are considered capable of. Including the ability to shape-shift and adopt the form of a bear.'

'That's impossible,' Josse stated flatly.

Her only answer was a soft laugh. 'Yes, Josse. Of course it is.' Then she yawned, released his hand, turned on her side and, after a murmured 'Goodnight', settled herself for sleep.

A bear man. God's boots, Josse thought, whatever will she have me believe next? He smiled; perhaps she had been teasing him, seeing how far-fetched a tale she could tell him and still be believed.

The problem with that was that, although he knew she would not hesitate to tease him about most things, her beliefs and the ways of her people were the exception. But a man who could turn into a bear! No, no, no, it was just not credible.

He lay, warm and comfortable, with the woman he loved and his beloved, adored child beside him, listening to the night forest sounds all around. The rushing water, the soft footfalls of the horses, the faint stirring of the wind in the treetops. There was the sound of a hunting owl . . . and there the faint and distant squeak of some small rodent, the sure sign that the bird had just found its supper.

I am a long way from my known world out here, he thought sleepily. The rules by which I live my life may not apply here, where the spirits of the wildwood hold sway. His eyes closed and, in the sort of split-second dream that comes when sleep is close, there and gone before it is really registered, he seemed to see a misty-edged figure that appeared to be made of smoke, blurred and vague all but for the eyes, which were bright and pierced like fire. His own eyes wide open again, he stared out into the darkness, his heart thumping. But then, as sleep took him again, he remembered Joanna's words: *I have his protection.*

They were Joanna's words, aye, and he recognised them. Which was odd, really. It might have been because he was drifting into sleep, but he thought he heard the words spoken in slightly different form and in a man's voice: *You have my protection.*

Funny what you dream about, Josse thought with a smile. Then he too was fast asleep.

A long way away, back in the Great Wealden Forest of southern England, a man went in peril of his life.

He was taking a risk this evening in riding alone but frequent habit had removed the threat of danger – they never saw a soul on the track – and now he was feeling all but invincible. It was his custom to ride home through the gathering darkness of the warm summer nights, talking idly with his companion when, as he usually did, he had one and relishing the exercise after a busy day, enjoying the soft dusk air on his face, the rapid and skilful swooping of the bats and the sounds of the forest as its inhabitants settled for the night.

It had been a good day. Well, they were all good days now. Everything was going smoothly and his predictions were proving to have been accurate, if a little on the cautious side. Oh, admit it, he said to himself, smiling broadly, it's far, far better than I dared hope for and so far shows no signs of grinding to a halt.

He made a mental note to order more supplies. If he put in his request early tomorrow morning then with any luck the goods should arrive by—

There was a sound in the deep woods over to his left.

He drew his horse to a halt and sat quite still, listening.

Nothing.

But no, there was something. Was that a person, moving stealthily through the shadowed undergrowth . . . ?

Afraid now, he kicked his horse to a trot, then to a canter. Fool, he berated himself, so to ride your luck, when simply by making certain you obeyed your own rules, this could have been avoided!

This. What *was* this? Fighting down the panic, telling himself he was running like a frightened child away from some dread thing that wasn't even there, he slowed to a walk and listened again.

He could hear no sound but those that he and his horse were making.

He smiled, shaking his head at his own foolishness. Soon be home now, he thought cheerfully, and what a welcome I'll get when I put this little lot – he patted the heavy leather bags hanging from his saddle – down on the table before her. Her dark eyes will light up, she'll tell me how clever I am, then she'll get up, take my hand and walk me over to where she has set out good food and costly wine to greet my return.

He had noticed with appreciation the improvement in the cuisine of his household. Why, he thought now, his pretty wife must be enjoying the delicious food and the costly wines as much as he, for he was sure she was putting on weight. She would not like that, he was convinced of it, for she wore her gowns in a style to show off the contrast between her full breasts and her tiny waist. But the more rounded contours of her body certainly pleased him . . .

Perhaps tonight she would invite him back to her bed. It had been so long, so very long, since he had lain with her. While he could accept that, in her eyes anyway, there had been reasons before why she should withhold her favours, surely that no longer applied now? He had found the goose that laid the golden eggs and she, perhaps even more than he who was working so hard to ensure those eggs kept coming, was enjoying the benefits. Even that bitch of a mother of hers must grudgingly have to admit to herself, even if not to anyone else, that her son-in-law was turning out better than she had hoped.

Why, then, he wondered miserably, did he feel like a stranger in his own home? Why, on his regular visits back to the house to bring home the takings and check that all was well, did he have the distinct feeling that both women would have preferred it if he stayed at the shrine? Dear God – a surge of anger flared swiftly through him – did they think he *liked* living out there among the whining, whingeing pilgrims and the sweating, deceitful toughs who guarded the property? The pilgrims moaned about everything from the aches and pains that had driven them to the tomb to the quality of the food, ale and accommodation that he offered; the toughs were singularly dull-witted and to a man they stank. Was it unreasonable to expect a bit of a welcome from his wife and her mother when he came home for a bathe, a decent meal and a good night's sleep? Especially when, each time he returned, he brought yet more money with him?

His earlier happiness had evaporated. Maybe I won't go home, he thought mutinously. Maybe I'll turn left when I quit the track that runs around the forest and instead of going home, head for London. I'll find a nice little house and a comely woman to share my bed, and I'll dress us both in fine velvets and silks and find the longest, showiest plume for my hat that money can buy.

It was a pretty picture but its appeal did not last long. There was only one woman he wanted in his bed; the trouble was, she did not appear to want him in hers.

He sighed. He thought, I'll just have to—

He did not complete the thought. At that moment a sound immediately behind him startled his horse, which leapt forward in alarm. Clinging on – he had lost a stirrup – the man tried to gather the horse but it was alarmed and had the bit between its teeth. The dim light beneath the trees hid what awaited man and horse a short distance along the track, so that the first the man knew of it was when the rope stretched across the path at neck height took him under the chin and threw him backwards off his horse.

The horse, thoroughly terrified now, galloped off down the track, stirrups and money bags banging against its sides and adding to its panic.

The man lay quite still on the track.

After a moment a broad-shouldered figure materialised from out of the darkness under the trees. He stepped quietly on to the path, where he bent down over the prostrate figure and felt for a pulse, the stout club that he held in his other hand held ready.

There was no pulse; the encounter with the taut rope had broken the victim's neck, just as the big man had predicted. Quickly he rolled the body off the path and a good distance into the undergrowth, pushing aside brambles and lodging the corpse deep in a thicket. He spent a few moments making quite sure he had left no sign that the vivid, surging greenery had been disturbed. Then he padded softly back along the track and located the place where he had tied the rope, deftly unfastening it and coiling it up in order to loop it over his shoulder. Pausing for only an instant to sniff at the night air and without another look at the shady and secluded spot where he had left his victim, he melted back into the forest. He would walk in the shelter of the trees and the undergrowth until he came upon the horse which, or so he guessed, would soon recover from its panic and slacken its pace until some tasty-looking clump of green and succulent summer grass caught its attention. When he came across it, grazing peacefully by the side of the track, the man would step out from beneath the trees and catch hold of its reins.

For now, the important thing was to get away from here. Leaving the body of the dead man to cool in the darkening night, he went silently on his way.

# 9

Josse and Joanna spent all of the next day travelling through the Brocéliande forest. Observing keenly, Josse noticed another difference between the Breton woodland and the Wealden forest: here there was not that sense – so very strong in the Great Forest – of a large area where the outside world was made to feel unwelcome; it always felt as if the Wealden Forest were the zealously guarded and personal preserve of those creatures, animal and human, who lived within. Here, in contrast, roads and tracks criss-crossed the forest and there were even small settlements growing up in woodland clearings. Mankind seemed more welcome here, and it did not appear that his attempts to fell a few trees and cultivate a patch for himself and his family were treated with such threatening hostility.

They stopped at one of the forest settlements to fill up their water bottles at the village spring and to purchase food. At first Josse had been anxious about advertising their presence in this way. Were anyone from Dinan to be hunting for them and chance to come this way, one of the villagers would surely report that yes, they *had* seen a man and a woman travelling with a small child, adding details of when the strangers had arrived and which way they had gone. But then Josse, Joanna and Meggie had to eat; he put his misgivings to the back of his mind.

They bought bread, a hunk of rather crusty cheese, dried meat strips and some of last autumn's apples. These were rather sharp but refreshing to a dry throat. Josse also bought a stone jar of cider, stowing it away in his pack with the aim of bringing it out with a flourish when he and Joanna had their evening meal.

His mind and body were full of her, singing with the delight of her. And she felt the same; he would have sworn she did, for her eyes kept returning to his and each time she gave him a sort of secret smile. Once, as if some particularly powerful reminiscence were stirring in her mind's eye, she even blushed.

Tonight, he promised himself, will be even better than last night . . .

Joanna was finding it quite difficult to recall that she and Josse were here for a reason, and that reason was not for the two of them to enjoy a sort of holiday out in the forest. She had both longed for and dreaded the moment when at last they would become lovers once again; she had known it would happen – had *wanted* it to happen – but she could not help the slight sense that she was somehow betraying a newer alliance in this re-forging of an old one. What would her people say if they knew she and Josse had made love and would continue to do so? What would the bear man think?

My people, she told herself firmly, would be happy for me. They – we – do not regard sex as the world does, as something strictly reserved for the marriage bed and, more often than not, the payment a woman makes in exchange for her keep; the duty she performs for her husband in order that she will bear him a son to whom he may pass on his wealth and his property. We see sexual joy as the gift of the Goddess, which is why we celebrate her major festivals by making love with whoever catches our eye. And as for the bear man . . . She shrugged, for she did not know. What she guessed, however, was that had there been any obligation on her to keep herself chaste for him, then doubtless somebody would have told her.

She wore the claw that was his symbol and that marked her out as blessed by his having chosen her. It was no secret that she had lain with him.

She thought about him now, smiling as she recalled Josse's predictable response to being told that her only other lover was a man who could turn himself into a bear. Never mind, dear Josse, she thought lovingly; it's not imperative that you accept every aspect of my new life and you certainly don't have to wrestle with the truly incredible ones.

Even Joanna sometimes found it hard to accept the concept of the bear man.

As they rode on through the afternoon, always following the same generally southerly direction, Joanna repeatedly checked the unfolding landscape against the markers stored in her mind. She had been told what to look out for, not having trodden this road before; when, the previous year, she had travelled from the north coast of Armorica down into the Brocéliande, she had set out from further west than Dinan. But her people knew how to give foolproof directions and that ability, together with her own growing skill at finding her way, gave her the confidence to know that she would not lead her small party wrongly.

As evening approached, she saw ahead the line of hills which, growing up into a dome, formed a sort of crown right in the heart of the Brocéliande. Even though they were not approaching from exactly the same direction, she recognised its shape and knew for sure that she had not led them astray. Tomorrow, she thought, tomorrow I shall try to find a track that leads to the south-west, for over there lies Folle-Pensée.

But that was for tomorrow. There was yet tonight.

She and Josse lay together in the darkness a short distance away from Meggie, fast asleep in her blanket, for they had just made love again.

She sensed that there was something on Josse's mind. Reaching up her hand to stroke his hair away from his hot forehead, she said gently, 'What is it, my love?'

She saw his brown eyes turn to look into hers. The golden lights in his irises caught the faint glow from the fire. He said without preamble, 'I have come looking for you in the forest, three times since you told me about Meggie. You said then that I might come to see you, yet each time I came, I could not find you.' He gave a short laugh. 'Twice I couldn't even find that hut of yours when I came looking.'

She had known he would speak of it sooner or later. Such was their intimacy that she was glad it was sooner, so that – with any luck – they could discuss it and get it out of the way. She thought for a moment and then said, 'I did warn you that I might not always be there to be found.'

'Aye, but three times!'

Oh, she thought, but I have hurt him. 'I am sorry,' she said gently. 'It was never my wish to cause you pain. On two occasions I genuinely was not there.' And these, she reflected, would be the times he had not been able to locate her hut, such was the power of the concealing force that she was now able to cast around the spot when she was absent.

'What of the third time? Were you hiding inside, keeping Meggie quiet in case she heard me and called out?'

There was bitterness in his voice and she ached for him. 'No, Josse. It was not like that. I knew you had come, I will not deny it, for I was close by and could have emerged from my seclusion so that we might have spent some time together.'

'But you didn't.'

'No,' she agreed. She was thinking furiously, determined to find the right words to make him understand. 'I was very deeply involved in what I was doing. Some things that I have been taught to do require a great deal of concentration – it's almost as if I leave my own body and travel in my mind to some other place or some other reality.'

'And that's what you were doing when I came to find you?' Despite himself, he sounded curious.

'Yes. I was on what we call a soul journey, although perhaps spirit journey describes it better.'

'Were you far away?'

'In a way, yes I was. I had gone back to the land beyond the seas from which we believe that our ancestors originally came, and that was drowned beneath the waves.'

She had his attention now; she sensed it. But she had not predicted what he would say next. With almost a reproof in the words, he said, 'And what of Meggie when you are off on your spirit journeys? Who watches out for her and makes sure she does not wander off or fall in the stream or into the hearth?'

Oh, Josse, she wanted to say, Meggie is a child of the wildwood and has far too much sense to do any of those things. But then he was the child's father and he had a perfect right to make sure she was safe. Again weighing her words, she said calmly, 'When it is a matter of merely a short period of intense concentration, I put Meggie in the hut and fasten the door if I am at all concerned for her. When I know that my attention will be elsewhere for a longer time, I ask one of the others to look after her for me.' That was true, as far as it went, and indeed Joanna had asked Lora more than once to do just that service. What she kept to herself was that, when the Great Festivals came round, increasingly Meggie went with her and joined in the worship and the celebrations.

Meggie, as so many of Joanna's people had kept pointing out, was a very special child . . .

Josse was silent. After a moment she said, 'What are you thinking about?'

He laughed, but she sensed behind the brief sound an underlying unease. 'I think I just acted like a real father and

I'm wondering whether I ought to apologise for even suggesting that you don't know how to look after our daughter.'

'Josse, you *are* a real father.' She hugged him tightly, feeling his strong heartbeat pump against her bare chest. 'And there's no need to apologise for something you have every right to ask.'

They lay close, breathing to the same rhythm, and she sensed that he was relaxing more with every breath. But then, tensing slightly again, he said, 'Do they – your people – know Meggie's mine?'

'Of course! I'm very proud of the fact, and so will she be when she's old enough to consider such things.'

'They don't object?'

Now it was her turn to laugh. 'No, why should they?'

'Oh – I just wondered if they preferred children to be – er, to be fathered by men of the tribe.'

I had forgotten, thought Joanna, how the world thinks. She realised how thoroughly she was becoming one of them, her people, that a reminder of the ways of the outside world should so pull her up short. 'It is up to a woman to choose who fathers her child,' she said. 'We have a special ceremony wherein the male spirit of the people is put into a chosen woman' – he went to say something, but stopped himself – 'but, other than that, it's our own decision. Sometimes children are conceived in the celebrations that follow one of our festivals, and those children are regarded as the Goddess's particular gift.'

'But – what about property? Land? How do you decide who owns what? I mean, normally a wife bears children for her husband and they inherit, if they're sons, that is. But . . .' He drifted to a confused stop.

Oh, but the gap between how he saw the world and how she now did was just so vast! 'We don't really have property like that,' she said kindly. 'Our life is very different. And as for a woman's children inheriting their father's name and wealth, our system is not like that at all.'

'Isn't it?'

'No. Josse, we trace our descent solely through the female line.'

He thought about that. Then he broke his rather shocked silence with one word: 'Why?'

She wanted to laugh, it was so obvious. But she didn't; in the same kind tone she said, 'Because only a woman knows with absolute certainty who fathered the child she bears.' Even she, she wanted to add, will not know for sure if she has made love with more than one man at the time of conception. But she didn't speak the thought aloud. Poor Josse was looking quite sufficiently aghast already. 'Therefore,' she concluded, 'it is far more reliable to record our families through the women than through the men.'

His silence was far longer this time. Then he said wonderingly, 'God's boots, but you're quite right. I never thought of it quite that way.' Raising himself up on one elbow, he looked down at her, grinned and said, 'Aren't your people wise?'

'Oh, yes,' she agreed. She was both touched and pleased that he had made the remark; he was going to meet some of her people tomorrow at Folle-Pensée – and probably powerful ones, at that – and for him to be able to put aside his perfectly natural prejudices and admit to being impressed by their wisdom even before encountering them was surely a good omen.

Tomorrow.

One way or the other, she thought sleepily, it promised to be quite a day. Turning away from him, nestling her bare bottom into the angle of his belly and his thighs, she drew the blankets around them both and, smiling as she felt his arm creep around her to pull her close, shut her eyes.

The next day was as warm and sunny as its predecessors. Joanna and Josse broke camp early – he had copied her ways the first morning and now could leave a patch of forest innocent of the marks of their presence almost as well as she could – and by mid-morning were well on the way. Meggie was riding with her father; intrepid child that she was, she expressed a preference for the *big* horse and appeared to take a real delight in sitting up there in front of Josse, securely held but with the height above the ground giving the illusion of danger.

Josse loved to have her there with him. The two of them chattered away incessantly and had developed a series of favourite games of which Meggie never tired.

'Josse?' Meggie said.

'Yes, Meggie?' He pitched his voice low, as if the matter was of seriously grave import.

She allowed a small tension-creating pause. Then, ecstatic as yet again her trick succeeded, she shouted, *'Nothing!'*

He tried to do it too but somehow she knew what was coming; 'Meggie?' he ventured.

And his daughter, shrieking with delight, answered, 'Nothing, Josse!'

So their unhurried progress through the sunlit glades and the heather-covered open spaces was accompanied by the sound of laughter. There was birdsong on the air; to Josse, the sound of his child's merriment sounded like the fluting of some particularly melodious warbler.

They stopped for lunch – the day was now very hot and they had ridden for a while out in the full sunshine – and when they had eaten, sitting relaxed in the shade of a stand of beech trees, Joanna made Meggie lie down on the cool, mossy grass where, despite her protests that she wasn't a bit tired, she promptly fell asleep.

'Are we almost at this place, whatever it's called?' Josse asked in a low voice.

'Yes. I'm fairly sure it's over the next small rise, then about another couple of miles,' Joanna replied. 'And it's called Folle-Pensée.'

'Foolish thought? Mad thought?' Josse suggested.

'Yes, I suppose just that.' She paused, then said, 'We have among our people healers of both body and mind, and they say that the waters issuing from the spring at Folle-Pensée can help when patients are troubled by strange thoughts. Me, I think it's the skill and the patience of our healers that makes them well.'

'Aye.' Josse was sure she was right. He was thinking of something similar that he had once observed and presently he said, 'I once met a young mother who believed she was unfit to care for her child. There was no reason for this belief, for she was intelligent and competent and in fact her little boy was thriving. Sister Euphemia – she's the Hawkenlye infirmarer' – Joanna nodded – 'said she'd seen such conditions before in new mothers and that it was often just a matter of listening to their fears and not dismissing them out of hand, then treating them with kindness and patience until they began to feel better.'

Joanna was looking at him with interest. 'I have met the infirmarer,' she said, 'and what you say merely enhances the impression of her that I have already formed.' She dropped her eyes, frowned and then, looking straight at him again, said, 'Josse, doesn't it strike you that fundamentally we are all striving for the same thing?'

He had an idea what she was trying to say. 'Go on.'

'Well, your nuns and monks are good people who look after the sick and the troubled and who don't spare themselves in trying to help others. Hawkenlye Abbey is not so very different in essence from Folle-Pensée, nor from other special centres that I've seen and been told about where my own people strive to drive out the demons of mental and bodily sickness so that their patients can resume happy and healthy lives. Yet were I to say as much to someone such as the terrible old priest whose stinking and unwholesome presence bedevilled my days when I was wed to Thorald, he would have accused me of possession at best and heresy at worst.'

Josse waited a moment before speaking. Then he said, 'Joanna my sweet, as I'm sure I must have said to you before, it's unwise to judge the whole church by one foul-minded and frustrated man. You've met men and women from Hawkenlye; I don't suggest that you take them as the norm, for in their way I believe that they are as unusual as your stinky old priest, but I would venture to say that maybe you could try to see them as the good face of the church, and that as such they can perhaps do a little to redress the balance for you who have experienced the most evil one.'

She opened her mouth to say something but apparently changed her mind. Giving him a very sweet smile, she said, 'I'll try, Josse.'

They sat for some time longer in the deep shade. Josse closed his eyes and dozed. Then he sensed Joanna getting to her feet; as he opened his eyes and looked up at her, she met his gaze and said, 'Time to go. Will you wake Meggie, please?'

They packed up, mounted and rode out into the sunshine. As before, Joanna was in the lead; watching her, Josse thought the set of her shoulders suggested a certain tension. It's important to her, he reflected, this meeting between her man from the world of the outsiders and her new people. Well, I shall strive not to let her down.

Meggie, slumped against him, had her thumb in her mouth and was still sleepy. Just when I would have welcomed her chatter as a distraction to my increasing sense of apprehension, Josse thought with a grin, she decides to lose herself in her dreams. Hugging her close, he squared his shoulders and tried to still the increasingly wild pictures that his mind was throwing up.

Reality was quite different from imagination. The tiny settlement of Folle-Pensée lay hidden away at the end of a track that twisted and turned through the trees, among which outcrops of the local stone – reddish-pink granite – stood out starkly. The path opened out into a wide clearing, in which were set several simple dwellings made of wooden stakes and brushwood as well as a collection of squat, ground-hugging little cottages made of the local granite. On the far side of the settlement there was a path whose edges were marked with stones; this led off into a particularly dense area of forest, where tall trees – pine, birch – overshadowed holly, broom and gorse. Watching Joanna closely, Josse saw her turn to the entrance to the secret path and give a low bow of reverence.

Then she slid off Honey's back; he wondered whether to do the same – wasn't it good manners to wait to be asked? – but then she looked at him and gave a quick nod, so he dismounted as well, reaching up and taking Meggie in his arms. Joanna was walking slowly up to the largest of the stone cottages and just as she put out her hand to tap on the partly opened door, it was flung wide and a man appeared in the entrance.

Josse's first impression was of vigour and glowing health; it was only at the second glance that he noticed the man had to be all of sixty, for the leathery skin of his beaming face was deeply lined and his long, smooth hair and neatly groomed beard were perfectly white. He was dressed in a flowing robe the colour of a clear evening sky.

He threw open his arms and had enveloped Joanna in a warm embrace; 'Beith,' Josse heard him mutter, 'Beith, how good to see you returned to us!' Then he added something in a low voice that Josse did not catch.

With the old man's arm still around her shoulders, Joanna

turned to indicate Josse. 'Huathe, this is Josse. And Meggie of course you already know.'

The white-haired man put out a hand and gently touched Meggie's round cheek; she gave him a coy smile. 'Yes, indeed. You, little one, are growing well.' Then, turning intent blue eyes on to Josse, he said, 'Josse. I am very glad to meet you.'

There was quite a long pause, during which Josse felt as if various bits of him were being inspected individually. It was a weird sensation, as if careful probes were being sent through his head and chest. He made himself stand quite still and tried hard not to resist the gentle inspection. His response must have been the right one for, after a few more moments, the white-haired man nodded, stepped forward and embraced both Josse and Meggie, still held firmly in her father's arms. Then, standing a little away, the man said, 'I will let it be known that you are to be given every courtesy while you are here with us. Welcome to Folle-Pensée.'

Feeling that he ought to make a reply, Josse said, 'Thank you – er – Huathe.' Was it all right to call him by that name? Then he held out his hand which, after a pause and a quick smile, Huathe took in both of his own. The old man's skin was firm and cool – Josse was put in mind of Sister Euphemia's touch when she tested a hot forehead for fever – and somehow the sensation was instantly reassuring.

'I will show you to your accommodation,' Huathe said. He led them to one of the shelters that stood on the far side of the clearing, a short distance away from its nearest neighbour. Opening the door, he ushered them inside.

'We eat our evening meal when the sun goes down,' he said. 'Until then, make yourselves comfortable; feel free to walk in the forest if you wish, although I would suggest that you do not stray too far.'

With no explanation as to why they should not, Huathe gave

them both a nod, then, pulling the door to behind him, left them alone.

Josse put Meggie down on the clean-swept, beaten-earth floor, then turned slowly round as he looked about him. The hut was simply furnished: a wooden-framed bed topped with a straw mattress and some blankets; a long, low table; a bench; a stone circle in which firewood and kindling had been laid ready; a shelf on which were some pottery mugs, a jug and a pair of horn-handled knives.

And that was all.

Josse noticed that Joanna appeared to be waiting for him to comment. With a smile he said, 'It's delightful. It reminds me of your little hut in the forest. It smells the same – your people are so clean, I imagine that all their dwellings are full of the scent of herbs and growing things.'

She looked flatteringly pleased by his small compliment. 'Yes they are,' she agreed. 'I'm glad you like it.' Then, unfastening her pack, she said, 'I want to wash out some of Meggie's and my clothes, then I'm going to bathe.'

He sensed that an unspoken invitation hung in the air. Aware of having worn the same undergarments for rather too long, he said, 'Is it all right if I do the same? I have a change of linen in my pack.'

'Of course.' Then, blushing and for all the world like some urban housewife, she said, 'Give me the garments; I'll launder them for you.'

She took him outside and showed him to the place where the people bathed. A stream came hurrying down out of the forest and a pool had formed where an upthrusting band of rock ran across the stream bed. Josse stood hesitant on the edge of the water; Meggie was already wriggling out of her clothes.

Joanna laughed softly. 'It's all right, Josse. Everyone bathes here and the sight of a naked body isn't going to upset or embarrass anyone.'

Except me, he thought. But Meggie was paddling into the water and it looked as if it might be quite deep on the far side; Josse quickly removed tunic, shirt and hose, then, trying not to think about it, waded into the pool after his daughter.

When, having finished her washing, Joanna joined them there some time later, Josse had forgotten his awkwardness and was thoroughly enjoying himself. Even the presence of others did not spoil it; Joanna nodded a greeting to the man, the two women and the youth who came to bathe with them and Josse, copying her, did not so much as glance down to make sure that the water adequately concealed his private parts.

Out there in the wildwood, it just did not seem to matter.

# IO

Twelve of them, including Josse, Joanna and Hauthe, sat down to eat the evening meal. They sat on benches and on the ground around the wide outdoor hearth. The food was simple – flat bread, goat's milk cheese, small, sweet onions and a dish of mixed stewed vegetables strongly flavoured with garlic – but there was plenty of it. Accompanying it was cider out of earthenware jars, sparkling and sweet and fragrant with the strong scent of apples.

When the food had been cleared away, Huathe signalled that the people should stay where they were. Then he rose to his feet and walked forward to stand beside the embers of the fire, roughly in the middle of the circle of his audience. Then he said, 'Here are Beith and her daughter Meggie, who were with us in the early spring of last year. With her is Josse, who has accompanied her from England. All three are our guests and are to be accorded a welcome.' There was a brief murmur of conversation and Huathe waited until it had died down before continuing. 'They have come for a particular purpose, which I shall now outline to you.'

Joanna had been prepared for something like this. Knowing the ways of her people as she was beginning to, she had expected that the unusual mission that had brought her and Josse to the Brocéliande would not be treated as some hushed-up secret. They had not broadcast it back home in the forest but then the community there was so very much more numerous . . . She waited to hear what Huathe would say.

His announcement was brief and to the point: 'An un-scrupulous man is making money fraudulently,' he began. 'In a forest in the south of England, he claims to have found the bones of Merlin.' There was a gasp from someone in the circle, quickly suppressed. 'He has invited the credulous to view the bones, implying that their various hurts and sick-nesses will be cured. There is a charge for viewing this grave and all profits are going into the young man's pocket.' Indicating Josse with a wave of his hand, Huathe went on: 'The man Josse here represents the Abbey of Hawkenlye, a place where the needy receive genuine care. The rival attraction referred to as Merlin's Tomb is taking people away from the Abbey's true healing to seek help where there is none to be had.'

Huathe paused to let his people digest what he had told them so far. Then he said, 'It has been decreed that we show Josse the place in the forest here that is commonly known as Merlin's Fountain and which, according to local legend, is the true burial place of the great enchanter.'

'But—' a man's voice began.

Huathe turned to face the speaker. 'Yes? You wish to comment?'

'The spring of Barenton is Nime's place,' the man said nervously. 'It is she who blesses the precious water and whose power we feel up there.'

Huathe smiled. 'We know that, or perhaps I should say that is what we understand,' he said patiently. 'There is power there; that is undeniable. We should accept that, to others, the source of this power may have a different name. To Out-worlders, who are not blessed with the understanding of the forces of this Earth that has been bestowed upon us, it is perhaps easier to understand if the power is dressed in the guise of a man.'

'But Merlin—' the man began.

Huathe fixed his bright eyes on to the speaker. 'It is enough for the present to acknowledge that to many people, the spring of Barenton is the dwelling place of the figure known as Merlin,' he said firmly. 'Tomorrow, Beith and I will take Josse up to the spring in the forest and give him a small sample of its power. Then he may return to the Abbey at Hawkenlye and report that the tomb in the woods there in the south-east corner of England cannot be the burial place of Merlin, since he and his magic lie here in the Brocéliande, where one has but to approach the place of his interment to feel his power.'

The protester in the seated circle bowed his head. 'As you wish, Huathe,' he said meekly.

'That is decided, then,' Huathe murmured. 'So be it.'

Joanna was awake early the next morning. She lay for some time, feeling Josse's comfortable, warm bulk at her back. Then, as the light waxed, she got up, went to wash and then woke Josse. She offered him some food – she wasn't hungry, for the knot of tension in her belly was making her feel slightly queasy – and he ate his way through two pieces of bread and a hunk of cheese.

Meggie was to be left with one of the women in the settlement. As Joanna was clearing away the breakfast, there was a soft tap on the door and Meggie's temporary guardian put her head in. With a smile Joanna led the child up to the woman, who crouched down and spoke kindly to her. Then, as the woman led her away to play with another child sitting outside a nearby hut – the woman's own daughter, presumably – Joanna made herself turn away. She'll be fine, she told herself. And Josse and I won't be away long.

Josse was brushing crumbs off his tunic. She grinned. 'You look very handsome,' she said. 'I see you've done your best to smarten yourself up for the occasion.'

He ran a hand over his hair. 'Should I wear my hat?'

Now she laughed aloud. 'Dear Josse, no. There's no need for that. If you're ready, we'll go and find Huathe.'

Soon afterwards Huathe was leading the way off along the path that led into the deep forest. Joanna, senses alert, stared about her, remembering it all so well from her previous visit. The year was much more advanced this time – high summer as opposed to early spring, when her first, powerful impressions had been formed – which made everything look different. The trees were thickly leafed and the vistas in among them consequently much reduced. There was the same sense of watchfulness, however; that uncanny and slightly unnerving awareness of unseen eyes steadily regarding her that had affected her so powerfully before.

They were climbing steadily and now and again the stream that ran from the summit of the hill could be seen over to their right; it could be heard all the time. Joanna felt the power of the place steadily overcome her. Watching Josse, whose apprehension she could feel coming off him in waves, she wanted to go to him and take his hand. But he might see such a gesture as suggesting that she thought him weak and needed her strength, so she held back.

Josse, I never think you're weak, she said to him silently. Quite the reverse.

They came to the top of the low hill and once more she looked out on the clearing. There was the mighty oak that stood alone in the glade; there the long white banner lifting and fluttering on the slight breeze; there the hawthorn bush that so resembled a crouched old man. There was the great granite slab that guarded the spring . . . and there was the fountain itself, the clear, cold water ever bubbling up out of the earth to pool briefly before trickling away down the hillside.

Huathe touched Josse's arm, making him jump; Joanna saw him start. 'There, Josse, is the power place,' he said softly. 'See the large, flat stone? It is granite and it is the spot where the forces that govern this special clearing are concentrated. The unwary' – dropping his voice, he leaned confidentially closer to Josse – 'they come to scare themselves, jumping on the slab and then, when the unexpected happens and frightens them silly, wishing they had had more sense.'

'What happens?' Josse whispered.

Huathe smiled. 'Oh, they see visions of terrible things. The visions are produced within their own heads; they see what they expect to see, and one man's demons are different from another's. We help those for whom the terrors prove ungovernable. We understand a little of the power of this place and we are happy to share what knowledge we have in order to help people who have been affected by it.'

'And this – this slab marks the burial place of Merlin the Enchanter?' Josse asked. 'I heard one of your people mention another name, although it was not familiar to me and I cannot now remember what it was.'

'It is not important,' Huathe said smoothly. *He will not mention the name of power,* Joanna thought with a private smile, *not when he has gone to such pains to make sure Josse has forgotten it.* 'To the inhabitants of this land – ourselves excluded – this is indeed the tomb of Merlin, by whom they mean the mystery figure who was the legendary King Arthur's magician, seer and sage. Merlin, so the story goes, found his way here to the forest pools and the spring of Barenton where the fair folk came to bathe, and here he met Viviane, descendant of the goddess of the hunt, whom he knew had been made to love him just as he loved her. According to his own prediction, he would be enslaved by his love for her. She showered him with questions, for she had heard tell of his power and was hungry to learn. In exchange for her promise of love he made magic, causing a castle to rise out of the very earth, surrounded by fair lawns and fruit trees where birds sang unbearably sweet songs. Their love for each other grew and, in time, he taught her all that he knew, including the knowledge of how she might keep him for ever more a prisoner of love. Some say that, such was his love for her, he went willingly to his perpetual imprisonment; whether or not that is true, for good or for ill she pent him up beneath a great granite slab over which stands guardian a hawthorn tree that, over time, has taken on the appearance of a stooped old man.'

Joanna, under the spell of Huathe's skilful, hypnotic tone, felt her eyes drawn to the spot where the hawthorn stood above the spring. Josse, similarly affected, actually walked a few hesitant steps towards it.

'Then Merlin was a real person?' he said doubtfully. Joanna felt a stab of sympathy for him; the conflict between logic and the force of Huathe's seductive tale was not an easy one.

Huathe hesitated. 'In a way, yes he was,' he said carefully. 'Legends, Josse, tend to arise out of the need of the people who create them. King Arthur represents the common identity of a threatened race who were driven to the western edges of northern Europe; he is their hero and his magician is the figure to whom they turn for aid, support, wisdom and learning. He was, after all, Arthur's teacher and, by extension, he becomes the teacher of the people, the bestower of wisdom and arcane knowledge.'

'But—' With a shrug Josse stopped, clearly at a loss.

'Most races have some tradition by which their forefathers received instruction from a godlike figure back in the infancy of the tribe,' Huathe went on. 'If you like, Josse, look upon Merlin as simply that: the personification of the mystical process by which knowledge comes.'

'So you're saying,' Josse murmured slowly, as if still puzzling it out, 'that it doesn't really matter what you call this – this person who imparts wisdom? That he – or she, I suppose – may be called by a variety of names but always serves the same function?'

'Yes!' Huathe said delightedly. 'Precisely that, and the name of this person – this *being*, perhaps, for she or he is commonly accorded godlike status – will vary according to the mythology of the people.'

'Then—' Josse's frown deepened, then cleared. 'There is a power of some sort buried in this hilltop, under that granite slab, and some people call it by the name of Merlin.' Huathe made as if to speak but, with a look of apology, Josse held up a hand. 'And therefore, as far as my own mission is concerned, I may report back that insofar as Merlin can be said to exist, then he lies buried not in the Great Wealden Forest close by Hadfeld but on top of a rounded hill in the Brocéliande.' He shot Huathe a quick glance. 'Yes?'

'Yes,' Huathe agreed.

'And because it's a power that's buried and not a person, then actually there is no physical entity *to* be buried, either in the British forest or anywhere else!' Josse finished triumphantly. 'Have I got it right?'

Huathe smiled, tentatively at first and then more broadly. 'Yes.' Laughing, he added, 'Oh, Josse, what a relief to have someone who so readily understands!'

'I don't understand,' Josse said flatly. 'But my comprehension isn't important. What is important is that I now know that they are not Merlin's bones buried in the Hadfeld tomb.' He flashed Huathe a brief smile. 'I don't believe he lies buried *anywhere* and, since right at this moment I'm not feeling any sense of awe or dread, I have to admit I'm also very dubious about the power that you say is interred here.'

Huathe watched Josse silently. Joanna, barely able to breathe, sent him a silent, urgent message: *Oh, be careful!*

For a few tense moments nothing happened.

Then Huathe stepped over to the vast granite slab. He put out a hand and lightly touched the hawthorn bush, bowing as if giving it due reverence. He seemed to be murmuring under his breath, or perhaps chanting; Joanna heard the quick hum of words that she did not understand. Then he jumped up on to the slab and, standing up tall and straight, threw out both his arms.

Now surely even Josse must have felt the power for Joanna was almost crushed by it, driven to her knees with her arms crossed over her head as she tried to shield herself from what felt like a sudden downward pressure as if the fierce, wild wind of a storm front were coming straight down from the sky. There was an intense flash as fire scoured across the treetops and she thought she heard the sound of rushing water; risking a quick terrified glance, it seemed to her that the gentle trickle of the spring had become a torrent, uncontrolled and endlessly renewing itself until all the land would be drowned. And from the ground beneath her there came a sound as of rocks breaking open, of deep cataclysmic chasms rending the very earth.

There was something else, too: a dazzling, pulsing energy throbbed in the air, steadily waxing until, brilliant as the heart of the sun, it overcame thought, emotion, even sense until finally she knew that in its presence she was nothing.

She fell forward on to the ground and buried her face in her hands.

After an endless time silence fell and she heard Huathe say gently, 'Enough.'

Slowly she straightened up. Josse was lying on his side a short distance away; she ran over to him, cradling him in her arms. He opened his eyes and stared up at her; he looked stunned. 'Josse, dearest, I—' she began.

But Huathe strode over and, with a gesture, commanded her to stop. Then, eyes on Josse, he said, '*That* was the power that is pent up in this hilltop. It comprises Air, Fire, Water and Earth. What you experienced at the end was the Quintessence, which is the fifth force and that elemental matter from which everything is made that is made and that permeates everything that is of the heavens and the earth.'

Josse was struggling to sit up. He looked, Joanna thought with vast relief, as if he had suffered no lasting hurt. He was glaring at Huathe and he did not look at all happy. 'And that's what the ignorant refer to as the power of Merlin the Enchanter?' he demanded.

'It is,' Huathe acknowledged.

Josse put both hands up to his temples, rubbing at the skin as if his head ached. Joanna would not have been at all surprised if it did; hers was pounding like a ceremonial drum beat. Then he lowered his hands and very slowly stood up. His brown eyes fixed on Huathe's, he said with a faint smile, 'Very well. I believe you now. There *is* something here.'

But Huathe did not return the smile. Instead, his expression deeply disturbed, he turned to Joanna. Leaning down so that his mouth was close to her ear, he whispered, 'The power must not be abused, for it is terrible in its wrath. Nime was right to pen it up.' Then, standing up again and addressing Josse: 'You must find a way to stop the sacrilege that is being perpetrated in your British forest.' He paused, lowering his head and screwing up his eyes for a moment as if he too were in pain. Then he continued, 'You, Josse, are the one whose task it is. It is you who must convince those who have to be convinced that this presumptuous new Merlin's Tomb is nothing but a moneymaking sham perpetrated by a foolish young man who is risking his life by dabbling with powers that he does not understand.'

Silence fell. Joanna, realising that her tension had prevented her breathing except in shallow little gasps, let her shoulders slump and then took a deep, restorative breath. Poor Josse, she thought. He suffers, and yet still he does not really know what it is that inhabits this place. But does he understand enough to fulfil his mission? Fleetingly she wondered which of her people had come up with the idea of bringing Josse here and why; had they believed Josse would have a look, be terrified out of his wits and rush home claiming not only to have seen the real Merlin's Tomb but to have felt its dangerous power? Surely not, for Josse's nature and quality were known to them – to some of them, at least – and they would therefore know he would not have reacted in that way.

Joanna had developed a great respect for her people and it slowly dawned on her that the predicted outcome of Josse's visit here was probably this very thing that had in fact just happened. He had seen – been shown – enough for him to go home with a convincing argument. Nobody had underestimated his intelligence by treating him like a gullible yokel chewing on a straw; instead the plan had been formed whereby he was initiated into a piece of knowledge that surely was normally kept within the tribe.

Which meant that someone – and Joanna suspected that it was the Domina – had considerable respect for old Josse . . .

She felt a surge of love for him, standing there a stranger and an outsider in this magical, enchanted place, yet straight-backed and courageous. If he was feeling fear at all, which, despite everything, somehow she doubted, then he was not allowing that fear to show.

Suddenly another thought struck her, one that brought with it a sadness so acute that it was like a knife in her heart. They had now done what they had gone there to do. The mission had been achieved and now they would go home. Josse would return to the Abbey, the Abbess and whatever he did in his ordinary life; she would go back to the hut in the forest. And this, this lovely, happy time of travelling with him, talking to him, eating, sleeping, making love with him, *loving* him, would recede in her memory until it was just a beautiful dream.

Josse was talking quietly to Huathe; she was glad, for it gave her a moment to let the tears fall before she wiped them away and prepared to face him.

Eventually they left the hilltop, Huathe leading with Josse and Joanna following. Josse reached for her hand; gratefully she took it. He looked at her for a long moment. Then he murmured, 'That was quite a display. Frightening things seem to happen among your people, Joanna. Things that the rest of us don't even dream of.'

She did not answer. There was not in truth anything she could say.

'But,' he added, speaking now out loud and with a dignified authority, 'say what you will, *I* don't believe Merlin the Magician is buried up there.'

They set out from Folle-Pensée after eating the midday meal. Huathe saw them off, standing by the horses while Josse and Joanna fastened their packs and the bags full of food that the people of the settlement had pressed on them. Then Josse swung up into the saddle, taking Meggie from Joanna's arms and sitting her down in front of him. Huathe was watching the two of them; he must have realised Josse is her father, Joanna thought, and if the resemblance between them hasn't struck him before, it will now.

Then Huathe came over to her, briefly touching her hand and then leaning forward to put a kiss on her forehead. 'You are strong, Beith, and your way is clearly marked out,' he said very quietly, right in her ear. 'But do not shut this good man out of your life, for in so doing you would rob your child of a fine father.'

'I cannot see clearly what will happen,' she whispered back, and to her distress there was a sob in her voice.

'No, perhaps not,' he said. Then, a serene smile on his wise old face, he added, 'But I can.' Then he gave her a blessing, watched as she mounted the golden mare and then, stepping back, waved as they headed off along the track leading out of the settlement.

Turning as they rounded a bend, Joanna saw Folle-Pensée disappear from sight.

Josse, deep in thought, rode along listening to Meggie's chatter and giving her only cursory replies; not that she seemed to mind. He was relieved to have completed the mission on which he had been sent, even if he still did not fully understand all that had happened. I'll see the Abbess, he thought, and tell her what I was shown. I'll be able to say with total honesty that I've seen a place called Merlin's Tomb, that without doubt it's a place of strange and terrifying power and that it's believed here in Brittany to be the true resting place of King Arthur's magician. Will it be enough to persuade Gervase that he must stop Florian of Southfrith's fraudulent scheme? If it's not, he realised, then it's the best I can do.

I do not believe, he told himself, that Merlin is there beneath that stone slab any more than I believe those are his bones that lie in the tomb from which Florian is making so much money. But then who am I to say?

With a shrug, he decided to stop worrying about it. Which was easy, when there was a far more pressing problem to be addressed: how was he going to be able to bear to say goodbye to Joanna and Meggie when they all reached home? This dismal prospect had been obsessing him ever since yesterday when, on leaving the fountain on the forest hilltop, it had suddenly occurred to him that, with the job done, it was time to leave.

Despite Meggie, despite being with Joanna, he had barely smiled since that moment of realisation had come.

They made good time for the rest of that day, stopping in the early evening and making camp in a circle of pine trees whose needles made a dry, comfortable bed. The next day they had an early start, which proved just as well since a summer storm blew up in the middle of the afternoon, so severe that there was no question of going any further. Joanna located a reasonably adequate shelter for them in a place where a stand of beech trees grew out of a rocky shelf. The ground around the trees' thick roots was hollowed out into a small cave and there was enough room for the three of them to crawl inside out of the rain. While Joanna rubbed Meggie's hair dry with a piece of linen and set about spreading out blankets and preparing food, Josse removed the horses' saddles and bridles, hobbling them to prevent them straying too far, and then came to join them in the little cave. Joanna cut some fronds of bracken and by arranging them across the cave mouth, managed to keep out the rain. It was so heavy that, fortuitously, it was falling straight down.

They sat huddled together watching the storm. The heavy black clouds were massing right above and the flashing lightning was coming almost simultaneously with the crashing sounds of the thunder. Putting his arm round Joanna and pulling both her and Meggie close – the child, to his relief, seemed more fascinated by than afraid of the raw force of the violent storm – Josse reflected that he didn't envy anyone unlucky enough to be caught out in the open.

Someone else shared his thought, someone who was suffering from those very conditions that made Josse so glad of the meagre shelter.

The tall man pulled his soaked garments closer around him – not that it did any good – and leaned closer into the trunk of the yew tree beneath which he had hastened to hide when the storm broke. He must be thankful for the weather that had caused his quarry to halt the day's journey early, he told himself, for he had all but lost the trail.

Those he pursued rode on horses; he was on foot. He was lean, fit and strong and he could keep up his economical, loping trot for hours on end if he had to, and indeed for most of the journey there had been no problem. The few times when they had increased their pace and left him behind, he had always managed to pick up the signs of their passing and follow them. He had hidden just short of the settlement they had visited and, when they were taken up to that strange fountain on the hilltop that exuded such a powerfully strong force, he had observed without being seen.

Or so he thought.

His orders had been to follow them, watch where they went and what they did there. He had been told what to look out for. Those whose work he did had explained how he should set about making the ultimate decision. It was good that they trusted his judgement. The thought gave him a sensation of pride that was quite novel, for normally his duties were clear-cut and simple, so that their commission was in the nature of a trained animal going through a routine task, so familiar that neither thought or discretion were required.

He had observed closely, thought about what he had seen and, after long and careful consideration, reached his decision. They must die; he had heard enough to convince himself of that. And they must both die, for if one were left alive they would shout the tale of the slaying of the other to all prepared to listen. And that must not be allowed to happen. It had been impressed upon him that this business must be concluded with the utmost secrecy, with not even the slightest footprint left that might lead anyone who came asking awkward questions back to the man who had carried out the slaying and, even more crucially, to those who had sent him.

He baulked at the idea of killing the child. There was surely no need for that; she was small and would be incapable of describing what she had seen. She he would bundle up, her eyes bound so that she could not see his face, and he would take her to some village on the edge of the forest and leave her on a doorstep.

Yes. That was the plan.

He slid his back down the trunk of the yew tree until his buttocks rested on the ground. Then, eyes intent on the hollow beneath the beech trees, he waited. Sooner or later the right opportunity would present itself and he would carry out his ultimate orders.

It was merely a matter of time.

# II

The body was brought to Hawkenlye Abbey because those who found it – three days after the murder and stinking to high heaven – did not know what else to do with it. The men whose unpleasant lot it had been to smell out the corpse were merchants; a trio of Essex men on their way back to the markets of London after a visit to northern France. They had heard of the new attraction in the forest close to Hadfeld and taken a brief detour to go and see it for themselves. People back home loved to hear tales of faraway places and the three men had congratulated themselves on their foresight in making sure that, this time, they would be returning armed with a story good enough to ensure that they would be stood drinks in the tavern on the day they reached home.

And that had been *before* they found the body.

The tomb they had found in a state of some confusion: queues of men, women and children of all ages and in all conditions stood in a line patiently waiting to be admitted through the gap in the fence, yet as the merchants' turn approached they detected unease among the stoutly built and mean-looking men who guarded the place. And when the youngest of the merchants ventured a question concerning the discovery of those impressively large bones, one of the guards had shot a nervous glance at his companion and said not to ask him, *he* wasn't the one with all the clever answers, to which the other guard had muttered something about their job being to safeguard the tomb, wait to be told what else to do and then collect their wages, and God alone knew when *that* was going to happen.

The three merchants had dutifully waited their turn and crept forward to look at the giant's bones in their stony grave, each of them feeling the same sense of shock and, as one of them put it, 'a sort of trembling on the skin'. All three of them were far from being cowards, each having had his share of the sort of dangers common to the life of a travelling man, yet to a man they were glad to walk away from the tomb and its silent, inert occupant, who somehow managed to emanate a sense of threat, of menace.

The men purchased bread, cheese and mugs of some reasonably tasty small beer. Then, as they finally set off, they decided that the weird things they had experienced might be exaggerated a little when the tale was told; with any luck, they might get their beer bought for them for more than one evening . . .

Their noses had led them to the putrefying body quite soon after leaving the tomb. They had hacked their way into the huge clump of brambles and, not without damage to their hands, wrists and clothing, managed to extract it.

One of the merchants had unfolded a blanket out of his pack, which he had nobly sacrificed (nobody, not even a man without a sense of smell, would want to use that blanket again, with all those stains from where the dead flesh was seeping foul liquids) for the purpose of wrapping up the body. They slung the noisome parcel over the man's horse – he opted for riding pillion behind one of his companions, close proximity to the corpse being best avoided as far as possible – and quickly got on the road. The three knew of Hawkenlye Abbey and, being God-fearing men, decided that it was the obvious place to deposit their unwelcome burden. One of the men half-heartedly suggested returning to the Tomb of Merlin that they had recently left – it was certainly closer – but the others were of the opinion that Hawkenlye was altogether a holier and therefore more honest and trustworthy place. The three men had each gained the impression that there was something distinctly odd about Merlin's Tomb.

The merchants reached Hawkenlye in the mid-afternoon. The man who had wrapped the body slid down from his friend's horse and, approaching the nun on duty beside the gate, asked to speak to the abbot.

'You're strangers,' the old nun said, fixing him with sharp eyes.

'Yes,' he agreed. 'We know *of* Hawkenlye Abbey, Sister, but not a lot *about* it.'

'Then,' the porteress said grandly, 'I shall excuse your ignorance and inform you that the person in charge here is the Abbess Helewise.'

The man made a graceful bow. 'My apologies.'

'No need for that,' the nun replied. Eyeing the other two merchants and the blanket-wrapped body, she sniffed and added, 'Follow me.'

Helewise, her work interrupted by Sister Ursel's knock, listened to the merchant's tale as she strode beside him back to the gate. Standing beside him, eyes on the body on the horse, she said quietly, 'You found him on the southern fringes of the forest?'

'Yes, my lady Abbess, in the middle of a bramble thicket. It was only the smell that gave him away.'

Helewise was thinking it was quite likely that other passers-by had smelt the corpse but, less Christian than these three merchants, had, in St Luke's words, passed by on the other side. Turning to the man standing beside her, she said, 'You could have left the body where it lay and avoided both the unpleasant task of bringing him here and also the delay it has afforded you.'

The merchant looked quite shocked. 'But, my lady, he might have died unprepared! We could not have left him there to rot in unhallowed ground with his sins heavy on him.'

'You have done well,' she said. 'I will summon some of the lay brethren to transport the body to the infirmary, where the poor soul will be prepared for burial. As for yourselves' – she glanced at the man's scratched hands – 'I will ask my infirmarer to arrange for your wounds to be treated. And will you take refreshment with us before you go on your way?'

The merchant glanced at his companions, then said, 'Thank you, my lady, but, as you imply, we have already lost time. With your leave, we'll have our hands bathed and then we will depart as soon as we can.'

'Of course.' Helewise caught Sister Ursel's eye and, as the nun hurried to her superior's side, quickly gave orders that Brother Saul and two or three of the others be summoned. Then, beckoning to the three merchants and leading them over to the infirmary, Helewise forced herself to gather her thoughts.

She was trying to work out what Josse would have done under the circumstances. A body had been found, on which there might or might not be means of identification. It had been concealed, which in all likelihood meant that the dead man had not met his end by natural means. Unless, of course, he had felt unwell and slipped unconscious from his horse . . . But then he would hardly have crawled into a bramble thicket to die, now would he? she reminded herself crossly. The deep scratches on the hands of the merchants who had extracted him bore witness to how dense that thicket had been and, by a natural progression, to the unlikelihood of the body having been in there for any purpose other than concealment. Which meant that the poor soul had probably been murdered and that his killer had hidden the body.

Josse, she decided, would extract every scrap of information that he could from those who found the body. Especially since, in the case of these three merchants, it was likely that they would not be available for further questioning once they had proceeded on their way.

Entering the infirmary, she briefly told Sister Euphemia what had happened, alerting her to the fact that she was just about to have a very smelly dead body to deal with. She added that the three merchants required treatment for cuts to their hands and the infirmarer summoned one of her nursing nuns, who quickly fetched hot water and oils and clean linen cloths and set about her task.

Watching the veiled head bent over the first man's bleeding wrist, Helewise said, 'Now, my friends, please relate to me the whole story and omit no detail, however small.'

It sounded very businesslike – also quite dramatic – but for all that, once the three men had told their story, interrupting each other, butting in with additional observations, Helewise was really still no wiser than she had been to begin with. It boiled down simply to the merchants having left the Tomb of Merlin – one of the men offered the opinion that the guards on duty there had seemed ill at ease – and shortly afterwards, perhaps four or five miles along the track and still very close under the eaves of the forest, smelling the stench of death. They had quickly located its source and, with barely a glance at the body, hastily wrapped it up and loaded it on to one of their horses.

'Sorry, my lady,' one of the merchants said. 'But that's all we can tell you.'

She nodded her acceptance. 'Very well. Thank you for what you have done and please rest assured that I shall summon our priest, who will do what he can for the poor dead man's soul. We shall bury him here at Hawkenlye unless someone comes forward to claim him, and we shall pray for him.'

The man's eyes filled with tears. 'He could do no better than be buried here,' he said. 'I can think of nowhere finer nor more fitting to await the Day of Judgement than here with you and your good nuns.'

Helewise bowed her head. 'Thank you. Now, if you are all ready, I will see you on your way.'

A short time later, Helewise was back in the infirmary, in a curtained-off cubicle at the far end of the long room. Hot water and lavender oil bubbled in a little pot over a candle flame, giving off a strong, cleansing scent, and Sister Caliste had prepared bunches of rosemary that now hung above the body on the narrow cot. She stood beside Sister Euphemia and Sister Caliste as the two nursing nuns first unwrapped the blanket and then set about carefully removing the corpse's garments.

The dead man was dressed in a fine velvet tunic which, before his body had begun to leach discolouring fluids into the fabric, had been scarlet red in colour, trimmed with gold braid. His undershirt was of linen and he had clearly been wearing it for several days, for it was sweat-stained and grubby around the collar and cuffs. His hose were of good quality but, like the tunic, scratched and torn by the brambles. His boots had suffered similar damage, although even the mud, the scuffed toes and the deep scratches in the high-quality leather could not disguise the fact that the boots must have cost a goodly sum. His tangled hair had been recently trimmed and looked dark in colour, although as Sister Caliste began to wash it, it was revealed to be a reddish chestnut shade. At a nod from Helewise, Sister Euphemia gently lifted the right eyelid. The dead man's eyes had been light grey.

When the corpse had been stripped, thoroughly washed and covered up to the chest with a linen sheet, the three nuns stood looking down on the dead man. The body was already bloating and the veins were prominent and slightly greenish in colour. The face had swelled a little but, despite the disfigurement, it was still perfectly obvious that he had been a very handsome man.

Helewise was staring at a large bruise on the front of the neck. Pointing, she said quietly, 'Sister Euphemia, could this be what killed him?'

The infirmarer bent closer. Then, with a soft exclamation, she beckoned to Helewise. 'Look, my lady,' she whispered. 'There, on the right side of the throat beside the main area of bruising. Can you see?'

Helewise leant over the corpse. Sister Caliste tapped her gently on the hand and offered a sprig of rosemary; she had been squeezing it to make it release its fragrant oils and now Helewise, giving the young nun a grateful smile, held it to her nose. It helped, a little.

She made herself concentrate, forcing down the nausea. I must help this poor soul, she thought, and I will not be able to do so if I am crouched outside the infirmary vomiting up my midday meal. Now, let me see if I can make out whatever it is that Sister Euphemia's sharp eyes have spotted . . .

After a moment she said, 'Yes. There are faint marks like a plait, or a braid. Of course!' Straightening up, she stared triumphantly at the infirmarer. 'A rope.'

'Aye, that's what I'm thinking,' Sister Euphemia agreed.

'Was he hanged, then? Throttled?' Helewise could not help but envisage both possibilities, harrowing though the visions were.

'I think not, my lady.' Sister Euphemia frowned. 'If either were the case, the rope marks would extend far further around the neck. No, what I reckon is that he's run at some speed into a taut rope, perhaps stretched across a path, and the force of it hitting his throat broke his neck.' Glancing down at the dead man with compassion in her face, she added quietly, 'He'd not have known much about it. Quicker than the hangman's noose, that would have been.'

'There is some comfort in that,' Helewise agreed. She was thinking hard, trying to decide what to do next. A well-dressed young man, found murdered close by the new venture of Merlin's Tomb, and— Suddenly she recalled something that one of the merchants had said. *The guards at the tomb seemed ill at ease,* were his exact words.

Why should that have been? Did they know about the dead man lying in the bramble thicket just a few miles away? Good Lord, had one of them killed him? Had he been a visitor to Merlin's Tomb who had somehow annoyed one of the guards, done something, said something, that had earned him his death warrant? But *what,* for goodness sake?

Oh, she thought, oh, how I wish that Josse were here!

But he's not, the cool part of her mind replied. You have brains, you've worked together with Josse many times to work out the solution to puzzles more complex than this one. And what do you always do when at a loss? You search out more information.

'I shall ride out to Merlin's Tomb tomorrow,' she announced. 'Sister Euphemia, can you spare Sister Caliste?'

'Aye, my lady, for we are quiet just now and I have enough pairs of hands to do all that is necessary without her.'

'Thank you. Sister Caliste, you will accompany me. We shall take Brothers Saul and Augustus. Oh.' Belatedly she realised that, with Joanna's mare absent in France, they only had three mounts, the Abbey cob, a pony and a recalcitrant old mule who went by the name of Mole.

Sister Caliste must have appreciated the difficulty. 'You and I could ride together on the cob, my lady,' she suggested. 'It is not far to the tomb, I believe, and neither of us is very heavy.'

A kind remark, but inaccurate, Helewise thought, hiding a smile; Caliste was slim and lightly built but she herself was a broad-shouldered, tall woman.

'I think, Sister, that instead we will dispense with one of the lay brothers,' she said. 'Go and find Brother Augustus, please, and tell him to prepare the cob, the pony and the mule after Tierce tomorrow morning and be ready for an early start. You can ride the pony, Augustus must do what he can with the mule, and I shall ride the cob.'

Sister Caliste bowed low in compliance. Not quite quickly enough, Helewise noted, to hide the lively excitement in her eyes engendered by the prospect of the outing.

The weather the next morning was all that an English summer day ought to be. Sister Martha had helped Brother Augustus prepare the mounts and now the three animals stood ready, Augustus holding the mule and Sister Martha the pony and the cob. Helewise stepped forward and the nun gave her a leg up on to the cob's back. 'We call him Baldwin,' she said. 'Sometimes he responds to his name, sometimes not.'

'I see,' said Helewise. The cob shifted beneath her and she patted his thick neck. He was an inelegant horse, nothing like as enjoyable a ride as the mare Honey, but then, Helewise reminded herself sternly, I am not going on a pleasure jaunt.

Caliste and Augustus were now also mounted; with a nod, Helewise kicked the cob's sides and led her little party through the gate and off on the road that led around the forest.

There was no need to ride in silence and Helewise let her two younger companions chatter away to each other, although in the main she did not join in. She was very aware that she had an important role to play today and she was trying her best to convince herself that she was up to it.

They reached the track that branched off into the forest glade where Merlin's Tomb was to be found and joined the queue of people waiting to file past it. But only until they reached the first of the barriers; here Helewise, suppressing her surprisingly intense desire to go on and catch a glimpse of those bones, addressed the heavily built man on guard duty and asked to speak to whoever was in charge.

The man looked her up and down, only belatedly according her, in an awkward and grudging bow, the respect that as a habited nun was her due. Then, with a sniff, he rubbed at his broken nose with the back of his hand and said, 'Reckon that's me. What d'you want?'

'I am not prepared to discuss the matter out here in the open where we may be overheard,' she said quietly. 'Is there somewhere more private where we might go?'

He glanced around. Then, evidently spotting whatever he was looking for, he called out, 'Jack! Oi, Jack, come over here.'

A man in a stained leather jerkin walked unhurriedly across to them. 'What?'

'Watch the gate here for me. I've got to talk to the nun here. She wants a word in private.'

The man in the jerkin gave Helewise an assessing look. Then, turning to his companion: 'All right, Hal, but don't be long about it. I'm meant to be off duty and I'm about to get myself something to eat.'

'I'll take what time I want,' the first guard said, swiftly rising anger turning his fleshy, deeply scarred face an unhealthy shade of purplish-red. 'You answer to me, Jack, and don't you go forgetting it!'

Then, puffing out his chest like a cock in the barnyard, he said grandly to Helewise, 'Follow me, if you will, Sister.'

He led the way back along the track for a short distance before taking a narrower path off to the left. There was just about room for Helewise and her companions to ride, although she felt the undergrowth scratch against the fabric of her habit and once a branch of hazel pushed quite hard into her leg.

The path opened out into a clearing where cut widths of tree trunk had been set out, presumably to serve as seats. The litter of hard crusts of bread, rinds of cheese and one or two coarse, cracked earthenware mugs lying around on the trampled grass suggested that it was the place where the guards went to take their refreshment breaks.

'Now,' the guard said, looking up at her through calculating, narrowed eyes, 'will you dismount, Sister, so that we may speak?'

Brother Augustus slipped off the mule's back and, keeping hold of the reins, said, 'Friend, this is the Abbess of Hawkenlye. You must address her as my lady Abbess.'

The guard looked quite impressed and his thin lips twisted in a gap-toothed grin. 'Sorry, my lady Abbess, didn't know who you were.'

'It's quite all right,' Helewise said.

'Right. Now, then. What can I do for you?'

'A body has been brought to the Abbey,' she said without preamble. 'It is that of a well-dressed and handsome young man and it was found in a bramble thicket some four or five miles from here. A party of merchants found it, locating its place of concealment by the smell; the victim had been dead for some days. Since the body was found quite close to Merlin's Tomb, I must ask you if anyone corresponding to this description has recently visited the tomb.'

The guard had heard her out in silence, his face unreadable. When she finished speaking he said, 'What was he wearing and what did he look like?' Helewise told him. 'Did he have a horse?'

'No mention was made of a horse.' She had been careful not to say how the man had died, just as now she made sure not to offer the suggestion that any horse the dead man might have been riding would surely have eventually made for home when its owner failed to remount and kick it on again.

The man was frowning. Then he said neutrally, 'Our master is missing. Hasn't been seen for four days now.'

'You mean Florian of Southfrith?' Helewise tried to keep the shock out of her voice. Was the body at Hawkenlye that of Florian? Unbidden she heard in her mind the Domina's voice: *There are things that could be done.* But the guard was speaking; stamping down the whirling thoughts, she made herself listen.

'The very same,' the guard said. Now he sounded like a gossip avid to impart news. 'He was busy in the afternoon and early evening four days back counting his takings. He was going to bag up the money and take it home after the last visitors had gone. Well, other than the few who stopped over. If we had any that night, that is. I could check,' he offered. He was, Helewise noted, being considerably more co-operative now that he knew who she was. Rank does indeed have its uses, she thought wryly.

'Was it generally known that he was to ride home with the money?' she asked. 'If indeed he rode?'

'He rode all right. Had a fast-paced bay gelding that must have set him back a tidy sum,' the guard said. 'And as to it being known, aye, I reckon it was. It's no secret how much he's taking here, my lady Abbess, nor, I reckon, that he usually takes the money home two or even three times a week. People have eyes to see the coins changing hands and brains to do the adding-up.'

'He was in the habit of taking the money away with him unescorted?' she asked. It seemed very foolhardy.

The guard shook his head. 'No. It was more usual for one of us guards to go with him, and he picked us special like, on account of we all know how to handle ourselves in a fight and have no qualms over bearing arms and using them if we have to. But that night, nobody could be spared. I remember now' – he nodded enthusiastically – 'we'd been busy and there were a party of seven staying over. Florian, he said we had to help out. He didn't want folk going away and saying they hadn't got their money's worth, see, so Jack and me and the others, off we went to the accommodation huts to dole out food and shake up mattresses.' His look of disdain told her what he thought about that.

'So quite a lot of people would have known that he was to take a large sum of money home with him but with no bodyguard,' she mused.

'I can guess what you're thinking, my lady, but it weren't as risky as it sounds on account of that bay of his,' the guard said. 'It went like the wind and Florian said he could outrun anyone as tried to apprehend him and rob him.'

'I see.' What, Helewise wondered, became of the horse? Had it indeed returned to Florian's home? But if so, then why had nobody raised the alarm? A riderless horse coming in late at night must surely have sent Florian's wife and her mother into a veritable panic of alarm.

Perhaps it did, Helewise thought. Perhaps they sent for help and even now a search party is out looking for Florian. A search party that for some reason has not yet got as far as Hawkenlye Abbey. Which, considering the Abbey's fame hereabouts, must be a very odd search party indeed.

Her next move was now clear. 'Thank you for your help,' she said to the guard. 'Now one last request: tell me, if you please, how I may find Florian of Southfrith's dwelling place.'

The directions were easy to follow and presently Helewise was leading her companions through the gate and into the courtyard of Florian's Hadfeld manor house. There was a row of tethering rings set in the wall and, dismounting, Helewise tied her mount's reins. Brother Augustus and Sister Caliste did the same. Then, turning slowly to look about her, Helewise took in the scene.

There was a new extension under construction and the half-built walls were keeping a team of men busy. She could hear them talking; occasionally someone would call out a request for some tool or item of building material, to which there would be a cheerful response. A happy work force, she thought, doing a skilful job in fine weather for good wages.

She crossed the courtyard to the steps leading up to the main building, sensing Augustus and Caliste falling in behind her. Mounting the steps while her companions waited at their foot, she knocked on the stout door. After quite a long wait – she was just about to knock again – the door opened.

The woman who stood on the step staring out at Helewise with hostile eyes and an arrogant tilt to her chin was dressed entirely in black. Her hair was drawn off her face and covered with a little close-fitting black silk cap, over which was pinned a long, dark, semi-translucent veil which fell forward over her forehead almost as far as her eyes. In a voice that had the harsh timbre of a cawing crow, she said in heavily accented English, 'Yes? Who are you?'

Helewise announced herself. Then, feeling her way cautiously, she said, 'I wish to speak to the wife of Florian of Southfrith, whom I understand to be master here.'

The woman made a sound that sounded as if she did not think much of this understanding. 'He's – not here,' she said.

'As I say, it is his wife to whom I wish to speak,' Helewise repeated politely.

The woman studied her, dark eyebrows drawn down. Then: 'You can't. She has taken to her bed.'

'Is she sick?'

'She is . . .' The formidable woman hesitated. 'Sick, *oui.*'

'I am sorry to hear that,' Helewise said. 'Perhaps we can help? Sister Caliste here is a nursing nun and skilled in the healing arts.'

'My daughter can see nobody,' the woman said firmly. 'She is . . .' Again, she seemed to be searching for the right words. It could be, Helewise thought, because she was unaccustomed to speaking English. Alternatively, it could be because she was weighing what she said extremely carefully so as not to give too much away . . .

I am not going to stand here on the doorstep like some pedlar trying to sell his wares, she decided. She drew in a breath and then said quietly, 'The body of a young man has been brought to Hawkenlye Abbey. I have just come from Merlin's Tomb, where I was told that Florian of Southfrith has not been seen for four days. The description that I gave to the guard there at the tomb appears to match that of your son-in-law and so I am very reluctantly forced to inform you that I believe the young man lying in our infirmary awaiting burial is indeed Florian.'

The woman's face might have been carved from marble for all the reaction the features displayed to this terrible news. After a moment, the thin mouth opened and, lapsing into her mother tongue, she said, 'It is as I feared, then. Primevère keeps saying that I am foolish to worry, that it is merely that he stays for more days out at the tomb in the forest – he is in the habit of remaining there for several days at a time, so eager is he to ensure that everything runs well – but me, I say we should send men to look for him. Now, alas, it seems I was right to be concerned.'

Helewise, trying to follow the rapid French – a language that nowadays she spoke infrequently – silently gave her brain a sharp nudge and replied in the same tongue. 'Perhaps it would be wise for someone from your household to view the body to make quite sure it is that of Florian,' she suggested. 'If your daughter is already sick, then it would be unkind to risk upsetting her for nothing if the dead man proves to be someone else.'

The woman in black considered this for some time and then gave a curt nod. 'It is sensible,' she conceded. She thought further, frowning. Then: 'I shall come myself. Wait here.' Then she closed the door.

Helewise turned and slowly descended the steps. 'That is Florian's mother-in-law,' she muttered to Augustus and Caliste. 'She is going to return to Hawkenlye with us to view the body. She seems certain it's Florian but we will wait for proof before she breaks the news to his wife.' Dropping her voice still lower, she added, 'The girl's name is Primevère.'

'Primrose,' Sister Caliste breathed. 'How pretty.' Her face fell into dismay. 'Oh, the poor girl! It's dreadful for her, isn't it, my lady? And she doesn't even know yet that he's dead!'

'Indeed not,' Helewise agreed, 'for the mother says her daughter is still making herself believe that nothing is amiss; that Florian is merely staying on for a few more days at the tomb in the forest. And already Primevère lies sick in her bed, although what ails her I do not know. Perhaps it is anxiety about her husband. That would be readily understandable, for all that she may profess not to be concerned.'

'Did you ask about the horse, my lady?' Augustus asked softly.

'No, Gus, I didn't. Do you think I should?'

'Oh!' The young man seemed surprised and embarrassed to have his opinion sought. Then, sensibly, he put the reaction aside and answered the question. 'Well, seems to me as if the horse can't have turned up, else the alarm would have been raised.'

'Quite so,' she said.

'If on the other hand the horse came home alone and nobody thought to wonder what had become of the rider,' Augustus went on, 'then that might very well be something we ought to investigate. Why, I mean, did nobody go out looking for him?'

'How would we know if the horse *did* come home?' whispered Helewise.

Augustus glanced around him. 'Stable block's over there, I reckon.' He pointed to a long building that went away at right angles from the far side of the house. 'While we're waiting, I might just go and stretch my legs before we set off for the Abbey. A fast bay gelding, didn't the guard say?'

Helewise found herself smiling. 'Yes, Gussie. I believe he did.'

She watched as, with a convincing air of nonchalance, Augustus strolled off in the direction of the stables. He stretched, gazed around him, even plucked at the rear of his habit to pull it away from where the perspiration of the ride had made it stick to his buttocks. He's very good, she thought.

Presently he disappeared around the corner of the stable block. As Helewise waited to hear what he would find out, she discovered that her hands were sweating.

# 12

Augustus came sauntering back from his little walk, still wearing the same expression of vaguely disinterested nonchalance, shortly before the door to the house reopened and the woman in black emerged. She descended the steps, looking across towards the stables with a deep frown creasing the pale skin of her forehead. Presently a groom appeared leading a bay.

Augustus, standing very close to Helewise, murmured in her ear, 'That horse is a mare. There are two more bays in the stables and both are geldings.'

'Oh.' Florian and his household, it appeared, had a fancy to possess matching horses. 'Not very informative, is it, Gussie?'

'Not at all, my lady.'

Observing his look of concentration, as if in the midst of puzzling out a problem, it occurred to Helewise to wonder why they should even harbour the faintest suspicions about the death of Florian. Strange, though, how they did . . .

The woman in black was saying something to the groom, who helped her to mount. Helewise nodded to Augustus and Sister Caliste, and the three of them crossed over to where they had tethered their horses and also mounted up. The woman in black kicked her mare and rode up close to Helewise: 'I am Melusine,' she said grandly. 'As such you may address me.'

Helewise raised an eyebrow. 'Very well.'

Then, for the sooner they reached Hawkenlye the sooner this prickly, arrogant woman could be escorted back to where

she belonged, Helewise stuck her heels into the cob's sides and
led the way at a smart canter off on the road to the Abbey.

There was scarcely any conversation on the homeward journey. They reached the Abbey and Helewise sent Sister Caliste
and Brother Augustus off to find some food, for it was a long
time since they had eaten and she realised they must be
ravenous. Augustus offered to take the four horses off to
Sister Martha in the stables and gratefully Helewise accepted.
He's a good lad, she thought; even now, when he's tired,
hungry, dusty and thirsty, he remembers to put the needs of
other creatures before his own.

Then, addressing the silent and stone-faced Melusine, she
said, 'Come with me to the infirmary and I will show you the
body found in the forest.'

Melusine walked beside her the short distance across to the
infirmary. It was cool and fragrant inside; as Sister Euphemia
had earlier pointed out, the nursing nuns were not very busy
and there was an air of peaceful tranquillity about the place.
Sister Euphemia, spotting her superior standing in the doorway, came over and gave her a bow.

'My lady Abbess, welcome back,' she murmured.

'Thank you. Sister Euphemia, this woman is called Melusine and she is the mother of Florian of Southfrith's wife. Our
enquiries at the Tomb of Merlin and at Florian's house have
led us to the tragic conclusion that our dead man here in the
infirmary may well be Florian. Melusine has come to identify
the body.'

Sympathy flooded the infirmarer's face and she put out an
instinctive comforting hand to the woman in black. Melusine,
however, drew herself apart, and Sister Euphemia's hand fell
back by her side. 'He is in the recess at the far end,' she said
neutrally. 'Follow me, please.'

Helewise and Melusine followed her steady steps the length

of the long room. The mingled smell of rosemary and lavender intensified as they approached the recess but it could not disguise the terrible stench of the putrefying body. Sister Euphemia turned and gave them an apologetic smile: 'We were about to move the poor soul to somewhere more private,' she said quietly. 'We may not have many patients in the infirmary but the few we do have should not be subjected to a constant reminder of their own mortality, especially when they are sick or wounded and correspondingly anxious.'

Nor indeed should you and your nuns, Helewise thought.

Sister Euphemia drew back the curtain, letting it fall again as soon as Helewise and Melusine were inside the recess. Then she stepped forward and folded the sheet down to reveal the dead man's face.

It was a shocking sight; Melusine gave a sharp intake of breath. Then: '*Oui. Ce n'est que trop vrai, malheureusement.* That is my son-in-law, Florian of Southfrith.'

Then she turned, strode out of the recess, along the infirmary and out through the door.

'Oh, dear,' murmured Sister Euphemia.

'Time to remove the body, Sister,' Helewise said. 'Have him taken to the crypt – it's cool there – and send someone to fetch Father Gilbert. We have an identity for our dead man and we shall pray for him. Now we must bury him as quickly as we can.'

Sister Euphemia was nodding. 'Quite so, my lady. Leave it to me.'

Helewise briefly touched her arm. 'Thank you, Euphemia.' Knowing the infirmarer would not ask, she supplied the information anyway: 'I shall offer the lady some refreshments, and then I shall escort her back to her home. The sooner she is away from here, the better.'

'Take someone with you,' the infirmarer urged. 'We now know that it's a local man that's been murdered, my lady, and for all we know it could be over some matter that affects all of us in the area. His killer may still be lurking nearby and you must take care.'

'I will,' Helewise assured her. 'I will ask two burly lay brothers to ride either side of us.'

With a nod of approval, Sister Euphemia returned to her task. As Helewise left the infirmary, already she could hear her voice summoning help for the removal of the dead body.

Melusine was all for setting out back to Hadfeld immediately but Helewise, whose stomach was growling with hunger, insisted that both of them ate and drank something before they left. Melusine did no more than pick at the fresh bread and the dish of stew with vegetables and chicken pieces but, Helewise observed, she did considerably more justice to the mug of fine red wine, accepting two refills.

Brothers Saul and Augustus were waiting for them when they emerged from the refectory; this time Augustus was riding the pony and Saul the mule. Augustus had a stout cudgel over his shoulder. He was obviously taking his bodyguard duties seriously.

'Do you mind making the journey again, Gus?' she asked him. 'Are you not tired?'

'You're making it a second time too, my lady,' he replied promptly. 'If you're not tired, neither am I.'

She gave him a grateful smile. She had a very soft spot for young Gussie.

Melusine kept up her silence for several miles. Then, when they were perhaps halfway home, she glanced over her shoulder to make sure that the two lay brothers were out of earshot and said abruptly to Helewise, 'You will hear it from someone sooner or later so it may as well be from me. I was not entirely in favour of my daughter marrying him.'

It seemed an extraordinary remark to make out of the blue and under the circumstances; Helewise could not help wondering if perhaps the three large mugs of strong wine had made Melusine uncharacteristically rash. 'Indeed?' she replied warily. 'You speak of your late son-in-law, I assume?' She laid faint but unmistakeable emphasis on *late*; it would do no harm to remind this extraordinary woman not to speak ill of the dead.

But Melusine did not notice. '*Oui*. He wasn't good enough for Primevère.' She gave her characteristic lift of the chin. 'My late husband was Theobald of Canterbury; I am from Angers and I am an heiress in my own right. Oh, the Southfriths are a good family, I do not say otherwise – four generations back, Florian's ancestor was a close friend of Richard Fitzgilbert de Clare, and *he* was King William's man. The Southfriths have thrown up some decent people down through the years and indeed Florian's two elder sisters are good women. The eldest one, Edith, entered a convent in north Kent where I am told she does well. The younger one, Matilda, is wed to Hugh de Maubergeonne and she lives in Poitiers.'

Wondering what might be the purpose of this sudden torrent of information, Helewise said, 'I see.'

But Melusine gave no sign that she had heard. 'Florian was spoilt by his mother and both his sisters,' she stated flatly. 'He was ever a silly, pretty boy and they doted on him for his good looks and his courteous manners, bringing him up to believe that he could have anything he wanted and that even the best wasn't good enough for the likes of him.' She turned dark and angry eyes on Helewise. 'He lied to me, my lady Abbess. He led me to believe that he was far richer than he really was, that he owned property of which he is in fact only a tenant, that he had connections at court and among the country's prominent families.' The scowl intensifying, she went on, 'He faced strong competition for my daughter's hand, for it is well known that I am a wealthy woman and Primevère is my only child. Not only that but my daughter is extremely beautiful – many a man fell in love with her and longed to claim her as his bride. But like many a woman before her, she was taken in by a handsome face and it was Florian that she would have.'

'If they were happy together,' Helewise put in, the monologue briefly stopping as Melusine paused for breath, 'then was it so bad for Florian to have exaggerated his means? For him to have—'

'But they were not happy,' Melusine hissed vindictively. Briefly she met Helewise's eyes, as if to gauge her reaction to the harsh words. 'I believe in facing facts, my lady,' she said. 'I am a realist and I do not fool myself. Oh, to begin with there was the usual ecstatic period when they couldn't keep their hands off each other, but that soon came to an end as Primevère realised just what sort of a man she had chosen. He was deeply in debt, having borrowed vast sums in order to maintain his pretence of being a rich man.' She snorted. 'And there was the ransom – fool that he is, Florian went to the collectors and put the money right into their very hands!'

'He had no choice,' Helewise protested. 'Everyone had to pay up.'

'But to go and *offer* it like that!' She made a sound that sounded like *pouff!*, clearly expressive of her disgust. There was a brief pause. 'Then, of course, he found the bones out in the forest.' There was, Helewise noticed, a slight exaggeration on *found*. She stored that interesting little fact away for future reference. 'And we all know what happened next. Florian comes home with bags and bags of coins and suddenly Primevère can have anything her heart desires in exchange for a mere snap of her fingers.'

'So they did recover their original happiness before he died,' Helewise said softly, almost to herself. 'That is something for which to be very grateful, for Florian's sake in particular.'

'Eh? Happy, you say?' Melusine frowned. 'You'd have thought so, yes, for Primevère loves pretty garments and new shoes and she was overjoyed that they started on the new building work so quickly. This little bay mare he bought for her and that I'm riding today is a lovely animal, too.' She broke off, the look of puzzlement intensifying. 'Yet it was not enough, for I who know my daughter well judged that still she was contemptuous of Florian, that the initial flame of her love and desire for him was not rekindled. Why, I am all but certain that he no longer shared her bed. And that, my lady, is the strangest thing of all, for I believe that—'

She stopped. Just like that, in mid-sentence, she bit back whatever she had been about to say. With a cunning and slightly cruel smile, she said, 'Enough. Your cellarer keeps a fine wine, my lady Abbess, and the hot sun on my head adds its contribution, so that I am not entirely myself and I speak when I should stay silent.' She kicked a sharp heel into her mount's side, making the animal start. Kicking again, she urged the horse into a trot, then a canter.

She is all of a sudden eager to be home, Helewise thought. Very well. We will hasten on to Hadfeld, where I will do my utmost to ensure that I see this enigmatic daughter with my own eyes. This Primevère, who is sick enough to have taken to her bed, undoubtedly – for all that she denies it – out of anxiety over her husband's absence, yet who, according to her mother, has no love for him despite his sudden generosity.

It was both an exciting and a slightly alarming prospect.

They reached Florian's Hadfeld house in mid-afternoon. Leaving her horse with Brothers Saul and Augustus, who sensibly found a patch of shade on the side of the road beneath an oak tree under which to wait, Helewise made sure that she was right beside Melusine as the latter went up the steps and into the hall; short of banging the door in Helewise's face, Melusine had no option but to admit her.

'I will come with you as you break the news to your daughter,' Helewise said smoothly, sticking to Melusine's side like an armed escort. 'She will be distressed and I may be able to offer comfort.'

Melusine eyed her shrewdly and Helewise had the distinct feeling that she knew exactly what Helewise was up to. But she nodded her agreement. She led the way across the hall and up a couple of steps on the far side, through a deep arched doorway and along a short passage that appeared to lead into an upper chamber. As they approached, Helewise thought she heard the low murmur of voices.

Melusine could not have helped but hear too. She called out something in French, the words rushing out too fast for Helewise to catch; she was, however, almost sure that they were a warning. A warning to Primevère that her mother was not alone but was bringing with her the Abbess of Hawken-lye? That Primevère should therefore prepare a very good excuse for entertaining company when she was supposed to be sick?

Helewise followed Melusine into the room. They entered via a gracefully curved stone arch and, a little way along the same wall, there was another arch, this one covered by a heavy hanging, which possibly led down to the kitchen quarters. Casting quick eyes around, she took in clean rushes thickly strewn on the stone floor and costly wall hangings that gave off the distinct smell of new wool. Tall beeswax candles stood on a chest set back against the wall at the room's far end. In the middle of the room stood a high bed covered with costly bedclothes and on the bed, propped up on a mountain of snowy-white pillows, lay a young woman.

Other than for her, the room was empty.

Melusine was glaring at her daughter. '*Que fais-tu?*' she

demanded. Then, switching to the common tongue: 'Here is the Abbess Helewise of Hawkenlye, come to visit you.'

Helewise studied the woman on the bed. She was slim and slight, although the swelling breasts that strained against the violet silk of her gown were generous. Her face was pale – very pale; perhaps she was really sick with some wasting disease – and her eyes, slightly slanting, were darkest blue. Her hair was long, loose and black and, belying the pallor, shone with health.

She said, her voice totally composed, '*Ma mère*, our neighbours sent the old family servant with a little gift for me.' With a casual nod she indicated a posy of sweet-scented pinks and violets that lay on a small table next to the bed, beside them a glass bottle of some pinkish substance. 'Rose syrup,' said Primevère languidly. Then, eyes on Helewise: 'Ranulf of Crowbergh and his household are both our neighbours and our friends. Do you know them, my lady Abbess?'

'No,' Helewise replied.

'They are worthy people. Sir Ranulf, who is the head of the family, had heard that Florian has not returned from the tomb in the forest for several days and, concerned in case I was anxious, sent word to offer his help.'

Melusine hissed a sharp remark in French – translating, Helewise realised she was demanding why Primevère had not had the sense to get up and receive this servant in the hall, as a lady should – had she no shame? – to which Primevère gave a wan smile and replied, also in French, that she was still feeling too sick to risk rising from her bed. Especially, she added with a yawn, for a servant.

Helewise drew Melusine aside so that she could speak privately to her. 'We must tell her,' she murmured.

Melusine nodded.

Primevère watched them, her eyes going first to her mother, then Helewise. 'What's the matter?' she demanded. When neither woman answered, slowly her face took on an expression of dread. Then, her lips trembling, her eyes flew back to her mother's face and she said in a tiny voice, 'Oh, it's not true, tell me it's not true!'

Melusine stepped forward and, perching on the bed, took her daughter's hands in hers. She muttered something in French: *It's true, yes, he is dead, and his body was taken to Hawkenlye Abbey, where I have just returned from seeing it.*

She added something more – perhaps a word of comfort – but whatever it was, Helewise could not hear over the torrent of hysterical sobbing that rose in a crescendo of dreadful sound from the stricken Primevère. Melusine patted her daughter's hands, offered a handkerchief, a drink of water, but Primevère, eyes squeezed shut and leaking a flood of tears, batted her blindly away. She tried to speak, eventually getting the words out: 'Dead! Florian is dead! Oh, and here I lay, wasting time in polite pleasantries with my neighbour's fussy old serving woman, all the time not knowing that my beloved husband was lost to me!'

Helewise, affected by the girl's outpouring of grief, moved over to the bed and crouched down beside Primevère. 'My dear, you were not to know that anything was amiss,' she said. 'Your mother told me that you had convinced yourself all was well and that Florian's absence was merely because he was too busy at the tomb to come home.'

'Yes, yes, that's what I thought!' sobbed Primevère. 'But I was wrong, wasn't I?' She had opened her eyes and was staring fixedly at Helewise. 'All the time he lay dead and I did not know!' Then, wiping her cheeks with the back of her hand, she asked plaintively, 'When did he die, my lady?' She took a sobbing breath. 'And *how*? Did he have an accident? A fall?'

Anxious to help in any way, even if it meant answering painful questions such as this one, Helewise quickly said, 'We think it happened about four days ago. I spoke to a guard at the tomb, who told me that Florian was heading for home late in the day bearing bags of coins. He did not do as he usually did and detail one of them to ride with him because all the guards had their hands full looking after the overnight guests. But, as the guard pointed out, Florian rode a fast horse and he must have been confident that he could escape from any attempt to waylay him and rob him.'

'Is that what happened?' Primevère whispered.

Helewise glanced at Melusine. Was it, she wondered, the right moment to tell this poor, grieving young woman the brutal details of her husband's death? Would it not be better to reveal the nature of his murder in a day or two, when she was over the first terrible shock?

But Primevère caught the look and, before Melusine could respond, she fixed Helewise with a stare and said in a surprisingly authoritative voice, 'You must answer my question, my lady. I have a right to know how my husband met his death.'

'Indeed you do,' Helewise said soothingly, 'and I thought only to spare you further pain at this dreadful time.'

'I wish,' said Primevère, the tears falling freely, 'to be told.'

'Somebody was lying in wait for him,' Helewise said, agonising for her. 'It appears that his habits were well known and presumably some opportunist had discovered that, on that particular night, Florian was to ride without a bodyguard.' It suddenly occurred to her in a flash of illumination that perhaps one of the guards had been paid for that very information – perhaps, contrary to what she had been told, it had been the guards themselves who had stated that they were too busy with the overnight guests for any of them to accompany their master home . . .

But that was not a thought to share with anybody just yet, particularly poor Florian's shocked and weeping widow.

Who was now staring at her with wide eyes in a deathly pale face, waiting for her to go on. 'They attacked him and stole the money?' she whispered.

'They did,' Helewise confirmed.

'Could they not have just robbed him?' Primevère murmured pathetically. 'When they had got what they wanted, could they not have just left him there? Oh, but to *kill* him!' She dropped her face in her hands, her shoulders heaving with the extremity of her pain.

'I am so very sorry,' Helewise said softly. 'I shall pray for you, my dear, and for Florian.'

'Florian,' Primevère said, slowly raising her head. Then she wailed, 'Oh, *oh*, what am I to do? What is to become of me?'

'You have your home and your husband's wealth,' Helewise said, wanting nothing more than to make the poor young woman realise that things could be worse. 'Believe me, my dear, I see many women who, on the death of a husband, lose everything else as well and must henceforth depend on charity for their daily bread. It is no comfort now, I know that, but in time it will be and you will be reassured by having the blanket of your husband's fortune to shelter you from the cold.'

'She speaks true,' Melusine added. Her voice taking on an unexpected and not entirely convincing sugary tone, she added, 'Listen to her, Primevère, and tell yourself that poor Florian would be deeply distressed to see you thus, he who so loved to look into your lovely eyes and admire your pale beauty.'

Primevère dropped her face in her hands again and sobbed even harder. Catching Helewise's eye, Melusine said quietly and with cool dignity, 'Thank you, my lady, for all that you have done. I will look after my daughter now.'

She bent her veiled head over her daughter's wild hair. Helewise got to her feet and, with one last glance, left the room and tiptoed away.

It was a great relief to rejoin the two monks and get away from Hadfeld. The brothers knew better than to question her but she told them briefly what had happened. Saul, his own eyes moist with sympathetic tears, said it was dreadful, quite dreadful, and he didn't know what the world was coming to. Augustus said nothing. When, a little later, Helewise caught his eye, he said, 'Saw someone ride away after you went into the house, my lady, although we only got a quick glimpse.'

'Yes. I was informed that there was a visitor. It was the serving woman of a neighbour of theirs called Ranulf of Crowbergh.'

'A *serving* woman?'

'Yes.'

'Hm. She rode a fine horse for such a person. It was a bay gelding. Seems such horses are two a penny hereabouts.'

Helewise thought about that. Then, for in her experience bay geldings were two a penny almost everywhere, she put it from her mind and, urging the cob on, set a pace sufficiently fast to ensure that they would arrive back at Hawkenlye well before the long summer daylight began to fade.

# 13

In the Brocéliande forest, Josse and Joanna made their way steadily northwards. It was the morning after the storm; the weather was once more fine and hot and the rain had given everything a shine as if newly painted.

That morning they had set out before the sun had climbed far into the sky. The rain having driven them to seek shelter so early the previous day, they had turned the setback into an advantage and all had had a long night's sleep; Meggie had wakened them soon after sunrise saying there was something moving around in the forest below the shelter and oh, *please* could she have something to eat because she was starving?

While the child had been preoccupied with eating, in between mouthfuls sipped from the hot herbal infusion that Joanna had prepared, Josse, speaking very quietly into Joanna's ear, asked if the mysterious something moving was likely to be real or a product of Meggie's half-awake, half-dreaming mind.

Joanna had shot him a keen glance. 'I'd say she imagined it, mainly because she doesn't seem at all frightened. Only . . .' She hesitated.

'Only what?'

Joanna's eyes on his were wide and wondering. 'Only I thought I heard something too.'

'What sort of something?' he demanded, the rush of adrenalin making him speak more sharply than he intended. 'And why,' he added softly, 'did you not wake me up and tell me?'

Her face melted into a smile. 'So you're determined to be our bodyguard, bless you,' she murmured. 'Josse, it's all right. I'm quite used to taking care of Meggie and myself all on my own, you know. And the reason I didn't disturb your exceptionally deep sleep to tell you I'd heard noises was that I wasn't sure if I was dreaming. And when, wide awake, I listened again, there was nothing.'

He pondered that. 'Do you often wake in the night when sleeping in the open?'

'Hardly ever. We – my people usually feel safe when out in the wilds and the depths of the forest. Safer than when we have to be close to civilisation,' she added wryly.

'Is it because you all seem so—?' No, he thought. Now was not the moment to question her about the dangers that the outside world might or might not present for her, even given that such dangers really did exist. And, he added honestly, given also that I really want to know about them when, all the time she is apart from me, I do not see what I can do to protect her.

No. There was a more pressing matter.

'D'you think, then, that these nocturnal noises – if they were real and you and Meggie didn't dream them – were made by something that your sleeping mind perceived to be a threat? Not, for example, by a natural source such as some animal that is active in the dark hours making its way back to its burrow?'

'A threat?' She shrugged. Then, considering what he was suggesting, said thoughtfully, 'If there really was a noise, then yes, I'd agree with you and say that, for all that I did not truly feel afraid, it was made by something or someone that does not belong in the forest at night.'

Her words went through his head over and over again as they rode under the increasingly hot sun of the July day. They were still deep in the forest – Joanna estimated that they should reach its northern fringes that evening – and the trees provided welcome shade. They also provided a thousand places where someone following the little party with evil intent could hide himself. Josse kept his hand close to his sword hilt. As ever, the dual presence of a sharp dagger in its scabbard on his belt and a sword by his side was enormously reassuring. Whoever he is, just let him try, he thought grimly. I'll be ready.

They stopped for the night in a shallow dell just beneath the summit of the rounded hump of a low hill. Birch trees grew; there was a trio of them set almost exactly so as to give a roughly circular space in their midst. Joanna, recognising a place where the spirit forces waxed strong, knew that by pitching their camp in the birch-circled dell she would be able to call on unseen helpers for aid should it become necessary.

All day she had felt eyes upon her. Perhaps on Meggie or Josse; she could not really say. But she had been puzzled by her own reaction, for sometimes she felt that the eyes were kindly and benevolent, sometimes that they held at best hostility, at worst . . . She had not let herself dwell on that.

The trouble was that she had now guessed who might be behind this stalking presence in the woods. The more she thought about it, the more likely it seemed. But having solved the mystery brought no relief whatsoever: quite the contrary, for the man she had in mind was vicious, ruthless, had no respect for the law and was out for her blood.

All the time they had been on the outward journey and at Folle-Pensée, her delight in being out in the wildwood with Josse had been overwhelming, so that practically everything else had been drowned out. But now that they were once more close to the outside world, she had remembered that disturbing scene in the inn at Dinan.

*It's too many years that my poor brother has gone unavenged,* he had said, *but at last the day of reckoning has come.*

And was he – no, not him; more likely some hired killer – now out there in the undergrowth, biding his time and waiting for the perfect moment to strike? She had been terrified on that awful night in the inn that he meant to have her arrested and thrown into jail so that they could accuse her of murdering her husband and hang her. But in truth, all that she recalled of Césaire told her that it was not really his way to act according to civilisation's rules. It was surely far more likely that he would just have her quietly killed. After all, what honest man would simply accept Césaire's word that she had had a hand in Thorald's death? It just did not seem possible that she could be arrested, tried, convicted and executed on such slim evidence. Nothing could be proved against her and, with Thorald rotted in his grave these many years, *he* wasn't going to speak out against her and back up Césaire's accusations by confirming that yes, his wife had loathed him and had in all likelihood been behind his death.

No. If Césaire wanted her dead, then this was the only sure way.

She frowned, for still her reasoning did not satisfy her. If indeed whoever was out in the forest following them, spying on them, was indeed Césaire's hired killer, then why did she not feel afraid *all the time*? Why did her moments of alarm always seem to be tempered with another thought? A thought, moreover, that did not arise from her own mind but one that seemed to say, loud and clear like someone speaking quietly in her ear, *Do not worry, you will be safe.*

Perhaps it's the spirits of this forest, she thought. Perhaps they read in the very fabric of time and place what will happen. They see the threat and the danger, yet they also see that Josse and I together will defend ourselves and our daughter and emerge unharmed. They know I can and will fight if I need to and they are aware of Josse's strength and courage, of his great protective love for me and for Meggie.

She was still not totally happy with the explanation. But she had a feeling it was the best she was going to come up with.

In the dell between the birch trees, Josse built a small fire and Joanna prepared food. Aware that they would be back in inhabited regions tomorrow and able to purchase supplies, she was lavish with the portions and shared out the last of the victuals given to them by the people at Folle-Pensée. It was a feast and soon Meggie was drowsy and yawning, lying relaxed in her father's lap, one thumb in her mouth and the fingers of her other hand delicately pulling at and twiddling the hairs on Josse's forearm.

She adores him, Joanna thought. And as for his feelings for her, well, I have rarely seen a man so love a child. Mind you, she reminded herself, I have few examples of fatherly love by which to judge. But then she did not really feel she needed such comparisons; Josse, she knew full well, would be equal to the very best of them.

She got up, moving quietly so as not to disturb Meggie, and set about packing up the remains of their supper. She made sure that, apart from the blankets that they would use overnight, everything was neatly stored away ready for the morning.

At the back of her mind – and steadily making its way to the front – was the unwelcome thought that whatever noise she had heard the previous night was quite likely to come again; perhaps from closer at hand this time. And if she was right, and the source of the noise really was what she believed it to be, then it would be as well if they were able to take to their heels just as fast as Josse could remove the horses' hobbles and saddle up.

She returned to the little camp among the sheltering birches.

Looking up at the trees, she selected the largest of the trio and went to stand close beside the beautiful trunk. Guard us, Lady of the Woods, she said silently, you whose powerful spirit is present in these graceful, silvery trees. Stay with us, please, and let no harm come to Josse, to Meggie or to me. Then she took the sharp knife from its sheath on her belt, nicked the flesh on the inside of her elbow and allowed seven drops of her blood to fall to the ground at the roots of the tree. She stood for a few moments, head bowed, her concentration profound. Then, feeling the warm flow of reassurance, she went back to Josse and Meggie.

The child was asleep already, rolled up in her soft blanket and snoring gently. Josse looked up with a smile. 'You missed story time,' he remarked.

'What tale did you tell her this evening?'

'One about a little girl riding through the woods on an enormous horse that was very special because, if he had to get away from his enemies, he could grow wings and fly high up above the treetops.'

'Did she like it?'

'Aye, she did. She wanted to know if Horace could grow wings.'

Joanna felt a chill run down her back. Trying to sound casual and unconcerned, she said, 'Does she think he's going to need them?'

Josse met her eyes. 'No, Joanna. She feels no threat at the moment, I'm certain of that. In fact—' He stopped.

'What?'

Josse was looking perplexed. 'Well, I probably should have mentioned this earlier, but when she was riding with me this afternoon, she said there was someone following us but that we couldn't see him because he was magic and therefore invisible.'

Joanna was horrified. 'Do you think there really was some-one there? Oh, and Meggie *saw* him?'

Josse put out his arms and she sank against him. As ever, the sheer bulk of his broad chest and the steady thump of his heart did much to reassure her. 'No, she saw nothing,' he murmured into her hair, kissing her to punctuate the words. 'She said, as I just told you, that he was invisible.'

'Then how could she have known he was there?' she whispered.

Josse shrugged. 'It was just a game, Joanna. Didn't you have imaginary friends when you were little?'

'Yes, but it's different for Meggie.'

'How is it different?'

She baulked at the enormous task of explaining how Meggie's extraordinary heritage made her a child who had a power to see, hear and sense things that were undetectable to others. But then she is his child too, she reminded herself. Doesn't he have the right to know? 'Because,' she said slowly, 'Meggie's imaginary friends are in all likelihood inhabitants of the spirit realm. Oh, Josse, don't look like that' – his expression was aghast – 'they wouldn't harm her for all the world! They wish only to protect her – she's very special, you know.'

He relaxed again, but she sensed that he was only partly reassured. 'So you keep telling me,' he grunted. Then, his tone still gruff, he added: 'We have another long day's riding tomorrow. We should sleep.'

She settled down beside him. He had turned his back and she read his mood: he was emanating distress and she was sure it was because she had just been speaking of that other world that was her and Meggie's true home. The world of the forest people, with all its magic, mystery and secrecy.

The world to which she and her daughter would soon be returning. The world where, no matter how much he loved Joanna and Meggie and they him, Josse could not follow.

No wonder he had turned away from her.

Struggling to control the grief that rose up in her, Joanna tried to relax into sleep.

Out in the dense forest at the foot of the low hill, the tall man waited. He had kept his distance today for he had sensed that the child felt his presence. It was strange, because she displayed no fear, but all the same he had seen her brown eyes with the dancing golden lights turning his way more than once and he knew he must not risk following the little party too closely.

He had the strong sense that they were now near to the forest fringes. Tomorrow, perhaps quite early in the day, they would emerge into the world of well-used tracks, small hamlets, villages and, eventually, towns. It would then be much easier, if he made some mistake, for a man on the run to melt into the crowd.

He had no real fear that he would make a mistake, for he knew what he must do and the task held no terror for him. He must take life, yes, but then he served a stern and uncompromising master and he had been given his orders. It was not for him to question what he was instructed to do. The deaths, he had been firmly instructed, would be marked down on his master's account and not his own.

He would strike tonight. Then, if anything did go wrong – again he reminded himself that he did not believe it would – he could readily and swiftly escape into the world beyond the forest. Yes. It was good to have an emergency plan, even if he was not going to need it.

Time passed. Dawn was not far off but for now it was fully dark and he had known there would be but a sliver of moon tonight; he had been watching the steady waning for these past few nights. Scarcely a moon and no light save the bright starlight; conditions were perfect.

He drew his long knife. Its blade was honed to razor sharpness; it was not his intention to cause his victims unnecessary suffering and when he struck it would be with a sure, strong hand. They would die quickly; perhaps even before they woke.

For a killer, he was a merciful man.

Stealthily he crept out from under the hazel bush where he had hidden himself. One step, two, three, his feet falling so softly on the springy forest floor that even the most acute ears would not have heard a sound. Onward and upward, beginning now to climb the base of the hill where his prey had made their camp.

A sound from his left. He froze, as still as the tree trunks on either side of him. He listened, ears straining.

Nothing.

He crept on. The slope was steeper now and he went more slowly. Fit as he was, even he might pant for breath if he attacked the hill too fast. In any case, the snail's pace was better because he was less likely to put a foot where it ought not to go. Such as on to a twig, which might snap under his weight. A small sound in the daytime, when the forest was alive with noise, but now, in the silence of the night, it would be like a man shouting in an empty church.

On, on, up the slope. He could see them now. The man and the woman lay close, her head resting on his shoulder. It was a position that spoke eloquently of trust and tenderness but the tall man was unmoved. He had trained himself long ago to remain aloof from human emotions. The child lay curled up beside her mother, tightly wrapped in a blanket. That was good, he thought dispassionately, for it would be a simple matter to tie her up in the bedding, cover her face and take her with him when he fled the scene.

He moved closer. Earlier they had made a fire – he had seen its flames – and now he could feel the heat from its still-glowing embers. By its light he saw that they lay on the far side of the makeshift hearth.

He studied them. The man had settled half on his back, face up to the stars, neck exposed. The woman was on her right side. The tall man stood lost in careful thought; soon his mind was made up. He would step around the fire and strike swiftly, first at the throat of the man, then through the ribs on the woman's left side and straight into her heart. It would be just as he had hoped: they would not even wake up.

Then he would swiftly pick up the child and set off out of the forest, running as fast as he could until, coming to the first hamlet or outlying cottage, he would check for the signs that the place was inhabited and then leave his small burden on the doorstep.

Then he would go home.

He drew his knife. The metal made a tiny, harsh little hiss as it emerged from its scabbard. He pulled it clear and weighed it in his hand, letting it settle until it felt like an extension of himself.

Then he struck.

In the same instant Joanna shot up screaming like a vixen and Josse, already on his knees and rapidly pushing himself on to his feet, grasped his sword and his dagger from where he had hidden them beneath the blankets.

Even as Josse's fighter's brain coolly sent instructions to his limbs, he found the time for a swift prayer: *Thank God for Joanna's acute sensitivity, so that she knew danger was approaching and gave us the time to be prepared.* Without that forewarning, he would now be lying there with his throat cut.

He was trying to get an idea of their assailant, peering, eyes straining, in the dim light of the fire's last embers. A man, tall, strong, lean and smelling of the outdoors. Knife in his right hand; left hand empty. Dark, deep eyes, no expression.

And so very dangerous; in those first few seconds, Josse realised he was facing an opponent who was at least his equal.

He tried to thrust with his sword; his great advantage was that his main weapon was longer by far than his enemy's knife. But the tall man had realised this too and he leapt nimbly out of Josse's reach, coming down from his jump and in the same movement switching his knife to the other hand and bringing it down on Josse's sword arm. Josse felt the sudden sharp pain as the blade dug into his flesh, then adrenalin took over and, howling, he straightened his left arm like a spear and aimed the knife at the man's throat.

The man jerked to one side and Josse's blade caught his shoulder; the difficulty that he had in withdrawing it told him that the wound was deep. Joanna, seeing that their attacker was hurt, leapt on his back and tried to cut into his neck with her own knife, slicing off half of his right ear; with a cry of pain he flung her off. She fell heavily, her head thumping loudly against the ground, and lay still.

There was no time to go to her. Instead Josse lunged again at the tall man, who took his hand away from his ear – pouring blood – and struck out at Josse; neither Josse's nor Joanna's onslaught had managed to dislodge the deadly knife from his hand. Josse kicked out with his right foot, feeling his boot make contact with something soft in the man's crotch. Again, the assailant cried out in pain, abruptly crouching over and in on himself, cradling his genitals in his free hand.

Josse bent to retrieve his sword, taking it in his left hand. A right-hander, still he was efficient with his left; strong enough, he prayed, to deal with a man wounded in shoulder and crotch and bleeding profusely from his ear. He launched himself on the tall man but at the last moment the man ducked down under the swinging sword and, half-crouching, ran off down the hill.

Josse hesitated. What should he do? Pursue the attacker or follow his heart and his every instinct and go to Joanna?

But if she is still alive, he reasoned – she is, she *is*! cried his heart – then my duty is to slay our assailant, for if he is allowed to get away he may strike again. Making himself turn his back on both Joanna and Meggie, who was now awake and rubbing her sleepy eyes, little face creased with fear and sobbing her distress, Josse plunged away down into the forest.

He thought he could hear the tall man ahead of him. He could hear *something* . . .

He made himself stop.

But what he could hear was not the right sort of noise. It just did not sound like a badly wounded man fleeing for his life.

It sounded . . . Josse's eyes widened in alarm. It sounded like a very large animal quietly moving through the under-growth.

Had whatever creature it was been attracted by the smell of blood? It was quite possible, for the deep wound that Joanna had inflicted must be pumping it out. What creature could it be? A carnivore, surely, for otherwise it would not follow the trail that promised fresh meat.

A very large carnivore.

A wolf? Bigger than that. A bear? *Were* there bears here? He knew the creatures were to be found down in the Pyrenees, that desolate mountain wilderness far to the south. But here in Brittany? Josse did not know.

He moved on along the faintly marked track, trying to calm his alarmed heartbeat, seeking to keep himself concealed as best he could. The animal, if there is an animal, will go for the easier prey, he told himself. I am quite safe.

He did his best to believe it.

He crept forward.

He clutched his sword in his left hand, the lighter dagger in his right; that arm, now that the white-hot heat of the fight had passed, was beginning to hurt so badly that it was all he could do not to moan with the pain. You keep quiet, he ordered himself.

Movement ahead, sudden, unexpected: a dark shape coming in fast from the right, in the darkness nothing more than an impression of great speed and huge bulk.

Dear God, Josse prayed, what in heaven's name *is* that?

He stood quite still, eyes hurting as he strained to see. In the faint starlight he could make out little but an impression of a darker shadow against the gloom; a black shape with the terrible power to strike paralysing fear into all who saw it.

Then why, Josse thought wonderingly, am I not afraid?

The whirlwind of emotions and the pain of his wound were making him dizzy. It was with quickly fading vision that he saw the final act.

In his confusion he must have been unaware that he had gone on moving steadily onwards. But suddenly the tall man was only a few paces ahead, standing quite still with his back to Josse and his eyes on something that slowly rose up on the faint and twisting track before him.

Something made of the darkness that grew and grew, upwards and outwards like a great cloud of black smoke that expands as it rises.

Josse stepped back, but his fascinated, horrified eyes were incapable of looking away.

The tall man had both hands up to shield his face; he stood as if nailed to the spot, perhaps transfixed by some power emanating from the *thing* that rose up high over his head. Then there was a glimmer as the light from the heavens briefly shone on something that flashed down through the air and struck at the tall man, once, twice, a third time.

There was a heart-stopping shriek that quickly degenerated into a gurgling sob.

Then there was nothing.

The tall man slumped to the ground and lay crumpled like a

pile of rags. Tearing his eyes away, Josse looked fearfully up at the black shape.

It had gone.

Somehow, in the brief moment that Josse had looked down at the tall man lying on the deep leaf litter of the forest floor, the thing had slipped away.

It must have . . . Josse tried to think. But something, some strange force that hummed in the air all around him, arrested the thought so that he couldn't remember what had been in his mind.

Another thought smoothly slid into its place.

*Joanna!*

With a cry, Josse spun round and, making himself ignore his pain, raced back the way he had come, along the narrow animal track and up the hill. Then, gasping, blood pouring down his arm and dripping off his hand, he burst into the dell beneath the birch grove.

# 14

In the small room at the end of the cloister at Hawkenlye Abbey, Helewise's mind was distracted from her duties by one persistent and overriding thought: who killed Florian of Southfrith?

Sorely missing Josse's stimulating presence, she tried to think how the two of them would approach this question were they together and working side by side on the problem, as they had so often done in similar cases in the past. After some thought, she decided that the first thing to attack was why he had been killed. Drawing an old scrap of vellum towards her across her table and picking up her stylus, she dipped it in the ink horn and wrote *Why was Florian killed?*

Florian had discovered bones that he claimed were Merlin's. The tomb, which might or might not be genuine, had already made Florian a very rich man and therefore the first reason for his death must surely be robbery. She wrote down the word, putting in brackets *horse* and *bags of money*. Both horse and money were, according to Florian's mother-in-law Melusine, missing. It was perfectly reasonable to assume that both were now in the possession of whoever had slain Florian.

What other possibilities were there? Helewise gnawed at the end of her stylus. If robbery were not the motive, who else might want to see the back of Florian?

A thought occurred to her. She was reluctant to accept it but then, in the absence of both Josse and Gervase, it was for the moment up to her to work on this problem on her own. Filling her stylus with ink, she wrote *The Forest Folk*, underlining it and then adding *They are disturbed by the Tomb of Merlin.*

If the Domina's people resented the presence of a commercial and probably fraudulent enterprise so close to the forest lands which they held sacred, Helewise thought, then might not one of their number take matters into his or her own hands and quietly dispatch the man behind it? The forest people had been known to kill when something or someone treated their holy places with contempt, as Helewise well knew, for she had once discovered a body with a flint-tipped spear in its back. The dead man had disturbed something that he should have left alone and seen something that he was not supposed to see; the forest people had not allowed him to live to tell the tale.

But the Domina had, after consultation with Helewise, agreed on a very different and far less violent method of stopping Florian's activities. In the midst of her preoccupation, Helewise paused to send some thoughts Josse's way, wondering how he was getting on over there in Brittany and praying – without very much hope, she admitted to herself – that he would not even now be storing up great sorrow for himself when the time came, as it inevitably would, for him and Joanna to part.

Making herself return to her notes, she thought, but this killing might have been done without either the Domina's knowledge or consent. There must surely be other powerful figures among the forest people; might not one of them have decided that this business of going across to Brittany to view and verify the true Merlin's Tomb was taking altogether too long? And in any case there was no guarantee that Josse and Joanna's mission would be successful. Joanna might not succeed in finding the place, or Josse might not actually be able to convince himself that Merlin was buried there any more than he was in the forest near Hadfeld.

The bones. Those giant bones . . . Her mind slipped away and she found herself imagining them, wishing she had yielded to the temptation to go and have a look while she had been at the tomb. If they were not Merlin's, then whose were they?

*They give off a force*, Josse had said. He told her he had felt he was in the presence of a great power that he did not understand.

Were they the bones of a saint? Helewise wondered. It was unlikely that a saint would have been buried out in the forest, but then Josse believed Florian had found the bones elsewhere and reburied them at the tomb site. Had he robbed a churchyard? Broken into a reliquary? But no – if some church was missing its valuable relic – and she had never heard of a whole skeleton, only a finger bone or perhaps a couple of ribs; in rare cases, a skull – then surely word would have spread of the outrage?

Perhaps the bones were those of some holy man whom the church had not recognised but who nevertheless had power . . . But that was sacrilege, she told herself firmly, for to worship bones – or anything else for that matter – without official sanction surely must amount to raising false idols.

A giant. Josse said the man would have been taller than him by a third of his own height.

Do I believe in giants? Helewise asked herself. Again she wished she had seen the bones with her own eyes, for she was struck with the idea that the huge skeleton might be nothing but a clever fraud; Florian might have cobbled together the bones of more than one man, perhaps also including animal bones.

She flung down her stylus in frustration; she was getting absolutely nowhere.

She made herself set out on a different approach. What other facts did she know of Florian of Southfrith?

She made a new heading – the dead young man's name –

and then wrote down all that she could recall of the facts told to her by Melusine. He was the youngest of three with two elder sisters, one a nun somewhere in north Kent, one well married and living in France; Angers, wasn't it? No – Poitiers. She wrote it down. He had been married to Melusine's daughter Primevère – her only daughter – for two years. He had boasted of wealth in order to win the young lady's hand in the face of stiff opposition; his means later proved to have been exaggerated and he had further impoverished himself by hurrying to give his contribution towards King Richard's ransom before he was even asked. Primevère was an heiress – Helewise heard in her mind Melusine's haughty tones as she said *My late husband was Theobald of Canterbury; I am from Angers and I am an heiress in my own right.* So Primevère would never have been a pauper, even had Florian not come up with his great money-spinning scheme, for the doting and wealthy mother would have swooped down and rescued her precious child long before Florian spent the last of his pennies on her.

The vague idea that had been growing in Helewise's mind – to do with the possibility that Primevère, on her mother's own admission bored with her new husband, might have had him killed in order to enjoy his money without having to endure him – faded away and died. It just did not work for, if Primevère had in truth been ready to leave her husband, she could have gone to her mother, explained simply that she was tired of Florian and the two of them could have moved away and set up home together elsewhere. Not being in need of her husband's money, why on earth would Primevère want him dead? And anyway Helewise only had Melusine's word for it that Primevère no longer loved her husband; to Helewise, the young woman's grief had seemed only too real.

Perhaps Melusine had reasons of her own for claiming that her daughter's marriage was dying, if not dead . . .

Something suddenly occurred to Helewise. She saw again the pretty picture of Primevère lying on her bed, apparently sick, with her pale face supporting the claim. Yet there had been that fall of luscious, extravagant, gleaming hair. And, now Helewise came to think of it, the young woman's eyes had been bright, the whites shining and clear; apart from the pallor, Primevère had looked the picture of health.

Supposing – just supposing – she had only been pretending to be sick? It must be possible to create the image of pale cheeks; why, a small amount of flour would surely do the trick.

Although she simply did not know why Primevère, lucky enough to be well, might wish to pretend she was sick, nevertheless Helewise wrote down *Primevère: what ails her and is she genuinely unwell?*

Then she sat back and stared at her list.

And she realised that, a considerable time spent in deep thought notwithstanding, she didn't seem to have come up with anything very helpful. Also, that she had absolutely no idea of what to do next.

I have spent far too much time on this already, she rebuked herself sternly. In order that my musings shall not be entirely wasted, I must worry my thoughts to a conclusion and then leave the matter alone and get on with my work.

She tried to still her whirling mind, hoping that a moment's serenity would allow some sense or pattern to emerge from the chaos. She laid down her stylus, folded her hands, closed her eyes and, deliberately relaxing the tension in her neck and shoulders, laid her head back against her tall chair.

After some time she thought, but I have been making this far more complicated than it is, for surely by far the most likely answer is that someone – a visitor to the tomb, or, as I was beginning to suspect when I was with Primevère, one of the guards – knew that Florian would be alone when he carried away his takings that night, followed him until he was well away from anybody who might hear him cry out and then hurried on ahead to set up the rope that broke his neck. Why, I have only to look around me to see what poverty there is in this land of ours. People are desperate, as is demonstrated by the way in which they are flocking to the so-called Merlin's Tomb in the hope of some miracle that will give them a helping hand. Why, then, should I seek to complicate what is almost certainly murder for gain, the gain being a good horse and several bulging bags of money?

She kept her eyes closed, trying to maintain the state of deep and clear-sighted concentration. At first it seemed to her that she had convinced herself that the obvious solution was the right one. But then, like the first fluffy cloud in a clear sky that heralds a storm, the face of the guard at the tomb to whom she had spoken slid into her mind, swiftly followed by that image of the pale-faced Primevère reclining against her pillows.

Someone at the tomb might well know more than has yet been revealed; she would send Augustus and Saul over there to ask around. As for herself, she would give Primevère a little time to recover from the shock and the grief of Florian's death, then she would ride back to Hadfeld and, with an experienced nurse beside her such as Sister Euphemia if she could be spared and Sister Caliste again if she could not, visit the young widow on the pretext of trying to help her in her sickness and her sorrow.

She was just thinking resignedly that in truth she had not yet finished with this killing when a new realisation seared across her mind, temporarily driving everything else out: with Florian dead, Merlin's Tomb would surely now be closed and the pilgrims would come back to Hawkenlye.

The great surge of relief that this happy thought brought with it was swiftly and very thoroughly displaced by a flood of guilt. How can I of all people, she demanded in silent anguish, be glad of anything that comes about because of such a death?

That poor young man had his neck broken and his body thrown into the bushes to rot, and here am I feeling *happy*! She was horrified that, even after all her years as a nun and a Christian, still such a thought could have got through her guard. Getting up, she left her room and went across to the Abbey church where, in its empty and lofty silence, she prostrated herself before the altar and begged first for forgiveness for her wicked thought and then for the Lord's mercy on the soul of Florian of Southfrith.

In the small hours of that morning, Josse knelt over the body of Joanna as she lay on her back in the dell in the Brocéliande forest, biting down on the keening howl of grief that was trying to burst out of him. She lay pale and unmoving just where she had fallen and he was not sure that he could detect any signs that she was breathing. Meggie was watching him from the snug burrow of her blanket, her brown eyes wide; she did not speak and had made no move to rush to her mother's side.

Josse did not know what to do.

He had been crouching there above her for an immeasurable time that could have been hours or just a few moments and, as the light of dawn waxed around him, he noticed that blood from the wound on his right forearm had dripped down on to Joanna's cheek, running down her neck to pool in the hollow above the place where her collar bones met. My blood, he thought distantly, staining her pale skin. He tore his eyes from her and looked at his arm. The blood was beginning to congeal.

He thought, I must do something to help her.

He laid his sword and his dagger carefully down on the mossy grass and then, using his left hand in an effort to spare himself any more pain from his right, very gently he edged his fingers behind her head.

There was a large lump at the base of her skull. Feeling

around, he discovered that by bad luck she had fallen on to a boulder lying in the grass. Her head seemed to have been jerked backwards, the boulder pushing her neck forward while her head fell back behind it. His exploring fingers went on across her head, tangling in her thick, soft hair, but he found no other wound.

He put his cheek to her mouth, trying to detect any drawing-in or expulsion of air. He thought he felt a very faint breath, but it could have been a product of his own fierce need. Bending down further, he laid his ear against her breast, just over her heart . . .

. . . and, after a few unimaginably terrible moments, heard a heartbeat.

It was faint and worryingly irregular, but it was there.

His world had just begun turning again.

He leapt up and hurried across to where Meggie lay beside the remains of their fire. 'Meggie, I need your mother's blanket because she's hurt and we must keep her warm,' he said to the wide-eyed child, trying to keep his voice cheerful. 'Then when I've made her comfy, you and I will build up the fire. Will you help me do that, Meggie?' Solemnly Meggie nodded. 'That's my good girl,' Josse said approvingly. Then, catching up Joanna's blanket and his own as well, he went back to her.

He did not think he ought to move her, tempting though it was to draw her closer to the fire. He had seen people with concussion before and he knew from experience what could happen if an unconscious man unable to say where he was hurting was dragged along the ground. Once in his soldiering days a man had fallen from his horse and landed on his head. The troop had been in a hurry and the commanding officer had snapped out to two of the man's comrades to pick him up and sling him across his saddle. When the man had rapidly recovered consciousness, it was briefly to scream out with agony before the blood in his lungs drowned him: his fall had broken three ribs, one of which had, as he was lifted and put on his horse, punctured a lung.

I will not let such a fate be Joanna's, Josse told himself. Very tenderly, disturbing her as little as possible, he tucked both blankets around her prostrate body. He felt her bare feet – they were icy – then, as he began to rub them, called out softly to Meggie.

'Sweetheart, come here,' he said. 'Mummy's feet are cold and she needs them to be warmed up. Will you kneel here – just here, aye, that's right – and put her feet very carefully in your lap? Aye, like that – very good. Now, put your hands around them and, *very, very gently*, rub some heat into them.'

He knelt back and watched as his daughter did exactly as he had ordered. Then, satisfied, he gave her a smile, bent down and kissed the top of her head and then hurried away to see about building up the fire.

Not long afterwards he was back by her side. Meggie had done her job well and now Joanna's feet were far less chill to the touch. 'Well done, Meggie,' he said approvingly. In addition, the fire was now blazing and the warmth from its flames could be felt even from where the three of them were, some four or five paces away.

'Hungwy,' Meggie announced.

'You're hungry?' She nodded. Of course you are, Josse thought, wondering if he could steel himself to leave Joanna's side to prepare some food. What could he fetch that would take the least time? Their provisions were low but there were some strips of dried meat, the last of the flat bread and a couple of apples. Not much for a hungry child, but at least she could have all of it; Josse didn't think he'd ever want to eat again.

He leapt up, fetched the bag in which Joanna carried the victuals and was back again in an instant. He delved in the bag and, extracting some meat and a hand's-span-sized piece of bread, gave them to Meggie. She chewed her way rapidly through the food, swallowed and said, 'More.'

From the grass Joanna's voice said, 'More, *please*.'

And Josse, knowing better than to fling himself upon a possibly wounded woman, had to content himself with saying gently, 'Joanna. Welcome back.'

As she struggled to sit up, telling the anxious Josse very firmly that there was nothing wrong with her but a headache and she would mix up some herbs and soon put *that* right, she felt something damp on her face and neck. She put up her hand and it came away coated with blood. Oh, Great Mother, I am wounded after all and, if it gives no pain, it must be deep and grievous indeed . . .

But Josse, eyes watching her every move, spoke quickly. 'Joanna, it isn't your blood – there is no wound to your head or neck except the bump on the back of your skull.'

'Then what is—' She broke off, for what she had just caught sight of had answered her question. 'Josse, I must see to your arm.'

'But—'

'Now, Josse, for the cut slices deep and if it starts bleeding again, I may not be able to stop it.'

She got to her feet, unable quite to prevent the wince as the pain from her head seared through her. He noticed that, too, and put out a hand to hold her back. But it seemed that his strength had suddenly left him, for even as he tried to grab her, he sank back on to the grass.

She looked down at him, nodding. 'Yes, dear Josse. Lie there until I have done what I can for you. Meggie – oh, Meggie, hello, dearest! Have some more to eat – yes, help yourself from the bag. Now,' she added to herself, 'what should I do first?'

He had mended the fire, she noted, and she put a small

amount of water on to boil. While it heated up she fetched her leather satchel and took out several small packets: comfrey, Lady's Mantle, herb bennet, horsetail and lavender; styptics and an antiseptic with which to treat that gaping wound on Josse's arm. Also, because she knew she would be a more efficient and observant healer without the thumping headache, she set out white willow and a tiny pinch of the dangerously poisonous but highly and swiftly efficacious monkshood for herself.

As soon as the water began to steam she poured a little into the small wooden cup that she reserved only for healing and into which she had already put some drops of lavender oil. Then, returning to Josse, she gave the bowl and a clean piece of soft cloth to Meggie and told her to bathe away the blood.

Josse looked up at her, horrified. 'She's only a child!' he hissed. Looking down at the cut on his arm — it was, Joanna had to acknowledge, not a pretty sight — he added, 'She shouldn't have to do this!'

'She's a healer and in her own time she's going to be a fine one,' Joanna replied calmly. 'Also, as you are about to find out, she has an exceptionally gentle touch.' Then she went back to the fire.

The water was now boiling and quickly she poured some on to the mix of analgesic herbs in her drinking cup, swirling the mixture round and round to make the plant substances release their power and to cool the water a little. Making a face at both the ghastly, bitter taste and the still-hot water, she swallowed it down. Then, knowing that it would soon bring relief and in the meantime trying to ignore the crashing pain in her skull, she set to work to prepare the mixture that would knit Josse's flesh together and, with any luck, heal that awful cut without the need of stitches.

Some time later, her headache all but gone and Josse's arm bound up in clean cloth — she had after all had to put in three stitches, an operation that Meggie had observed with keen interest and that Josse had borne with great courage, only crying out once – the three of them sat under the shade of the birch trees eating the small amount of food that Meggie had left in the bag.

'Now, dear Josse,' Joanna said when there was not even a crumb remaining, 'tell me what happened this morning just before dawn.'

She had been dying to ask ever since she had come round but, appreciating that there were more important things to do and that, moreover, there no longer seemed to be any imminent danger, she had reined in her curiosity and got on with what she (and, increasingly, Meggie) did best. But now that she had done all that she could, she had to know.

Josse was gazing out over the forest and for a while did not answer.

'Josse?' she prompted.

He turned to her and, smiling, reached for her hand with his unbandaged one. 'I do realise,' he said gently, 'how much you must want to know. It's just that I'm not sure how to tell you because I don't know what *did* happen.'

'Ah.' She had an idea that she knew why this might be. To prompt him, she said, 'We sensed that someone was out there, approaching the hillock, and—'

'*You* sensed it,' he corrected. Then, in a fervent whisper, 'I'm still giving thanks for you and your weird abilities.'

She squeezed his hand. 'Me too. So, someone attacked us and we both leapt up and laid into them, you with your sword and dagger, me with my knife.'

'You all but cut his ear off,' Josse remarked.

'Did I?' She had but a vague memory of pouncing on their assailant's back and wielding her blade. 'Pity. I must be losing my touch because I was going for his throat. Then what happened?'

'He flung you off and you fell flat on your back. I thought – hoped – you might only be winded but in any case I couldn't do anything for you just then because—'

She heard the apology in his voice. 'Of course you couldn't,' she agreed calmly. 'Your priority was to kill our attacker before he killed us.'

He gave her a grateful smile. 'You always were a very reasonable woman,' he murmured. 'Anyway, I chased off after him down the slope and away along some narrow and winding animal track and suddenly he stopped. When I caught up with him there was something, some*one* maybe, standing right in front of him.'

'A man? An animal?' She was now almost certain she was right.

He shrugged, the deep frown betraying his confusion. 'I don't know. While I was in pursuit I thought I heard some very large animal running through the undergrowth, keeping pace with me. Then, when I saw that great shape of darkness rising up in front of the attacker, I – Joanna, it – he – was *huge*.'

I was right, she thought jubilantly. I just *knew* he was out there – I sensed his presence. Oh, perhaps he's been with us ever since Folle-Pensée! He must have picked up that we were in danger and he did not leave us until he had removed that danger.

She had not a single regret over what had happened, for the man sent by Césaire had undoubtedly meant to kill her and probably Josse and maybe even Meggie – oh, Meggie! – too. Nevertheless, she who had seen her rescuer as both man and as bear knew how his very appearance could strike cold terror in the heart, even when he was in his benign aspect. In furious fighting mode, rising up to his full height on those incredibly powerful back legs, deadly claws extended to strike, he— But she stopped herself. It was too frightening even to think about.

Trying to calm the thrill of excitement coursing through her, she said, 'Did he kill the man?'

'I'm not sure,' Josse replied. 'I think so. The starlight seemed to flash on a weapon of some sort – it was something I've never seen before, almost like a knife with multiple blades – and I caught an image of terrible violence, although the picture wasn't clear in my mind and I'm at a loss to know what really happened.' Slowly he shook his head. 'The man who attacked us fell and I watched to see but he didn't get up again. When I looked up the dark shape had vanished.'

'Did you not check that the man was dead?' she demanded; she had to know, had to be sure they were safe now.

He looked at her and she could not read his expression. 'No, Joanna. He was down and that was all that mattered. Me, I had other things to see to.' There was a brief pause. Then: 'I thought – I was terrified that you were dead.'

She understood. Her moment of anxiety-induced anger vanished and she saw the scene from his perspective.

Dear, loving, loyal Josse.

She leaned against him, turning her head so that she could kiss the bare flesh at his throat. 'Dearest Josse, I have a skull like a rock. It takes more than falling against a stone to kill me.'

'Don't say—' he began.

But it was enough; there was no need to say any more.

She stopped him with a kiss.

# 15

As the sun rose to its noon height, Josse insisted that he was well enough for them to get moving and proceed with their journey back to the coast. Joanna would have liked him to rest for the remainder of the day for she was afraid that, despite Meggie's careful bathing, the wound was at risk of developing the hot, red inflammation that told of the onset of the often fatal infection in the flesh. As yet the area around his wound was cool to the touch. Perhaps he would be all right even if they did set off now, for he was strong and healthy and men such as he seemed, in her experience, to fight off deadly infections better than their weakling fellows.

Besides, she herself had an urgent reason for moving on. Césaire wanted her dead badly enough to have set an assassin on her trail; having encountered the man, she knew that she was right in her assumption that Césaire would not do the deed himself but hire another to do it for him. But now, were he to become anxious as to what had happened to that assassin, he might very well despatch a second and she and Josse might not be so lucky again. If they left now they might make ten or a dozen miles before stopping for the night; very likely, more. And they surely could not be more than a couple of days from the coast, although for obvious reasons they could not now aim for Dinan but must turn north-westwards and take the longer road to one of the ports that lay further along the coast.

Josse was one-handedly removing the horses' hobbles, and

Meggie was helping him. He would not, Joanna thought, be able to put on their saddles and bridles; since he really did seem determined to set off, she hastened to finish packing away their belongings and, after kicking out the last embers of the fire and throwing the circle of hearth stones back into the undergrowth, she shouldered her satchel and her pack and went to help him.

Studying the sun's position, she steered them to the west of the track that would lead out of the forest in the direction of Dinan. At first Josse did not notice; he must be suffering, she thought with a stab of empathetic pain, for normally he is acutely aware of direction. Eventually he said, almost apologetically, 'Shouldn't we turn slightly to the right if we're heading for Dinan?'

Reining in, she said, 'Josse my love, we're not. I believe I know who attacked us last night. I think it was someone hired by Césaire.'

So total had been Josse's immersion in their mission in the Brocéliande that, she observed with amusement, he had to think for a moment to recall who Césaire was and why he should want them dead. Then: 'Your husband's brother. Of course.'

'My *late* husband's brother,' she amended. 'He threatened me in the inn at Dinan and said I'd got away with it too long, or words to that effect. He always was a dreadful man – a bully and a coward, one of the worst combinations there is.'

'Just the sort to send another to do his killing for him, do you think?'

'Oh, yes. That would be Césaire's way.'

Josse was frowning. 'You really think he still carries a sufficient grudge against you to kill you now, all these years afterwards? He must in truth have loved his brother.'

She gave a short, harsh laugh. 'Love had nothing to do with it.' She hesitated, then, giving Josse a slightly guilty look, said,

'After Thorald died, I left as quickly as I could, as I believe I told you?'

He nodded. 'Aye, you did. Before any of your horrible in-laws could stop you, was what you said.'

She grinned. 'Yes, they were a family who were quite without redeeming features and I loathed every one of them.' She paused. 'What I did not tell you, however, was that before I left, I went to Thorald's secret hiding place and helped myself to a large bag containing silver coins and some heavy pieces of gold jewellery. That's why Césaire wants revenge: not because he thinks I had a hand in Thorald's death but because I took the family treasure that he reckons should have gone to him.'

Josse whistled. 'Was it a very big bag of silver?'

Her smile widened. 'Very.'

They rode on, for some moments not speaking. Then he said, 'Where do you suggest we go instead of Dinan?'

Dear Josse, she thought, with a rush of love for him. Not one word to the effect that it was a dishonest act to steal from my husband, never mind having actively worked towards that very convenient accidental death. So stout is his support of those he loves that whatever I did, I think he would find a good excuse for my behaviour.

But he had asked her a question.

'Well, I've turned us north-west now in order to avoid both Dinan and Léhon, which lies to the south of the town and is the place where Thorald had his estates. We will pass well to the south-west of the Rance and with any luck, anyone searching for us will not be able to find us.'

'Can we keep within the forest? Does it extend as far as the coast?'

'I don't know,' she admitted. 'Let's keep on this heading and find out.'

\*

They were in luck for, although the forest thinned occasionally and in some cases, around hamlets and villages, petered out entirely, sooner or later the track would once again disappear beneath the trees.

Out in the wildwood, they saw not a soul.

Towards the end of the afternoon they passed a village called Yvignac, whose church's strange round tower they had been using as a landmark for some miles. There a baker sold them fresh bread straight out of the oven and mouth-wateringly fragrant. They also purchased milk, cheese, cider and apple tarts. On the far side of the village the forest closed in again and soon they came across a clearing close to the track where they stopped and fell upon the food. Josse was clearly in great pain – riding a large horse, even a well-mannered one, was no fit task for a man with such a wound – but, despite Joanna's urging, he flatly refused to stay there in the clearing and make camp for the night. He was good for many miles yet, he claimed stoutly. Although she would rather by far have lit a fire, made up an analgesic remedy and helped his agony, there was nothing for Joanna to do but agree. She did, however, insist that Meggie rode with her.

They rode on until at last the long daylight began to fade. Then, with the clear sky above deepening to a blue so piercingly beautiful that it seemed like the heavens' gift, Josse announced that he'd had enough.

Joanna had to help him down from Horace's back. They were on a track leading north-north-east along a river and quickly she found them shelter under a long, straggling hazel hedge and made Josse comfortable in his blanket. His forehead felt heated but the arm, thank the Great Ones, was still cool. She built a fire, gave Meggie careful orders as to how to tend it, and then slipped down the river bank to collect water. Her most important task was to mix up a pain-killing remedy for Josse and she was going to get it ready as fast as she could and not make him suffer a moment longer than he had to.

The slow-moving water, when she thought to taste it, was brackish: it must be a tidal inlet, which meant they were close to the sea.

We can follow the inlet up to the coast, she thought, visualising the action, where in whatever port we come to, we shall find a boat to take us back to England. Then Césaire will not be able to find me, and Josse, Meggie and I will be safe.

Back in England, also, she and her daughter would have to part from Josse. But she didn't allow herself to dwell on that.

Instead she concentrated on tomorrow. It would be the time of greatest danger for, even if Césaire had not discovered that his assassin was dead, he might in any case be watching the ports since he would be able to reason as well as she could that returning via Dinan would be foolishly risky. What can I do? she wondered as, having fed Josse the analgesic, she watched him slide into a light sleep. How best can I keep us safe?

Safe.

Without any conscious prompting, an image of her little hut in the forest slid into her mind. She felt utterly safe there, for as well as being right out in the wildwood she had set it about with spells for safety and for concealment. Nobody – not even Josse, whom she loved – could find it if she did not want them to. But she was not in her hut now: she was approaching the north coast of Armorica with someone hunting for her who wished her dead.

Against her will she saw more images. Horrible images, of the arrest, trial and execution of a woman condemned for killing her husband by witchcraft. The woman had been kept awake far beyond her endurance, her body naked and shaved of hair from when they had searched for the Devil's Mark. She bore both physical wounds from her long torment and also mental wounds, for they had raped and abused her. Now, still naked, she was being led out to the thick stake surrounded by brush and bundles of wood where, very soon now, they would tie her up and burn her to death.

She saw the woman's face and the woman was her.

She gave a low moan, and felt a great keening wail rise up in her throat.

She gritted her teeth and kept her silence. I will not allow this weakness, she commanded herself fiercely. His man did not succeed back there in the forest, either in killing me or Josse my protector, or in taking me prisoner and marching me off to Dinan. We killed the killer, Josse and I. Josse is wounded now and cannot fight as he did then, so it is up to me.

Slowly she rose to her feet, careful not to disturb either Josse or Meggie, sleeping peacefully beside her father. Then, already beginning on the long, low chant that would carry her into the right frame of mind, she delved into her leather satchel and began assembling the tools and the ingredients she would need.

Then she began to work her spell.

In the morning they followed the inlet down to the sea. To Joanna's relief, Josse looked better after his night's rest. She had ensured, by slipping a light sedative into his herbal infusion, that his sleep was profound; the sleeping draught, combined with strong pain-killing herbs, had knocked him out like a felled ox and both she and Meggie had been disturbed by his snoring. But now she had her reward for interrupted sleep, for here was dear old Josse, bright-eyed and claiming the pain was much reduced, holding out his arm to show her that his wound seemed to be healing well.

So far, so good.

On the right bank of the inlet, on a promontory guarding the bay, was a great castle, granite-built, threatening. Neither knowing nor caring to whom it might belong, Joanna and

Josse ignored it and instead went down to the shore, where several boats of varying size were tied up along a wooden quay. Their requests for passage for two adults, a child and two horses seemed doomed to failure until one man, an ageing sailor missing one eye whose face was chestnut-brown and deeply seamed with creases, offered the remark that his wife's cousin's son had a boat and that sometimes – only sometimes, mind – he sailed over to England, where he knew a man with a weakness for Breton oysters. He might – just might – be setting off on such a venture quite soon and he might see his way to taking some passengers. For a consideration, naturally.

After parting with the price of several flagons of cider and the meals to go with them, Josse managed to elicit the information that the seaman's relative by marriage sailed out of somewhere called St Cast and that this port was maybe another four, five miles up the coast; they couldn't miss it, claimed the old sailor, and his wife's cousin's son was called André and his boat was the *Sacrée Vierge*.

Josse, Joanna and Meggie rode on. They found both André and his boat and, just as the old man had said, André was loading boxes of oysters. He eyed his would-be passengers, nodded and suggested a price for their fare to England. It was not unreasonable but for pride's sake Josse haggled and beat him down a little. Then, for André was eager to utilise the tide and the south-westerly wind to the very best advantage, Josse and Joanna got the horses on board and into the hold and, sitting up in the prow with Meggie held securely between them, watched as the *Sacrée Vierge* slipped her moorings and pulled away from the shore.

The wind strengthened as they entered open water and soon the sails were scooping it up, filling and billowing over their heads. The boat was a smallish craft, lightly built, and she sped along as if she were flying. André, relaxing somewhat now that they were well on their way, came to pass the time of day and told them the ship was bound for New Shoreham, where his lordship the lover of Breton oysters lived. They expected to make landfall in time for supper the next day, André said, adding that there would be little point in even contemplating the voyage unless it were at a time when conditions meant it could be accomplished swiftly. Even his magnificent and freshly collected oysters, he said, didn't keep longer than three days.

After supper Josse and Joanna settled Meggie down to sleep, wrapped in her blankets between them in their place in the prow where she would be perfectly safe. The little ship neither pitched nor rolled and Josse reckoned that they were in for a comfortable night.

Putting his undamaged left arm out so that Joanna could lean into his shoulder, he said quietly, 'Have we, think you, accomplished what we set out to do?'

She raised her head to look at him briefly before relaxing against him once more. 'I had almost forgotten our mission,' she replied. She reached to kiss his throat. 'These past few days with you have been a joy.' She laughed briefly. 'Not to mention the slight distraction of someone trying to kill us.'

He did not want to dwell on how wonderful their time together had been because that thought would lead directly to a far less happy one: that it was about to come to an end. So, acknowledging her remark with no more than a squeeze and a soft kiss dropped on the top of her head, he said, 'But what of the reason why we made this journey?'

She thought for a moment and then said, 'It's up to you, Josse. The Abbess and the Domina hoped that by showing you the place known in Armorica – Brittany – as Merlin's Tomb and by telling you the legend attached to it, you would be convinced and therefore able to state conclusively that the Brocéliande tomb is the true one and the one in the forest at

Hadfeld must therefore be a fake.' She paused. 'Are you so convinced?'

Slowly he shook his head. 'I wish I knew, sweeting. Your people at Folle-Pensée are good, honest souls and they would not *tell* me that I must believe in the spring being Merlin's burial place.'

'No, we leave that sort of command to the church,' she murmured. 'Our way is to set out what we believe and then let others make up their own minds. In our view, all men and women have been given a brain and it is up to every one of us to make up his or her own mind on matters of faith. To us the concept of telling people that they *must* believe or else they'll suffer damnation is faintly absurd since faith comes from the heart, not the head, and it simply doesn't work that way. Besides,' she added, warming to her theme, 'who wouldn't claim to believe in just about anything if the alternative were the threat of being roasted in hell for eternity with devils sticking red-hot pitchforks in your private parts?'

Josse chuckled. 'I can think of one or two priests who would fall into a swoon at the very idea of independent thought on matters of faith.'

'So can I,' she agreed wryly.

He was still pondering her original question. Had he seen enough to say without doubt that Florian of Southfrith's tomb was nothing more than a confidence trick? He did not know. There was nothing fraudulent about the tomb at Folle-Pensée, that was for sure, and he had been left in no doubt that there was a power source there beneath the vast granite slab and in the sparkling water. If he was honest with himself, that moment when Huathe had stood up on the stone and summoned the elements had scared Josse more than virtually anything in his life. He had been a fighting man, aye, but you knew what to expect with a flesh-and-blood opponent. That – that spirit, or presence, or whatever it was at the spring in the Brocéliande

was not of this world, or if it was, it was from a part of it that
Josse had neither experienced before nor wished ever to meet
again.

It dwelled, he thought, in Joanna's world.

He had been given, he realised, a unique vision into the place
that she now inhabited. It was a privilege – aye, he recognised
that well enough. But it also brought him immeasurable sorrow,
for it made him see just how different her life now was from his.
From anybody's, come to that, who did not share her world.

*Do not think of that*, a calm voice seemed to say in his head,
*for there is nothing you can do but accept.*

He felt his pain lessen and fade away and, after a moment,
he found himself scratching his head and trying to recall what
he had just been thinking about . . .

The tomb, he thought. I was comparing Merlin's Tomb
with the power of that spring out in the Breton forest. But then
he had felt power from the great bones in the forest near
Hadfeld, too, although he was as sure as he could be that
whatever caused it had nothing to do with Merlin and everything to do with Florian making false claims for something he
did not begin to understand.

God's boots, but it was difficult!

She had sensed his mental turmoil – bless her, she always
knew when he was in any kind of distress and would try to
comfort him – and, snuggling against him, she said, 'Josse?
May I make a suggestion?'

'I wish you would,' he said fervently.

She laughed softly. 'Well, both the Abbey and the forest
people are desperate to see the new site at Hadfeld closed
down, the Abbey because the tomb is drawing away pilgrims
from the healing spring in the Vale and from the skilful hands
of the nursing nuns, and the forest people because the presence of a money-making business on the sacred soil of the
forest is, in their eyes, sacrilegious. Yes?'

'Yes,' he agreed.

'You were sent out to Armorica to see with your own eyes another place where it is claimed that Merlin lies entombed. It seems to me that you have to decide which of the two is the more authentic.'

'There's no question but that it's the one in the Brocéliande forest,' he said instantly. 'It's clearly ancient; it's been a place of veneration for generations and there's undoubtedly a force there, identified by local tradition as the magician Merlin. The Hadfeld site, on the other hand, is brash and brand-new and I have a strong suspicion that Florian didn't find the bones where he said he did but brought them in from elsewhere. No. I may not be totally convinced that the place at Folle-Pensée is Merlin's Tomb, but then I'm not sure that I believe that there ever was a magician called Merlin and even if—'

'Josse,' she interrupted gently, 'would it not be a good idea to stop right there? Slightly earlier, actually, with your first remark.'

He thought back. 'That I'm in no doubt that the tomb in the Brocéliande is the more authentic?'

'Exactly. The rest is a matter of belief and that, as we have just been suggesting, is up to the conscience of each individual.'

He was nodding. 'Aye. Aye, you're right, Joanna.' He hugged her close. 'I can tell the Abbess Helewise just that, can't I? That way I won't be telling her a lie.'

'No, you won't,' she agreed. Returning his hug, she added, 'And I know how important that is to you. Not lying to her, I mean.'

He did not know how to answer. The issue of the Abbess was something that he sensed was somehow unresolved between himself and Joanna. Should he raise it now? If he did, what would he say? Yes I love her, but not like I love you? That would be the truth, but would Joanna want to hear him admit to loving another woman, whatever form that love took?

He could not make up his mind.

Then Joanna said very softly, 'Josse, I know. And it's all right.'

Which seemed to him to be all the answer he needed.

Behind them in the Brocéliande forest a man patiently awaited death.

He had been there, slipping sometimes into unconsciousness, for a long time – dawn through to noon, then sunset and now night again – for he had been strong and fit, trained to endure hardship without complaint, and it would take many days for the life force to leak out of his fatally wounded body.

As he lay there, past pain and instead affected with a growing numbness, he distracted his mind from his fast-approaching end by thinking back over his last mission.

The one that had at long last brought him face to face with death and made him the loser.

Those whom he obeyed had commanded him to locate a particular man and woman; why he must do so was not explained and he had not expected that it would be. The third member of the little group was a child. His mission had been to watch and follow the party, awaiting the right moment to strike, and he had carried it out without deviation for many weary days, for ever performing the delicate calculation of how close to trail them without being seen while balancing this with not losing them.

He was good at tracking people, which was why he had been selected for the job.

This mission had been special, for he was only to kill the man and the woman if certain conditions were met. It had been left to his judgement to make the decision but what doubts he might have had were allayed by the demeanour of the pair; when it came to it, little judgement had been called for because both the man and the woman had shown perfectly clearly – by the man's words as they came down from the spring, by their expressions, by the slump of their shoulders, by the woman's tears that she tried so hard to conceal from the man – just what they were thinking.

Those telling details had signed their death warrants. They had to die, that was plain, and so he had waited until the conditions were right and then made his move.

He went back in his mind to the fatal night.

They had known he was approaching, although he had no idea how. He was as silent as the darkness. Well, it was no use worrying over it for it made no difference now. He ought to have been successful, even after the woman had leapt up and shrieked at him and the man had gone for his weapons, and the fact that he had managed to disable the man's sword arm ought to have increased his advantage over them. But then that she-cat had leapt on his back with her knife in her hand and that had been the beginning of the end.

She'd cut off the lower part of his left ear.

Also, although he had not realised this until much later, her savage cut had in fact found the target that she must surely have been aiming for; the knife's point had gone into his neck in front of and just below his ear and nicked a blood vessel. Not the major one whose severance meant almost instantaneous death as the brilliant red blood spurted out; no. In that sense he had been fortunate, for her knife had found the little tube that carried the lesser flow of purplish blood. He must have started bleeding simultaneously from his ear and his throat and, the major wound being the more painful, he had not at first noticed that he was also bleeding from the neck.

Then he had turned and fled off down the gentle slope, plunging down into the forest in the hope of evading the man, who unfortunately seemed quite prepared to attack with his sword in his left hand as in his right: he must, mused the dying man, be an ex-soldier, although nobody had thought to tell him so.

I could have escaped, he thought, and perhaps attacked again another day, had I managed to evade him and hide away while I patched myself up.

But he hadn't escaped.

Instead that terrifying black shape had risen up out of the forest floor right in front of him, appearing out of nowhere and frightening him so badly that he had felt his bowels turn to liquid. He had tried to defend himself but his attempts were as futile as a child waving its fist at an armoured knight: the black shape had swung a huge, hairy arm – *was* it an arm? – and the tall man's long knife had flown out of his hand.

I must by then already have lost more blood than I knew, he now thought wearily. I was delirious, seeing visions; how else explain the figure out of legend, out of nightmare, that put an end to my life?

The dark shape had towered above him as he cowered before it. Then, even as he began to form the words with which to beg for mercy – a mercy in which, in truth, he had little faith for he knew he did not deserve it – the man, or the animal, whatever it was, had extended a long arm at the end of which were sharp points that gleamed in the starlight.

The tall man had felt the flesh of his throat and chest open like butter under the knife and, looking down with horrified eyes, had seen the deep gashes tearing into him from just above his collar bone right down to his belly.

He had sunk, already fainting, to his knees.

As he slumped on the spongy forest floor dizzy and nauseated, trying to hold his flesh together and dam the great rush of blood but with the darkness already spreading in front of his eyes, he had looked up to face his attacker one last time; a man ought, after all, to know and recognise his final enemy.

But there was nothing there.

He had slept, or slipped into unconsciousness; it was hard to tell the difference now. Awake and aware once more, he realised that he could not feel his feet.

The insidious chill of death crept up his legs. He looked down at his hands, bloodstained from where he had clamped them to his destroyed chest.

Not long now.

What *did* I see? he wondered.

*Was* I seeing visions? Was my killer in truth no other than the man with the sword, dressed up in that horrifying guise by my own fevered imagination? Perhaps, perhaps.

But if so then why, the dying man wondered, did he have four parallel grooves in his flesh that looked for all the world like claw marks?

He sighed.

It was sad to die with an unsolved mystery on his mind.

But it did not look as if he was going to have any choice.

# 16

Helewise's first action after the early offices was to send for Brother Saul and Brother Augustus and request that they return to Merlin's Tomb in order to ask anyone prepared to talk to them one or two pertinent questions. Saul, whose expression did not look like that of a man readily able to distinguish a pertinent question from any other sort, began to frown but Augustus said straight away, 'Like did anyone notice some man hanging around and trying to find out which day Florian was most likely to be carrying home the takings and what time he was going to leave?'

Helewise beamed. 'Precisely that, Gus.'

Saul's tense face relaxed; he was evidently relieved that he now understood what was being asked of him. He nodded sagely and was about to speak when Augustus got in before him.

'We might also try to find out about the guards, my lady,' he said excitedly. 'They looked a tough bunch to me and, without wishing to blacken anyone's good name without due cause, it'd be pretty obvious to anyone that they'd likely be the best source of information regarding Florian's movements.'

'Yes, Augustus, that's right.' She shot him a smile, then turned to Saul. 'Brother Saul? Were you about to say something?'

'Oh – aye, my lady, but only that it'd be a relief to bring the killer of that poor young man to justice.'

'Saul, there must be no heroic attempt to solve this by

yourselves.' She looked from Saul to Augustus and back again. 'Florian was murdered by a cold-hearted and dispassionate killer who robbed him and threw his body in the brambles. Remember that.'

Saul and Augustus exchanged a glance. Then Saul said, 'We will, my lady.' And, as if they could no longer contain their eagerness for the unexpected outing, as one they bowed low, turned and hurried away.

For some moments after their hasty departure, Helewise sat staring at the door and wishing that she was going with them. She could have done; nobody would have questioned her motive in leading the little expedition. But she knew there was no need for her to go. Augustus was an astute young man who kept his eyes and ears open and who, for all his youth, seemed to know when people were trying to deceive him. And Saul – well, Saul was as solid as the very earth and as dependable as sunrise.

With a small sigh that even someone standing right in front of her would probably have missed, Helewise drew her accounts book towards her, reached for her stylus and got down to work.

The two lay brothers returned in the early afternoon.

'What did you discover?' she demanded as soon as they had come in and closed the door behind them.

It was Saul who spoke first.

'The place is all shut up, my lady. There was a handful of people hanging around in the clearing just inside the forest, where all those trees were cut down. We stopped short and tethered the horses, then edged our way nearer so that we could hear what was going on but not be seen. There was a cross-looking man in a dirty leather jerkin—'

'It was that fellow Jack, my lady, who came to relieve the gate guard when we visited,' Augustus put in.

She nodded. 'Go on.'

'The man in the jerkin was telling the people they couldn't visit the tomb' – Saul picked up the narrative – 'and that they should go back where they came from.'

'I see.' She could visualise the scene. She hoped that none of the pilgrims would suffer too badly from having made that abortive journey. She also hoped – and she knew it was unworthy – that all the people who were being frustrated in their desire to see Merlin's Tomb would sooner or later find their way here to Hawkenlye.

'The gate in that there outer fence – that's the post and rail one, my lady – the gate was closed and chained. Er – me and Gussie, we reckoned it wouldn't be too hard to climb over it, so we did. In fact it was quite easy, what with two of us, one helping the other.' He was watching her hopefully, as if keen to know they had done right.

'Well done, Saul,' she said. 'Then what?'

'Not far beyond the first fence we came to a second,' Saul continued. 'This one was much more of a barrier, my lady, because the spaces between the rails had been filled in with hurdles and it was that thick, we—' Saul broke off as Augustus leaned across to whisper in his ear. With an apologetic smile, Saul said, 'But then you know, my lady, since you've seen it for yourself.'

'Only from a distance, Brother Saul. Please, go on.'

'The gate in the second fence was also chained and to begin with me and Gussie didn't see as how we were going to get through. Then Gussie spotted a tree quite close to the fence, just about the only one around there that hadn't been felled, and he reckoned he could climb it and crawl out along one of the higher branches so he could see over the fence, if you follow me, my lady.'

'I do, Saul. And you managed this?' She turned to Augustus.

'Aye, my lady, though I've bruised my— Aye. Saul gave me a leg-up and I got hold of one of the lower branches, then I shinned up till I could reach the higher ones. I crept out as far as I dared, only then I began to hear the branch creaking a bit and Saul said to come down.'

'Saul was quite right,' she said gravely. 'If you had fallen inside the enclosure, Gus, how could Saul have come to your aid?'

'Exactly what I said myself!' Saul cried.

'What did you see?' She stared at Augustus.

'I saw the tomb,' he said simply. 'It was a long, wide depression and, inside it, huge great bones.'

'The grave was still open?' She was surprised; would not whoever had locked up the site have at least made some attempt to cover the bones? It seemed almost . . . shocking.

'Wide open, my lady,' Augustus said.

She could not control her curiosity. 'What did you feel, Gus?' she asked. Remembering what Josse had said, she added, 'Did the bones affect you in any way?'

Augustus pondered the question for several moments. Then he said slowly, 'I felt I was trespassing, and that's the honest truth. I felt I was staring at something that I had no right to see and I even felt that something was watching me and telling me to get away from there and leave the dead in peace.'

'*Did* you?' It might, she thought, have been no more than a lad who lived with monks having picked up their respect for the dead. On the other hand . . .

'Aye. I tell you, my lady, I couldn't get down out of that tree fast enough. Then me and Saul ran back to the track and to the place where we had left our mounts.'

'*Then*,' Saul interrupted, picking up the tale, 'we rode right up to the fellow in the jerkin, pretending we'd just arrived, and asked him if we could see the tomb. He'd seen Gussie afore, of course, that time he went with you and Sister Caliste, my lady, only we kept our hoods up and he barely gave us a glance, so I don't reckon there's much chance he recognised Gus.'

'That was clever,' she said admiringly. They *had* done well! 'What did he say?'

'He said Merlin's Tomb was closed and we should go away. Gus said but we've come all the way from the other side of the forest – which was true even if it implied we'd travelled much further than we really had – but the man in the jerkin just snarled a bit and said he couldn't help that and the tomb was still closed.'

'Did he not guess by your habits that you came from Hawkenlye?'

'He didn't seem to, my lady,' Augustus said. 'Truth to tell, he seemed preoccupied and even a bit scared-like and I reckon we could have worn crowns and carried sceptres and he still wouldn't have noticed.'

Smiling at the exaggeration, she said, 'What could he have been scared of?'

'Of being found out, if he had something to do with his master's death,' Saul said shrewdly.

'Hmm.' She considered that, recalling her own suspicions regarding the guards. Was it really so simple and merely a question of a ruffian guard becoming greedy and attacking and robbing his master? But if so, then the last place the man in the leather jerkin would be now was at the entrance to the tomb site; if he had killed Florian, in addition to the bags of silver coins he would also have a fast horse. He would be several counties away by now if he had any wits at all.

No. Common sense said that it was not he who had killed Florian. He might, however, have some idea who did.

And of course he had not been the only guard at Merlin's Tomb.

'Did you ask him any more questions?' She looked at Saul, eyebrows raised.

'Gussie did.' Saul grinned. 'Said he'd heard that the man who ran Merlin's Tomb had been robbed and murdered and was it true and did the guard know who was behind it?'

'Ah, the direct approach,' Helewise murmured. 'Brave of you, Gus. What was the answer?'

Augustus smiled ruefully. 'Told me to mind my own business, only he used an extra word that I won't repeat, my lady.'

'He knew it was true all right,' Saul put in. 'When he'd finished telling us to bugg— um, that is, to go away, he said we'd find out soon enough whether it was true and in his view it was just as well because he'd never felt happy about the tomb, he'd had more than enough of the place, he didn't even want to talk about it and he was leaving the district as soon as he'd seen off the last of the visitors.'

'So Merlin's Tomb is truly to close,' she said thoughtfully. Somewhere deep inside her, there was a profound relief. They will return to us, she thought, those people in need, and once again old Brother Firmin will dole out holy water and gentle kindness, and the monks and nuns will all do whatever they are best at to heal hurts of minds, bodies and souls.

She gave herself a shake: relief was all very well but it didn't solve the problem of who had killed Florian.

'Did you see any of the other guards?' she asked. 'Perhaps the one we spoke to, Gus, when we visited?'

Gus shook his head. 'No, my lady. Seems the man in the jerkin was left to do the job by himself.'

Was left . . . Something that had been nagging at her now came to the front of her mind. 'Who left him?' she wondered aloud.

'My lady?' Saul looked puzzled.

'Gussie just said he was left to do the job. Left by whom?'

Saul's frown deepened. 'Well, left on his own by the other guards who'd legged it, my lady.'

She smiled. 'I'm sorry, Brother Saul, I'm not explaining myself clearly. I meant with Florian dead, who is issuing the orders?'

Gus was nodding his understanding. '*Someone* must have told the guards to secure the place and chain up the two gates, and ordered one of them to stay to turn away visitors,' he said eagerly. 'Oh, Saul, why didn't *we* think of that? We could have asked him!'

'Don't worry about it, Gus,' Helewise said. 'Even if you did he'd only have told you to *go away* again.'

Gus picked up the emphasis and grinned. 'Aye, that's likely true. All the same . . .'

She got to her feet. 'No use in regrets, Gus,' she said briskly. 'The two of you have done well and I am most grateful to you. Now, off you go. Return to your duties and leave me to torment my brains wondering what to do next.'

They bowed and backed out through the door. As they left, she added, 'If you do come up with any bright ideas, please don't hesitate to share them with me.'

And, with murmurs of assent, they were gone.


She sat quite still, staring into space, not seeing any of the familiar objects, few in number, that furnished her simple little room. Her mind was racing as she tried to think what she ought to do next.

She could not control the insistent thought that kept saying, Merlin's Tomb is to close and Hawkenlye is safe! Soon they will begin to come back!

That is not all there is to this business, she reprimanded herself sternly. Florian of Southfrith has been robbed and murdered. Is his death to be written off with a shrug as the work of some vicious itinerant felon who has long fled the district?

She recalled her unspoken objection to Saul's suggestion

that the guard in the leather jerkin might have been involved in the crime: that, if he had been, he'd have fled the district long since. Surely the same applied to whoever it was who had really done the deed? There was that fast bay horse of Florian's to keep in mind, after all. Why would the murderer stay when he had the means to escape?

Suddenly she thought, but I am forgetting that Gervase de Gifford will soon be home! As relief flooded her, she wondered if it would be wrong of her to hand the whole sorry matter of the murder in the forest over to him.

I shall not abandon the business entirely, she decided. I shall carry out the action upon which I had already decided; in a day or so, I shall send for one of my nursing nuns and go to visit that poor young woman, Primevère. She will be calmer by then and more prepared to speak to someone other than her mother.

Having thus made up her mind on what she should do next, with considerable relief she went back to her work.

Two days later she had returned to her room after Nones and was wondering if now would be a good time to fetch either Sister Euphemia or Sister Caliste and ride over to Hadfeld when there was an abrupt knock on her door. It opened in response to her 'Come in!' and Josse stood before her.

He looked terrible. His face was lined and haggard and there were dark circles beneath his eyes. He carried his right arm awkwardly and she could see a linen bandage on his forearm.

There was not the slightest sign of his usual smile of greeting.

Her first reaction was a painfully forceful stab of guilt: I have sent him on a mission that has returned him to a state of intimacy with the woman he loves and now he has had to lose her all over again.

And it was all for nothing.

Before he could speak she had hurried around her table and, taking both his hands, she said, 'Josse, Florian of Southfrith is dead and Merlin's Tomb is closed. Forgive me, for the journey on which I sent you was unnecessary. Had we but waited, you need never have gone.'

He studied her for a few moments. His face was tanned from days spent riding out in the sun and his tunic, open at the neck, showed that the brown skin continued down across his chest; he's been riding out in the sun with few clothes, she thought before she could stop herself.

But his eyes were full of pain.

His hands, which had been limp in hers, suddenly squeezed. He said, with a curious formality that was never usually in his tone when he spoke to her, 'My lady Abbess, you have no scrying glass with which to predict the future. You asked me to do what at the time seemed the only possible thing that could be done to close the fraudulent tomb and willingly I accepted.' There was a brief pause, then, looking down, he muttered, 'Be consoled that, however I may be feeling now, I would not have missed the past couple of weeks for all the gold in the world.'

She felt tears in her eyes. She whispered, 'Oh, Josse,' then, before the emotion could make her add something she might later regret, she dropped his hands and, returning to the other side of her table, sat down heavily in her chair.

The best thing, she knew, would be to get going straight away on discussing what each of them had to report. The trouble was that neither she nor Josse seemed to know how to start.

Eventually it was he who broke the awkward silence. 'Florian of Southfrith is dead, you say?'

'Yes.' Briefly she told him the little that she could about the murder, adding that she had visited the young man's wife and spoken to his mother-in-law. 'It was she – her name's Melusine, she's a rich widow and a bit of a dragon – who came here and identified the body.' She went on to summarise what she had learned of Florian's background and circumstances.

Josse absorbed it all in silence, nodding occasionally. When she had finished, he said, 'I've met the mother-in-law. Well, I *saw* her, at any rate, that time I went to look for Florian at his house. So the young fool exaggerated his wealth in order to win his bride. Overspent, in debt and with an expensive wife, he must have been quite desperate for money.' He paused, wincing, and altered his position so that he was supporting his right arm in his left hand. She was about to make some comment – You're hurt! May we help? – but he did not give her the chance. 'So, when he found some old bones which by their very size looked strange and mystical, the idea of making some much-needed cash out of them must have come to him like a blessing from above. He created the tomb on the edge of the forest, not caring who he upset, and then all he had to do was stand there by the gate and take the coins pressed into his greedy hands by gullible pilgrims.'

'He's dead, Sir Josse,' she reminded him gently. 'Whatever he did wrong, he did not deserve to die out there in the forest.'

'Hmm.'

Josse, she thought, did not seem entirely convinced.

Something he had said returned to her. 'You appear to be in no doubt that the Merlin's Tomb near Hadfeld is a fake,' she said, trying to keep the sudden flare of hope out of her voice; how much simpler for the closure of the tomb to be universally accepted if it could be shown up to be nothing but a clever pretence! 'Does this mean that you have seen the magician's real burial place?'

He sighed. 'I have seen a place of great power which is known by the local people as Merlin's Tomb, aye. There is a great oak in the middle of a clearing in a forest and a vast granite slab from beneath which issues a healing spring. In those parts they tell how it was there that Merlin revealed the secrets of his magic powers to the woman that he loved and that she used the knowledge to pen him up and bind him to her for ever. He lies under a hawthorn tree, they say, and one such tree does indeed stand there close by the oak and the fountain.'

She felt an atavistic shiver run down her back. 'You saw where Merlin lies?' she whispered.

He smiled faintly. 'I saw where some say he lies,' he amended.

'But do you believe them?' she persisted; it seemed very important.

He shrugged. 'If I believed that Merlin was a real person then aye, I could accept that he was buried in that place, for I did in truth sense a great power there.'

'Then—' she began.

'But, my lady, remember that I also felt some force emanating from the great bones at Florian's site,' he said gently. Then, with another sigh: 'Perhaps I'm just gullible.'

'You're not gullible!' she protested.

Now his smile seemed to spring from genuine amusement. 'Thank you for that. But I think you may be being over-generous.'

She decided not to pursue that; she was quite sure he was speaking of something other than merely the matter of the two tombs. Oh, but he has endured so much! she thought, pity for him making her emotions churn. But it would be no kindness to do as she longed to do and express her deep sympathy and risk undermining him; she must, she well knew, stick to the practicalities.

She cleared her throat a couple of times and said, 'So, you made up your mind to return to us here at Hawkenlye and report that you had seen the true Merlin's Tomb over in the Breton forest, which meant that the place near Hadfeld must be nothing but a pretence?'

He hesitated. Then: 'Aye. Pretty much. I can't be entirely

certain, my lady, but then who could? I spoke long with Joanna's people over there – they're good people, speakers of the truth – and they refused to say unequivocally that their forest held the enchanter's bones. They' – his brow creased as he tried to find the words – 'they more or less said to me that this is what some people believe, and why that belief came to be, and then they left it to me to make up my own mind.'

'Nothing was definite, then?'

'No. But then, in matters of belief, is that not always so? We believe that Jesus is the son of God, came to earth, died and was resurrected, but there's no proof and so we can't say that it's definite.'

'It's in the Bible!' She heard the shock in her voice.

He smiled but did not speak.

And after a moment she thought, but he is right. Faith has nothing to do with reading things, or being told them. Faith is in the heart, not the head.

There was silence in her little room. Then, as the whirl of her thoughts finally dropped her gently back in the here and now, she realised that he was tired, dirty, perhaps in pain, probably hungry and thirsty and undoubtedly grieving. She said, 'I apologise, Sir Josse, for keeping you here talking for so long. Please, go and refresh yourself down with the monks in the Vale and, if necessary, ask Sister Euphemia or one of her nuns to look at that wound on your arm. When you are rested, come back and eat with us. Then I prescribe a good night's sleep.' Watching his sad eyes, she added hopefully, 'Things often look better in the morning.'

'Thank you, my lady,' he said courteously. 'I will do as you suggest.'

He turned to go but, at the door, stopped and looked back at her. 'What ought we to do next? About young Florian, I mean?'

'Sir Josse, *you* need do nothing, for you have done more

than enough already to help me in my concerns. Anyway' –
she tried to speak lightly – 'you have earned a good rest!'

'I don't want a rest,' he snapped back. Then, quietly,
'Forgive me, my lady. You meant well, I know. But I would
rather keep busy, if you don't mind.'

Her heart ached for him. Trying to sound brisk – for surely
now he really would break down if she offered him kindness
and sympathy – she said, 'Well, I plan to make another visit to
Florian's widow, Primevère. She is grieving, of course, and in
addition there seems to be some suggestion that she might be
unwell. I thought to take either Sister Euphemia or Sister
Caliste with me, then, if the young woman would agree to
being examined, help might be offered to heal whatever ails
her.'

He nodded. 'I see.'

'In addition, I feel that somehow it is important to discover,
if we can, just who is in charge of the Merlin's Tomb site now
that Florian is dead. Who, for example, gave the order to close
it? Who posted the guard at the entrance to turn would-be
visitors away?'

'Quite,' he said neutrally.

'I had been thinking of going this afternoon,' she went on,
'but it can just as well be tomorrow. Then, well rested after a
night's sleep, if you really want to you might accompany us?'

'Aye, I'll do that,' he said. Then, with a nod, he was gone.

She waited but he did not return. Presently Brother Micah
tapped at her door, bringing Sir Josse's apologies but he was
going to eat with the brethren down in the Vale, being too
weary to be very good company. He would present himself
tomorrow morning, Brother Micah went on, for the trip down
to Hadfeld.

He doesn't want to take the risk that I might question him
about Joanna, she thought. Poor Josse; I would not have

spoken of her until and unless he raised the subject, but he was not necessarily to know that.

A part of her felt terribly sad that he did not know her better than to realise it.

'Thank you, Brother Micah,' she said with a calmness she did not feel. 'Please send Sir Josse my best wishes and say I shall expect him early in the morning.'

Micah bowed his way out of her room.

Leaving Helewise – heart-sore and anxious for her old friend, deeply hurt that he chose not to be with her but to suffer alone – right back in the claustrophobic circle of her own thoughts.

## 17

Down in the Vale, Josse retired early to his usual place in the corner of the shelter but sleep was a long time coming.

He missed Joanna badly. He had spent so many nights with her curled up by his side and on most of them had slept the profoundly heavy and peaceful sleep that follows lovemaking. But it was not just her physical presence that he missed, important though that was; he also missed her lively mind, her sense of fun and, perhaps most of all, her mystery and her strong sense of power.

What a woman . . .

They had got into New Shoreham in good time the previous day, early enough to travel a fair distance before stopping to make camp for the night on the north face of the South Downs, in a shallow depression just below the summit of a line of hills overlooking the vale between the Downs and the ridges where the Great Forest began.

They had made a fire, eaten supper and then settled Meggie to sleep. Then, neither of them feeling ready for sleep themselves, Joanna had fuelled up the fire and they had sat there beside it, hand in hand, gazing out into the warm night.

'We are close to the Caburn,' Joanna said eventually, breaking a long silence.

'The Caburn . . .' He was sure he had heard the name but, preoccupied as he was, could not remember in what context he had heard it.

'Men built a fort there a long time ago,' she said dreamily. 'But it was used by humankind long before that. It's a place of power.'

'A place of power,' he repeated. 'Your people's sort of power?'

She shrugged. 'I don't know, but it all stems from the same source, and that is the Earth herself.' She leaned closer to him. 'In fact it's more *your* people,' she added.

He considered that for a moment and then, wonder dawning, began to think he might know what she was referring to.

It had been over a year ago, the previous February, when the Abbey had been stricken with the pestilence. Josse had been persuaded to use the Eye of Jerusalem, his late father's precious heirloom, and, reluctant to credit that there was any magical power in his bloodline, had been gently corrected by Joanna. There had been a woman, a forebear of his mother's, she had told him, who was recognised by her people as one of their Great Ones. He had not known exactly what that meant – still did not know now – but it sounded impressive.

'You refer, I believe, to this magical grand-dam of mine,' he said lightly.

'I do, and she was considerably further back in your ancestry than that.' There was no levity in Joanna's tone, he noted.

'Tell me?' he asked.

'Not much to tell,' she admitted. 'I only know that she was an ancestress on your mother's side, a native Briton, and that she lived close to here and tended the sacred fires on Mount Caburn.'

Josse tried to think what that might mean and failed. 'She was – she was pagan?'

'Of course. Six generations back, the new religion was by no means universally accepted in Britain.'

The new religion. She must mean Christianity. So she was

telling him that, not all that long ago, a woman of his blood had stood on the summit of a hill, very close to where he now sat, chanting incantations and feeding the sacred flame in the service of her gods.

For a moment an image appeared before him out of the darkness and the low flames of their own small fire suddenly seemed to grow immensely, searing up into the night sky in vivid hues of violet, purple and gold, while a tall woman in a pale robe, a circlet of silver around her head, cried aloud in a voice that sounded like singing.

He blinked and both woman and fire were gone.

Beside him Joanna laughed softly. 'If I'm right and you saw it too,' she murmured, 'then we just witnessed your grand-mother's great-great-grandmother going about her holy work.'

Slowly he shook his head, but more in wonder than in denial. Once, not so very long ago, he might have shied away from thinking about Joanna's strange power in his daughter's blood, never mind some equivalent force that came from his own forebears. But that was before he had spent this precious time in her company and grown to understand a little – just a little – of what she and her people truly were.

Now, far from being ashamed to think that his own blood contained elements of the same power, he was proud. Staring out in the darkness, silently he called out to that woman from so long ago, sending her his recognition, his blessings and his love. As if a warm arm had been slipped around him, he felt all three sentiments returned.

Soon after that they had made love – she, he was sure, also trying not to think that it might be for the last time – and settled down to sleep.

In the morning they had ridden back to Hawkenlye. She had slipped off the golden mare's back and silently handed the reins to him, for there was no place for a fine animal such as

Honey in Joanna's forest life and the mare was better off being useful at Hawkenlye. They had made their farewells brief – for Meggie's sake, they solemnly told each other – and he had watched as, with Meggie holding her mother's hand and twisting round so as to go on waving to him till the last possible moment, Joanna had set off along the track that led into the forest.

Then, his mind gone numb, he had returned to the Abbey.

Where now, with the sounds of the monks settling for the night all around him, he lay seeking respite in sleep from the grief of his loss.

Eventually he must have drifted off, only to wake with the dawn to the sound of Brother Saul muttering in his sleep.

With a sigh, he turned over on to his side and, to distract the natural drift of his thoughts, went back over everything that the Abbess had told him about Florian of Southfrith, his wife and his mother-in-law. Not that he could make himself care greatly, but then he had offered to go with the Abbess today and to give her what help he could in her noble attempt to find out who had killed the young man. The least he could do, he reasoned, was to try to appear interested. It would serve as a distraction, even if nothing else.

He presented himself outside her room after Tierce. The day was already hot and promised to become hotter; the sooner they began, the better.

He walked beside her across to the infirmary and waited while she sought out Sister Euphemia. There was a muttered conversation between the two women and at one point the infirmarer waved a hand to indicate the many empty beds. Then she called out to Sister Caliste, who appeared from a recess at the far end of the room. The infirmarer spoke to her, the young nun nodded eagerly, and then all three women came back to Josse.

Sister Caliste and Sister Euphemia were both looking at him with love and compassion in their eyes: God's boots, he thought, do they *all* know? But instantly he regretted the moment of anger. Kindness was, after all, not that common a commodity and a man should be grateful when offered it. He bowed briefly to the nuns.

'Both the Sisters will accompany us, Sir Josse,' the Abbess was saying, 'since neither has any pressing duties that require their presence here and both may be of assistance to Primevère, if indeed she is sick.'

'I shall be pleased of your company, Sisters,' he said gravely. 'Come, let us be on our way.'

But the infirmarer held back. 'The Abbess tells me you bear a wound, Sir Josse.' She nodded at the bandage on his right arm. 'May I tend it for you and see how it heals?'

He drew back his arm as if she had tried to grab hold of it. 'No you may not!' he cried. Too loudly and too forcibly; the three nuns were all staring at him.

But Joanna had wrapped that piece of linen around his arm; Joanna had stitched the wound after Meggie had bathed it and he knew, from the steady reduction in discomfort, that it was mending well. The sutures would have to be taken out some time but until then he didn't want anybody else to touch it, no matter how well-meaning they were.

He could not, of course, explain all that.

'I apologise for my rudeness.' He gave Sister Euphemia a curt bow. 'It's just that . . .' He stopped, at a loss.

But she gave him a loving smile and said quietly, 'It's all right. I understand.'

And he realised that there was no need for explanations after all.

Probably out of deference to Josse's feelings, they left Honey in the paddock. The Abbess rode the Abbey cob, Sister Caliste had the pony and Sister Euphemia was left with the mule which, before mounting, she had fixed with a very firm eye as if to say, now I'll have no nonsense from *you*. It must have worked for as they set out, Josse observed with a faint smile that he had never seen the mule behave better.

They rode along the track that circled the forest, staying in the shade of the trees whenever they could, and quite soon they came to the place where the road branched off south-east towards Hadfeld. Soon after that, the Abbess led the way through the gates into Florian's courtyard.

Josse noticed that the building work had progressed well since his previous visit. No doubt, he thought, because of that slim and rigid figure who habitually stood on the mounting block keeping an eye on proceedings. As she was doing this morning; today, she was dressed in a gown of violet silk whose tight, high waist accentuated her full breasts. She turned at the sound of their mounts' hooves and stared out at the quartet with imperiously raised eyebrows.

'Yes? Oh, it's you, Abbess Helewise. And – Sir Josse? That is your name, as I recall?'

'Aye.'

'And here is Sister Caliste' – the Abbess indicated the younger nun – 'and this is my infirmarer, Sister Euphemia.'

Primevère's dark blue eyes turned to the infirmarer and the hint of a smile quirked at the corner of her mouth. 'And to what do I owe the pleasure of this visit?'

'When we came to see you a few days ago, it was to bring the dreadful news that you had lost your husband,' the Abbess said gently. 'In addition to having to bear your grief, you were already sick and in bed. I have come, with these my trusted companions, to see how you are.'

There was a flash of something in Primevère's eyes, almost too brief to catch, but Josse, who was best positioned to see, thought that the swift expression looked like impatience, as if the young woman regretted having to be distracted from the task that currently absorbed her while she dealt with this nuisance that had just arrived in her courtyard.

But then she smiled widely and, stepping carefully down from her mounting block, holding her skirt high to avoid treading on it, she approached the Abbess and said, 'How very kind. Please, all of you, come into the hall and I will send for refreshments. It is a very hot day, is it not? Me, I do feel the heat so badly – it makes me feel weak and nauseous. As I am now well, as you will have observed, I have in fact attributed my previous indisposition to nothing other than too much sunshine.'

The four of them dismounted and Primevère clapped her hands to summon a groom. The lad – he was small and had the narrow chest and pale skin that spoke of malnutrition – took the reins of the horses, the pony and the mule and, with one or two apprehensive glances at Horace, led them off to the stables.

Josse hurried after him: 'He's a big horse but, treated with kindness, he's very well-mannered,' he reassured the boy. But his remark was met with a look of fear, swiftly replaced by stony-faced apathy.

All is not happy here, Josse thought. The lad is afraid, and here is the mistress, a very recent widow, who far from welcoming her well-wishers, seems almost irritated by their presence . . . He resolved to keep his eyes open and his senses alert.

Primevère led the way up the steps into the cool hall, where the woman in black – Melusine, Josse recalled; that was what the Abbess said she was called – sat on a bench under an open window. She was sewing some piece of embroidery in gloriously rich colours and talking in abrupt and rather curt tones to a man standing beside her.

She looked up as her daughter led the four visitors towards

her. 'Abbess Helewise,' she said, nodding up at the Abbess, 'and you I recognise . . .' Her eyes had swivelled to Josse and she was frowning. 'You came before, *non?*'

'Aye,' Josse said.

For a moment Melusine looked almost anxious. Then her face cleared and she said with evident relief, 'But of course, sir knight, you have come to offer your condolences on the death of my son-in-law! *N'est-ce pas?*'

Primevère said something very swiftly in French. As far as Josse could tell, for the young woman had sat down close to her mother and spoke very softly so that he could barely pick up the words, she was telling her that the Hawkenlye party had come to see how she was faring in her grief.

'Ah, but how very kind!' Melusine said. 'The charity of the sisters, is it not famous far and wide?'

The man at her side spoke for the first time. 'Indeed,' he said smoothly, 'and of all religious foundations, the reputation of Hawkenlye and its good people is the most highly esteemed of all.'

Josse turned to him, taking in the man's air of strength contained within an elegant and well-dressed body; the man's garments simply shouted *expensive*, from the closely fitting tunic of very fine wool to the soft leather boots and the hint of scarlet-died fur at the ends of the wide sleeves. Feeling Josse's intent eyes, the man met them and, smiling widely, said, 'I am Ranulf of Crowbergh, family friend to Florian and his household.' Josse might have been mistaken but he thought he heard a sudden intake of breath from the Abbess, standing close beside him. 'Sir Josse—?'

'Josse d'Acquin.' Josse gave a formal bow.

'Sir Josse.' Ranulf of Crowbergh returned it.

Primevère had moved across to and through an arched doorway at the far end of the room and her voice could be heard giving instructions to whoever was working there. She returned and, still the epitome of good manners, Ranulf of Crowbergh made a show of pulling up a seat for her and settling her upon it.

Primevère, after a swift look up at him, gave a little cough and said, 'You are most kind to concern yourself, my lady Abbess, over my grief and my sickness. The former nobody can help me with, although *Maman* assures me it is but a matter of time.' She gave a little sigh. 'As to my sickness, as I said, it was a simple matter of the heat. Now, why, you can see for yourselves that I am well!' She beamed around at her four guests and indeed, Josse thought, she looked the picture of health, from her glossy dark hair, shining like the coat of a well-groomed horse, to the clear eyes and the faint flush of pink in her cheeks.

'You were sick enough to be in your bed when last we saw you,' the Abbess reminded her kindly. 'And you were very pale; as I said, I was concerned for your health, which is why I brought with me our two nursing nuns here. Would you not like to speak privately to Sister Euphemia, or perhaps Sister Caliste, to discuss your—'

'No,' said Primevère very firmly. Then, with an apologetic laugh, 'You are so kind, *mes soeurs*, to have made the journey, but it is all for nothing for, as you see, today I am no longer the least bit pale! It is the heat, nothing but that, which occasionally makes me sick. As I told you just now, it does not suit me, yet I am forced to spend much time outside under the sun because, with no husband to bear the burden, it is I alone who must ensure that the builders do as they are told and do not try to take advantage of a poor, helpless widow.' She cast her eyes down and put a hand to her eyes as if wiping a tear.

Josse, on whom not one nuance of the speech was lost, reflected that the place where Primevère usually stood was, as he had noticed on his first visit, the one place in the courtyard that was *not* in the sun. But, bearing in mind all that this young woman was having to cope with, it would have been churlish to mention it.

Ranulf of Crowbergh was speaking, saying something about helping out Florian's widow and her mother whenever he could but, in addition, having the demands of his own household to see to. 'And, the dear Lord knows, it always seems that there are just not enough hours in the day for all that has to be done!'

A servant arrived with a jug of ale, so cold that droplets of water were condensing on its sides. He poured out mugs for the visitors and, after a swift enquiry, one for Ranulf of Crowbergh as well. The ale, Josse discovered, was excellent, light but very refreshing. He drank almost the entire contents of his mug and then, feeling awkward, held it in such a way that his hostess could not see how much had gone. She, however, watched him with observant eyes and gave him a little smile.

Neither the infirmarer nor Sister Caliste had spoken. Both stood a respectful couple of paces behind their Abbess. They too, Josse knew, had observant eyes. He wondered what impressions they were gaining of Florian's household.

Melusine was getting to her feet. A glance passed between her and her daughter and Primevère gave an almost imperceptible nod. We are about to be very courteously sent on our way, Josse thought. Putting down his now empty mug, he said, addressing Primevère, 'My lady, one thing puzzles us. We have heard that Merlin's Tomb is now closed and that visitors are being turned away.'

'Ah, I expect some of them have gone instead to Hawkenlye,' Primevère said with an understanding nod.

Neither confirming nor denying that, Josse went on, 'We are asking ourselves who, in the absence of your late husband, has made and implemented the decision to shut down the site? It had proved extremely popular, I am given to understand, and was clearly fulfilling a need for the people in these difficult times. Why, then, close it?' He looked from Primevère to her mother, then, finally, at Ranulf.

Whom he caught in what appeared to be an intense exchange of glances with Primevère. 'It was my decision, naturally,' she said calmly after a moment. 'The tomb was Florian's project and I had nothing whatsoever to do with it. It is no task for a woman and although it is possible that I might have engaged someone to run the place – why, my neighbour here has offered his help' – she looked up and gave Ranulf a smile – 'I do not care to go on being associated with it.' Meeting Josse's eyes she said, with a moving catch in her voice, 'Sir Josse, how could I possibly wish to take over a matter that was the cause of my beloved husband's death?'

She made a good point, he conceded, and he made her a swift bow in acknowledgement. 'I quite understand,' he murmured.

But I'll wager, he thought, that you have no such qualms over spending the vast amounts of money that the tomb has brought you.

The Abbess had also put down her mug. 'We must be going,' she said. 'But remember, please, that we are not far away. If, Primevère, you continue to be troubled by the heat, come and see us and I am quite sure that my infirmarer will be able to prescribe a tonic.'

'Thank you, you're most kind,' Primevère said. 'Now, let me see you on your way.'

She got up from her seat and, stepping forward, raised her chin and preceded the party out of the hall.

The groom was waiting in the courtyard with the horses and the Abbess, Josse and the two nuns quickly mounted. Primevère bade them farewell and, just as they rode off, Josse saw Ranulf of Crowbergh hurrying round to the stables. They had gone only a short way up the road when there was the sound of hooves from behind them and he trotted up to join them.

'I too must be about my work,' he said to the party in general, 'back to home, hearth and the bosom of the family, you know!'

'Indeed,' said the Abbess politely.

Then, surprisingly, Sister Euphemia spoke up. 'My lady,' she said to the Abbess, 'may I make a request?'

The Abbess looked surprised. 'Of course, Sister. What is it?'

'I ought to have asked the lady back there' – she jerked her head back towards the house they had just left – 'but somehow, what with her very recent bereavement, I didn't like to. I would so love to see for myself these bones we've been hearing so much about. May I ask you, sir' – she turned eager eyes to Ranulf – 'if you think it would be all right for us to make a detour to Merlin's Tomb before we return to Hawkenlye?'

Josse, wondering what was behind the request, studied Ranulf as he thought about it. The man seemed doubtful, which could, Josse acknowledged, be for a very good reason, if he had guessed that Florian's site in the forest was a fake. Any decent man would do his best to protect his dead neighbour's widow from such harmful gossip about her late husband. And on the face of it Ranulf of Crowbergh did indeed appear to be a decent man . . .

But then Ranulf's face cleared and he smiled. 'Of course it will be all right! Wait here – I will ride back and request to borrow the keys so that I may unfasten the chains. We can't have you shinning up over the fences, Sister!' And he gave her what was almost a flirtatious wink.

As he hurried back to the house, the Abbess was eyeing Sister Euphemia. 'Why do you want to see the tomb, Sister?' she asked.

The infirmarer shrugged. 'I can't really say, my lady. Just a feeling I have . . .' She didn't elaborate.

Josse, recalling those observant eyes, suddenly felt sure that the wise infirmarer, with her vast experience of people, had spotted something that the rest of them had missed. He spoke up, addressing the Abbess: 'My lady, I too would dearly like another look at those bones,' he said, 'especially since it's apparent that it will likely be the last chance for any of us to do so.'

'Although I too must confess to a certain curiosity concerning this place about which we have heard so much,' the Abbess said, frowning, 'we really should get back to Hawkenlye.'

'It's not far and it won't take long,' Josse said persuasively.

The Abbess smiled thinly. 'Very well. Since Sir Ranulf has already hurried off to see about accommodating your request, Sister Euphemia, I suppose that it would be discourteous now to say we have changed out minds and do not wish to visit the tomb after all.'

They sat and waited in a rather stony silence for Ranulf to return; Sister Euphemia caught Josse's eye and mouthed, 'Thank you.'

Presently Ranulf rejoined them and, still acting as if this were a cheery midsummer outing, led the way up to the forest fringes and along the track that led to Merlin's Tomb.

One guard remained, a yellow-haired youth whose thin shoulders suggested he was hardly up to the job. He was on duty at the gate in the outer fence, where presumably his orders were to turn away any last hopefuls, and he slumped in a half-crouch with his back against a post. Seeing and obviously recognising who was leading the approaching group, he instantly straightened up, brushing at his tunic and trying to kick the mug from which he had just been drinking away into the grass. 'Sir!' he hailed Ranulf. 'All quiet, sir!'

'Good, good,' Ranulf purred. 'I will pass on the news. Now,

man, these good people wish to view the bones, so kindly open up' – he threw down the keys – 'and admit us.'

The guard leapt to do as he was ordered, opening the first gate and then hurrying ahead of them down the path to unfasten the second, higher barrier. As they drew level with him he offered to hold their mounts while they went on into the clearing.

They dismounted and Ranulf of Crowbergh led them across the short turf to the open scar of the tomb. Then, stepping away, he waved a hand as if in invitation and all four of them approached.

Like a punch in the chest, Josse felt again the power of those huge bones. It was none the weaker for being experienced a second time; if anything, it was stronger. But then I am not the man I was last time I stood here, he thought. I have spent two weeks with a woman of the forest and some of her beliefs and her spirit – quite a lot of her spirit – seems to have rubbed off on me.

To distract his thoughts from her, he watched the three nuns as they looked down into the grave. The Abbess was staring unblinking at the skull, as if trying to imagine what the features had looked like in life; Sister Caliste, very obviously distressed, was praying; Sister Euphemia, her face impassive, studied the bones, shot a quick look at Josse, then slowly walked away.

After a few moments the Abbess, Sister Caliste and Josse followed the infirmarer back to the horses and, thanking Ranulf for granting Sister Euphemia's request, the Abbess mounted the cob and set off back up the path. At the place where it met the bigger track, she said, 'Our way is to the left so here we will bid you farewell, Sir Ranulf.'

He bowed. 'It has been a pleasure, my lady.'

'We will keep the lady Primevère informed as to progress into finding out who murdered her husband,' Josse said. Then, watching Ranulf, 'The sheriff of Tonbridge will be returning home soon and he will be keen to apprehend whoever robbed and killed Florian.'

Ranulf absorbed this, the smile still on his face turning now slightly puzzled. 'But I thought it was agreed that some passing thief saw the opportunity and, attacking poor Florian in the darkness, made off with both money and horse?' He laughed, shaking his head. 'The sheriff is a good man, I have no doubt, but even he cannot work miracles. Much as I hate to say it, I do not believe that the man who slew Florian will ever be found. Why, he's probably across the narrow seas by now and *hundreds* of miles away!'

Josse did not reply immediately; he noticed that his failure to agree seemed to be bothering Ranulf. Finally he said easily, 'No doubt you are right. Now, we must be on our way – farewell!'

He felt Ranulf of Crowbergh's eyes on his back as the little party rode away. It was not, he discovered, a comfortable sensation.

'Sir Josse?' the Abbess said.

'My lady?'

'It may well be of no importance,' she said carefully, 'but when Primevère spoke to me of her neighbour before I had met him, I believe that she implied he was older than he is.'

'Indeed?' He could not see why it should matter and the Abbess did not seem all that sure of herself. 'In what context did she make this attempt to mislead you?'

'Oh, I would not put it as strongly as that!' the Abbess said. 'It was just a vague feeling and the mistake may well have been mine.' She bit her lip. 'She referred to him as the head of a worthy household and spoke of fussy old servants, both of which gave the impression of a family headed by an elderly couple.' She made a wry face. 'Or so I believed. It seems I was misled.'

'And why should Primevère have wished to mislead you, my lady?'

Her frown deepened. 'I don't know . . .'

He waited but she said no more.

Nobody spoke again until they were nearing Hawkenlye Abbey. Then Sister Euphemia, who had been lagging behind apparently deep in her own thoughts, kicked her heels into the mule's sides and, drawing level with the Abbess and Josse, said, 'My lady, about those bones.'

'Yes, Sister Euphemia?' The Abbess was looking at her with an indulgent smile. 'Worth the detour, do you think?'

'Oh, yes, my lady,' the infirmarer said.

She paused. Then, surprising Josse with the firm conviction behind her words, stated baldly, 'Whoever else they may or may not belong to, those are not the bones of Merlin.'

'So Sir Josse also believes, Sister, having been shown a mysterious site in Brittany which appears to have a better claim to be Merlin's burial place. But—'

'Forgive me for interrupting, my lady, but that's not the point.' The infirmarer's face was flushed. 'Those aren't any man's bones. For all their size, I know I'm right because in this instance I know what I'm talking about.' She paused. Then she said, 'Those are the bones of a woman.'

# 18

'Sister Euphemia, how can you possibly be so sure?' the Abbess demanded.

They were back in the Abbess's room, she herself seated behind her table, the infirmarer, Josse and Sister Caliste standing in a row before her.

Sister Euphemia did not seem at all put out by her superior's impatient question. 'I have long worked as a healer, my lady, as you well know,' she replied calmly. 'Before I entered Hawkenlye, I was a midwife. I have laid out my fair share of dead bodies and sometimes those I prepared for their graves had been long dead. I know full well the differences between the skeletons of a man and a woman. There are two main things to look for,' she went on eagerly, 'first, the skull, where normally the ridges above the eyes are much more pronounced in a man than in a woman.'

'The skull had quite large brow ridges,' the Abbess remarked.

'Aye, my lady, but the woman in that grave must have been a veritable giantess and that doesn't surprise me. It's the other difference that makes me so sure.'

'And that is?' demanded the Abbess.

'The pelvis, my lady. It's one shape in a man, quite another in a woman. Stands to reason, really, when you keep in mind that a woman's designed to bear children. You need a good, wide opening between the bones to let a baby pass out and, believe me, I've seen what problems can crop up when a woman's too narrow down there. Why, sometimes—'

'Thank you, Sister,' murmured the Abbess.

'Sorry, my lady.'

'That's quite all right.'

There was a small silence. Then the Abbess said, 'So you are in absolutely no doubt that the skeleton in Merlin's Grave is female?'

'None whatsoever.'

Another silence, again broken by the Abbess, who, addressing the room in general, asked, 'Has anyone else a relevant observation to report?'

Josse held his peace. He believed he had noticed several things, but it would be interesting to see if either of the nuns had anything to offer.

Sister Caliste, flushing slightly, said, 'I have, my lady.'

'Go on, Sister.'

'I – oh, I'm probably wrong, but I thought that the lady Primevère was pregnant.'

'So did I,' said the infirmarer.

'Goodness!' the Abbess exclaimed. 'What grounds have either of you for your supposition?'

Sister Euphemia glanced at Sister Caliste and then, with an apologetic smile at her junior, spoke. 'You said that when you saw her the first time, she lay abed and pale, although the rest of her was a picture of health.'

'That's right, I did,' the Abbess agreed. 'I went back to Hadfeld with her mother after Melusine had identified Florian's body and together we went up to Primevère's bedchamber.'

'Could she not have taken to her bed out of grief?' Josse asked. 'It would also account for looking so pale.'

'But she was in bed and pale *before* she knew he was dead and, although it was true that he had not been home for several days, this was apparently not unusual and, according to her mother, Primevère was not unduly worried,' the Abbess said. 'I did wonder if she had deliberately made herself look pale, perhaps by dabbing flour into her cheeks, although why she should do such a thing I cannot say.'

'Such an appearance – pale face but otherwise a veritable glow of well-being – is typical of pregnant women,' the infirmarer assured them. 'A woman can be healthy as you like but still affected by sickness, usually in the morning although sometimes at other times; it depends on the woman. My guess, my lady, is that the first time you met young Primevère, she had the radiance of pregnancy but it was marred by her having just brought up her dinner.'

'It seems a slim fact on which to say with certainty that the lady is pregnant,' the Abbess protested.

'She is very full in the breasts,' Sister Caliste put in.

'Aye, and more so than when first I saw her almost three weeks back,' Josse added.

He smiled as, outnumbered, the Abbess sat back and threw up her hands. 'Very well!' she cried. 'Primevère is pregnant; I accept what you all urge me to believe. It does but increase my pity for the poor girl, since she must face the daunting prospect of bringing a fatherless child into the world . . .' She broke off, frowning.

'My lady?' Josse said.

She shook her head. 'It's nothing. Now,' she got to her feet, 'Sister Euphemia, Sister Caliste, thank you for accompanying me today and for your most valuable contributions. Please, now go about your duties and I am sorry to have kept you from them for so long.'

She waited until the two nuns' footsteps had faded away. Then, nodding to Josse to close the door, she said, 'So we must conclude that Florian of Southfrith committed a deliberate fraud in claiming that the bones that he found and planted in the forest were those of Merlin; it was nothing but a way to earn money.'

'I believe that is so,' Josse agreed. 'Were the young man not dead, he would have much to answer for before the sheriff.'

'When will Gervase de Gifford return?' she asked.

'I cannot say, my lady. He has had the time even by now to have visited Nantes and be well on the way home, especially if his ship had the same favourable wind which we – which I enjoyed.'

*We*, he thought. Joanna, Meggie and me.

He firmly closed his mind on that.

She had noticed; he knew she had. But, bless her for her tact, she did not pick it up. 'Will he call here on his way home to Tonbridge, think you?' she asked instead.

'He might, although I imagine that Sabin will be very anxious to get back to her old grandfather.'

'Then, Sir Josse, we can but wait for him and then pass the burden of resolving this sorry business of the shrine over to him. Whether he will feel any action is necessary, the originator of the fraudulent shrine being dead, your guess is as good as mine.'

'He may well feel that there is little point,' Josse said, 'unless he feels the matter of the shrine is relevant to the robbery and Florian's murder, for that is a crime whose perpetrator he will for certain wish to bring to justice.'

'Oh, Sir Josse, but of course! Is there, do you think, any hope that the murderer will be caught?'

'I don't know,' he admitted. It would have been unfair to add that he didn't much care.

She was watching him. 'A young man is dead,' she said gently. 'He may have been greedy and unscrupulous, but he did not deserve to die at another's hands. For myself, I believe we must pass on to Gervase de Gifford all that we know and have thought concerning who could have wanted Florian dead.'

'You are right, my lady,' he conceded with a sigh. 'When I get the chance, that is exactly what I shall do.'

Leaving the Abbess's room, he set off aimlessly in the direction of the Vale. But it was as yet only mid-afternoon; there were hours to go till bedtime and little down there to distract him. With visitors still a rarity, even the monks were reduced to mending things that weren't really broken and endlessly sweeping dust off paths that nobody trod.

I'll ride down to Tonbridge, he thought suddenly. I'll see if Gervase is back and if so, maybe he'll offer me supper while we discuss our journeys. If not, I'll drop in on Goody Anne and see what tavern fare is on offer this evening.

Brightening at the prospect – not much, but even a little was a help – he turned and headed for the stables. Sister Martha greeted him with a kindly smile and, despite his protests that there was no need for her to stop what she was doing since he could easily prepare his horse himself, had Horace tacked up and ready within moments.

Thanking her, he set off at a smart pace and was soon taking the turning down the hill that led to Tonbridge.

He knew Gervase was back even before he rode up to the door from the sheer amount of noise emanating from the house. There were voices – Sabin's and the thin, reedy tones of old Benoît – and a shout of laughter from Gervase. It would be good, Josse thought, to be among happy people.

A young lad rushed up to take his horse, giving him a shy smile of welcome, and Josse strode up the steps and into the house.

The old grandfather was sitting in his accustomed place on the bench by the hearth and Sabin sat beside him, holding both his hands and talking away very rapidly in her own tongue. Benoît was nodding and smiling, as if whatever she was telling him was good to hear. Gervase stood relaxed, a mug of wine in his hand which he was using to make occasional gestures as he backed up some remark of Sabin's. He has come on in his knowledge and use of his bride-to-be's language while they have been away, Josse thought; it was no surprise, for Gervase was a quick-witted and intelligent man.

It was Benoît who noticed Josse first. Hearing some small movement, he turned his cloudy eyes in the direction of the door and said, 'There's someone there!'

Sabin and Gervase turned, saw Josse and both rushed to greet him. He was hugged and kissed by Sabin, had his hand shaken and his back slapped by Gervase, and was then escorted to a seat beside Benoît and given a mug of the excellent wine. Benoît put his face right up against Josse's and said, 'Why, it's that fellow, what's-his-name!'

'How long have you two been back?' Josse asked Gervase when he could get a word in.

'We rode up from the coast and arrived soon after noon,' Gervase said. 'We looked out for you in Dinan, hoping to take ship home to England with you, but there was neither sign nor word of you.'

'No. We – er, we came back by another route.' He frowned at Gervase who, understanding, gave a swift nod. 'We'll speak of it later,' Josse muttered to him, and again he nodded.

'Did you find the proof that you went searching for?' Sabin asked.

'Aye, I suppose so, although it is irrelevant now.' He hesitated. Was it all right to speak of this before Sabin and the old fellow? Well, she was about to be the sheriff's wife and Benoît his father-in-law; they'd have to get used to violence, robbery and murder sooner or later. 'The man behind the tomb out at Hadfeld is dead,' he said baldly.

'How did he die?' Gervase asked.

Josse gave a thin smile. 'Not from natural causes, that's for sure. He was robbed and killed late one night on his way home from the tomb.'

Sabin was watching, her eyes wide. Benoît was muttering to himself about men not being safe even in their own beds; he did not seem to have entirely understood.

'Any idea who might have killed him?' Gervase asked. 'The motive was robbery, presumably?'

Briefly Josse related the story, including details of yesterday's visit to the young widow at Hadfeld. When he had finished, Gervase demanded, 'Who is this supportive and avuncular neighbour?'

'Ranulf of Crowbergh.'

The name was clearly familiar to Gervase. 'I see,' he said slowly.

'You know the man?'

'I know of him,' Gervase replied.

'You do not like him,' Sabin put in. 'I can tell from your voice.'

Gervase smiled at her. 'I wouldn't say that, although I do have reason to be suspicious of him.' He frowned. 'There may well be no justification for my suspicion, however, for as I say I have not met him and what I was told was hearsay, indeed little more than taproom gossip. It was never proved.'

Josse's curiosity was aroused. 'What was not proved?'

Gervase paused as if considering whether he would be right to repeat the rumour. Eventually he said, 'Try not to let this cloud your judgement, Josse, but for one thing, the image of Ranulf of Crowbergh as a contented family man is not quite right. He is a childless widower.'

'Ah!' One or two images that had puzzled Josse during the morning's visit now seemed rather clearer. 'When did his wife die and what happened to her?'

'She died late last autumn. Apparently she slipped and fell on a frosty path and cracked her skull against a stone water trough.'

'But?' There had to be a *but*.

'Oh, it's very likely that was exactly what happened,' Gervase said. 'Nobody saw but the path was certainly icy, she had good reason to be walking along it, and it appeared that the fatal wound on her head was made by the corner of the trough.'

'Why, then, the rumours?' Sabin demanded. 'The poor man surely had enough to bear, losing his wife so suddenly and in such a manner.'

'True, my love,' Gervase said, 'and I would agree with you and condemn such loose talk were it not for two things. One, Ranulf now has his wife's fortune at his disposal in addition to his own. Two, there is a suggestion – quite a strong one – that he held back from giving the help that might have saved her. She was unconscious and she bled to death and there is nobody to corroborate Ranulf's claim to have been away from home when the accident happened. His horse was in the stable and he said he was out on foot with his hawk, yet, unusually for him for they say that he and his falcon are an efficient pair, he returned home empty handed.'

'But if he was using his hunting expedition to explain his absence then surely he would have made quite sure he came home with a good catch!' Sabin protested. 'He must have foreseen that people would doubt him.'

'Perhaps,' Gervase said.

'And what possible reason could he have for wanting his wife out of the way?' she went on, quite cross now on this innocent stranger's behalf.

But Gervase and Josse exchanged a look; Gervase, Josse thought, could furnish a reason as well as he could himself.

Sabin urged Josse to stay to supper and, after some token resistance, he accepted. Smells had been wafting through from the kitchen for some time now and his stomach was rumbling loudly enough for the others to hear. Gervase had always kept a good table; with Sabin in residence, the quality of the cuisine had soared up to first class.

Before they sat down to eat, Gervase suggested to Josse that they go outside to check that Horace was being well tended; it was a totally unnecessary expedition but Gervase, Josse guessed, wished to question him in private about his return journey.

Out in the evening cool of the courtyard, Gervase said, 'Was it to avoid Joanna's accuser that you did not sail from Dinan?'

'Aye.'

'Was there – oh, this is difficult, Josse, but was he justified in believing Joanna was behind the death of her husband?'

'No,' Josse said firmly. He knew Gervase wanted him to elaborate but he wasn't going to.

Gervase let out an exasperated sigh. 'You're as bad as Sabin,' he grumbled. 'She admitted that Joanna revealed quite a lot about her past that night in then inn at Dinan, but she said it was in confidence and totally refused to tell me anything.'

Josse sensed that it was not mere curiosity that made Gervase so keen to know. He was, after all, a man of the law. Taking pity on him, he said, 'Gervase, Joanna was wed against her will to a cruel old man who made her life a misery. She wanted him dead – of course she did! – and she consoled herself by envisaging ways in which he might die. That does not amount to murder any more than does wishing someone dead.'

'The wish might be the more potent weapon, when we speak of a woman such as Joanna,' Gervase muttered.

'Aye, but back then she hadn't come into her full power. And since when was anyone accused of murder simply for wishing to be rid of someone they loathed? Great heavens, most of us would be on trial sooner or later if that were the case.'

There was a silence. Then Gervase said, 'You're right, of course, Josse. So, go on with your tale. What happened when we left Dinan?'

'Joanna's brother-in-law – a man named Césaire de Lehon – set someone to follow us and the man tried to kill us on our way back from the Brocéliande.'

'Good God! You weren't hurt?'

'No.' Josse glanced down quickly to ensure his sleeve covered the bandage; there was no need to mention his wound to Gervase and for some reason he felt compelled to minimise the drama. 'Joanna somehow sensed his approach and we were able to fight him off.'

'Did you kill him?'

'I? No. But I am almost sure that he is dead.'

'Did Joanna kill him, then?' Gervase's voice had dropped to a whisper.

'No, no.' Josse waved away the suggestion. 'We – er, we had help. From one of the forest people over there. I believe it – I believe he had been following us, protecting us. He came to our aid when we were in danger.'

Sensing that Josse did not want to say more, Gervase tactfully ceased his questioning on the matter. Instead he said, 'So you set sail from another port?'

'Aye, St Cast. We were lucky and picked up a small, light craft that utilised every breath of a strong south-westerly and got us home as fast as flying.'

'And after that—' Again, Gervase stopped. Josse, who did not want to think about *after that* any more than he did about the attack in the forest, was grateful.

Josse broke the small silence. 'What will you do about the death of Florian?' he asked without much interest. 'Will you go along with what everybody else seems to think and decide that, with the killer very likely miles away by now, there's little point in doing anything?'

'Josse, I hope you know me better than that.' There was a mild reproof in Gervase's voice. 'Tomorrow I will visit the widow – what is her name?'

'Primevère. She's extremely lovely, pretty tough and she's pregnant.'

'Ah. And just bereaved, poor soul. I will tread carefully with my enquiries and try not to upset her.'

'Her grief comes and goes,' Josse said bluntly. 'It may sound cruel, but I'll wager she may well lament the loss of the money that her husband was bringing in rather more than that of the man himself.'

'It does sound cruel,' Gervase agreed. 'You should not—' But he bit back whatever reprimand he was about to issue, instead clapping a hand on Josse's shoulder. 'Come and eat, my friend,' he said. 'Sabin has done wonders for the fare on offer in my house and we have some delicious French wine. Then, if you wish, we will make up a bed for you and you shall stay the night.'

'Thank you,' Josse said. 'The food and the drink I accept with pleasure but if you will excuse me, I shall ride back to the Abbey later. I have,' he finished with a deep sigh, 'much on my mind and a ride in the cool night air will do me good.'

The meal lived up entirely to expectations and, for the time that Josse sat at Gervase's table, watching the sheriff's benevolent smile as he listened to Sabin chattering away happily about their forthcoming wedding, some of the cheerfulness rubbed off on him and he felt his spirits lift. In order to keep Sabin talking – she had an entertaining way with her – Josse asked about the visit to her former mistress in Nantes.

'The Duchess looked well,' Sabin replied, 'and there was no sign that the malady is accelerating in its progress through her poor body. When I explained my plans, she did not protest overmuch that she must lose me. Us, I should say,' she corrected herself, glancing at Benoît. 'Then I asked if I might present Gervase to her and he quite won her over with his charms!' She laughed delightedly.

'You exaggerate, sweetheart,' Gervase protested.

'Oh, no I don't,' Sabin flashed back. 'Anyway, she said she was not a woman to stand in the way of love and she gave us her blessing.'

'She has found another to help her in her sickness?' Josse asked.

'Yes,' Sabin answered. 'I was able to reassure myself that Grandfather and I leave her in good hands.'

'And now I have my beloved books and equipment with me once more!' Benoît put in with a cackle. Turning his all but blind eyes towards Josse, he added, 'The books, I admit, are nowadays of more use to Sabin than to me and they will be hers entirely one day. But I still have skill in my hands and my sense of smell is as sharp as ever; I can be of use here, even in my infirmity.'

'You can, Grandfather,' Sabin assured him affectionately. 'And I still have much to learn from you.'

They will be happy, Gervase and his bride, Josse thought. Even the presence of a blind and often crotchety old man under Gervase's roof did not appear to be a drawback and, indeed, Gervase seemed genuinely fond of the old boy. But, pleased for his friend and his bride though he was, the contemplation of others' marital bliss was a difficult one for him to bear just then.

He took his leave when the last jug of wine was empty. Benoît bade him farewell from where he sat; Gervase and Sabin went out into the courtyard to see him on his way.

'I will call at Hawkenlye after going to see Primevère tomorrow,' Gervase said.

'We will expect you,' Josse replied.

He swung up into the saddle and Horace took one or two steps towards the gateway. 'Ride safely,' Sabin said.

Expressing his thanks with a bow, Josse was about to depart. But then, perhaps prompted by all the empty hours of tomorrow with nothing much to fill them and so distract his thoughts, he looked down at Gervase and said gruffly, 'I don't mind coming with you to see Primevère if you like.' Struck with the idea that the offer needed explanation, he said, 'The Abbess Helewise and I have discussed Florian's murder at some length and it might help were I to pass on our thoughts to you as we ride.'

Gervase, good friend that he was, seemed to pick up more than Josse's words said. 'Nothing I'd like better, Josse.' He gave an encouraging smile. 'I'll ride along by the Abbey and collect you.'

Josse nodded briefly, then wished them both goodnight and, the familiar ache for Joanna already returning, rode off into the darkness.

# 19

Helewise knew that she could no longer put off sharing her suspicions with Josse. Early the next day she sent one of the nuns to seek him out down in the Vale and, very shortly after the summons, he tapped at her door and entered her room.

His face was grey beneath the suntan and his eyes looked sunken and dull, the lids slightly puffy. He said, his tone unenthusiastic, 'My lady Abbess? You sent for me?'

She longed to speak of the subject that just had to be uppermost in both their minds but she held back. We are old friends and have deep affection for each other, she told herself. If he wants to ease his pain by sharing it with me, he will. All the time he chooses to keep it to himself, I cannot say a word.

Although it grieved her, she made herself smile and said, 'Yes, Sir Josse. I am uneasy in my mind about several things concerning our visit yesterday to Primevère and I hoped you might be willing to discuss them with me.'

'I am at your disposal,' he said expressionlessly. Then, a very small amount of enthusiasm entering his voice, 'That is, until Gervase arrives, for I have offered to go with him to Hadfeld today.'

'I see.' That's good, she thought; he will at least have something positive to occupy him. 'Then before he collects you, let us walk outside in the sunshine while we talk,' she suggested, getting to her feet; the prospect of spending any time with this new, sad Josse within the confines of a small room was nothing short of awful.

She led the way across the cloister, around the end of the infirmary and towards the rear gate. Passing it on their left, they walked on, turned right when they met the far wall of the Abbey and, a little way along it, settled on a stone bench overlooking Sister Tiphaine's herb garden. There, after a few moments' contemplation of the sweet plant smells encouraged by the sunshine, she spoke.

'Primevère did not wish it to be known that she is pregnant,' she said. 'She excused the pallor and the nausea by saying that the heat did not agree with her.'

'Aye, I noticed that, too,' he said, a faint stirring of interest in his voice. 'For all that she said she was affected by standing outside in the sunshine watching the workmen, her vantage point on the mounting block is in fact in the shade. And people as dark as she, I have observed, tolerate the heat better than their fair-haired and light-skinned counterparts.'

'True. And did you notice her reaction when I said I had brought two nursing nuns to see if they could help cure whatever was wrong with her? She knew full well that an experienced healer such as Sister Euphemia would be aware of her condition straight away, and indeed Euphemia spotted it without so much as the briefest examination.'

'Aye. I also noted the care with which she descended the mounting block; she does not want to risk losing this baby, my lady.'

Wondering if he was edging towards the same conclusion that she had reached, she nodded. She was about to speak when he said, 'The young groom was uneasy. Something is going on there that goes amiss with the servants. It is not, I would say, a happy place.'

'Yes, and Primevère's mother looked alarmed to see us at first,' she agreed. 'I wonder why? Was she aware that Florian's scheme was based on a falsehood and did she therefore believe that we had come to make accusations?'

'I think, my lady,' he replied, 'that her unease had more to do with the presence of Ranulf of Crowbergh in her daughter's hall.'

'But why?' she demanded. 'He and his family live close by and what is more natural than for a neighbour to help out at such a time?'

He frowned slightly but she noticed that he did not take up the point. Instead he said, 'I observed that Ranulf seems to make himself at home in Florian's house and he addresses its mistress by her Christian name.'

'So did I, but Primevère has said that the Crowbergh family were good friends to her and Florian.'

'Aye, that is so. But, my lady, it surprised me that he should be willing to spare the time away from managing his own household in order to lounge in his dead neighbour's hall.'

'Probably he has a very efficient wife,' she said, unable to keep a certain tartness out of her voice.

He turned to look at her. 'My lady,' he said quietly, 'he has no wife. She died last autumn.'

'She – *oh*!' The implications swiftly sinking in, she said, 'But he implied that he was a family man, I'm quite sure he did, and so did Primevère!'

'He is a childless widower,' Josse said neutrally.

'But that was not how it sounded – not only was there Primevère's initial implication that he is older than he really is, but in addition I was left in no doubt that when he left us he was on his way home to his wife!' Ranulf of Crowbergh was clever, she realised; without actually speaking an untruth, he had set in her mind the fact that he was married.

Not that marriage ever stopped anyone . . .

She jerked her attention back to Josse. 'He has money,' he was saying, 'both wealth of his own and that which he inherited from his wife.'

So he, she thought, who so kindly offered to extend his neighbourly duties to taking over the running of Merlin's

Tomb, was not concerned with the income when he did so. He had no more need of the money than Primevère, with her rich heiress mother.

'Yet Ranulf is well known at Merlin's Tomb,' she said thoughtfully. 'The guard recognised him instantly and was at pains to smarten up his bedraggled appearance and hide the ale mug from which he had no doubt just been drinking.'

'Aye. And Ranulf, I noticed, did not welcome the news that Gervase de Gifford was on his way home. I dined with him and Sabin last night and it was he who told me of the death of Ranulf's wife. Nor did Ranulf like my suggestion that Gervase is unlikely to drop the matter of who killed Florian without making some enquiries of his own.'

There was silence between them as their various observations and opinions sank in. Helewise thought about all that they had said. There was one thing that they had left out; Josse because he was not aware of it, she because . . . She was not quite sure, except that, if you looked at it one way, it was the piece that made the puzzle fit together.

Always providing, of course, that looking at it that way was the right way.

I will ask Josse what he thinks, she decided.

'There is something else,' she said, lowering her voice in the unlikely event that anyone might be listening.

He gave a quick grin. 'I had a feeling there was.'

'When I brought Primevère's mother here to view poor Florian's body,' she began, hardly registering his remark, 'I offered her some wine to restore her after the shock and to refresh her for the ride home. Actually she drank rather a lot and as a consequence spoke more freely on the way back than she probably intended to. She told me that Primevère no longer had any love for her husband.' She turned to face him. 'She said she was all but certain that he no longer shared her bed.'

Josse gave a slow nod. Then: 'But would she necessarily know? It's but the work of a moment to plant a child on a woman and a man does not ask his mother-in-law's permission before he beds his wife.'

'Yes, Sir Josse, I appreciate that, but Primevère and her mother do seem particularly close and Melusine has sharp eyes. I find that I can well believe she was right.'

'Well, I shall just have to bow to your feminine intuition on such matters, my lady.' He smiled again, slightly more genuinely this time, she thought. 'So, if it's not Florian's child she carries, do we need to look very far for the father?'

'It is a terrible accusation to make if she is – if they are innocent,' Helewise murmured. 'But then poor Ranulf is a widower, you tell me, and Primevère a very beautiful young woman—' With an effort she made herself stop.

But, glancing up at Josse and meeting his eyes, she thought that she had already said quite enough.

By mid-morning, Gervase and Josse were well on the way to Hadfeld. On the early part of the ride they had been discussing Ranulf of Crowbergh; Gervase had asked some relevant questions of a few well-informed men and he was able to report on his findings. He had discovered that Ranulf was in truth very wealthy, with extensive estates some miles to the west of Hadfeld and, or so it was said, an even larger property in France – it was near Le Mans, or so one man had insisted – where he bred war horses and finer-boned animals for regular riding.

'I am thinking,' Gervase observed, 'that perhaps, in addition to speaking to the lady Primevère, we ought also to pay a call on Ranulf of Crowbergh.'

'And I am thinking you're right,' Josse agreed with a grin.

All was quiet at the house of Florian of Southfrith. For once there were no workmen on the building site; although the new

construction was clearly not complete – far from it – there
were not even any workmen's tools or piles of stone lying
around. The courtyard stood empty under the sun, the air hot
and still and no movement except for the flutter of a pair of
doves in the shade beneath the mounting block.

Josse and Gervase tethered their horses and Josse murmured to the sheriff that, only the day before, the men had
been busy at work on the new building.

Gervase absorbed this with a nod. Then he led the way up
the steps and in through the partly open door, calling out to
announce himself and Josse.

At first there was no reply. Then there came the sound of
hurried footsteps from the passage leading off the hall and
Melusine appeared. Josse greeted her and presented Gervase
to her.

Studying her as she spoke the required polite phrases to
Gervase, Josse noticed that, for the first time in his admittedly
limited experience of her, she looked flustered. Her face was
flushed and her hair was less than perfectly restrained by the
black silk cap.

Gervase was asking to speak to Primevère, explaining that,
just returned from a journey, it was now his duty to find out all
that he could about the death of Florian.

'Primevère can tell you nothing,' Melusine stated flatly. 'She
knows no more than I do, which is that Florian went off to
Merlin's Tomb, he stayed away longer than usual and then we
were told that his body had been found in the forest.'

'I see. Nevertheless I should still like to speak to the lady
myself. Sometimes a seemingly irrelevant question can bring
to someone's mind some fact that they had quite forgotten
about until prompted, and I have known such small facts
become the key that unlocks the mystery.'

'My daughter is sick in bed and can see nobody,' Melusine
said. She put up a hand to tuck a thin strand of hair under her

cap and Josse was surprised to note that the hand trembled. 'She is in no state to answer questions, relevant or not.'

'She was perfectly well yesterday,' Josse remarked.

Melusine turned on him. 'Yes, so she was, till you and those tactless nuns came bothering her!' she cried. 'Questions, questions, and she a widow of only a week!'

'But —' Josse began, stung to angry protest at hearing the Abbess, the infirmarer and Sister Caliste slandered with the word *tactless* when their delicate and kindly offers of sympathy and help had been anything but. With an effort he restrained himself.

'The Hawkenlye sisters would indeed be most unhappy to learn that their visit had caused your daughter distress,' Gervase said smoothly. 'I am sure that was not their intention, for they are good women and work with all the goodness in their hearts for the benefit of others.'

Melusine gave a sniff. 'They mean well, I grant you.' Then, as if wanting instantly to shore up what might have been seen as a gap in her defences, she added, 'But you still can't see Primevère. She . . .' She hesitated. 'She is an unchaperoned widow now and I must take every care for her good name.'

Josse's fury almost spilled out of him at this thinly veiled insult; as if he or Gervase would take advantage of a sick and recently bereaved young woman! It was preposterous.

'We would not dream of intruding on her,' Gervase said smoothly. 'However, the fact remains that I must speak to her, sooner or later, so I shall ask you please to send word to me in Tonbridge when she is ready to see me.'

Josse thought he saw a tiny glint in Melusine's dark eyes and he was quite sure that some of the tension seemed to go out of her. Smiling now, she said, 'Of course. And I am sorry, both of you' – she turned so as to include Josse in her benevolence – 'that you have had a wasted journey. I would offer you refreshments but, alas, I am preoccupied with the care of my daughter.'

'We would not dream of putting you to the trouble,' Gervase assured her. 'We will leave you both in peace and I look forward to meeting your daughter soon.'

'Just as soon as she is well again,' Melusine agreed.

She saw them to the door and they were aware of her watching them as they mounted and rode away. She was still there, dark eyes following their departure, as they rounded the bend and rode out of her sight.

As if she must be absolutely sure that they had really gone.

On the way over to Ranulf's house – Gervase had been given directions before leaving Tonbridge – Josse told him what little the Abbess had discovered about Florian, his background, his family and his wife.

'His horse has not turned up?' Gervase asked.

'No.'

'Someone's lucky day, to apprehend a man with the intention of stealing his money only to discover that he rides a first-class horse into the bargain.'

'Perhaps the killer knew that already,' Josse suggested.

'You do not go along with the opinion that a passing thief was responsible for the crime?'

Josse shrugged. 'Perhaps.' Then he told Gervase of his discussion that morning with the Abbess and, when he had finished, Gervase gave him a very intent look.

'You believe that Ranulf is the father of the child that Primevère carries?'

'It seems likely.'

'And do you then extend the crimes laid at this man's door and suggest he murdered Florian?'

'It is a grave accusation, I know that well enough,' Josse replied. 'But aye, I feel we ought to keep it in mind when we speak to Ranulf.'

Gervase was frowing. 'So let us postulate,' he began slowly, 'that it happened like this. The lady Primevère, wed to a boastful youth who exaggerated his means, tires of his pretty face and turns him out of her bed. Then along comes a handsome neighbour, a mature man who has recently lost his wife, and she recognises in him everything that she thought to find in young Florian.'

'Is it not possible that he came along *before* he lost his wife?' Josse suggested.

'Ah, so now you would lay the murder of his wife at Ranulf's hands as well!' Gervase exclaimed. He shot him a warning glance. 'Have a care, Josse.'

'It was you who told me there were some who said Ranulf did not rush to his wife's aid when he might have done!' Josse snapped back. 'I merely point out that the time scale is relevant.'

'Yes, of course you're right,' Gervase admitted. 'It's just that I find myself reluctant to throw such dangerous accusations around in the open. Great harm can be done by the spreading of malicious gossip,' he added primly.

Josse made a show of looking all around him. 'Well, *I'm* not proposing to go spreading it,' he said. 'There's nobody to hear us here except our horses, and fortunately neither yours nor mine has the gift of speech.'

Gervase gave a short laugh. 'No. Sorry, Josse.'

'Hmm.'

When finally they rode up to the imposing manor house that was the dwelling of Ranulf of Crowbergh, it was to be met by another calm and peaceful scene in which every living thing appeared to have sought rest in the shade. Gervase called out and a boy came scurrying into the courtyard from what appeared to be the stables, a structure that ran along in a block joining the front wall of the yard to the house. Again

Gervase gave his and Josse's names and, as they both dismounted, asked to speak to the lad's master.

The boy stared from one to the other and said, 'He's not here.'

'I see.' Gervase frowned. 'Do you know when he will be back?'

'He's gone away,' the boy said. 'He's taking some horses over to his estate in France.'

Josse nodded. He had been told how the Conqueror had brought heavy horses to England in order to interbreed them with the lighter native horses; Ranulf, presumably, was doing the same thing by taking his English horses out to France. English stock was highly thought of nowadays, having been improved over the years by the introduction of those wonderful, fast and beautiful Arab horses that the Crusaders brought home. He thought, with a silent apology to good old Horace, just how much he would love such a mount.

Gervase nudged him quite hard in the ribs. 'When did your master leave?' he demanded. Josse brought his attention back to the present and waited for the answer.

The lad frowned ferociously and pursed up his mouth in an aid to concentration. 'Yesterday,' he finally said. 'It were late in the afternoon but well before sunset. He were aiming to sail on the evening tide.'

Alert now and probably thinking along the same lines as Gervase, Josse calculated rapidly. Ranulf had left them at the edge of the forest and as soon as they were out of sight he must have raced home, collected his horses and set off immediately for the coast. But why had he not mentioned that he was leaving? Under the circumstances, it was good of him to have spared the time to escort the Hawkenlye party to view the tomb and—

But suddenly Josse knew why Ranulf had not said he was about to depart for France; because it hadn't been planned.

And he also knew just when Ranulf had decided to go and he thought he knew why.

The stable lad was standing scuffing his boots in the dust, clearly waiting to be dismissed. Josse drew Gervase a little apart and said, 'I am thinking that it was the news that you were due home that made Ranulf decide on this sudden trip to his French estates, for he made no mention of it to us yesterday.'

Gervase looked grim. 'And I cannot help thinking that among the group of horses he has spirited out of England there might well have been a certain fast-paced bay.'

Josse emitted a brief curse. 'He's got away, Gervase.'

Gervase was already preparing to mount. 'He may still be at the coast,' he replied. 'I will—' He broke off.

Josse nodded, appreciating the difficulty. 'But where on the coast?' he said softly. 'Any number of ports harbour ships that sail from England to France. Where, Gervase, will you start? And to what purpose, when, according to the lad here, Ranulf fully intended to sail yesterday evening?'

Gervase flung his horse's reins into Josse's hand and strode back to the lad. 'Are you sure your master sailed last night?' he demanded.

The lad looked anxious. 'He *said* he was going to, sir. But I can't swear to it, not actually having seen him take ship, like.'

Gervase turned back to Josse, anger and frustration in his face. 'I must—' he began.

But the lad had raised his hand. Josse, noticing, said, 'What is it?'

'I could ask Peter,' the boy volunteered.

'Peter?' Gervase and Josse said together.

'He's head groom. He rode down with Master.'

Even from a couple of paces away Josse could hear Gervase grinding his teeth. 'Please ask him to come and speak to us,' he said through a patently false smile.

The lad trotted away and presently returned with a bow-legged man with a very tanned face, no hair and few teeth. 'You're asking about my master,' he said suspiciously. 'Who are you and what business may his comings and goings be of yours?'

With a sigh, for the third time that morning Gervase explained who he was. Peter gave a smug smile and said, 'You'll have a long wait if you want to ask questions of Sir Ranulf. He's in France. He sailed last night and before you ask, no, I don't know when he plans to return.' Then, curiosity overcoming loyalty, he burst out, 'What d'you want Master for, anyway?'

Gervase stared at him. Instead of answering, he said, 'Whereabouts in France are your master's estates?'

'How should I know?' Peter replied. 'I ain't never been there and I ain't likely to be going.' He spat on the dusty ground.

Gervase summoned his dignity and said frostily, 'When your master returns, send word to me.'

Peter gave a grunt that could have been an acknowledgement. Then he turned on his heel and, with the lad trotting behind him, stomped off back to his stables.

'I think,' Gervase said as they rode away, 'that we must go back to Hadfeld and insist on seeing the lady Primevère.'

Josse wondered whether to say what he was thinking. Oh, why not? he thought. We'll know soon enough in any case.

'We'll find the bird flown,' he said.

'What? Where will she have gone?'

'My guess is that at this moment she's either on board ship for France or else she's already there. Gervase, think!' he said urgently as the sheriff began to protest. 'The Abbess and the nuns and I last saw her around the middle of yesterday. After we left her, Ranulf finds out you're on your way home and will be making enquiries. He decides to make a run for it, taking

Florian's horse – which I'll wager money that Ranulf, being a breeder of fine horses, sold to him in the first place – to remove it from the scene. He pays a hasty visit to his mistress to tell her what's happening and quick as she can she dismisses her building gang – no point in having them do any more work when she's leaving – packs her bags, orders her horse prepared and races off to follow Ranulf so that she can sail with him on the same ship.'

Gervase was shaking his head. 'Josse, it all makes sound sense, as I have learned to expect when listening to you. But . . .' He paused, chewing at his lip. 'But I am still going to verify your theory by going back to Hadfeld.'

The courtyard and the house were, if anything, even quieter than on their previous visit. But the door was now closed; hurrying up the steps, Gervase banged hard on it with his fist.

After quite some time, Melusine opened it. To Josse's surprise, she invited them to come in.

'I must insist on seeing your daughter, madam,' Gervase said.

Melusine smiled thinly. 'You cannot.'

Gervase was making for the doorway giving on to the passage; Josse followed him

'Her room is up the steps and straight in front of you,' Melusine called after them.

They ran through the archway, up a couple of steps and along the corridor to the upper chamber. Bursting into the room, it was a matter of a brief glance to see that it was empty. The rushes on the floor had been disturbed and the bed, with its white linen, tumbled bedclothes and many pillows, had not been made. A chest at the far end of the room stood with its lid thrown open; it, like the room, was empty.

Melusine came to stand in the doorway with them. 'She has taken all her lovely new clothes,' she said conversationally.

'For all that he'll buy her more and better, still she's a woman and she wouldn't part with a new gown unless she had to.'

'When did she leave?' Gervase asked, although Josse guessed that he already knew the answer.

'Yesterday afternoon. He came for her and told her she must make haste and she did. I've never seen her go about a task so quickly or efficiently, but then it's not every day you flee the country with your lover, is it?' Her voice was poisonous with sarcasm; whatever had happened here, it did not appear that Melusine approved.

'Why were they in such a hurry?' Gervase said.

Melusine gave him a sideways look. 'I didn't ask,' she said coldly.

'Where have they gone?'

She shrugged. 'France, I imagine, although I didn't ask that either.'

'He has estates in Le Mans, I am told,' Gervase said.

Again, the shrug.

Gervase muttered a curse and, with one last look around the room, turned and strode back to the hall and out into the sunshine.

Josse and Melusine followed more slowly.

'This place wasn't Florian's, you know,' she said. 'It belongs to a relation and he used it as yet another way of persuading my daughter and me that he was a man of wealth.'

'He would be that in truth now, were he still alive,' Josse said. 'That tomb of his was bringing in money as if he was minting it.'

She turned down the corners of her mouth in a gesture of doubt. 'For a while, yes, it is true, much money could have been made. But sooner or later the truth would have emerged.'

'They are not Merlin's bones?'

Melusine laughed. 'Of course not.'

They were at the entrance now. Josse stopped, turning to Melusine. 'And what of you, madam?' he asked her.

She shot him a look, her dark eyes narrow with suspicion, and he thought her already pale face went a shade whiter. 'Me? What do you mean?'

'Your daughter has fled with her lover and your son-in-law is dead so, presumably, you will no longer wish to go on living here,' he replied.

'Ah, I see.' Melusine suddenly seemed to sag and Josse put out an instinctive hand to support her. For an instant she stood quite still, head bowed, then, rallying, she straightened up. 'I shall return home,' she said firmly. 'Do you know Angers, Sir Josse?'

'Er – no. Can't say I do.'

'My home, it is backed by low hills and overlooks the Loire.' Now her voice was dreamy, as if she were speaking of some beautiful place that she had loved very greatly, had lost and might not find again. 'It is comfortable and the weather is usually mild, the food is first rate and the wines of the Loire are without equal. It is a place of great serenity and beauty and now' – the dark eyes did a quick sweep of the courtyard, the modest house and the new building work and Melusine's down-turned lips seemed to sum up her opinion of what she was looking at – 'now that it is all over, I am impatient to return there.'

Angers, Josse was thinking, was not very far from Le Mans; these people had worked it all out. *Now that it is all over*, she had just said. Did she know, then, exactly what her own daughter and her lover had planned between them; what perhaps Ranulf himself had done? If so, then her attitude, he reflected, was more than a little callous . . .

'Have you no pity for Florian?' he asked quietly.

She considered the question, turning her head on one side. Then, dark eyes on Josse's, she said, 'No, not really.' Then: 'You see, I never really liked him.'

# 20

'What will you do now?' Josse asked the sheriff as they rode back to Hawkenlye.

'I am very tempted,' the sheriff said testily, 'to take a force of men and sail across to France, locate Ranulf's estate near Le Mans and demand that he accompanies me back to England to face an accusation of murder and robbery.'

'But how would you prove it, even if you could force him to come?'

Gervase frowned. 'There *must* be proof, Josse, did I only know where to look.'

'I very much doubt it,' Josse replied. 'Someone steps out of the darkness and kills a man on the forest fringes at dead of night. The man is robbed of his money bags and his horse and his body hidden in the bushes. Who on earth is to say who did the deed?'

'I might find the proof I need if I could locate Florian's horse,' Gervase said.

'Aye, now well on its way to some place where it'll be lost among dozens that look exactly like it,' Josse countered. 'Would you take Florian's groom with you and ask him to point out his late master's bay? And even if you could prove without a shadow of a doubt that Florian's horse is now in Ranulf's paddock, then there's nothing to stop either Ranulf or Primevère saying, oh, yes, the horse did turn up, minus the money bags, and we forgot to tell you, and since nobody here has any use for it we decided to send it out to join the rest of the stock out in France.'

'So, like hiding a tree in a forest, the animal is for ever lost among its fellows and will end its days happily breeding and making a rich man even more money.' There was a tinge of bitterness in Gervase's voice.

Josse grinned suddenly, remembering something the Abbess told him. 'Correct in all but one respect, Gervase,' he said. 'The horse was a gelding.'

There was silence between them for some time. Then Gervase said passionately, 'Dear God, but how I hate to see someone commit a crime and walk away a free man!'

Josse considered several replies. Then he said, 'I know, my friend. In this case, however, I think you're going to have to put up with it.'

Back at the Abbey, they both went to see the Abbess.

She was not alone in her little room: before her stood Ranulf of Crowbergh, and Primevère sat on the small wooden stool kept for visitors.

Josse, astounded, instinctively banged the door shut behind him and stood against it. Forgetting that he had left his weapons at the gate, as he and other armed visitors always did, his hand had flown to the place where his sword usually hung.

Gervase, face tense, squared up to Ranulf.

Who, with a smile, put up his hands and said calmly, 'Please, gentlemen, there's no need for violence.' Turning round to exchange a glance with the Abbess – who, Josse noticed, was sitting straight-backed and regal in her throne-like chair with a slight frown but no other sign of unease – he went on, 'Primevère and I have been experiencing the most agonisingly divided loyalties. I was all for our setting sail last night for France, where I had planned that we would lie low until – until matters had taken their course, with or without our intervention. Primevère' – he gave her a loving smile – 'has persuaded me otherwise and, since the decision really has to be hers, I have bowed to her wisdom.' He stood back, one hand to his heart, head lowered as if to say, I have said my piece and now it is up to others to explain.

Which, after a short moment of silence in which the mood was so full of tension that the very air seemed to crackle, Primevère did.

Gracefully she got to her feet, the luscious silk of her gown hissing as she moved and settling in generous folds around her feet.

'My lady Abbess, Sir Josse, and—?' She looked enquiringly at Gervase, who introduced himself.

Primevère smiled. 'Of course,' she murmured. 'Patient listeners, stand easy for I am going to tell you a story.' Briefly her dark blue eyes went around the group, a certain arrogance in her stance commanding their attention, then she began. 'It is of someone who was born to discontent; someone who, despite being brought up the pampered favourite in a comfortably wealthy family, still could not be happy, for their nature had a peevish streak of self-preservation that always said, I am worth more than this! This person grew to adulthood and became arrogant, adopting the attitude that they were so special that others ought to recognise this and treat them accordingly.'

She speaks of Florian, Josse guessed; she must indeed retain some love for him, for speaking of him in this way makes her look so very sad.

'This person became manipulative and cunning,' Primevère went on, 'and, with time and desperation, cunning turned to dishonesty and then, as the last vestige of conscience was lost, to evil. In pursuance of their own wicked aim, they no longer recognised right from wrong and did not know where to stop.'

The tomb, Josse realised; she refers to his heartless manipulation of gullible people by pretending to have discovered Merlin's bones.

'Now I will tell you the tale of someone else,' she was saying, 'a woman whose tragedy was that she fell out of love with the man she had married and could no longer accept him as a wife should, turning him out of her bed and, as time went by, shunning his conversation, even his very company.' She paused, eyes bright with tears, and Josse observed her pain as she spoke of her own experience. She must have felt the stab of empathy for, turning to him, she said softly, 'It was miserable for her, Sir Josse; how much worse it was for the man to whom she was wed.'

Gervase seemed to shake himself free from the spell of her words; stepping towards her, he said roughly, 'Madam, murder has been done and yet you would engage our sympathy for the perpetrators! Remember that—'

Surprisingly it was the Abbess who, raising her hand, said quietly, 'Please, Gervase. Hear her out.'

For an instant Gervase stood his ground. Then, with a faint bow towards the throne-like chair, he subsided.

'Thank you,' Primevère murmured. She had been slowly pacing the small room and now she stopped right in front of Gervase. 'The perpetrators,' she said, repeating his words. 'You refer, I think, to Ranulf and me, believing that I was the woman who tired of her husband and that I persuaded my lover to help me rid myself of him? I do not deny that Ranulf and I are lovers and have been since last winter. Ranulf lost his wife, you see, and although she did not love him, he still loved her and his grief at her death was compounded by the cruel rumour that instead of trying to save her life he had left her to die.' Now the deep blue eyes were hard as they stared up into Gervase's, as if Primevère were silently saying, you may not have started the rumours but you most certainly have passed them on.

For a brief moment Gervase looked sheepish. Then, rallying, he said coldly, 'I have only Ranulf's word for that.'

'Mine too,' Primevère said, 'for I was there that day and both Ranulf and I did what we could for her.' Gervase was about to speak but she anticipated his question. 'I did not speak up, and I was wrong. I would have done had Ranulf been arrested, but as it was it seemed best not to invite further slandering of his good name by advertising the fact that his neighbour's wife had been with him on the day his wife died.' Now Primevère spun round to face the Abbess. 'Ranulf and I have sworn to the Abbess Helewise that we were not lovers then, although neither of us can deny that we already loved each other.'

'And I believe them,' the Abbess said.

'But you are now,' Gervase said bluntly. 'You are pregnant, madam, are you not, and not by your husband?' There was a gasp and swift movement from the corner where Ranulf stood and he went to stand by Primevère's side.

'I am, and the child is Ranulf's,' Primevère replied. 'And—'

'Enough,' Ranulf said forcefully. His arm around her waist, he looked around the group, fixing Josse, the Abbess and Gervase in turn with a direct stare. Then, bending his head to hers, briefly he touched her forehead with his lips. 'Enough,' he whispered to her.

She looked up at him. 'I must finish,' she said.

He looked at her for a long moment. Then, shoulders slumping, he whispered, 'Very well.'

'You killed Florian, didn't you?' Gervase appeared to be addressing both of them. 'An unwanted husband was a hindrance at the best of times; even more so when the lady here was expecting an unwelcome child.'

Two heads turned sharply to face him and the protest ripped out of both Primevère and Ranulf: '*No.*' Ranulf was about to continue but Primevère whispered, 'Please?' and, with an obvious effort, he stopped.

'*Not* an unwelcome child,' she said with dignity, 'for, although conceived out of wedlock, this baby could not be more loved and wanted if he or she were the heir to the throne.

And' – now she faced Gervase again – 'for all that it must seem to you that for us to kill him was the obvious and rational solution, I have to tell you that neither Ranulf nor I had anything to do with the death of Florian. Should you doubt us, we can provide someone who knew that we were together on the night he was killed.'

'I'm sure you can,' murmured Gervase.

Ranulf's face darkened. 'Have a care,' he said. 'You make a vicious implication, and it can and will be proved to you that you speculation and guesswork are entirely wide of the mark.'

The slight emphasis on *speculation* and *guesswork* were, Josse thought, a calculated insult; since guessing and speculating were in truth exactly what he and Gervase had done, under the circumstances it seemed justifiable.

Primevère had moved her position so that she now stood between Ranulf and Gervase. With dignity she said again, 'Let me finish.'

And, after a tense moment, both men stepped back.

Josse, suppressing a flash of admiration, waited for her to complete her tale.

'Florian's death has set me free to marry the man I love and when Ranulf spoke just now of wanting us to sail over to France, he referred to his suggestion that the two of us go over to live on his estate near Le Mans for a time. We would have married quietly somewhere on the journey and at home Ranulf would have presented me as his new and pregnant bride. There we would have stayed until either those who killed Florian were caught and brought to justice or until the law gave up and stopped hunting for them.' She shot a glance at Gervase. 'But then we discovered who was behind the murder and it changed everything.'

'Who is it?' Gervase demanded. Then, furiously, as his anger finally boiled over: 'I have had enough of rambling tales that skirt and obscure the truth; if you really do know who killed your husband, tell me now or I shall arrest the pair of you.'

As the echoes of his harsh voice died away, nobody in the room doubted that he meant it.

Primevère bowed her head meekly. 'Very well,' she said quietly. Then she raised her eyes to meet those of Gervase. 'Florian's habits were well known,' she began, 'and everyone both at the tomb and at Hadfeld was aware that he came home two or three times a week with the takings. Usually he had a guard with him and so the first task of the murderer was to arrange it so that one night, Florian rode alone. A guard was approached; it was Hal, the one with the scars and the broken nose. The murderer, judging correctly that Hal was a violent man, had found out that he was on the run for killing a man in a fight, and that useful little fact gave the murderer power over him. Not that Hal needed much persuasion; a large share of the proceeds of the robbery was sufficient incentive to enlist his help.'

'But surely the killer wanted the money!' Josse protested.

'No, Josse,' Primevère said with a sad smile, 'for the person behind Florian's death was already wealthy. It was not for personal gain that my husband was killed.'

*The person was already wealthy.*

*Agonisingly divided loyalties.*

*The decision has to be hers.*

He thought then that he knew who had killed Florian of Southfrith and, meeting the Abbess's eyes, he saw in their expression that he was right.

'I spoke just now of someone who was deeply discontented and who, instead of sitting back in happy appreciation of all that life had provided, instead was compelled ever to strive for more: a larger house, a purer-blooded horse, higher status, more reverent awe from everybody else. When their own options grew fewer and fewer, this person turned the force of their driven nature to another, whose steps they tried to force along a certain path almost from birth.'

The tears were falling silently down her face; Josse, unable to witness such pain any longer, said softly, 'You speak of yourself, Primevère, and the person who has tried to put you in harness all your life is your mother.'

Primevère turned to him. 'She can't help it!' she protested. 'She acts out of love for me; although she never liked Florian she believed, as I did, that he was very rich and so she grudgingly accepted him. Then when she saw that I no longer loved him, she was delighted because it meant that, sooner or later, she would be able to persuade me to abandon him and our life of deepening poverty at Hadfeld, when she planned to take me back to France to marry a distant kinsman of hers who has high social standing and is wealthy beyond counting. She had, or so she told me, already written to the man to tell him about me.' She dropped her head in shame, as if she too were in some way responsible for her mother's actions. 'Then, of course, Florian came up with the idea of pretending he had found Merlin's Tomb and suddenly there was so much money coming in that I could have anything I wanted. I began to express doubts about leaving Florian and going to marry the new husband my mother had selected but not because, as she thought, I was tempted by Florian's sudden wealth.' She leant closer to Ranulf and he tightened his arm around her. 'It was because, even though I was married to Florian, I could not bear to go away and leave the man I love.'

'So your mother hired the guard Hal to kill Florian,' Gervase said slowly. 'She, then, is guilty of his murder.'

'She did not actually kill him!' Primevère cried. 'She's an old woman and she could not possibly have carried out such a brutal slaying!'

'But she paid someone else to do it for her,' Gervase said relentlessly. 'She must have told Hal to say to Florian that the guards were too busy that night with the visitors for any of them to accompany him home with the money. Then, as

Florian set off, Hal must have ridden hard and overtaken him, setting up his garrotte rope and then, presumably, spooking Florian's horse so that he rode full tilt into it. No doubt he'd have had a weapon of some sort with which to finish the job if the fall didn't kill Florian. Then he dumped the body, caught the horse and its precious bags of money and rode off into the night, finding some place to hide up until he could sneak over to Hadfeld and report back to Melusine.'

'Yes,' Primevère whispered. 'Yes, that's what happened.' A sob broke out of her. 'When *Maman* told me, she thought I'd be pleased.'

And that – the memory of that moment – was finally too much; Primevère turned her face into Ranulf's chest and collapsed into his arms.

'Do you want my help?' Josse panted as he ran after Gervase.

'No, Josse. I can have a band of men ready swiftly and there's no need for you to come as well.'

They reached the stables and Gervase was untethering his horse. 'Will you go after Melusine too?'

'Oh, yes,' Gervase said grimly.

'And what of Hal? He's now a very rich man and he rides Florian's fast horse, so—'

'His new wealth is what will give him away.' Gervase was in the saddle now, clearly impatient to go. 'He won't resist the temptation to start spending. I'll get him, Josse; you'll see.'

With a nod and a very faint smile – Gervase, Josse thought, was going to derive a certain grim pleasure from catching the two people behind the murder of Florian – he put heels to his horse and clattered off across the courtyard and out through the gates.

Thoughtfully Josse made his way back to the Abbess's room. Shortly afterwards she appeared in the doorway carrying a platter of food and a mug of wine. 'Sir Josse?' she said. 'Ranulf has taken Primevère to the infirmary to lie down and I have arranged for food to be sent in to them. Will you eat too?'

It was only then, with the prospect of food before him, that he realised how hungry he was. He went to join the Abbess and they sat down on a stone seat in the cloister outside her room while he ate.

'We have come to the end of this particular road, Sir Josse,' the Abbess said as he finished his meal.

'Aye.' He swallowed. 'Gervase seems to think he'll catch both Melusine and the guard Hal.'

She was slowly shaking her head. 'I still find it difficult to accept the fact that Primevère voluntarily gave up her own mother,' she said. 'It was a terrible thing that Melusine did, but the woman was so misguided that surely it almost amounts to a sickness, in which case we ought to pity rather than condemn her.'

'Perhaps,' Josse suggested gently, 'such a sentiment might form her defence, if and when she is put on trial.'

The Abbess turned to him. 'Oh, Sir Josse! To think of imprisonment and possibly even the gallows, when all her life she has been used to such luxury!'

He shrugged. He could not find it in him to feel quite the same sympathy. Instead he said, 'I think I may know why Primevère acted as she did.'

'Oh?'

'I think she may have inherited some of her mother's instinct for self-preservation,' he said. 'She realised full well that she and Ranulf were likely to be suspected of murdering Florian and so, before any questions could be asked or any arrests made, she got in first and revealed who really did it.'

'But her own mother!' the Abbess repeated.

Josse gave her a quick grin. 'Who no doubt guessed precisely what her daughter would do and is even now on her way across the Channel bound for home.'

'But then – will she not be brought to justice?'

Josse shrugged. 'Perhaps. Probably, aye.' He paused. Then: 'Gervase de Gifford is a very determined man.'

There was a short silence. Then she said, 'Well, the tomb is closed, thank the good Lord, and we here at Hawkenlye may now wait in happy expectation of our pilgrims returning.'

'Aye,' he agreed. 'Ironic, to think that our – my trip to Brittany was in vain since the tomb was going to shut down anyway.'

'Yes, I suppose so.'

Again, silence fell between them.

He thought for some time before expressing the thought that had steadily been growing in his mind. There was something that he very much wanted to do; he knew full well what was behind this final excursion that he had to make and he was quite sure the Abbess would have no difficulty in guessing this reason. But he decided to tell her just the same.

'There's one thing I would still like to see to,' he said, sipping at his mug of wine.

'And that is?'

'I want to have another look at those old bones,' he said.

'You do? Why?'

He was not sure that he could tell her, for he barely knew himself. 'Oh, I don't know, just a feeling I have. We now know whose they aren't, but I'd still like to see if I could discover where Florian found them and who they really did belong to.'

'A very big woman,' the Abbess said. 'Is that not enough, Sir Josse?'

'No, my lady. Perhaps it ought to be, but—' He shrugged. 'Somehow I sense that there is still more to this business.'

'Your instincts are usually sound,' she said loyally. 'Go and have your final look, sir Josse. If you set out now, you will be there and back again by sunset.'

## 21

He rode slowly along the track that led around the forest fringes. Horace was tired – so was he – but there was no hurry and the horse had been rubbed down and watered when they returned from the earlier journey. Besides, it was cool in the shade.

His mind and his heart turned constantly into the forest to where he knew – or assumed – she was, she and his little daughter. He wanted more than anything to turn in under the trees and, riding as hard as conditions allowed, go and seek them out. But he had promised her not to; not for the time being, anyway.

She too had felt the deep, searing pain of their separation; he knew that as well as he knew himself. They had both tentatively explored the ways and means by which they might contrive a life together but in each case the same stumbling block cropped up: she was a woman of the forest, only just starting to come into the power that was both her and her daughter's destiny, and her home was the wildwood. She had no desire to live among the Outworlders – she had experienced enough of that life to last the rest of her days – and even her love for him did not tempt her to try. He, for his part, knew that life out in the little hut in the clearing was not for him. I am, he had decided ruefully, too used to my comforts and to the security of four stout stone walls around me when I lay my head down at night. And as for all that magic stuff . . .

She would not marry him; he had asked her and, lovingly, tears in her eyes, she had gently turned him down. 'The answer, my beloved Josse, is the same as it was the first time you asked me.'

The best that they had managed to come up with – and even that, bearing in mind how very great was their sorrow, was not that good and brought little consolation – was that both of them would return to their usual lives and that he would visit her regularly just after the days of the solstices and the equinoxes (he had had to ask her when they fell). She would usually be at home then, she had said, recovering her strength after the ceremonies.

He did not want to know about those, which was just as well since she didn't tell him.

It was July now, less than a month past the summer solstice, and the next quarter day was not until late September.

How, he howled inside his head, am I to manage?

He rode on determinedly towards the site of Merlin's Tomb. It was good to have something to do and, as he drew close, he actually felt a tingle of excitement at the thought of having a closer look at the ancient bones.

There was no sign of the guards and the gate in the outer rail fence was still chained shut. Josse tethered Horace to the top rail, climbed the fence and walked on. The gate in the second, higher fence was closed but the chain had not been refastened. He pushed the gate open and slowly walked across the turf to the open grave.

Again, some force emanating from the huge bones seemed to reach out for him. But this time he had come prepared. Not allowing the fear to take hold, he strode on to the very edge of the gaping wound in the earth and, standing on the grave's lip, said softly, 'Lady, I do not know who you are but I have good news. This place is now closed and I give you my word that I shall do my utmost to find out where it was that you were brought from so that I may return you to your rightful place.'

He paused, listening intently.

Other than the sweet, treble song of a wren somewhere in the undergrowth, silence. Except . . .

Except what?

Straining his ears, it seemed to him for a brief instant that he could hear the sound of long, regular breathing. And a – what was it? A sort of pulse, slow and steady, as if the very heart of the earth could be heard beating.

He sank to his knees. He was tense and expectant, every sense alert. But, he realised in wonder, he was no longer afraid.

He edged forward so that he was looking down on the bones. They really were enormous and, were it not for the high esteem in which he held the infirmarer, he would have doubted her firm assurance that this skeleton belonged to a woman. If it was indeed a woman, he thought suddenly, then it was somehow even more of an outrage that her bones lay there exposed for all to see. He tried to think what he had with him with which to cover her, and recalled that he still carried his travelling blanket, rolled up and tied to the back of his saddle.

Running back to Horace, peacefully grazing by the outer fence, swiftly he unfastened the blanket and returned to the grave. Then, kneeling down again, he attacked the problem of how best to tuck it around the bones. The steep sides of the grave had been faced with stone at their lower levels – something he had not noticed before – and he now saw how skilfully the job had been done: the stone sides met the slab that formed the base at exact angles and the fit was so tight that very little earth seemed to have penetrated the pit. The dark metal plaque on the far side of the grave, with its false claim that these were the bones of Merlin the Enchanter, was propped up by a rough chunk of sandstone.

Sandstone, and it was unworked. Yet the lining and the base of the tomb were surely granite, beautifully shaped with loving care.

Something began to stir at the back of Josse's mind.

He leaned down into the grave. Half expecting a smell, he

detected nothing but a slight earthy tang, by no means unpleasant. Laying the blanket within reach on the graveside, he edged his upper body down over the lip of the tomb and, eyes alert, looked very carefully all around the bones, trying to see if anything lay beneath them.

With his head right down in the grave, he soon found what he was searching for.

There was virtually nothing left of the leather bag except for its top, where the leather was doubled over to hold the drawstrings. But its contents had proved more durable and now they lay in a tidy little group beneath the skeleton's right hip.

Unable to tear his fascinated eyes away, Josse silently enumerated them.

There was the clawed foot of some bird of prey: probably a kestrel, he thought. Next to this lay a knife made out of some metal that, during its long immersion in the ground, had acquired a greenish sheen; its handle was of bone and carved into the shape of a dragon. There was also a razor with a handle of stone, two small shells and a set of matching stones which, when Josse reached down and picked up a couple, had strange designs carved into them. There was also a collection of small animal bones and a large amber bead.

He pulled himself back out of the tomb and knelt on the grass. Then, making himself act before the enchantment took over and he could no longer make such decisions for himself, he reached for his blanket and, with all the tender care of a father tucking up his child for the night, laid it across the skeleton and fixed it as well as he could so that every part, except for the ankles and the feet, was now hidden from view.

The strange force that had filled the clearing seemed to fade a little, as if the respectful gesture had somehow diminished its potent anger.

And Josse, sweating and gasping, collapsed on the grass.

*

He lay there for some time, listening to the natural and very welcome sounds of the forest reassert themselves. The birds sang, a light breeze rustled the leaves and from somewhere near at hand he thought he heard water running.

He closed his eyes and some of the various anxieties that he had been carrying seemed to seep out of him, leaving him relaxed and drowsy. It was almost as if a soft voice was murmuring in his ear, saying *Sleep, sleep* . . .

He slept.

He was suddenly wide awake, disturbed by some faint sound that echoed through his head but that he could not identify. It had seemed to his dreaming mind that somebody had called his name, but that couldn't be right.

But then he heard it again. *Josse.*

And, sitting bolt upright so fast that his head swam, he found himself staring up at the Domina.

'What are you doing here?' Her voice sounded cold.

'I came to tell her that it's over. The tomb is closed and I was going to try to find out where he found her – where her true resting place had been – so that I could return her there.' He met the Domina's secretive eyes. *I have nothing to be either ashamed or afraid of,* he told himself firmly. Standing up – he felt at even more of a disadvantage crouched at her feet – he added, 'Only I now think I was wrong.'

'About what?'

'About thinking that Florian found the bones elsewhere and moved them here.' He paused, watching her closely. 'This woman has been here all along. Hasn't she?'

There was a long pause, and then very slowly the Domina nodded. 'Yes.'

'Who was she?' he asked eagerly. 'How—'

But the Domina did not appear to hear, or, if she had, she chose to ignore his question. 'The man Florian did indeed discover her grave,' she said. 'He came into the forest around the time of the spring equinox and he was in great distress, so severe that it was in his mind to make an end of his life and hang himself from one of the oak trees. He had been searching for buried treasure, having heard a rumour that coins had been found deep within the forest. He came across this clearing and noticed the hollow in its centre. He began to dig and instead of finding treasure, he found bones.' She looked away, into the tomb. 'A rib bone was detached and had been brought up near to the surface by some burrowing rodent. It was the end of this rib that Florian first found. Excited, for where there were bones there might also be valuable grave goods, he dug and he dug and he went on digging until he discovered that a whole skeleton lay buried here.'

She sighed, sadly shaking her head.

'And Florian's instant thought,' Josse said slowly, 'was how he could turn his discovery to his own advantage. In his desperate need for money, he came up with the idea of pretending that they were Merlin's bones – no doubt he, like everyone else, had heard about what the Glastonbury monks have done. Florian realised he could not claim that he had discovered the bones of King Arthur or his queen, since it's said they lie at Glastonbury, and so he settled on Merlin.' He shook his head. 'Who would have ever dreamed that this skeleton is that of a woman?'

'Your nun did,' the Domina observed drily.

'Aye, but then Sister Euphemia is vastly experienced in matters of the human body.' A thought occurred to him and he voiced it. 'You seem to know a lot about Florian's discovery of the tomb. Why, if you were aware of him and what he was doing here, did you not stop him?'

'Some of my people asked the same question,' she replied. 'Incensed as we all were by this sacrilegious intrusion into somewhere so close to our own sacred places, many of our young men wished to attack Florian and protect the site from further despoliation.'

'He is dead,' Josse said quietly.

'I know. We are not responsible for his death.'

'No, no. I didn't think you were. He—' But he realised that the Domina was not listening; the doings of Outworlders, he thought, had very little interest for her unless they conflicted with the lives of her people.

He went back over what she had just been saying; there had been something there, something he wanted to ask her about . . . Yes. That was it.

'Lady, you said that this clearing is close to one of your sacred places.'

'The entire forest is sacred.'

'Oh.' The vague idea that he had been forming drifted apart. 'Then – she – the woman in the grave – she is not one of the forest people?'

The Domina's eyes flashed to his and she said, 'No. She was here in an age before we inhabited these woods.'

There was only one question to ask. He whispered, 'Who is she?'

Again, the Domina appeared to consider her words before she spoke. Then she said, 'She belonged to a people known as the Long Men, for they were a race of uncommon height and strength. Their territory was between the Downs and the forest and they guarded their precious valley fiercely. They were seers, magicians, and, although their numbers dwindled in the great fight against the invader from the south, enough of them survived to return to some sort of prominence after the incomers had gone. The Long Men enjoyed a brief resurgence and some of their number were appointed seeresses and cunning men of the ancient kings of Sussex. They were admired and feared, and with good reason for, in the long years of their presence here, their powers that stemmed from the very Earth had grown and extended.'

'Where are they now?' Josse asked, his voice an awed whisper.

The Domina glanced at him. 'Their blood still flows in the veins of their descendants, but in the later years they were few in number and driven to choose mates from outside the tribe.' She gave a faint smile. 'Some men whose antecedents were from this area still stand out by their height.'

'A race of giants,' he said slowly. 'I always thought giants were only in the tales told to children by the fireside.'

'Do not dismiss such tales,' the Domina said, 'for at their roots there is always a grain of truth.'

He was shaking his head. 'They lived between the Downs and the forest,' he said, thinking back over what she had said, 'and so this – this place that you said was sacred – marked the northern limit of their land.'

'Yes.'

'Was that why she lies buried here? Because she was one of their most powerful ones and she guards the frontier of the area that her people claimed as their own?'

'It was their own. They had lived here since the dawn of time.'

'Aye. But I'm right, aren't I?'

The Domina risked another smile and he thought he detected a flash of approval in it. 'Yes, Josse. You are.'

His mind racing now, he went on, 'And on the Downs is there another such burial – perhaps of a man – that guards the southern border?'

'Yes, there is. But that one is more easily found, although very few people nowadays know that the marker that indicates the place stands above a man's body.'

He knew all at once to what she referred, for he had seen it with his own eyes and stared at it in wonder. 'You speak of the chalk giant,' he said.

'I do. The Long Man, do folk not call him?'

And, with a laugh of delight, Josse said, 'Aye, they do.'

He looked down at the huge skeleton. I know who you are and why I felt such power from you, he addressed her silently. And I know too now that I need not take you anywhere because here is where you are meant to be and where you will stay. 'Shall I fill in the grave?' he asked the Domina.

'There is no need,' she replied – rather swiftly, he thought, as if she wanted to make quite sure he did not suddenly start doing so.

'But we can't leave the bones lying there with only my old blanket to frustrate prying eyes!'

She made a pacifying gesture with her graceful hands. 'Others will perform the task, with the appropriate rituals.'

'People of your tribe?'

She hesitated. 'No, Josse. My people will not interfere, for the same reason that we prevented our own men from taking action to defend this place and this grave when first Florian intruded here. Those who will perform the necessary rite are *her* people.'

He baulked at accepting what he believed the Domina meant. Was she saying that there were still people of this long-dead woman's race who would appear out of the shadows and, praying and chanting, replace the earth over her? But no, that couldn't be right. Could it?

He stared at the Domina. With a moment's compassion softening her face, she said, 'You and Joanna almost lost your lives in the forest in Armorica.'

So Joanna had told her. Unless, of course, the Domina had used her mysterious gifts and *seen* what had happened with her own inner eye. 'Aye. It was an attack in the night and it was only because she – Joanna – sensed danger approach that we were on our guard and fought him off.'

The Domina watched him steadily. 'The assailant was not who you took him to be.'

'Not – but it made perfect sense! Joanna's brother-in-law said he'd make sure she didn't escape again; we all heard him!'

'Yes, I am sure that you did. But it was not he who tried to kill you.'

Josse tried to think but his mind was in a whirl. The Domina, with a faint noise of exasperation, said, 'What did you notice about the man?'

'Very little,' Josse said crossly. 'It was dark and we were fighting for our lives.'

'Did you gain no impression of him at all?'

'He was very tall, and—'

*Very tall.*

Then he knew.

'Yes, yes,' the Domina breathed. 'He is one of the few still alive of the old race and to him and his brethren falls the sacred duty of protecting the places that mark the northern and southern boundaries of his ancient race.'

'It was he who tried to kill us?' She nodded. 'But why?'

She raised her eyes to the sky, as if seeking inspiration. 'I do not know. They were aware of your mission to Armorica and would have guessed, I believe, that you sought proof that these could not be the bones of Merlin the Enchanter. They, even more than the Hawkenlye community or my own people, were desperate for the site to be closed down for, in addition to the fact that it was attracting far too may unthinking and uncaring visitors to a holy place, the very concept was a terrible affront to those who still remember she who really lies here.'

'But we had found the proof that we needed and we were on our way home to spread the word that Merlin's Tomb was a fake!' he protested. 'Why on earth should he try to prevent us doing the very thing that he too most wished for?'

Again she said, 'I do not know. I can only think that somehow he was led to believe that your mission had not been successful and that you had failed to find the necessary proof. But I—'

There was a movement behind her. And, before Josse's amazed eyes, two figures dressed in the colours of the forest materialised out from beneath the trees. One moment they were not there; the next, they were. Both were very tall; one stood a little to the fore of his companion, who leaned heavily on a staff.

The man with the staff had a bandage around his head and four very deep gashes across the front of his neck that disappeared down inside his green tunic.

And Josse, who knew exactly who he was, put a hand down to his sword hilt.

The man in the lead held up both hands, palms outwards, and said in a hypnotic voice, 'Do not try to draw your sword, knight, for you will not be able even to extract it from its scabbard.'

Josse tugged at his sword but the man had spoken truly and it would not come. 'What do you want with us?' he demanded.

'You have tampered with the bones,' the tall man said in the same chanting tones. 'None may do that and live.'

'I came here to help!' Josse shouted. 'We went to Armorica to seek proof that this was not Merlin's Tomb and to make sure it was closed down! We found the proof but, on our return, we discovered that the man behind the pretence was dead and the tomb already safe behind a secure fence.'

The tall man studied him for what seemed an age. Then he said, 'My brother here followed you all the way from this place to your destination. He had kept his ears and his eyes open and discovered that his quarry would be crossing the narrow seas and so he followed you until it was clear from which port you would embark. He noticed the party of monks waiting to board the vessel that you selected and it was easy to arrange his dark, hooded cloak so that it looked, to the superficial glance, like a monk's habit. He made a mistake on board the boat, for he allowed the woman to become aware of him. In his own defence, he had not expected her to be so sensitive and so skilled; usually, when he casts that aura of unobtrusiveness over himself, most people barely even realise he is there.'

'A monk!' Josse breathed. He could hardly even recall the party of monks, let alone details such as one of them looking slightly different from his brethren.

'He dogged your footsteps all the way to the fountain in the Armorican forest,' the tall man continued, 'and he followed you back on the homeward journey, right up until the time when he made his presence known to you.'

'I thought he was dead!' Josse stared at the man with the staff.

'Death indeed came looking for him.' The tall man eyed his companion with dispassionate eyes. 'He fought an assailant whose power was even greater than his own. He lay down in the forest in the land over the water and he waited for death. As he lay there he sent out his thoughts to those who sent him and they heard. They went to find him and they did what had to be done for him so that he might find a little strength. Then they bore him up to the coast and found passage over the water.' Again, that curiously disinterested glance at his wounded companion, as if the tall man's emotions were not in the least engaged by this harrowing tale of his brother's dogged and dangerous mission and his brush with death. 'I went to meet him on the shore beyond the Downs so that I could bring him home,' he concluded. Then, turning suddenly back to Josse, he drew a long knife from beneath his cloak.

'*No!*' Josse shouted. The Domina beside him stood unmoving; with a part of his mind wondering why she did not act – performing some kind of spell to release his sword from its scabbard would have been a start – he lunged forward towards the two men.

As he raced across the ground he sensed someone at his side. The Domina, he thought, at last spurred into action.

But it was not the Domina; it was Joanna.

She had something in her hand and he saw it was her wand with its brownish crystal. She pushed in front of him, screaming out some words that he did not understand, and two things happened.

His sword suddenly came loose from its sheath and, without an instant's hesitation, he raised it above his head in a two-handed grip and brought it down in a swinging blow of such force that the tall man's head must surely have been severed from his shoulders. Just as the steel made contact with the man's flesh, he experienced a sort of tingling in his hands. It extended right up his arms and he felt the muscles in his shoulders quiver. And his blade seemed to meet with no resistance whatsoever.

At the same time Joanna leapt on the man with the staff, knocking it away so that he slumped to his knees. Her own knife in her hand, she struck down in the direction of the man's throat to finish what she had begun back in the Brocéliande.

There was a sudden brilliant light in the clearing, so powerful – so painful – that it was as if the noonday sun had descended to earth. A white mist emanated from it and within the mist there seemed to be flashes of lightning. Josse, his sword still in his hand, could make out the shape of Joanna crouched close to him and he hastened across to her, putting his free arm around her. 'Are you all right?' he asked urgently.

'Yes!' She sounded surprised. 'But I have no idea what's happening . . .'

There was a clash in the milky-white haze above them and another flash of light, so searing that Josse threw himself on Joanna. His body covering hers, he closed his eyes tight against the pain.

He waited for the killing blow. There was *something*, some terrible pressure on his head. Then the world went black and he passed out.

\*

He was aware of the wren's song and he had an awful head-ache. But he was alive and so was Joanna; so close to her, he could feel her breathing. After some time he risked opening one eye. Then the other one.

The mist had gone, there was no sign of the two Long Men and the Domina stood beside the grave, alone.

Josse got shakily to his feet, putting out his hand to help Joanna up. Together they walked slowly forward until they stood before the slim, straight figure in the grey robe.

Joanna gave a gasp, pointing. Josse followed her finger. The grave had been filled in.

Before either he or Joanna could say a word, she spoke. 'I had to stop you for you would have killed them. One is already dying and the one who drew his knife to attack you just now does not deserve death, for he acted as a result of a mis-apprehension.'

'What?' Josse demanded, but he noticed that his voice sounded weak.

The Domina smiled softly. 'The man who pursued you had very specific instructions. He was to follow you, see where you went and what you did there and, if you believed you had found proof that the blasphemous Merlin's Tomb here in the forest was in fact the true burial place of the enchanter, then at all costs he was to prevent you reaching England with that information. For, they told him, if the man Josse returns saying that he has found proof that the bones there in Armorica are not those of Merlin, then we are done for and all hope is gone.'

'But what I was shown at the fountain near Folle-Pensée proved the very opposite!' Josse protested weakly; his head was hurting so badly that he could barely see.

'The tall man made a fatal mistake,' the Domina said. 'Observing the two of you as you returned from the fountain on the hilltop, he misunderstood the cause of the mood between you. He saw deep sadness on your faces, read distress in the very way you moved. Knowing that you, Josse, were connected with the Abbey, he appreciated that you must therefore have hoped for proof that Merlin could not lie buried in England because his true resting place was in the Brocéliande forest in Brittany. Your clear distress on returning from the hilltop, he reasoned, was all the proof he needed that the opposite had happened: he believed that you had been shown some totally unconvincing pretence at a tomb of Merlin, so that you were faced with the unwelcome fact that there was no reason now not to say that this site here was in fact the magician's true burial place. In addition to what he observed,' she added, 'he actually overheard you, Josse, speak the fatal words.'

'What words?' Josse demanded.

'As far as I recall from what I was told, the words were *Say what you will, I don't believe Merlin the Magician is buried up there.*'

'But I don't believe he's buried anywhere!' Josse protested. 'I didn't mean I wasn't convinced by the stone slab and the spring – I was, believe me!'

The Domina smiled. 'I do,' she said. 'Unfortunately, it was not I who had to decide.' She paused, staring from one to the other. Then, very softly, she added, 'You were both clearly affected by some strong emotion. That your sorrow had a very different cause never even crossed your assailant's mind.'

Josse's sword arm drooped. Putting his free hand to his thumping head, he said, 'How do you know all this?'

'The Long Men just told me,' she said serenely. 'They are sorry for the mistake and they hope that you will understand. They are not,' she added, 'well versed in the ways of men and women.'

But something was still not quite right . . . fighting the growing sense of confusion, Josse said, 'You prevented us from killing them, lady, *before* they told you this. Why did you—?'

Joanna, close beside him, dug her elbow into his side. 'Enough,' she murmured.

'They were about to attack us!' he cried, refusing to leave it. 'The one in the lead stopped me drawing my sword! And where are they?' He spun round, trying wildly to look in every direction at once.

'They've gone,' Joanna said, putting her arm round his waist and hugging him. She glanced at the Domina. 'I don't think they'll be back.'

'You will not see them again this day,' the Domina confirmed.

Josse sank to his knees, then, the agonising pain behind his burning eyes at last overcoming him, lay down on the ground. He was aware of Joanna's concern and he heard the Domina say quietly, 'Tend to your man, Beith, for he is hurting and he needs you.'

Your man, he thought. I like that.

He felt Joanna's cool hand on his head and then there were other small noises as she opened the leather pouch at her belt; he thought he heard that running water sound again. Presently something almost too chilly for comfort dripped on to his brow and then, pressing a little cup to his lips, Joanna whispered, 'Drink this, Josse.'

He drank. It was cool and tasted of moss. Or herbs. Or something. It made him very sleepy. He let himself relax on to the short grass. Something soft was placed beneath his head and he thought he felt Joanna's lips on his cheek in a tender kiss. This is all very pleasant, but I must sheathe my sword, he thought dreamily. The dew will fall and the blade should be covered . . .

Then he fell asleep.

# 22

Aware as if in a dream of Joanna helping him on to Horace's back, Josse sat slumped in the saddle as she led the big horse along narrow forest tracks, twisting and turning this way and that, until at last they reached her hut in its secret clearing. He felt a sharp stab of pain in his head as she got him off Horace and inside the hut, where it was all she could do to make him drink an infusion that she hastily prepared from her stocks of herbs on the shelves in the hut.

He lay stretched out on the sleeping platform and she covered him with soft blankets. He tried to keep his eyes open – there was so much he needed to know – but sleep was overcoming him relentlessly.

'It's all right, dearest Josse,' Joanna murmured.

'But how—?'

'No more questions till the morning,' she said very firmly. Then she lay down beside him, curled up against him and, immeasurably comforted by her warmth and her presence, at last he surrendered.

He woke to the lovely sensation of having his forehead massaged with a feather touch by very small fingers. There was the sweet, sharp smell of lavender oil. Seeing his eyes open, his daughter said, 'Does it still hurt, Josse?'

He was not entirely sure but he thought not. To test this out he raised his eyebrows and lowered them very quickly four or five times in quick succession, which amused Meggie so much that he did it several times more. Then she had to try, and in the resulting laughter one of them managed to upset the little dish of oil.

'Sorry,' he said to Joanna when presently she came into the hut. 'Some of the oil got spilled.'

She sniffed. 'It doesn't matter. This hut always smells of some remedy or another and lavender is one of the better ones.' She came up to stand in front of the sleeping platform. 'You look better. How's the head?'

'It's fine,' he assured her. 'Whatever you dosed me with last night has mended me.'

'Just a pain killer,' she said.

'A strong one, and it made me sleep like the dead.' She did not reply. 'Were you, I wonder,' he added softly, 'hoping that it would also serve to confuse me, so that I could no longer tell what really happened late yesterday from the weird and unlikely things that cropped up in my dreams?'

Her dark eyes were steady on his. 'Yes.'

'It didn't work,' he told her. 'I can still see that image of my sword swinging down in a blow that should have beheaded him, yet—' No. Whatever had happened next had completely gone, if indeed it had ever been there in the first place. 'And you with that lethal knife of yours, I could have sworn you cut the other man's throat.'

'Sssh!' She put a warning finger to her lips and belatedly he remembered Meggie, sitting just behind him. He turned but she seemed absorbed in making a very neat plait from the fringed ends of one of the blankets.

'Meggie, Josse and I are going outside for a while,' Joanna said. 'We won't be long, then we'll come back and I'll prepare some food. I've put a pot of water over the hearth to boil and, because fire and hot water can hurt, you must stay up there where it's safe, yes?'

'Yes. Stay,' the child agreed.

'She's very obedient,' Josse said as he and Joanna walked slowly over to the far side of the clearing.

'She's very sensible,' she replied. 'When I tell her to do or not to do something, I try to explain why, and usually – not always – she accepts without too much complaint.'

Something within Josse protested at the thought of a child not yet three years old being *sensible*. 'Does she never just play or be naughty?' He could hear accusation in his voice.

Joanna smiled, not to be ruffled. 'Oh, she does both of those.'

They had moved into the shade of a great oak tree. Birds sang in its dense green foliage and from near at hand came the rushing sounds of a stream. He said, 'So, what happened? Did the Domina turn those two men to mist just as our weapons struck?'

He had intended sarcasm, but surprisingly she nodded. 'Yes, sort of,' she replied. 'They had something to do with it too; the uninjured one is a very powerful man and his abilities far exceed those of his brother. Actually I think *brother* is not to be taken literally, only to imply that they are united in the clan. The men are, I believe, no more than distant cousins.'

As if, he thought, it made any difference. 'So why didn't the stronger one undertake the task of following us?' he demanded. 'For one thing, his greater power might have allowed him to realise the truth about what we found out at Barenton so that he wouldn't have launched his attack on us. For another, maybe if it had been he who fought that – that whatever it was that came to our defence in the Brocéliande, he might have emerged the victor.'

'He might,' she agreed. 'They would indeed have been more evenly matched.'

Still she seemed serene, quite unfazed by his angry comments. With an exasperated sigh, he said, 'Joanna, I don't understand supernatural powers and I never will. But, since it seems that twice recently people wielding such powers have tried to kill me, I do think that you might at least *try* to explain.'

She smiled. 'Of course. Yesterday the Long Men were angry because they thought people – you – were again violating the grave of their venerated ancestress. You weren't,' she added quickly, 'but they didn't know that. We – you and I – saw them and, recalling how the wounded one tried to attack us before, we defended ourselves, once the Domina had released what the Long Man had done to stop you drawing your sword.'

'What did he do?'

'Oh, that's actually quite simple. You could have unsheathed it all along but he had put the thought into your mind that it was suddenly impossible.'

'How could he possibly do that?'

'Josse, it would take all of today and tomorrow to explain, let alone to tell you how to do it. Just take my word for it that putting thoughts into someone else's head is quite easy when you know how.'

'Can *you* do it?'

'I can, yes, but I never do it to those I love.'

'Oh.' He could not for the moment think what else to say. 'Where was I? Oh, yes. The Domina knew that the Long Men would not wish to harm us once they knew the true story. Once they knew that the information we brought home from the Brocéliande *supported* the closure of Merlin's Tomb and not the opposite, because what you were shown there in the forest of Armorica confirmed your belief that the tomb here was a fake. Also, once they knew that you went there yesterday to apologise to the ancestress for what had been done, even though it wasn't your fault, and to try to make amends.'

'I suggested to the Domina that I could start to fill in the grave,' he recalled with a grin.

'I can imagine her reaction. That was a task of great honour reserved for the dead woman's own people. But you weren't to know. The Domina knew she must stop our attack on the men because, once everyone knew the truth, there was no more need either for them to try to kill us or for us to defend ourselves and retaliate.' She paused, then added quietly, 'The Domina is more far-sighted than most people and she no doubt saw what would have happened had your sword and my knife found their mark. Two of the Long Men would have been slain in their own sacred grove and, even though they are nowadays few in number, still the repercussions would have been terrible.'

'So she turned my man to cloud and my sword passed straight through him,' Josse murmured. He still could not believe it.

'It's mind control again, Josse,' she said earnestly. 'You thought you did things that, in reality, worked out rather differently.'

'I've been a soldier all my life!' he cried. 'I know when I'm swinging my sword down in a death blow and you can't tell me otherwise.'

She began to speak but then, with a nod, stopped; it was almost, he thought, as if she were listening to a voice within her head giving her instructions . . .

'Let us just be relieved that further harm has been averted,' she said calmly. 'Now, what do you want for breakfast?'

'I—' Breakfast? When his mind was still bursting with things he was desperate to know?

But she was already moving away back towards the hut. She held out her hand to him and, after a moment, he took it.

After they had all eaten, Joanna unwound the linen bandage and inspected the wound on his forearm. It had healed well and skilfully she removed the stitches.

Then there was no more reason for him to stay.

Joanna and Meggie went with him to the edge of the forest. He had announced he must return to the Abbey; 'She'll be worried about me,' he said.

Joanna did not have to ask who *she* was.

Dear Josse, she thought now as the moment of parting approached. He did not really understand one little bit of what had happened by Merlin's Tomb yesterday. She did not understand all of it herself; the level of power possessed by beings such as the Domina and the Long Men was as far beyond her own small skills as Saturn was beyond the Moon. But she, unlike Josse, had the great advantage of knowing that it was quite possible to learn how to do such things, provided you were prepared to devote your life to the process.

I am prepared for that, she thought. I shall miss Josse more than I can now know, I am certain of that. But my life is here. I have set my feet on the path and I cannot deviate now.

And he would be back.

The thought gave her a deep, secret joy.

They had emerged from the trees. Meggie had stooped down in the grass that began where the trees stopped and was picking daisies.

'Farewell, dearest Josse,' Joanna said, both his hands in hers.

'Take care, sweeting.' His eyes were wet.

Feeling the emotion rising, she tried to think of something to say that might lighten the mood. Ah, yes; she had the very thing.

'About that female antecedent of yours who used to tend the sacred fire on the Caburn,' she began. 'Remember?'

'Aye. What of her?' Despite himself, he looked interested.

'About you, taller than most men.'

'What are you talking about?' He frowned ferociously, then all of a sudden his face cleared and, wonder in his eyes, he said, 'She was of their people?'

She nodded, almost laughing. 'Indeed she was. They didn't let just anyone muck about with the Caburn fire.'

'Have you known all the time?'

'No, of course not – I knew hardly anything about the Long Men until very recently. The Domina told me yesterday. In fact, she said she told you too but you weren't listening.'

'She did no such thing!'

'*Some men whose antecedents were from this area still stand out by their height.* Don't those words sound familiar at all?'

'Er—' He hardly liked to think.

'She was referring to *you*, Josse.'

'So – that woman lying in the tomb is one of my forebears.' It was yet another thing that scarcely bore credence.

'Indeed she is.' She thought for a moment, then added, 'The Domina will have told the Long Men who you are. I shouldn't think they would object if, once in a while, you went back to the grave of your ancestress to pay your respects.'

He was shaking his head, giving every impression of a man too bemused and perplexed by a succession of wonders to know if he was on his heels or his elbows. 'I just don't know what to make of it all, and that's the truth,' he said.

She put her arms round him. 'Go now, my love,' she urged him. 'Go back to the Abbey, speak to the Abbess Helewise and reassure her that all is well, both at Merlin's Tomb and with you, which will be concerning her far more than some old bones in the ground.'

'She doesn't know that we—' he protested.

But she put a gentle finger up to his lips, silencing the words. 'Oh, yes, she does.'

She watched as, still looking as if he had been recently poleaxed, he walked slowly over to Meggie, gave her a hug and a kiss and said, in a remarkably cheery voice, that he would be seeing her soon. Meggie reached up to return his kiss and dropped her daisy chain around his neck.

With Meggie standing at her side and holding her hand, Joanna watched as he mounted Horace and, kicking the horse to a trot, descended the slight slope towards the Abbey gates.

Then, doing her best to sound as cheerful as Josse had managed to do, she blinked away her tears and said, 'Now, Meggie, time to go home.'

Helewise heard his footsteps coming along the cloister with vast relief and when he knocked on the open door and stepped into her room – he appeared to be wearing a daisy chain – she got up and hugged him.

'Sir Josse, I do apologise,' she said hastily, taking two large paces backwards. 'It's just that I was so very worried about you because I know how you and—' Flustered, she stopped abruptly and then tried again. 'That is, the brethren in the Vale said you did not come back last night and I feared some harm had come to you.'

He was watching her, deep affection in his brown eyes, smiling gently as if at some small private joke. 'What is it?' she demanded.

'Oh – nothing, my lady. I am very sorry to have caused you anxiety. I – er, I met some people I was not expecting at Merlin's Tomb but all is well there now. The site is indeed closed and the grave has been filled in.'

She stared intently at him. 'That is for sure?'

'Yes, my lady. Your Abbey is safe.'

Oh, thank God, she thought. 'Thank you, Sir Josse. I am more grateful than I can say.'

'No need to be grateful to me, my lady. The principal reason it's closed is because Melusine paid a killer to murder Florian, and so far it looks as if both of them are getting clean away with it.'

'Give Gervase time,' she soothed. 'He will not give up so easily, I know.' Then, remembering why he had gone back to the tomb the previous day, 'Did you find out whose the bones were?'

'Aye,' he said. She waited, but he said no more.

Well, perhaps it didn't really matter.

She read sorrow in every part of him. Walking slowly out to the stables to see him off – he had declined her offer of sharing the midday meal, saying that he really ought to return to New Winnowlands – she had a sudden vivid picture of him going back to that empty house.

Oh, Josse!

But what can *I* do? she demanded of herself. My work and my duty are here; I cannot make rash offers to ride over and visit him to see how he is and check that he's happy. Anyway, he probably won't be.

Impulsively she reached for his hand. 'Come back whenever you feel like company,' she urged him. 'Remember that you have many friends here who care about you very much.'

She saw tears in his eyes. He bent to kiss her hand and muttered something about knowing that right enough. Then he strode into the stable, emerged leading Horace and, with barely a nod in her direction, mounted and hurried away.

# POSTSCRIPT

*September 1195*

The mood of the forest was changing as the living things within it sensed the turning of the year; it was the beginning of the season that brought death and rebirth. Soon it would be the equinox and among the forest people, looking forward to celebrating the moment when Sun appeared to stand on the halfway point between his summer and his winter homes, excitement was rising.

The autumn equinox was marked by the festival of the second harvest. Lammas, in August, had celebrated the wealth of the land as expressed in the safely gathered crops; the wild ceremony that took place then was to celebrate the marriage of Lugh the Sun God with the Earth Mother. Lammas honoured the ripe grain and the bounty of the Earth, both her flora and fauna; the September ceremony was the one that gave thanks and praise to the very plants themselves and, for the forest people, this meant predominantly the trees.

At the equinox, the spiritual emphasis was upon the harsh fact that living things, be they plants or animals, had to surrender their own lives in order that the humans who preyed on them might flourish. Death was an inevitable fact of life; the equinox ceremony gave the grateful people the chance to honour the harvested crops and the slaughtered animals – few, in the case of the forest people – whose flesh would be salted, dried and preserved for the lean months. It was, more than anything, a festival of thanksgiving.

Mabon, her teachers had informed Joanna, was the sacred child of Modron the Divine Mother and, because his life cycle was endlessly played out in the passage of each year's seasons, he was at the same time both the youngest and the oldest. Embodiment of fertility, his fate was written out. He was the Star Child, Son of the Goddess; even at his birth at the Winter Solstice, the time when the light returned, joy at his coming would always be tempered by the knowledge of his death that would come at the harvest, when he would be cut down with the corn.

Joanna, excited along with everyone else as the day of the festival approached, had heard faint and vaguely disturbing rumours that this year the ceremony was going to be different, although she had no idea what this might portend. But there had been violation within the forest; the spirits of the place had not – or so the Great Ones of the tribe decreed – forgiven or forgotten. Florian of Southfrith's scheme had failed and he was dead; his killer too was dead, caught, tried and hanged within two months of his crime. The woman who had hired the man to kill for her had evaded justice; the sheriff of Tonbridge had followed her to her home in France and done his utmost but wealth, privilege and position had protected her. It seemed she had some very powerful friends . . .

Most importantly for all who dwelt within the forest, the Long Men had contrived to conceal once more the filled-in grave of their giant ancestress and, on the surface at least, all appeared to be well.

But this was an illusion.

The forest people had sought out the Long Men secretly and had conversation with them. The Long Men, threatened, battered and traumatised by all that had happened to them already that fateful year, had at first been unwilling to communicate in any way; they had hidden away, so skilfully that it had taken the Domina and her two companions some days to find them. The discussion that followed had been brief and afterwards the Domina forbade any mention of what had gone on, a stricture that was not truly necessary since none of the forest people would have contemplated asking questions of her companions and they certainly did not dare approach her.

It was not only Joanna who was in the dark about what was to happen at the equinox: for all that some strange and unusual orders had been given out that led to much speculation, hardly anybody else had any more idea than she did about what form the ceremony was to take.

Speculation and excitement steadily mounted until the tension could almost be heard straining and singing in the air.

In the mid-afternoon of 21st September Joanna wrapped Meggie warmly in her new wool cloak – the sun was shining out of a clear sky but there was a chill in the air – and fastened the child's leather sandals. She stood back to have a last look at her daughter to ensure that she looked her very best. Meggie's curly brown hair – recently washed and trimmed – was glossy from brushing and her dark eyes with the strange golden lights shone with excitement. Her face was rosy and she could not suppress her smile. Joanna, who had been very anxious in case the little girl would be scared and apprehensive, reflected wryly that she need not have worried and could easily have saved herself the several broken nights of the past week. Far from being nervous, Meggie looked as if she couldn't wait to begin.

Quickly Joanna drew on her white robe, buckling the leather belt and settling her knife in its sheath. She swung her cloak over her shoulders, did up the brooch that fastened it and then, looking down at Meggie, silently raised her eyebrows as if to say, ready? Meggie nodded vigorously and, holding tight to Joanna's hand, led the way out of the little hut and off along the track that led to the clearing where the people had been commanded to assemble.

There was the faintest buzz of talk among the mainly silent group beneath the trees. Nobody had actually forbidden conversation, but such was the sense of awe in the suddenly heavy air that somehow words seemed inappropriate. Joanna stood a little apart, Meggie beside her almost as still as her mother, and waited.

The order, when it came, was unexpected: the people were to make their way due south through the forest to a clearing on the far side.

A clearing which from that brief description, Joanna thought as she strode off behind a group of two men and an older woman, must surely be in the general vicinity of the place where the ancient bones lay . . . And all at once she realised both that the celebrations really were going to be different this year and also why that was.

The thought was both thrilling and frightening.

They came to the clearing.

It was not the one in which the giantess lay buried; it was some hundred paces away, further into the forest and so well hidden that Joanna, who had visited the area, had had no idea it was there. It was not large – perhaps twenty or thirty paces across – and the trees that surrounded it in an almost perfect circle were all mature and majestic oaks. Between them the undergrowth had been cleared, so that their thick trunks had the appearance of regularly spaced pillars.

It was a place that set an atavistic chill in the heart; it was a place, Joanna knew in her very soul, of strong magic.

The fires had already been lit. Their slow-swirling smoke was spiralling up into the trees and there was a soft, continuous rustling sound emanating from the leaves as, with the life-moisture now drying out of them, they brushed together.

In the middle of the clearing, close to the huge trunk of a long-fallen oak that Joanna guessed would serve as both the platform for the performers and the throne-like perch of the greatest of the elders, was a glorious display of autumn produce. There were apples, pears, berries and nuts in wicker baskets; shallow trays of flat, unleavened bread; small platters of seeds and pulses; bundles of dried herbs. By way of decoration, the vivid colours shining in the soft light like splashes of sunshine, there were wreaths and garlands made out of small branches of oak, beech and sweet chestnut, the leaves turning to russet. There was also a great sheaf of corn.

As the Great Ones of the tribe walked in solemn procession to take up their places, Joanna and Meggie slipped into the circle of people who stood around the oak trunk with its backdrop of living flame. The signal was given and the long chant began; soft and slow at first, it seemed no more than an intensification of the natural sounds of the forest. But gradually the pitch rose and the tempo increased and, from somewhere out of sight, the rhythm was picked up on a drum. Steadily, irrepressibly, the hymn of quiet and respectful praise escalated until it was a shout of joy, an outcry of deep-felt gratitude and profound appreciation from the hearts and the throats of all the people. *We greet you, praise you, honour you and thank you*, chanted the tribe, *you who have given up your lives that we may live*. The long lists went on and on – plants, fruits, vegetables, trees that produced foodstuffs, firewood and building material; small creatures, large creatures, goats, sheep and cattle – and each named benefactor was given its due thanks.

The ecstatic song came at last to its climax and conclusion, the last few words being uttered in a triumphant shout that set echoes ringing through the clearing and out into the night. As they died and silence fell, it seemed that the darkness crept in to fill the vacuum. The fires had burned low and, for a short time, nobody moved.

It was the instant of perfect stillness.

Then a voice cried out, the fires were quickly stoked and as the flames rose high once more, the tribe seemed to let out the collective breath it had been holding. All at once excited talk and laughter filled the air; the unseen drummer changed his tempo into a dance rhythm, somebody began to play a lively tune on a pipe and the people, greeting one another as if they hadn't met for weeks, joined hands in a swirling, whirling chain and began to dance.

And then, after the dancing, came the feasting.

Some time later, they sent for Joanna. They took Meggie by the hand and told her to wish her mother goodnight then, allowing time for no more than a swift kiss and hug, they led her away, part of the quiet procession of people slowly leaving the clearing and heading back towards their dwellings on the other side of the forest.

Soon they had all gone and only five people remained in the clearing: the Domina; two cloaked and hooded figures who, from their size, appeared to be male; a nervous-looking, grey-haired woman of about sixty and Joanna.

Her first thought as she looked at the four silent figures was that there must have been a mistake. There stood the Domina with two of the other Great Ones; a trio whom she knew to be held in deep reverence by the people, for they were profoundly wise and one of them at least was a bard, one of the special few who memorised the long history, legends and genealogies of the people and recited them from memory.

What on earth, Joanna wondered, am I doing here?

She was just about to approach one of the group to point out that surely she ought to have been dismissed when it occurred to her that this was no mistake: hadn't someone just sought out her and her daughter specifically to take Meggie home?

She was meant to be there, then.

She waited.

After some time, when the last faint sounds of the people's progress through the forest had long faded, the Domina stepped forward into the centre of the clearing and spoke.

'We have come here to honour the spirits of nature at this time because of the violation that has happened here,' she began, her voice sonorous and low, pitched just loud enough for her audience to hear and no louder. 'We have celebrated all together and our prayers and our goodwill have made up a little for what was done. But this' – she glanced round the group with piercing eyes – 'has been just the beginning. There is another task that must be done and for this we now must march south. Come!' She smiled brilliantly. 'Let our hearts be joyful, let our legs bear us swiftly and let us take strength from one another. Come!'

Swirling her cloak around her and picking up a stout staff, she turned and strode out of the clearing. Without a word the two elders fell into step behind her, the woman following them.

Joanna took up her place at the rear of the group and, trying to still the wild speculation racing through her mind, made herself concentrate on the simple, hypnotic process of this strange and unexpected night march.

On they walked. The forest was far behind them now – Joanna, glancing over her shoulder, could make it out as nothing more than a dark outline against the starry sky to the north. The moon had risen in the east, illuminating the scene with silvery light. They had descended into the strip of low land that ran roughly west to east between the forest ridges and the South Downs and now, even as her eyes stared at the folds of the hills ahead, she sensed that they were beginning to climb.

Soundless as ghosts, they passed sleeping villages and hamlets and so little did any of their essence spill out on to their surroundings that even the guard dogs did not hear them. Such was the way of the forest people when they wished to keep their doings a secret; Joanna, intent on moving as silently as her older and more experienced companions, experienced a sudden sense of belonging and a fierce flood of pride.

They were marching now up a track that ran between high hedges of bramble, bryony, ivy, ash and elder. Here and there briar roses sent out long, straggling suckers; in the dim light the dense black sloes looked like dark eyes. Joanna fought the sense that someone might creep up on her from behind and, to distract herself from her fear, she made herself go back to the question of just why she had been brought. The Domina and the other two elders naturally had to be here; the man who was the bard had been included undoubtedly so that he could see, remember and record what came to pass. The other man was possibly also a bard, or in training to be one, and as for the grey-haired woman . . . Joanna visualised the woman's face and suddenly she knew both what the woman's special skill was and also why she had been commanded to come.

The woman laid out the dead.

Oh, but then *who has died?* The question seemed to shriek aloud inside Joanna's head. Close on its heels came another, one which had endlessly repeated itself for the past three hours or more: *Why am I here?*

Neither question looked like receiving an answer in the foreseeable future. Her breath coming harder now, Joanna gritted her teeth and marched on.

They passed another village; Joanna made out the shape of a small church with long, low buildings attached. An abbey? She did not know, although it seemed likely.

Then, about a mile further along the track, suddenly the Domina plunged off to her left, presumably through a gap in the hedge. The others followed – the gap was narrow and overgrown, as if little used, and Joanna felt the long, sharp scratch of a bramble on the back of her hand – and it seemed as if the branches and the foliage of the hedge closed together again behind her. She could not resist turning round to look but instantly regretted it.

The hedge grew straight, thick and uninterrupted.

There was no sign of any gap whatsoever.

Suppressing a moan of terror, Joanna hurried after the rest of the group.

They were climbing in earnest now, over rough pasture that was dotted with dents and small hillocks. Panting, eyes down on the ground in an attempt to avoid the worst of the uneven terrain, it was some time before Joanna raised her head to look where she was going.

She knew, even before she made out the huge white outline gleaming in the moonlight. She knew because she had been here before and she had been told about this place. Its relevance struck her with such force that she almost laughed aloud as she thought, *Of course!*

They were on the lower slopes of Windover Hill and above them, soaring over them and looking down on them lay the vast shape of the Long Man.

They had told her, those wise and aged ones who had the task of instructing her in the ways of the people, that this site had long been revered. Here the first settlers had found the precious flint; there were flint mines over to the left, halfway up the hill beyond the Long Man's outreaching right arm and the staff that he held in his hand. To his left, beyond the tall staff that he held in his other arm, there was a chalk pit where once, countless generations ago, the ancestors had extracted their building materials. There was a burial mound on the hill itself, to the Long Man's left. Over his head there was a tumulus, although even her all-wise teachers had told her very little about that; perhaps they *knew* very little . . .

She stared up at the figure. He stood facing her, legs firmly planted and feet apart, arms outstretched and in the great hands those two mighty staves, held parallel so that, had there been a third staff joining them together at the top, it would have looked for all the world as if the Long Man stood in a mystical doorway, the guardian what lay beyond.

No. She did not want even to begin to think about where such a doorway, cut into a lonely chalk hillside, might lead. Not she, who was still so full of life . . .

The Domina had stopped. She had reached the depression left by the quarried chalk and now she stood on its lip. Turning, she faced her followers, the heights of Windover Hill behind her and to her left, a few short paces away, the steep drop down into the chalk pit. She looked at the two men and gave an all but imperceptible nod, at which they took up their positions on either side of her.

They are to stay close to her, Joanna thought with a flash of understanding, so that they see what she sees and so that the record that is added to the sum of our people's long tale comprises the precise, same visions that the Domina sees.

The grey-haired woman had sat down on the springy turf. She seemed very tired; the journey had exhausted her. Joanna wondered briefly why the Domina did not command that she stood up again but quickly realised why this was: the grey haired woman was not there to observe and record. Her skills were in another field altogether.

What about me? Joanna almost asked the question aloud.

It seemed for an instant that she must have done for the Domina turned, beckoned to her and said, 'Come here. Step forward when I do and remain beside me. Be watchful.'

Joanna hurried across the short distance separating her from the Domina. She felt eyes on her – fierce in their concentration and oddly penetrating – then the Domina turned and walked slowly on up the hill towards the figure of the Long Man. When she stood at his feet, she stopped.

Beside her, Joanna stopped too. She did not dare turn around but she sensed the two men just behind her.

They waited.

The moon went behind a cloud and it was profoundly dark.

After what seemed a very long time, her eyes fixed on the summit of the hill high above detected movement. Or so she thought; she had been staring so fixedly that it was hard to be sure. She looked away, blinked a few times and then looked again and this time there was no room for doubt.

At the top of the hill three figures had appeared to stand in dark silhouette against the night sky. All three looked very tall, although the central figure was shorter. As Joanna stared, the lower parts of their bodies disappeared, merging into the black background of the hill. They have set off down the hill; either that, she thought with a wry smile, or they're melting into the ground . . .

She sensed the Domina beside her grow tense.

Again, they waited.

The moon suddenly came out from behind the cloud. Now Joanna could see them, those three tall figures, moving slowly and steadily down the hill. To her shocked amazement, for it seemed like the worse sort of sacrilege, they walked straight over the Long Man, down through the outline of his head, across his broad chest, his belly and his groin. There they stopped briefly and two of the figures gave a low bow, as if in respect for this the progenitor of their people.

Now they were moving on again, in a straight line that bisected the space between the Long Man's legs and led directly to the Domina standing between his feet.

There they stopped, the two taller men now shoulder to shoulder and concealing the third behind them.

For some time the two men stared at the Domina and she at them. Joanna, observing closely, had recognised the pair some time ago: they were the wounded man and his kinsman, the men who had come to the clearing where their ancestress lay interred. But now that she could see them clearly she saw that the wounded man's condition had deteriorated.

He looked dreadful. His eyes were sunk in his head and his deadly white face was covered in sweat. He was breathing in snatched gasps and each breath seemed to be a great effort. The three-month-old scars across his neck and down his chest were brilliant red on the pale skin.

He is dying, Joanna thought. He will die tonight, and his death was foretold. That is why we have brought the woman with us, so that she can prepare his body for burial here with his ancestor.

What did it feel like, she wondered, to know the very hour of your death?

She shivered. It was an uncomfortable thought.

The unwounded man was, it appeared, once more to be the spokesman. With a grave bow to the Domina, he said, 'Welcome. Here beside me is my brother, the long thread of whose life is coming at last to its end. On this night of the equinox his spirit will go to meet his forefathers and we shall bury his body here in the place that is sacred to us.'

The Domina nodded. 'So be it.'

Joanna was watching the wounded man. It seemed very cruel and unthinking to speak of a man's imminent death in his hearing and she wondered how he would react. To her surprise his ravaged face wore a look of serenity and as she watched his thin, cracked lips broke into a smile of such deep joy that she was moved to her soul.

He is ready! she thought, amazed. More than ready; he is eager.

The Domina made a small gesture to the tall man – a sort of inclination of the head – and, with a nod as if in acknowledgment, he said, 'Yes, all is ready. Follow me.'

He moved on down the hill, the wounded man beside him. The Domina set off close on his heels, Joanna at her side, and the two bards and the third tall man followed behind, from where Joanna could hear their footsteps.

They went around the lip of the chalk pit and then down a steep path that descended into its depths. In the ground there was a long, narrow hole: the wounded man's grave.

At first, nobody spoke.

The wounded man seemed all at once to collapse, slumping to the ground as if every last vestige of strength had finally left him. With a deep sigh, he sat and then lay on the edge of the grave. He stretched out his long legs and crossed his arms on his breast. Intent on his face, Joanna saw his eyes close and a look of bliss soften the gaunt features. His breathing deepened, each breath longer, longer, the time between the out breath and the in breath getting steadily longer and longer until at last there was an out breath after which no in breath came.

The tall man knelt down beside his kinsman, first putting fingers to his throat, then bending over the long, inert body, putting his cheek right over the partly open lips, one hand on the breast above the heart. He crouched like that for some moments and then, straightening to his full height, he said, 'It is over.'

The Domina gave a bow. Then, turning, she called out softly and the grey-haired woman appeared out of the darkness. The Domina nodded and the woman, with a quick glance at the tall man, unfastened the leather bag at her waist and set about her task. The Domina, after watching for a short time, moved away across the bottom of the chalk pit, up its lower far side and on down the hill, only stopping when she was out of sight of the grave.

The tall man had come with her, as had Joanna and the two bards. The man who had accompanied the Long Men must have stayed at the graveside, for Joanna could not see him.

Perhaps it was he who would put his kinsman in the grave and shovel the chalky soil on top of him.

The Domina was speaking; Joanna turned her attention to the words.

'Your brother is blessed,' she said to the tall man, 'for he died in the service of his people, carrying out the sacred task entrusted to him. He acted in accordance with what he believed to be the truth, and not a one of us can do better. There is no resentment among my people for the harm that your brother would have inflicted on one of ours, for we understand and we forgive. We have come here on this sacred night of the autumn equinox to observe your kinsman's death, to honour his passing and to speak the words that will speed his worthy warrior soul to the halls of his forefathers.' She held out her right hand, palm uppermost, and, after a moment, the tall man put his hand palm down upon it.

'Let there be trust, understanding and peace between the Long Men and the forest people,' the Domina intoned, her low voice thrumming on the air.

And the Long Man, his eyes bright with what might have been tears, echoed the words: 'Trust, understanding and peace.'

The two of them stood thus, palm to palm, for some time. Then the Domina relaxed and seemed to diminish until she was no longer a figure of power but simply an old woman in a silvery cloak on a dark hillside. With the change in her something went out of the atmosphere – something strange and very powerful that had held the night in stillness and utter silence all around them – and slowly the ordinary sounds came back.

Joanna, stretching muscles that had cramped from the intensity with which she had maintained her tense pose, heard the sound of earth being shovelled. And she knew that her guess had been right: the grey-haired woman had finished her ministrations, the dead man had been laid in the Earth and now the third of the strange men was filling in the grave.

The Domina looked at the tall man, eyebrows raised, and he said, 'Yes.'

Side by side the two of them led the way back over the lip of the chalk pit and down to the grave. It had been about half-filled and now the two bards picked up implements – they looked like the shoulder blades of deer – and helped the third tall man complete his task.

Even with three of them, it took some time.

There was something very familiar about the third tall man . . .

Once again the Domina read Joanna's mind. Touching her arm, she said softly, 'Did you not recognise him until this moment?'

'No,' Joanna admitted. *Why not? What's the matter with me?*

The Domina smiled. 'I am pleased to hear it,' she murmured. Then, as if sensing Joanna's incomprehension: 'I told you to be watchful and you obeyed, bending all your concentratation to the matter in hand to the exclusion of everything else. Even' – the smile deepened – 'to the presence on this hillside of someone who is very special to you.'

'How could I not have noticed *him*?' Joanna muttered. Eyes fixed on the broad back, an urgent thought occurred to her. 'Has *he* noticed *me*?'

'Of course not,' the Domina said. 'But then, as you have seen, it is relatively easy for us to hide from unsuspecting men things that we do not wish them to see.'

'Why is he here?' Joanna felt she ought to be able to work it out but the shock of seeing him had unnerved her.

'He belongs here,' the Domina said simply. 'Do you not recall?'

Beside her the tall man, roused from his deep silence, stirred. 'He is one of us,' he confirmed. 'We chose him for this task so that he should be recognised by the few of us that remain on this Earth.'

Slowly Joanna nodded.

For some time they stayed there in the chalk pit. Finally the task was done and Joanna watched as both the tall man and the Domina stood beside the new grave and together chanted long strings of words that seemed to weave through the dark night like two threads of gold and silver.

When they were done, each stepped back from the grave, bowed to the other and then turned and walked away. Behind the Domina the two bards and the grey-haired woman fell into their places; the Long Man walked away alone.

Leaving just the two of them alone in the chalk pit.

He came towards her, his expression tentative. She opened her arms to him and his smile broke out like the first rays of the dawn sun, still some hours away. She hugged him tightly, pulling him close, and felt her body mould itself to his. He put a strong hand on her chin then bent to kiss her.

There was no need for words; as one they slowly climbed out of the chalk pit and set off along the track that would take them back to the forest. But not yet; after only half a mile or so, they found a place where a narrow trail led into a copse and, there on the woodland floor soft with newly fallen leaves, they made love.

Afterwards, waking soon after dawn from their brief but intense sleep, at last he spoke. He said, taking her quite by surprise, 'I knew you'd be there.'

'*Did* you?' Her voice fully reflected her amazement. 'But the Domina said she'd hidden me from you so you didn't see me!'

'She may have *said* she'd hidden you' – he bent his head to kiss her and she snuggled into his shoulder – 'but it doesn't necessarily mean she did so. She's not always right, you know,' he added.

'So you—'

He stopped her words with another kiss. 'Sweeting, it wasn't exactly that I saw you,' he admitted, 'more that I expected we'd meet each other, sooner or later and somehow or other. They sought me out to ask if I would be prepared to do this thing, you know.' His face creased in a frown. 'They said that there was a rift that must be healed. Harmful intent had been directed at me and by doing my bit this night I could indicate my forgiveness.'

'You came willingly?' she asked.

He looked down at her, right into her eyes. 'Oh, aye. I came willingly all right.'

'But—' She was struggling to understand. 'These things surely do not concern you? Rifts needing healing and all that?'

He grinned. 'No, I can't say that they do.'

'Then why were you so keen to come?'

'Because they said I wasn't the only one who had been threatened – you had been too. Then I knew you'd be there and after that there was no holding me.'

'You – you went off into the wild lands with the Long Men and you spent half the night digging and filling in the grave of a man who tried to kill you, just because you reckoned you and I might get the chance to be together?'

'Aye,' he said softly. Then: 'You promised, Joanna, that we would meet at the year's festivals, and last night was the equinox.' He was holding her close, his large, warm hand moving across her shoulder and down towards her breast, and already she felt herself begin to open to him again. Sensing her response he kissed her, deeply, long. Pausing briefly for air, he added, 'And you were always a woman who kept her promises.'

Then they were making love again and there was no time for another word.